D0348576

Robert Ludlum is one of the world's bestselling authors and there are more than 300 million copies of his books in print. He is published in 32 languages and 50 countries. As well as blending sophisticated plotting and extreme pace, Robert Ludlum's novels are meticulously researched and include accurate technical, geographical and biological details. In addition to the popular titles in the Covert-One series, Robert Ludlum's best-known books include *The Scarlatti Inheritance*, *The Chancellor Manuscript* and the Jason Bourne series – *The Bourne Identity*, *The Bourne Supremacy* and *The Bourne Ultimatum* – among others. Visit Robert Ludlum's website at www.orionbooks.co.uk/Ludlum.

James Cobb is the author of, amongst others, the Amanda Lee Garrett thrillers and is an avid student of military history and technology. He is a member of the United States Naval Institute and the Navy League. He lives in Tacoma, Washington.

Also Available

The Bourne Series
The Bourne Identity
The Bourne Supremacy
The Bourne Ultimatum
The Bourne Legacy
The Bourne Betrayal
The Bourne Sanction
The Bourne Deception
The Bourne Objective

The Covert-One Series
The Hades Factor
The Cassandra Compact
The Paris Option
The Altman Code
The Lazarus Vendetta
The Moscow Vector
The Arctic Event

Road to . . . Series
The Road to Gandolfo
The Road to Omaha

The Matarese Series
The Matarese Circle
The Matarese Countdown

Standalone Novels
The Scarlatti Inheritance
The Osterman Weekend
The Matlock Paper
Trevayne
The Rhinemann Exchange
The Cry of the Halidon
The Gemini Contenders
The Chancellor Manuscript
The Holcroft Covenant
The Parsifal Mosaic
The Aquitaine Progression
The Icarus Agenda
The Scorpio Illusion
The Apocalypse Watch
The Prometheus Deception
The Sigma Protocol
The Janson Directive
The Tristan Betrayal
The Ambler Warning
The Bancroft Strategy

Also by James Cobb

Robert Ludlum's™
THE ARCTIC EVENT

A **Covert-One** Novel

Series created by **Robert Ludlum**

Written by **James Cobb**

An Orion paperback

First published in Great Britain in 2007
by Orion
This paperback edition published in 2007
by Orion Books Ltd,
Orion House, 5 Upper St Martin's Lane,
London WC2H 9EA

An Hachette UK company

Reissued 2010

A CIP catalogue record for this book
is available from the British Library.

Printed and bound by
CPI Group (UK) Ltd, Croydon, CR0 4YY

The Orion Publishing Group's policy is to use papers
that are natural, renewable and recyclable products and
made from wood grown in sustainable forests. The logging
and manufacturing processes are expected to conform to
the environmental regulations of the country of origin.

www.orionbooks.co.uk

Dedicated to Donald Hamilton
and his creation, Matt Helm
(The real Matt Helm, not the Hollywood version)

PROLOGUE

March 5, 1953

The Canadian Arctic

Nothing lived on the island. Nothing could.

It was a jagged ridge of raw, storm-savaged rock thrusting through the ice and freezing waters of the Arctic Ocean only a short distance from the Earth's magnetic pole. A shallow crescent twelve miles in length from east to west, it tapered from two miles in width at its broadest point to a quarter mile at its tips, with something of a cove on its westernmost end. Two prominent peaks rose out of its narrow, boulder-strewn coastal plain, a glaciated saddleback joining them.

Lichen and a few tufts of stunted, frost-burned sea grass clung to bare existence amid its fissured stone. A few kitti-wakes and fulmars would roost on its cliffs during the brief arctic summer. The occasional seal or walrus would haul out on its gravel beaches, and the rare lordly polar bear would pad ghostlike amid its freezing fogs.

But nothing truly lived there.

The island was one of the myriad crumbs of continent scattered between the northern coast of Canada and the Pole. Collectively they were called the Queen Elizabeth Archipelago, and each was as bleak and blizzard blasted as the next.

For the bulk of its existence, the island had been unknown and unvisited by humanity. Some far-ranging Inuit hunter might have seen its peaks rising above the sea smoke on the distant horizon. If he had, the necessities of survival for himself and his tribe had prevented any further investigation.

Or possibly some Victorian-era arctic explorer caught up in the vain quest for the Northwest Passage might have sketched the island onto his crude map with a mittened hand. If so, his had been one of the ice-doomed ships that never returned.

The island and its sisters did not enter into the affairs of mankind until the coming of the appropriately named Cold War. The Queen Elizabeth Archipelago was photo surveyed in the late 1940s by the United States Air Force as a precursor to the construction of the North American Air Defense Command's Distant Early Warning radar line. The island gained a name then. The bored military cartographer who added it to the world's charts dubbed it Wednesday because it had to be called something and because its survey run had passed over his desk in the middle of the week.

Not long afterward, Wednesday Island received its first visitation.

A williwaw was blasting down from the Pole through the primordial darkness of an arctic winter, its winds screaming around the island's peaks, scouring the snow from their northern faces, leaving the black basalt naked to the storm.

Possibly that was why the island went unseen until it was too late.

Faintly, the sound of powerful aircraft engines came from the north, riding with the wind, growing swiftly in intensity. But there was no one to hear their thunder as they passed low over the island's coastline. Too low. The roar of the engines suddenly increased, spurred into a howl of desperation-born power.

The howl ended abruptly in the harsh, tearing slam of metal hitting on ice, and the eternal winds shrieked in triumph.

Wednesday Island ceased to be a point of concern for another half century.

CHAPTER ONE

The Present Day

The Canadian Arctic

Clad in Day-Glo orange parkas and snowmobiling suits, the three rope-linked figures leaned on their ice axes, forcing themselves up the last few yards to their goal. They had made their climb on the southern face of the ridge, its bulk shielding them from the prevailing wind. But now, as they struggled over the lip of the small, bare rock plateau at its peak, the full blast of the polar katabatics raked them, the wind chill driving the effective temperature from merely below freezing to well below zero.

It was a pleasant autumn afternoon on Wednesday Island.

The pale, heatless ball of the sun rolled along the southern horizon, filling the world with the strange, grayish glow of the weeks-long arctic twilight.

Looking down at the surrounding ocean, it was difficult to tell island from sea. The pack was closing in around Wednesday, the new, living ice buckling and jumbling up on the beaches. The only leads of free, dark water to be seen trailed behind the drifting icebergs on the horizon as they resisted the frozen constriction of the coming winter.

To the east, the driving winds had drawn a snow squall across the far end of the island, blurring the second, taller mountain into an ominous dark bulk hinted at behind a ragged curtain of mist.

The vista was that of hell with the furnaces shut down, yet the three who viewed it were of the breed who found such sights exhilarating.

The team leader threw his head back and challenged the

wind with a wild wolf howl. 'I claim this mountain by right of conquest and hereby name it . . . What in the hell are we going to name it anyway?'

'You were first man up, Ian,' the smallest of the three climbers pointed out, her voice muffled by her wind mask. 'So by rights it should be Mount Rutherford.'

'Agh, no! This should not be!' the third member of the climbing team protested. 'Our lovely Miss Brown is the first lady to climb this formidable peak. It should be Mount Kayla.'

'That's very sweet, Stefan, but it still won't rate you more than a handshake back at the station.'

Ian Rutherford, an Oxford biology major, chuckled. 'I suppose we shouldn't worry about it. No matter what we might name it, we'll just end up calling it West Peak as we always have.'

'You suffer from excessive realism, Ian.' Stefan Kropodkin, of McGill's cosmic ray research program, grinned into the heavy woolen muffler that covered the lower half of his face.

'I think we need a little realism at the moment.' Kayla Brown was in geophysics at Purdue. 'We're already an hour off our schedule, and Dr. Creston wasn't too happy about us coming up here in the first place.'

'Another man with little romance in his soul,' Kropodkin grunted.

'We still have enough time for a few photographs,' Rutherford replied, unslinging his rucksack. 'Cresty certainly can't object to that.'

They saw it as they cautiously worked around the perimeter of the tiny plateau, and it was the sharp eyes of the little geophysicist-to-be from Indiana who made the discovery.

'Hey, guys, what's that? Down there on the glacier.'

Rutherford peered down into the saddle between the peaks. There was something there, just barely visible through the snow haze. He shoved his goggles up and pulled his binoculars out of their case. Being careful not to allow their frigid metal to touch his facial skin, he peered through them.

'Bloody hell! There is something down there!' He passed the field glasses to his friend. 'What do you think, Stefan?'

The Eastern European looked for a long time. Then he lowered the binoculars. 'It's a plane,' he said wonderingly, 'a plane on the ice.'

CHAPTER TWO

Huckleberry Ridge Mountain Warfare Training Center

Lieutenant Colonel Jonathan 'Jon' Smith U.S. Army, MD, stood with his back to the edge of the cliff and took his final look around.

It was beautiful up here. From this point, one could look southward along the western slope of the Cascade range, the mountains all stone blue-gray, snow-frost white and forest evergreen. Shreds of mist hovered protectively over the lower slopes, and the golden glow of the sunrise streamed through the notchbacks of the ridgeline. With a further twist of his head he could include the distant, shattered cone of Mount St. Helens in his field of vision, a thin haze of steam cupped in the volcano's gaping crater.

It reminded Smith of long-past summers in Yellowstone, and the childhood pride and thrill of packing into the back-country for the first time with his father and Uncle Ian.

The air especially, chill, sweet, and biting with life. He took a last deep breath of it, relishing the experience, and stepped backward off the edge of the precipice.

His horizon rotated a smooth ninety degrees, and the climbing harness gave him a reassuring hug as the thick green nylon rope laced through his carabiners took up the strain. With his weight held by the rappelling brake and the cleated soles of his Danner 'Fort Lewis' mountain boots braced against the lichen-mottled black basalt, he stood on the vertical face of the cliff. He was still new enough to the experience that he grinned with exhilaration. By God, this was better than lab work!

'Okay, Colonel,' the loud-hailer-amplified voice of the

instructor echoed up from the base of the cliff, 'push off and take it easy.'

Above, Smith's fellow students, clad in the same forest camouflage that he wore, peered over the cliff edge. This was the big drop, the 150-foot rappelling descent. The slack of the rope trailed away below him, and Smith gave it a final clearing flick. Then he snapped his legs straight, shoving away from the rock and allowing the line to feed through the brake.

In Smith's continuing efforts to balance the wildly diverse aspects of his life, that of soldier, scientist, physician, and spy, this mountain warfare course had been a resounding success.

Over the last three weeks, he had thrown himself into the challenge of the program with a growing enthusiasm, hardening his body with the muscle-cracking wilderness training regime and clearing his thinking after too many days spent buried in the Fort Detrick laboratories of the U.S. Army's Medical Research Institute of Infectious Diseases.

He had revived atrophied combat skills and had learned new ones: rough-terrain orienteering, hostile-climate survival, camouflage, high-angle marksmanship. And he had been introduced to the art of mountaineering. Smith had learned how to use crampons, pitons, and a rock hammer and more critically, how to trust in the rope and the harness, placing in abeyance the instinctive human fears of the fall and the high place.

The rappelling line zipped through the steel loops, the palm of Smith's heavy glove warmed, and his boots jolted against the rock twenty feet farther down the face. He felt his eyes narrow and his face tighten as the adrenaline surge hit, and once more he pushed away and sheered off another forty feet of cliff.

'Easy, sir,' the voice from below warned.

For a third time he pushed off, hard, allowing himself to plummet, the rope screaming and the rappelling brake smoking.

'Easy, Colonel . . . Easy . . . Easy! . . . I SAID EASY, GOD-DAMN IT!'

Smith braked hard, arresting his fall. Pulling himself upright, he dropped boots-first the last few feet to the fir-needle duff at the cliff base. Backing off the bottom end of the rope, he rubbed the scalding heat pulse out of his glove and onto the thigh of his fatigues.

A stocky ranger sergeant in a sand-colored beret came up behind him. 'Begging the colonel's pardon, sir,' he said sourly, 'but I hope you realize that an officer can bust his ass up here just about as bad as an enlisted man or an NCO.'

'I'll take your word for it, Top,' Smith grinned.

'Then when I say 'EASY, SIR,' I damn well mean it!' The climbing instructor was a twenty-year veteran of both the Seventy-fifth Ranger Regiment and the famed Tenth Mountain Division and thus was a rather privileged individual, even to a light colonel.

Smith sobered and undid the chin strap of his helmet. 'I hear you, Sergeant. I got a little full of myself up there. Bad idea. Next time it'll be by the book.'

Mollified, the instructor nodded back. 'Okay, sir. Beyond being a little wild, that was a good descent.'

'Thanks, Top.'

The instructor went back to overseeing the next student down, and Smith withdrew to the edge of the clearing at the cliff base. Shedding his helmet and harness, he removed a floppy boonie hat from his cargo pocket, slapping it into shape before settling it over his dark, short-trimmed hair.

Jon Smith was a man doing his early forties well: broad-shouldered, narrow-waisted, and taut-muscled from both his recent bout of training and an instinctively vigorous lifestyle. He was handsome in a strong, man's way, his tanned features fine-planed, intent, and somewhat immobile – a face that kept secrets well. His eyes, an unusual shade of dark blue, had the capacity to cut across a room with a penetrating focus.

Taking another deep pull of the clean mountain air,

8

Smith sank down at the base of a towering Douglas fir. This was a world he had lived in once. During an earlier phase of his career, before going into research and USAMRIID, he had done a tour with U.S. Army Special Forces as a combat medical officer on forward deployment with the Teams. It had been a good time, a time of challenges and comradeships. It had been a time of fears and despairs as well, but all in all, a good time.

A random thought had been creeping into his consciousness over the past few days: What about going tactical again, maybe for another tour in Special Forces? What about going back to the real Army for a while?

Smith recognized it to be only a random fancy. He was too senior for the field anymore. The best he could manage would be a desk job, a staff posting, probably right back inside the Washington beltway.

And then, he must confess, he was good at his current researcher's position, and it was a critical one. USAMRIID was America's first line of defense against both bioterrorism and the evolving global disease pool, and Smith was at the cutting edge of that defense. Important duty, undeniably.

And finally, there was his other tasking, the one not listed in his open service record. The one that had been born out of a megalomaniac's nightmare called the Hades Project, and the death of Dr. Sophia Russell, the woman he had loved and had planned to marry. That was a duty not to be denied, either, not if he was to know peace with himself.

Smith leaned back and relaxed against the moss-sheathed trunk of the fir tree, looking on as his classmates took their turn at the long line. Still, today was a good day to be a soldier.

CHAPTER THREE

The Camp David Presidential Retreat

The Camp David Presidential Retreat was located some seventy miles outside of Washington, DC, in a carefully isolated section of the Catoctin Mountain Recreation Area.

Its origins extended back to the turbulence of the Second World War, when, concerned about the safety of the presidential yacht, *Potomac*, the Secret Service requested that Franklin Delano Roosevelt find a new, more securable vacation and rest site in the Washington area.

Such a site was located in Maryland's forested hill country, a summer camp for federal employees built in the mid-1930s by the Civilian Conservation Corps as a pilot reclamation project for marginal wasteland.

As a holdover from the days of the *Potomac*, the camp was staffed by the United States Navy and Marine Corps, a tradition that continued to the present day, and it was originally code-named 'USS *Shangri-La*.' The retreat did not gain the name 'Camp David' until the 1950s, when it was retitled in honor of President Eisenhower's grandson.

Many critical pieces of diplomacy and statesmanship had taken place at the retreat, such as the historic Camp David peace accords between Egypt and Israel. But for all the meetings or conferences reported by the national media, there were others unreported and shrouded in the deepest secrecy.

Dressed casually in chino slacks, polo shirt, and golfing sweater, President Samuel Adams Castilla looked on as a Merlin helicopter in the dark-blue and gold livery of the presidential squadron sidled in over the helipad, its rotor wash stripping scarlet leaves from the treetops. Beyond the inevitable wary perimeter guard of Marine sentries and Secret Service agents, Castilla waited alone. There was no formal diplomatic greeting planned. No ruffles and flourishes. No onlooking members of the White House press corps.

Castilla's guest had requested it.

That guest was now disembarking from the idling helicopter – a stocky, heavy-jowled man with short-trimmed gray hair and a blue pin-striped suit of European cut. It was worn as if it didn't fit comfortably, as if the wearer was accustomed to a different kind of garb. The instinctive way he started to answer the salute of the Marine sentry at the foot of the helicopter's stairway suggested what that other garb might be.

Castilla, a former governor of New Mexico and still tall, slim, and square-shouldered in his fifties, strode forward, his hand extended. 'Welcome to Camp David, General,' he said over the idling whine of the Merlin's turbines.

Dimetri Baranov, commanding general of the Thirty-seventh Strategic Air Force Army of the Russian Federation, returned a solid, dry-palmed handclasp. 'It is an honor to be here, Mr. President. On behalf of my government, I thank you again for agreeing to meet with me under these . . . exceptional curcumstances.'

'Not at all, General. Our nations share many mutual interests these days. Consultation between our governments is always welcome.'

Or at least necessary, Castilla added silently.

The new non-Soviet Russia provided the United States with almost as many challenges as had the old USSR, just in different ways. Corruption-racked, politically unstable, and with its economy still struggling back from the ruins of Communism, the fledgling Russian democracy was perpetually threatening either to backslide into totalitarianism or to collapse altogether. Neither outcome would be favorable for the United States, and Castilla had sworn neither would happen on his watch.

Over considerable resistance from some of the old-school Cold Warriors and congressional budget-cutters, Castilla had rammed a series of thinly disguised foreign aid bills through Congress, working with Federation President Potrenko to plug some of the more critical leaks in the Russian ship of state. Another such bill was undergoing debate at this time, with the issue still very much in doubt.

The last thing the Castilla administration needed was a new Russian complication. However, on the previous evening, a Russian diplomatic aircraft had touched down at Andrews Air Force Base. Baranov had been aboard, bearing a sealed letter from President Potrenko, naming the general as his personal representative and authorizing him to negotiate with President Castilla on 'an urgent point of mutual national concern.'

Castilla feared this scenario could mean nothing but trouble. Baranov confirmed his fears.

'I regret the information I bear may not be so very welcome, Mr. President.' The general's eyes flicked downward for a moment to the locked briefcase he carried.

'I see, General. If you would care to accompany me, at least we can be comfortable as we discuss it.'

The Secret Service teams unobtrusively shifted their observation positions as Castilla led his guest around the rock-lined fishpond to Aspen Lodge, the presidential residence at Camp David.

A few minutes later the two men were seated at an Adirondack-style table on the lodge's broad porch, a quietly efficient navy steward serving hot tea, Russian style, in tall silver-filigreed glasses.

Baranov took a polite, disinterested sip. 'I thank you for your hospitality, Mr. President.'

Castilla, who on a warm fall day probably would have preferred a cold Coors, nodded an acknowledgment. 'I gather, General, this matter is rather time critical. How may we assist you and the Federation?'

Baranov removed a small key from the pocket of his vest.

Placing the briefcase on the table, he unlocked the latches and removed a folder. Deliberately he laid a series of photographic prints on the tabletop. 'I believe, Mr. President, that you might recognize these.'

Castilla took up one of the prints. Frowning, he adjusted his titanium-framed glasses and studied it.

It was a grainy black-and-white blowup from a video frame, showing a stark, ice-sheathed backdrop, possibly a glacier's surface. The wreck of a large four-engined aircraft lay centered in the image, essentially intact but with one long, straight wing twisted and buckled back from the crash impact. Castilla was enough of an aviation expert to recognize the wreck as that of a Boeing B-29 heavy bomber, the same kind of aircraft that had been used to bombard Imperial Japan in the closing days of the Second World War and that had delivered the first nuclear weapons against Hiroshima and Nagasaki.

Or so it appeared to be.

'The mystery plane,' some media outlets were calling it. Others were referring to it as 'the Polar Lady-Be-Good.' A scientific expedition on an isolated island in the Canadian Arctic had spotted the wreck on a mountain above their base, and these long-range telephoto images had been flashed around the world by the Internet and the global news networks.

It was the hot feature story of the day, and speculation about the aircraft and the aircrew that had flown it were rife.

'I recognize the picture,' Castilla said carefully. 'But I am curious as to how this antique aircraft might be a matter of concern for our two nations.'

Castilla already knew that the mystery plane was a point of concern for the Russians. It had been mentioned in his recent national security briefings as a peculiar blip on the scope of the National Security Agency.

Over the past few days the Russian government had become frantic over the so-called mystery plane. NSA Internet monitors had noted a massive spike of activity on the part of certain known Russian Federation intelligence nodes, producing hundreds of hits on global infonews sites covering the crash. Hundreds more hits were being generated on sites involving the multinational science expedition that had discovered the wreck, the historic tables of organization of the U.S. Air Force and its record of arctic operations.

Castilla would let the Russians provide their own explanation, although both he and his intelligence advisors had their suspicions.

The Russian kept his eyes fixed on the photographs covering the table. 'Before I answer that, Mr. President, I must first ask you a question.'

Castilla took up his own filigreed glass. 'Please feel free.'

Baranov tapped one of the photo prints. 'What has the United States government learned about this airplane?'

'We have learned, rather remarkably, that this was not an American Superfortress,' Castilla replied, taking a drink of his tea. 'The archives of both the U.S. Army Air Force and U.S. Air Force have been carefully examined. While we did lose a small number of B-29 aircraft and their B-50 derivative over the Arctic, all of those downed bombers have been located. In fact, all Boeing B-29s known to have served in the U.S. inventory have been accounted for.'

Castilla set his tea glass down. 'Some eighty-seven Superfortresses were also provided to Great Britain in 1950. The Royal Air Force called them the Washington. The British Air Ministry has been consulted, and none of their Washingtons were ever lost or even flown over the Canadian Arctic, and all of the aircraft were eventually returned to the United States.'

Castilla looked levelly across the table. 'Does that answer your question, General?'

Baranov didn't look up for a long moment. 'I regret that it does, Mr. President. I must also now, regretfully, inform you that this aircraft may very well belong to us. It could be Russian. And if this is so, it could possibly represent a definite threat to both of our nations and to the world as a whole.'

'How so, General?'

'This aircraft may be a Tupolev Tu-4 heavy bomber, code-named by NATO "the Bull." It is an aircraft very . . . similar to your B-29. They were used by our Long Range Aviation Forces, or rather by the Long Range Aviation Forces of the Soviet Union, during the early years of the Cold War. On March fifth of 1953, one such aircraft, radio call sign Misha 124, disappeared on a training exercise over the North Pole. The fate of this aircraft was unknown to us. All radio and radar contact with the bomber was lost, and the wreck was never located.'

Baranov took a deep, deliberate breath. 'We fear this mystery plane may be the Misha 124.'

Castilla frowned. 'And why should a Soviet bomber lost on a training exercise over fifty years ago be considered anything more than a relic of the Cold War?'

'Because the Misha 124 was not a simple bombing plane; it was a strategic biological weapons platform, and at the time of its disappearance, it was fully armed.'

In spite of the warmth of the afternoon and the hot tea he had consumed, Castilla felt a chill ripple down his spine. 'What was the agent?' he demanded.

'Anthrax, Mr. President. Weaponized anthrax. Given your nation's recent concerns in these matters, I'm sure you recognize the disastrous potential.'

'All too well, General.' Castilla scowled. The megalomaniac with an elementary biological laboratory and delusions of godhood; the whiff of powder sifting from an opened envelope those were images to haunt a President's mind.

'The Misha 124 was equipped with a dry aerosol dispersal system,' Baranov continued. 'The bioagent was carried in a sealed stainless steel reservoir mounted in the aircraft's forward bomb bay. Should an in-flight emergency take place, the standard operating procedure would have been for this reservoir to be jettisoned over the open sea or, in this

15

instance, the polar ice pack. But, from the photographs available to us, it is impossible to tell if this procedure was successfully carried out. The reservoir and the agent it contained could still be in the wreck.'

'And still dangerous?'

Baranov lifted his hands in frustration. 'Very possibly, Mr. President. Given the subfreezing polar environment, the spores could conceivably be as deadly today as they were when first loaded aboard the aircraft.'

'Good God.'

'We urgently desire the assistance of the United States in this matter, Mr. President. Firstly, to ascertain if this . . . problem actually exists, and then to deal with it if it does.'

The Russian's hands wandered amid the photographs on the table. 'I trust, Mr. President, you can understand why my government feels secrecy in this matter is imperative. The revelation that an active and dangerous biological-weapons system of the former Soviet Union has been found on the North American continent could further strain relations between the current Russian Federation and the United States at this critical hour.'

'To say the least,' Castilla mused grimly. 'The Joint Russian-American Counterterrorism Act would go right out the door. Beyond that, any terrorist group or rogue nation on the planet who learned of the Misha crash would leap at the chance to acquire a biological-warfare arsenal simply by picking it up off the ground. And by the way, General, how much active agent are we talking about here? How many pounds, or rather, kilograms?'

'Tons, Mr. President.' The Russian's expression was stony. 'The Misha 124 was carrying two metric tons of weaponized anthrax.'

The Marine Merlin growled away over the treetops, returning General Baranov to Washington, DC, and the Russian embassy while Samuel Adams Castilla walked slowly back to Aspen Lodge. His Secret Service guard held distant cover. It was obvious to the team leader that the POTUS desired only the company of his own thoughts.

A new figure was seated at the table on the lodge porch: a smallish, graying, slope-shouldered man in his sixties. An anonymous kind of individual who worked hard at his anonymity, Nathaniel Frederic Klein did not at all resemble the classic image of a spymaster. At best, he could manage retired businessman or schoolteacher. Yet he was both a service-hardened veteran of the Central Intelligence Agency and the director of the single most secret intelligence-gathering and covert-action force in the western hemisphere.

Early in his first term, President Castilla had been confronted by what had become known as the Hades Program, a ruthless bioterrorism campaign that had caused the deaths of thousands around the world and that had come within a hairsbreadth of killing millions. In his postcrisis assessment of the incident, Castilla had come to certain ominous conclusions about America's capacity to deal with such threats.

The American intelligence and counterintelligence communities, by their sheer size and breadth of responsibility, were becoming clumsy and bureaucratically overburdened. Critical information was being 'stovepiped' and was failing to reach its needed destinations. Petty interdepartmental jealousies created unnecessary friction, and a growing number of professional political ass-coverers strangled operational initiative, crippling America's capacity to react to a rapidly changing global situation.

Castilla's had always been an unconventional administration, and his response to the Hades incident had been unconventional as well. He had chosen Fred Klein, an old and trusted family friend, to create an entirely new agency built around a small, handpicked cadre of specialists, military and civilian, from outside the regular national intelligence community.

These 'mobile cipher' agents were carefully chosen both for their exceptional and unusual skills and capabilities and for their lack of personal commitments and attachments.

17

They answered only to Klein and Castilla. Financed from national 'black' assets outside the conventional congressional budgetary loop, Covert One was the personal action arm of the President of the United States.

That was why Castilla had Klein standing by during his conference with the Russian general.

A beverage cart had been wheeled out beside the table, and a pair of shot glasses, one filled with an amber fluid and the other with water, sat at each place.

'Bourbon and branch, Sam,' Klein said, lifting his own drink. 'It's a little early in the day, but I thought you might need one.'

'I appreciate the thought,' Castilla said, sinking into his chair. 'You heard it all?'

Klein nodded. 'I had a clear pickup on the shotgun mike.'

'What do you think?'

Klein smiled without humor. 'You're the National Command Authority, Mr. President. You tell me.'

Castilla grimaced and lifted his drink. 'As it stands, it's a mess. And if we aren't exceedingly careful and extremely lucky, it's going to grow into a vastly larger mess. For certain, if Senator Grenbower gets his hands on this, the Joint Counterterrorism Act is as dead as fair play. Damn it, Fred, the Russians need our help, and we need to give it to them.'

Klein lifted an eyebrow. 'In essence we're talking about American military aid to the former Soviet Union, monetary and advisory. That still doesn't sit well with a lot of people.'

'A Balkanized Russia wouldn't sit well, either! If the Russian Federation disintegrates, as it is threatening to do, we could find ourselves facing Yugoslavia squared!'

Klein took a sip of whisky. 'You're preaching to the choir, Sam. The Russian devil we do know is better than the several dozen we don't. The question, again, is, how do you want to proceed?'

Castilla shrugged. 'I know how I wish we could proceed: with a squadron of Strike Eagles armed with precision-guided thermite bombs. We incinerate the damn thing where it sits, along with anything it might be carrying. But it's too late for that. The global media knows the aircraft exists. If we simply destroy the plane outright and without a viable explanation, every foreign affairs reporter on the planet will start digging. Before we know it we'll be facing a congressional investigation – just what we and the Russians don't want.'

Klein alternated a taste of whisky with a sip of branch water. 'I think an investigation may be the first step, Sam. At least our investigation. Everyone could be getting ahead of themselves here – you, me, the Russians. There may not be a problem at all.'

Castilla lifted an eyebrow. 'How do you figure that?'

'The emergency procedure the Soviet aircrew was supposed to follow: the jettisoning of the bioagent reservoir. For all we actually know, that load of anthrax may have been rotting on the bottom of the Arctic Ocean for the past half century.

'The discovery of the wreck of a fifty-year-old Soviet bomber on an arctic island, even if it had been outfitted as a biowarfare platform, would not be an insurmountable difficulty. As you pointed out, the plane itself would be just a Cold War anecdote. What supplies the "flash' to the problem, what makes it politically indigestible, is the possible presence of the anthrax. We have to find out if it's still aboard the aircraft. We have to find out fast and we have to find out first, before some war-bird enthusiast or extreme tourist decides to have a look inside that wreck. If the bioagent isn't aboard the plane, then everyone can relax and we can turn the entire question over to the Smithsonian Air and Space Museum.'

'What's your proposal, Director?' Sam Castilla was not Sam Castilla now. He was the President of the United States.

Klein opened a thin file folder that had been resting on the table beside him. It contained hard-copy printouts downloaded from the Covert One database in the few minutes following Baronov's departure. 'According to the information available from the leader of the scientific expedition on the island, no one has yet actually reached the crash site. They've only photographed it from long range. This could prove exceedingly fortunate both for them and for us.

'Mr. President, I propose that we insert a small Covert One action group equipped for mountain and arctic operations. We include a biowarfare specialist, an expert on Soviet-era weapons systems, and the appropriate support personnel. We have them assess the situation and advise us on what we're actually facing. Once we have some solid intelligence to work with we can develop a valid response scenario.'

Castilla nodded. 'It makes sense to me. When do we bring Ottawa into the loop? This island – Wednesday, I think it's called – is in the Canadian Arctic. It's their territory. They have a right to know what's going on.'

Klein pursed his lips thoughtfully. 'You know the old saying, Sam. "Two men can keep a secret as long as one of them is dead." If we want to be serious about security in this matter, we have got to limit dispersion.'

'That's a hell of a way to treat a neighbor, Fred. We've had our disagreements with the gentlemen up north, but they are still an old and valuable ally. I don't want to risk further damage to that relationship.'

'Then let's try this,' Klein replied. 'We advise Ottawa that we've been approached by the Russians about the possibility that this downed mystery plane might be Soviet. We say that we aren't sure about this. There's a chance that it still could be one of ours and that we want to insert a joint U.S.-Russian investigation team to establish just who the aircraft belongs to. We'll keep them advised as to what we discover.'

Klein lifted another sheet of hard copy from the file. 'According to this, NOAA and the U.S. Coast Guard are supplying logistical support for the multinational science expedition on the island. The team leader is Canadian, and he's already acting as the on-site representative for the Canadian government. We can suggest using him as our designated liaison as well. We can also ask for the expedition leader to keep his people well away from the downed aircraft until the arrival of our team, to prevent the disturbance of . . . say . . . historic relics and forensic evidence.'

'That could kill several birds with one stone,' Castilla agreed.

'The Canadian government's resources are stretched very thin across their arctic frontier,' Klein continued. 'I suspect they'd be quite content to have us tidy up this little question for them. If there isn't an anthrax problem, then what they don't know can't hurt us. If there is a problem, then we can bring in the Canadian prime minister for the development-of-resolution phase.'

Castilla nodded. 'I think that will be an acceptable compromise. You mentioned a joint Russian-American team. Do you think that's advisable?'

'I suspect it will be unavoidable, Sam. They'll want to be hands-on with anything that concerns their national security, past, present, or future. As soon as we inform Baranov that we are initiating an investigation of the crash, I'm willing to bet he's going to insist on there being a Russian representative with our people.'

Castilla tossed back the last of his whisky, making a face at its bite. 'That brings us to the next big question. Are the Russians giving us a square count on this? We know they sure as hell weren't on the Bioaparat incident.'

Klein didn't answer for a protracted moment. 'Sam,' he said finally, 'whether he answers to a czar, a premier, or a president, a Russian is a Russian is a Russian. Even post–Berlin Wall, we are still dealing with a nation where conspiracy is instinctive and paranoia is a survival mechanism. Right now, I'm willing to wager you a bottle of this good bourbon that we are not being told the whole story.'

Castilla chuckled under his breath. 'Wager not taken.

We'll work to the assumption that an alternative agenda will be in play. It will be up to your people to discern just what it is.'

'I already have a couple of good primary ciphers in mind, but I may have to pull in at least one outsider specialist to back them up.'

The President nodded. 'You've got your usual blank check, Fred. Pull in your team.'

CHAPTER FOUR

Huckleberry Ridge Mountain Warfare Training Center

Throughout the morning, small-unit war had raged across the alpine meadows and forested slopes of the Cascade range. Rock scuffed, devil's club burned, and with their camo face paint streaking with sweat, Jon Smith and the other three members of his trainee fire team dropped into cover behind a rotten fir log.

The ridge crest lay perhaps fifty yards beyond and above their position in the tree line, up an open slope dotted with ghost-pale snags and shaggy with low brush cover. Just beyond that crest would be another open slope and another tree line and, just possibly, another fire team similar to their own. Another group of classmates designated for the day as part of Red Force, the enemy.

Nothing moved save for a few dried grass stems in the hint of a breeze. Smith, his eyes fixed on the ridge crest, began to struggle out of his rucksack harness. 'I'll be back in a minute, Corporal. I want to see if we might have some company over on the far side.'

'What do you want us to do, sir?' His assistant team leader, a gangly young paratrooper from the Eighty-second Airborne, inquired. He and the other two members of the combat patrol lay spaced out in the forest duff beside the log.

'Just sit tight,' Smith replied, distracted. 'There's no sense in anyone else breaking cover.'

'Whatever you say, sir.'

Smith slithered over the top of the log. With his rifle resting across his forearms, he began to belly-slither up the slope to the crest. He'd already plotted his crawl path through the open terrain, a weaving course that would take best advantage of the deepest brush clumps and largest downed logs to maximize his concealment.

Smith took his time, mentally projecting and plotting each inch of the crawl, down to how his movements would affect each individual overhanging branchlet and twig. A hunting python would have created a greater disturbance as it oozed to the ridgeline.

Objective achieved. He held the high ground, and the far side of the ridge opened out below him. More brush tangles, more storm-stripped logs, and another line of evergreens, deep sun shadows puddling beneath their low-set branches. Hugging the earth, Smith eased the SR-25 out ahead of him. Flipping the protecting lens caps off the telescopic sights, he wormed forward a final foot, clearing his firing arc.

His weapon was something new since the last time he had served with the Teams. A creation of master gunsmith Eugene Stoner, the SR-25 was referred to as a tactical sniper's rifle. Scope sighted and firing the 7.65mm NATO cartridge through a semiautomatic action, it fed from a twenty-round box magazine. Possessing considerably more range, accuracy, and stopping power than the conventional assault rifle, the SR was also light and handy enough to be carried as a primary weapon, at least for a man of Jon Smith's size.

Over the past couple of weeks Smith had become fond of the potent brute and had been willing to put up with the extra carrying weight and barrel length in the field, amiably arguing the SR's finer points with his fellow trainees. Now he intended to put its qualities to use.

Slowly Smith tracked the sighting reticle across the tree line at the bottom of the ridge. Any potential target would presumably be as concerned with concealment as he was.

Once upon a time, in a more chivalrous day, stretcher bearers, medics, and military doctors had been classified as noncombatants. They were barred from carrying weapons and participating in active combat, yet they were also shielded by the theoretical Rules of Warfare, rendering them invalid targets on the battlefield.

But with the coming of asymmetrical warfare there had also come a new breed of enemy, one who obeyed only the laws of savagery and who viewed a Red Cross brassard only as an excellent target. In such an environment the Marine motto of 'Every man a rifleman' became a matter of necessity and common sense.

Smith completed the first scope sweep without result. Swearing silently, he tracked back. Those bastards had to be down there somewhere.

There! A minute movement at the base of that cedar. A head had tossed, maybe shaking off one of the endemic yellow jackets. Now Smith could just make out the outline of half a camoed face, peering around the tree trunk.

A couple of meters away, the outline of a second well-camouflaged form snapped clear in Smith's mind, stretched out beneath a brush tangle. There'd be more members of the fire team, but these two would have to do. He'd already stayed fixed for too long. They'd be hunting for him as he'd been hunting them. Time to hit and git!

The man behind the cedar was the harder shot. Smith would drop him first. The sighting crosshairs jumped back to the doomed soldier's forehead, and Smith's finger tightened on the trigger.

The Stoner crashed out a single shot, but the only thing that lanced downrange was an invisible pulse of light. Keyed by the noise and recoil of the blank cartridge, the beam from the laser tube clipped beneath the rifle's slender barrel licked out, tagging the sensors on the targeted man's MILES harness.

MILES, the Multiple Integrated Laser Exercise System, was the U.S. Army's means of keeping score in its grimly realistic war games. A dazzling blue strobe light began to flicker beneath the cedar tree, declaring to the world that someone had just 'died.'

There was a convulsive movement beneath the adjacent brush pile, and Smith shifted targets, firing a three-round raking burst. A second strobe light announced a second termination.

Smith rolled back from the ridgeline. Good enough for government work. Now to get out . . .

The forest line below him exploded in automatic weapons fire, and blue MILES strobes behind to blink in the tree shade.

He had taken too long! Someone had circled in behind the rest of his patrol! Smith crouched up, trying to regain situational awareness. The firefight seemed to be raging in the forest directly below him. He could go laterally along the ridge and disengage . . . No, damn it! That was his team down there!

Breaking cover with his rifle lifted, Smith ran downslope toward the tree line, trying to dodge and weave. A squad automatic weapon rattled out a long burst, and the light on Smith's MILES harness blazed on; the audial warning proclaimed him a dead man.

Smith drew up, thoroughly disgusted with himself.

The blank fire ended, and a man emerged from the trees: the same noncom who had worked with Smith on the long rappel. He'd been one of the instructor/observers monitoring this phase of the day's exercises. 'You're all dead, Colonel,' he yelled. 'Let's break for lunch.'

It would be a ranger's lunch: a Hooyah energy bar and a long swig of tepid water from a hydration pack, the slayers and the slain collapsing to rest side by side beneath the trees.

Nor was it 'rest' in a pure form. Such a concept was alien to the program. Weapons and equipment had to be cleaned, ammunition pouches reloaded with more blank cartridges, maps studied, and critiques received on the morning's drills. But it was a chance to unhelmet and unharness and sit in the shade, an opportunity to ease burning lungs and aching muscles for a few precious minutes. A luxury, but one Smith refused to enjoy.

Grimly he spread a poncho out on the forest floor, not for himself but for the SR-25. Breaking out his gun-cleaning kit, he began to knock down the rifle, removing the powder residue from its components. He'd fired only the two shots, but it gave him something to do while he raged at himself.

The ranger instructor crossed to where Smith sat cross-legged on the poncho, and took his own seat on a nearby log.

'Would the colonel care to tell me how he fucked up, sir?'

Smith stabbed a loaded cleaning rod down the SR's barrel. 'I failed to watch my back, Top. While I was fixated on the target on the far side of that ridge, I let the Red Force elements come in behind me. It was stupidity, just plain stupidity.'

The noncom scowled and shook his head. 'No, sir. You're missing it. It was something more stupid than that. You didn't let your troops cover your back, or cover their own.'

Smith looked up. 'What do you mean?'

'I mean you didn't use your team, sir. You didn't deploy them into overwatch positions; you just told them to stay put. You might have been able to get away with that with an experienced noncom as your assistant team leader. He'd have set up a defense perimeter automatically, without having to be ordered. But you had a green kid with you who assumed his superior officer was supposed to be doing all the thinking. You didn't take your troop quality into consideration. That was your second mistake.'

Smith nodded his agreement. 'What else?'

'You could have used another set of eyes up with you on the ridge. You might have acquired your targets faster and been out of there faster.'

Smith didn't consider arguing the points. You didn't argue when you knew you were in the wrong. 'Points all taken, Top. I blew it.'

'Yes, sir. You did. But it was the *way* you blew it . . .' The sergeant hesitated. 'Begging the colonel's pardon, but may I speak off the record?'

There was a formality in the ranger's voice, the kind often used by a noncom when bringing a potentially sensitive subject up with a superior.

'I'm here to learn, Top.'

The instructor studied Smith out of thoughtful, narrowed eyes. 'You are an operator, aren't you, Colonel? The real shit, not just a pill roller getting his ticket punched.'

Smith stalled, lightly oiling the dismounted bolt of his rifle, considering his answer.

Covert One did not exist. Smith was a member of no such organization. Those were absolutes. Yet this grizzled Special Ops trooper would no doubt be a master at seeing through bullshit. Likewise, Smith had come here to learn, especially about himself.

'I'm telling you that I'm not, Top,' he replied, selecting his words carefully.

The ranger nodded. 'I get what you're saying, sir.'

Now it was the instructor's turn to pause in thought. 'If you were an operator,' he went on finally, 'I say that you've worked solo a lot.'

'What would make you say that?' Smith inquired cautiously.

The ranger shrugged. 'It sticks out all over you, sir. In a lot of ways, you're good. And I mean damn good. You've got all your personal moves down solid. I've rarely seen better. But they're just *your* moves. You kept trying to do it all yourself.'

'I see,' Smith replied slowly, replaying the morning's exercises in his mind.

'Yes, sir. You forget your people and you forget to think for your people,' the noncom continued. 'That setup you ran on the ridge this morning probably would have worked just fine for one man, but there was more than one of you. I don't know exactly what you're doing in this man's Army, Colonel, but whatever it is, it's making you forget how to command.'

Forgetting how to command? That was a stark assessment for any officer – a brutal one, in fact. Could it conceivably be a valid one?

It was a startling thought, but it was entirely possible, given the peculiarities of his career path.

USAMRIID was not a conventional Army unit. The majority of its personnel were civilian, like his late fiancée, Dr. Sophia Russell. Directing a research project at Fort Detrick was more akin to working in a major university or a corporate laboratory than in a military installation. It was a peer-among-peers environment that required tact and a mastery of bureaucracy more than a command presence.

As for that other peculiar facet of his life, by the very nature and structure of the job, mobile cipher agents frequently operated alone. Since being drawn into Covert One in the aftermath of the Hades crisis, Smith had worked with a variety of allies in the field, but he had not borne the burden of being directly responsible for them.

It was one thing to make a bad call and get yourself killed. It was quite another when that failed call caused the death of someone else. Smith understood that. There had been a time in Africa years ago, before Covert One, when Smith had made such a failed call. The personal reverberations and pain of that decision lingered to this day. It was one of the things that had diverted Smith into the rarified world of medical research.

He slid the oiled bolt back into the SR's receiver. Had that move been a form of cowardice? Possibly. It would be something to take a long and hard look at.

'I see what you mean, Top,' Smith replied. 'Let's say that particular requirement hasn't come up with me recently.'

The instructor nodded. 'Maybe so, sir, but if you keep wearing those oak leaves, it will. You can bet your ass on it.'

Or someone else's.

Smith was still pondering the instructor's words when an alien sound intruded into the forest quiet: the muffled purrgrowl of a powerful two-cycle engine. A camouflaged all-terrain vehicle appeared through the trees, tearing up the trail from the Huckleberry Ridge base camp.

The young female soldier braked the ATV to a halt in the grove short of the mountain warfare class. Dismounting, she jogged toward them.

Smith and the ranger sergeant got to their feet as the courier approached.

'Colonel Smith?' she inquired, saluting.

'Right here, Corporal,' Smith replied, returning the salute.

'A call came in for you at base camp, sir, from the officer of the day at Main Post.' She produced a piece of white notepaper from the breast pocket of her BDUs. 'As soon as possible you are to call this phone number. He indicated it was very important.'

Smith accepted the slip of paper and glanced at it. That was all that was required. The number was one that Smith had long ago committed to memory. It was not so much a phone number now as an identifier and a call to arms.

Smith refolded the paper and stowed it in his own pocket, to be burned later. 'I'll need to get back to the fort,' he said, his voice flat.

'That's been arranged for, sir,' the courier replied. 'You can take the quad down to base camp. They'll have a vehicle waiting for you.'

'We'll take care of your gear, Colonel,' the instructor interjected.

Smith nodded. It was likely he wouldn't be back. 'Thanks, Top,' he said, extending his hand to the noncom. 'It's been a good program. I've learned a great deal.'

The sergeant returned the solid handgrip. 'I hope it'll help, sir . . . wherever. Good luck.'

The highway leading down to Fort Lewis snaked through the forested foothills of the Cascades, passing a series of small towns undergoing the economic conversion from logging to tourism for their sustenance. The sixth-largest Army post in the United States, Fort Lewis served as the primary staging facility to America's defense commitments in the North Pacific and as the home base for the Army's cutting-edge Stryker brigades. Scores of the massive eight-wheeled armored fighting vehicles could be seen occupying the post motor pools and rumbling down the access roads to the firing ranges.

The fort also served as home for the Fifth Special Forces Group, the Second Battalion, Seventy-fifth Rangers, and a squadron of the 160th Special Aviation Regiment. Thus, the members of the base cadre were well acquainted with the requirements and necessities of covert operations.

The officer of the day didn't ask questions when Smith checked in at the headquarters building. He had been advised to expect this sunburned and bearded stranger in sweat-stained camouflage. He had also been ordered by the highest of authorities to grant Jon Smith every possible assistance.

In short order, Smith found himself seated alone in a headquarters office with a secure communications deck on the desk before him. He dialed the contact number without consulting the note he had been given. On the East Coast of the United States a phone rang in a facility the public believed to be a private yacht club in Anacosta, Maryland.

'Yes.' The answering voice was a woman's, toneless and crisply professional.

'This is Lieutenant Colonel Jon Smith,' he said with careful deliberation, not for the human at the far end of the circuit but for the voice identification system that would be monitoring the call.

The device's verdict must have been favorable, for when Maggie Templeton spoke again it was with considerably more warmth and animation. 'Hello, Jon, how's Washington? The state, that is.'

'Very green, Maggie, at least the half I've been in. I gather you and the bosses have something for me.'

'We do.' The professionalism crept back into her voice.

Margaret Templeton was more than Fred Klein's executive assistant. The widow of a CIA field operative and a veteran of her own years at Langley, the slender, graying blonde was, for all intents and purposes, Covert One's second in command. 'Mr. Klein wants to brief you personally. Are you set up to receive hard copy?'

Smith glanced at the desktop laser printer connected to the secure deck, noting its glowing green check lights. 'Yes.'

'I'll start sending you the mission database. I'm putting you through to Mr. Klein now. Take care.'

'I always try, Maggie.'

As the desk printer started to purr and hiss, the phone clicked, and Smith visualized the connection jumping from Maggie Templeton's integrated workstation/office with its bristling array of computer and communications accesses to that second, smaller, starker room.

'Good morning, Jon.' Fred Klein's voice was quiet and instinctively controlled. 'How's the training going?'

'Very well, sir. I only have three days left to go on the course.'

'No, you don't, Colonel. You've just graduated. We need to put that training to work right now. A problem has developed that you are uniquely positioned to deal with.'

Smith had been bracing for this ever since receiving his contact notification. Still, he had to suppress a sudden shiver. It was happening again, as it had happened so often since Sophia's death. Once more something, somewhere, had gone terribly wrong.

'What's the situation, sir?' Smith inquired.

'Your specialty, biological warfare,' the director of Covert One replied. 'Only on this occasion the circumstances are somewhat unusual.'

Smith frowned. 'How can biowar ever be considered anything but unusual?'

A humorless chuckle came back. 'I stand corrected, Jon. Let me escalate that to exceptionally unusual.'

'How so, sir?'

'For one, the location – the Canadian Arctic. And for the other, our employers.'

'Our employers?'

'That's right, Jon. It's a long story, but this time around it appears we're going to be working for the Russians.'

CHAPTER FIVE

Beijing

Randi Russell sat in the Cantonese restaurant that opened off the Hotel Beijing's large and somewhat careworn lobby, breakfasting on dim sum and green tea.

She had worked inside Red China on a number of occasions for the Central Intelligence Agency, and oddly enough, she had found it a comparatively easy operating environment.

The mammoth PRC state security machine was ever present, purring and clicking away in the national background. As an *idowai*, a foreigner, every taxi or train ride she took would be recorded. Every long-distance telephone call would be monitored, every e-mail read. Every tour guide or translator or hotel manager or travel agent dealt with would answer to his or her assigned contact within the People's Armed Police.

So totally pervasive was this mechanism that it actually began to work against itself. As a spy, Randi was never tempted to let her guard down or become sloppy with her cover, because she was always acutely aware she was under observation.

This morning, her observers would be seeing a decidedly attractive American businesswoman in her early thirties, dressed in a neat beige knit dress and a pair of expensive but sensibly heeled pumps. Short, tousled golden-blond hair framed her face, and her open farm girl's features bore only a light touch of cosmetics along with the dusting of freckles across the bridge of her nose.

Only another member of the profession might note the

irregularity, and then only by looking deeply into her dark brown eyes. There could be seen the hint of an internal bleakness and an instinctive, perpetual wariness of the world around her – the mark of one who had been both the hunter and the hunted.

Today she hunted, or at least stalked.

Randi had chosen her table in the cafe with care, her position giving her an uninterrupted band of vision that cut across the hotel's lobby between the elevator bank and the main entrance. She scanned it only from the corner of her eye. As she nibbled and sipped, her attention appeared to be focused solely on the open and totally irrelevant business file on the table in front of her.

Intermittently she would glance at her wristwatch as if counting down time to some appointment.

She had no such appointment. But someone else might. The previous evening she'd committed the Beijing traffic schedules for Air Koryo, the North Korean national airline, to memory, and she was moving into a potentially hot time frame.

Randi had been covering the lobby for almost two hours now. If nothing happened within the next fifteen or twenty minutes, another member of the CIA cell assigned to the hotel would take over the surveillance, and Randi would disengage before her lingering became a cause for suspicion. She would spend the rest of the day doing suitable junior executive busy-work around the Chinese capital, all of it essentially as meaningless as the report she was reading.

But she had the duty now, and she caught the passage of the two men through the lobby.

The smaller, slighter, and more nervous of the pair was dressed in blue jeans and a crisp khaki-colored nylon windcheater, and he carried a battered computer case as if it was a precious thing.

The second man, taller, burlier, and older, wore a poorly cut black business suit and an air of guarded grimness. A person familiar with Asian ethnology might have been able to identify them both as Korean. Randi Russell knew them to be so. The man in the suit was an agent of the North Korean People's Security Force. The man in the wind-cheater was Franklin Sun Chok, a third-generation Korean American, a graduate of the University of California at Berkeley, an employee of the Lawrence Livermore Laboratories, and a traitor.

He was why she and an entire task force of CIA operatives had been positioned across the width of the Pacific: to oversee his act of treason and, if necessary, to assist him in carrying it out.

Unhurriedly Randi closed her file and tucked it into her shoulder bag. Removing a pen, she ticked her room number onto the bill on the table. Rising, she crossed into the lobby and dropped onto the trail of the two men.

Outside, the hotel's taxi marshal was feeding a line of guests into the swarm of cabs clumping up on a smog- and car-clogged Dong Chang an Jie Street.

Sun Chok got into the cab first, moving quickly. The North Korean security agent paused before following, sweeping a last jet-eyed stare around the hotel entrance. Randi felt that cold gaze brush past her.

She kept her own eyes averted until the Korean's cab pulled away. Given the timing of their movement, Randi knew where they must be bound. She wasn't unduly concerned about maintaining continuous contact. A minute or so later, using a hesitant Chinese several grades below her actual grasp of the language, she instructed the driver of her own cab to take her to Beijing's Capital Airport.

As the little Volkswagen sedan struggled through the hysterical traffic of Beijing's Forbidden City district, Randi flipped open her tri-band cellular phone, hitting a preset number.

'Hello, Mr. Danforth. This is Tanya Stewart. I'm on my way out to meet Mr. Bellerman at the airport.'

'Very good, Tanya,' Robert Danforth, the manager of the Beijing office of the California Pacific Consortium, replied.

'He should be coming in on the Cathay Pacific flight nineteen, or at least that's the last word we had. No guarantees. You know how the Los Angeles office is.'

'I understand, sir. I'll keep you posted.' Randi snapped her phone shut, having completed her carefully scripted verbal dance.

Robert Danforth was actually the senior agent in charge of the CIA's Beijing station, and the California Pacific Consortium was a front company used to provide cover for transient agents operating in northern mainland China. As for Mr. Bellerman, he existed only as a justification name inserted into routine Consortium business traffic over the past few days.

The cellular call had served two purposes. For one, it would explain Randi's actions to PRC State Security, should their curiosity be aroused. For the other, it would advise her superiors that two years of carefully crafted counterintelligence work was about to reach fruition.

When Franklin Sun Chok first appeared as a blip on the CIA's screens, he had been a graduate student of physics at Berkeley, employed at the huge Lawrence Livermore Laboratory complex in the Bay Area. A studious and intensely earnest young man, his after-hours interests and concerns included international disarmament and his ethnic heritage.

Neither of which was particularly out of place for a young American academic, but given the highly secretive nature of much of Lawrence Livermore's work, it had rated him a spot check by laboratory security. Alarm bells rang.

Sun Chok was found to be associating closely with a small Korean nationalist group on the Berkeley campus, a group promoting, loudly, the national unification of Korea and the withdrawal of the United States military from the peninsula. It was also an identified front organization for North Korean espionage in the United States.

Randi's cab drew up in the long line of vehicles feeding through the tollbooth access to the airport expressway.

Perhaps a dozen cars ahead, she spotted the taxi carrying Sun Chok and his security escort. All was still on track.

Sun Chok had been placed under intensive covert surveillance. He was tailed, his apartment was searched and bugged, and his telephone and Internet traffic was closely monitored. In short order it was confirmed that he was indeed spying for the North Korean government.

The evidence was adequate for an arrest warrant, but an alternative had been decided upon. Franklin Sun Chok's betrayal would be put to good use.

Randi glanced at her wristwatch and frowned. If this traffic didn't break soon, both she and the Koreans would be in trouble. Then she told herself not to be silly. The next flight to Pyongyang wouldn't be going anywhere until its VIP passengers were aboard.

No doubt to the delight of his North Korean controllers, Franklin Sun Chok was given a promotion at the Lawrence Livermore facility, complete with a handsome pay raise, a private office, an executive assistant, and a deeper access to the laboratories' secrets. In reality, he was being encapsulated in a technological fantasyland of the Central Intelligence Agency's creation.

For over a year, Sun Chok was fed a carefully metered diet of solid, valid, low-grade information: research breakthroughs that were destined to be openly published in science journals in months to come, and minor military secrets that would be secret only until the next round of congressional budgetary hearings.

As eager and as innocent as a baby bird gobbling an offered worm, he had relayed this information to his contacts, building their confidence in him as a valid resource.

When U.S. intelligence assets monitoring North Korea's internal R & D programs began to see this fed information being put to use, they knew that the Sun Chok line was being trusted. It was time to drive home the dagger.

Beijing Capital Airport looked little different from any other modernistic airline terminal anywhere else in the world. Drawing up at the departure entries, Randi caught only a glimpse of the Koreans as they entered the terminal, but that was as she wished it. If she couldn't see them, they couldn't see her.

Barring the usual large number of assault rifle-carrying People's Armed Police, airport security was actually lighter than at an American airport. Randi was permitted access to the concourses after only a single pass of her shoulder bag through an X-ray machine. She had nothing to be concerned about here. She carried neither weapons nor any James Bondian gadgetry. None were needed for this tasking.

With the hook solidly set in the North Korean jaw, Franklin Sun Chok was 'cleared' to an even higher security level and assigned work on a major new project involving the national antiballistic missile defense network. Information began to cross Sun Chok's desk that hinted tantalizingly at possible countermeasures to the system.

On the evening before Sun Chok left on his annual vacation from the laboratory, he remained late in his office, 'cleaning up his desk.' As CIA observers looked on cybernetically, Sun Chok accessed and downloaded a long series of secure data files on the antiballistic missile network.

Unknown to him, each of his illicit computer accesses was diverted to a carefully doctored alternate file set, prepared just for this moment. Then, instead of heading for Las Vegas as he had told his coworkers, Sun Chok had driven north, for the Canadian border.

Clearing security, Randi strode through the luggage-burdened crowds. She was less apparent here, for Capital Airport handled all the international traffic for Beijing, and many of the tourists and business travelers bustling around her now were American or European.

Cathay Pacific had been chosen as the preferred carrier for the mythical Mr. Bellerman because its boarding gates were located immediately adjacent to those of Air Koryo. Crossing to the Cathay Pacific waiting area, she took a seat that gave her a peripheral view of the North Korean gate.

Once more she removed the false file from her shoulder bag and focused her false attention upon it.

Sun Chok's flight across the Pacific had been a long and tortuous one: from Vancouver to the Philippines, from the Philippines to Singapore, from Singapore to Hong Kong, and from Hong Kong to Beijing. Pyongyang was not an easy place to get to from anywhere. Twice during the journey, Franklin Sun Chok had been contacted by North Korean agents, who had passed him falsified passports, visas, and identification, and in Hong Kong he'd picked up his escort from the People's Security Force.

At each stop Sun Chok had also acquired a CIA shadow. A network of American agents had been deployed to cover the primary Pacific travel nodes, monitoring the traitor's transit. In Singapore, the local station chief had even been forced to hastily intervene with the local authorities when a sloppily forged document had almost led to Sun Chok's arrest.

Randi Russell would be the last link in this chain. She would oversee Franklin Sun Chok's final passage into darkness.

Covertly she studied the youthful traitor. He kept glancing back down the concourse. Did he still fear some last-minute pursuit? Or could he be thinking back to San Francisco Bay and the apartment, life, and family he would never see again? Emoting to some idealized political principal was all well and good, but it was quite another thing to live out its reality.

Randi Russell knew full well what this reality was. She had been on the ground inside the last 'workers' paradise.' The experience still occasionally made her wake up bathed in a chill sweat.

She wondered if the young man was having second thoughts about his decision. Could it be that his fashionable intellectualist's disdain for the United States was starting to wear thin? Could he now be sensing a ghost of what had made his parents flee to the Western world?

If so, such considerations were coming too late. Another delegation of black-suited North Koreans had been standing by at the Air Koryo Jetway, a security team from North Korea's Beijing embassy. They closed around Sun Chok, a few curt words were exchanged, and the American was hustled down the extendable Jetway to the waiting airliner, past the Chinese People's Police officer, who was careful to not see him or his escorts.

Randi caught his eyes as he looked back one last time, and then he was gone.

She closed her eyes and sat unmoving for a long moment. Mission accomplished.

She knew what would happen next. The information contained within Franklin Sun Chok's laptop computer and within Sun Chok himself would be poured into the North Korean ballistic missile program. The information would promise leads in the direction of a foolproof countermeasures system that could defeat the U.S. antimissiles and leave the cities of the American West Coast open to attack.

But one after another, each promising lead would reach a technological dead end after devouring a precious percentage of the North Korean military budget and thousands of equally precious research and development man hours.

Eventually it would become apparent to the North Koreans that they had been duped, that their intelligence coup had, in fact, been a time bomb planted within their armaments program by the United States.

North Korea's 'Dear Leaders' would be displeased. Specifically, they would be displeased with Franklin Sun Chok. The displeasure of the 'Dear Leaders' would not be trifling.

Randi snapped her eyes open. If she were not careful with her memories, the cold-sweat nights would return.

From the concourse windows, she watched as the elderly Ilyushin jetliner climbed away from the airport on the final leg of Sun Chok's last journey. Returning to her seat, she waited for the next Cathay Pacific flight to come in and unload before making her call.

'Mr. Danforth. This is Tanya Stewart out at Capital. Mr. Bellerman wasn't on his flight. What should I do now, sir?'

Translation from agent doublespeak: the package has been successfully delivered.

Danforth sighed theatrically. 'Los Angeles strikes again! I'll look into it, Tanya. In the meantime you'd best get back here. Something's come up.'

'What is it, sir?'

'They need you back in the States as soon as possible. At the Seattle office.'

Randi frowned. The States as soon as possible? This was a deviation, and a radical one. Upon completion of this assignment she was supposed to ease out of China over a period of days, maintaining her businesswoman's cover. And what the hell was in Seattle?

'I'm already setting up your travel arrangements,' Danforth continued. 'You'll be flying out this evening on Asiana to Seoul, and from there by JAL. There will be a reservation waiting for you at the SeaTac Doubletree.'

'I see, Mr. Danforth. Should I swing by the office?'

'Yes. I'll have your tickets, and we can go over the outlines of this new project. You'll be met by a Mr. Smith in Seattle. He's with one of our associate firms, and you'll be working with him on a joint venture.'

Randi frowned. Mr. Smith? The Agency would never use a cover name like that. It must be the real thing.

Her frown deepened. It couldn't be. Not again.

CHAPTER SIX

San Francisco Bay

The diseased mind known in the Bay Area as the 'BART rapist' settled back in his seat and luxuriated in the contemplation of the next woman he would destroy. The big Bay Transit Authority SuperCat passenger ferry was just backing away from the Market Street terminal, and he would have a full fifty minutes for his contemplation before their arrival in Vallejo. It pleased him that she was already his possession but still totally unaware of it.

The Bay Area's public transport systems were his private stalking ground, and as with all his previous half-dozen assaults, this one would be a work of art, in its inception and execution and in his evasion of the police, a thing of great beauty. The actual debasement of his prey would merely be the delicious frosting applied to a master baker's cake.

He never used the same persona twice. For this act he would be a cross-bay business commuter, recently moved from the city to the wine country north of the bay. His falsified identification would support the cover story, as would his assumed appropriate appearance: graying temples and wire-framed glasses, sweater and slacks and an expensive tweed jacket with suede elbow patches, Birkenstocks and dark socks. It would all match the image conjured in the mind of any stupid policeman or security guard who might question him.

Even the contents of the paper bag he carried primly on his knees would be justifiable to any random police check: two pint tins of interior enamel paint, a selection of small paintbrushes, a few cards of hardware screws and cupboard hooks – all things a new DIY home owner would be justified in possessing – complete with a purchasing slip drawn on a downtown San Francisco decorating store.

In such company, the roll of duct tape and the box cutter would be totally unremarkable.

He had taken equal care with his past assaults. In the last, he had been the grimy mentally deficient street person, and in the one before that, the slovenly truck driver, and so on. The police didn't have a clue whom they were truly pursuing.

A pity, in a way, that he could not be admired for his artistry and his genius.

Riding the thunder of its hydrojet drives, the SuperCat cut northeastward across the bay, its twin bladelike bows slicing cleanly through the low swells. Beyond the ferry's windows, shore lights glittered on as the misty dusk settled. This was the eight o'clock run, the last of the day, and the ferry's commodious passenger bay with its multiple rows of seating was three-quarters empty.

The woman whom he had honored with his attention sat in the front row to port. Contentedly munching a crisp apple purchased from the ferry's snack bar, her attention was lost in the book resting on her crossed knee. She was beautiful, as were all his ladies – the rapist was, after all, a connoisseur. A tall brunette, she was slender but full-breasted, her long midnight black hair worn up in a neatly pinned chignon. She was somewhere in her thirties, with flawless, creamy skin, lightly tanned and glowing with health.

Her eyes were gray, and they had glinted with good humor as she had bantered with the snack bar attendant. She was a regular. Every Tuesday and Thursday she crossed on the ten o'clock morning run from Vallejo and returned on this, the last evening boat.

What she did in the city, he wasn't quite sure. But she was clearly a woman of fashion and means; her clothes were always of superb taste and quality. This night she wore a trim gray cord pantsuit that matched her eyes and stiletto-heeled black boots.

He might allow her to keep those boots after he destroyed the rest of her clothing; they would add something to the experience.

She always read her way across the bay with a book taken from the briefcase she inevitably carried. In his weeks of preattack surveillance he had made a point of positioning himself to see the book titles as a method of getting inside her head, of deepening his advantage.

But what he had seen had puzzled him: Anthony M. Thornborough's *Airborne Weapons of the West*, *The Greenville Military Manual of Main Battle Tanks*, and the like. Tonight's book was a crumbling yellow-paged volume in some Germanic tongue. From its illustrations it was concerned with cavalry warfare. Such topics were inexplicable for such a refined and totally feminine individual, and totally inappropriate. He would punish her for her interest in them.

The ferry slowed as it nosed up the Mare Island shipping channel, with the blazing city lights of Vallejo to starboard and the scattered work arcs of the old Mare Island Navy Yard to port. The great turbocharged diesels grumbled down into an idle as the catamaran came off plane. They were turning in toward the docking slips, the floodlights of the ferry terminal glaring in through the forward windscreen.

The BART rapist gathered himself. It was time for the final act.

He held back, just keeping his prey in sight as they descended the boarding ramps and passed by the big octagonal terminal building. He knew precisely where she was going. His rented minivan was already parked beside her dove gray Lincoln LS sedan out in the far parking lot of the terminal. Away from the lights of the terminal, he paused to hastily transfer the box cutter and duct tape to his jacket pockets, depositing his shopping bag in a trash can. He left the purchasing slip in the bag. Let the police chase this yuppie commuter; he would dissolve in a matter of a few more hours.

Perhaps he would become a Seventh-day Adventist missionary next.

His prey was crossing the broad asphalt expanse of the emptied parking lot now. The only thing that could delay her fate was the presence of some unexpected onlooker nearby. But no, the environment was entirely favorable. A few automobiles hissed past, uncaring, on the streets, and a small group of weary workers clumped at the bus stop a full block away. Probably even a scream would go unacted upon.

He hastened his steps, starting the rush that would close the distance as she reached her vehicle. In moments she would be in the shadowy gap between the car and the van, fumbling in her shoulder bag for her keys, diverted, ultimately vulnerable. Moments later, with wrists, mouth, and ankles taped, she would be under a concealing blanket on the floor of his vehicle.

But then the tall brunette stepped past the driver's door of the Lincoln. Turning abruptly at the front bumper, she put her back to the concrete bulkhead of the parking lot. Allowing her briefcase and shoulder bag to slip to the ground, she faced him, her arms loosely crossed over her stomach. In the dimness, she seemed to be smiling a wry, derisive smile.

'Morally, I should just let nature take its course,' she said, her voice a contralto rich with the same wry derisiveness, 'but I really don't need this kind of complication in my life.' Her voice dropped an octave. 'So I'll say it just once. Go away and leave me alone.'

She . . . was . . . discounting . . . him. She viewed him and all his arts and efforts an irrelevancy to be shooed away. The elemental hate at the core of his being boiled up, sweeping away his warped pretensions.

His hand plunged into his pocket, the box cutter's razor wedge of blade snicking open as he drew it. He stepped forward, spitting out his first vile epithet.

She moved, her arm sweeping in a flat, inhumanly fast blur. Something struck him sharply in the abdomen with a soft whucking sound. For a moment there was just the shock of impact; then came the impossible, searing pain. Instinctively he dropped the box cutter and clutched at the agony, his fingers closing over the slender metal haft of a knife buried in his stomach.

This . . . was not . . . in the plan.

His legs buckled, and he went to his knees on the cracked asphalt, the bits of gravel biting through his trouser legs, faint echoes of the agony in the center of his body.

Paralyzed by the pain, he heard footsteps click closer with deliberation. 'Excuse me,' that wry, now utterly terrifying voice said, 'but I believe that's my property.'

Then the boot heel rested against his shoulder, putting him flat onto his back with a sharp shove. There was a final impossible explosion of pain as the blade was twisted from his punctured stomach, and all consciousness faded.

A few minutes later someone dialed 911 from a waterfront public telephone and asked for the police department. The dispatcher picking up the call heard a pleasant contralto voice say, 'You will find a recently retired rapist in the C lot of the ferry terminal. He needs an aid car rather badly. If you do a DNA match with the BART attacker, you may be pleasantly surprised.'

Valentina Metrace, professor of history, PhD, Radcliffe and Cambridge, hung up the phone and walked back to her car at the curb. As the sleek sedan whispered toward the Redwood Parkway, she called up a disk on the CD player, and a Henry Mancini collection pulsed softly from the multiple speakers.

Fourteen miles into the North Bay wine country, the Lincoln turned off the highway and drew up in front of a steel grille security gate in a gray-pink stuccoed perimeter wall. An understated bronze plaque was mounted beside the gate:

SANDOVAL ARMAMENTS COLLECTION
Museum Hours: 10:00 to 5:00 Tuesday through Saturday.

The dab of a key card retracted the power gate, granting the professor entrance. She eased the car down the entrance loop road, past the F2H Banshee jet fighter banking on its gate guard pedestal, and the Matilda infantry tank on its display slab, to the turnoff drive that led to her quarters.

The Sandoval arms collection had been initiated at the turn of the previous century as the personal hobby of the wealthy scion of one of the old Californio families. Over the four generations since its inception, it had taken on a life and a justification of its own as one of the largest historical archives on weaponry and the tools of warfare in the United States.

A number of perks came with its prestigious curator's position, including the neat little California mission bungalow behind the sprawling complex of display buildings, libraries, and restoration laboratories. Parking in its carport, Metrace paused for a brief techno-ritual before passing through the sliding glass doors that led into the kitchenette. The multiple rows of check lights for the museum compound's extensive network of security systems all glowed green on the exterior alarm station.

Snapping on the kitchenette's indirect lighting, she set her briefcase and shoulder bag on the carmine-tiled breakfast bar. It was good to be home, even with complications. With a sigh, she shrugged out of her jacket and slipped the elastic band of the nylon concealed-carry sheath over her left wrist. Drawing the slender black-bladed throwing knife from the sheath, she examined the shimmering blade edges for bone or belt buckle nicks.

She bit her lower lip and considered. She couldn't have just left the superb little weapon in its target; she'd hand-machined and balanced it in her own workshop. Besides, as with all the knives she made, her initials were scripted in silver on the blade. Admittedly a vanity on her part.

She'd wiped it off on her attacker's jacket, but that wouldn't be at all adequate in these days of CSI. An overnight soak in a panful of gasoline would eliminate any

DNA trace evidence on the knife, and the sheath could go into the fire, but if her erstwhile rapist didn't do the world a large favor and terminally hemorrhage before the paramedics got to him, he might be able to give the police her description and license number.

She sighed again. There was no getting around it. She was going to have to contact her controller, just in case there was any rap-chilling to be done. Bay Area prosecuting attorneys could be peculiar at times, even in cases of flagrant self-defense. It might be suggested that she should have gone to social counseling with her attacker before implanting four inches of steel in his duodenum.

Mr. Klein wouldn't be at all happy if this incident went public. He much preferred that his mobile ciphers maintain a decidedly low profile in their private lives. And as a professor of history, she was supposed to know only *about* weapons, not about how to use them.

She set the knife and sheath on the breakfast bar and crossed the hall to her office. She kept her private collection here. A built-in gun cabinet took up one entire end wall, and more razor-edged steel glittered on display against the dark cherrywood paneling, a number of the blades bearing her silver signature. The polished horn of a great sable antelope curved saberlike above the mission-style desk.

The overall air of the room should have been masculine, yet it wasn't. A subtle stylistic femininity had been imprinted upon it – subtle, yet dynamic and profoundly individualistic.

Sinking down behind the desk, the professor found a recorded message light glowing on her answering machine: a call on her unlisted private number. She pushed the caller ID key, and an Anacosta, Maryland, area code flashed up. Her brow cocked. She didn't need to contact Covert One. Her alternate employers were trying to contact her.

CHAPTER SEVEN

Russian Long Range Aviation Headquarters,
Vladivostok, the Russian Pacific Maritime Provinces

Major Gregori Smyslov braced a hand against the dashboard as the GAZ command car lurched over the potholed base road. Glancing out of the moisture-streaked side window, he frowned at the passing vista of dilapidated barracks and abandoned operations buildings under a sodden lead-colored sky. Serving here must have really been something . . . once.

The huge air base complex was a ghost of what it had been. Only a few of the hundreds of hardstands lining its broad runways were still occupied. Where once entire regiments of sleek swept-wing Sukhois and Tupolevs had staged, only a couple of understrength squadrons remained on alert, nervously watching the Chinese border.

The remainder of the vast facility hadn't even been mothballed, just abandoned to the wind and the rot and the foxes.

Smyslov was a New Russian. He could recognize the elemental fallacies at the heart of Communism that had led to the collapse of the USSR, and he still had the hope of seeing the eventual success of a free and democratic Russia in the twenty-first century. But he could understand the bitterness in the hearts of some of the old hands. They could remember the days of power, of respect – days when they weren't a joke in the eyes of the world.

The command car drew up in front of the Pacific Air Forces headquarters building, a massive windowless bastion of rust and water-stained concrete. Dismounting, Smyslov dismissed his driver. Turning up the collar of his greatcoat against the chill hiss of the rain, he strode up the puddle-mottled walkway to the main entrance.

Just short of the great bronze doors he paused and knelt, picking up a stony fragment from the pavement. It was a small chunk of concrete, freshly flaked from the facing of the headquarters building. Such disintegration was an endemic problem with much of the old Soviet architecture. Smyslov applied pressure, and the concrete crumbled between his gloved fingers. The Russian officer smiled without humor and shook away the wet, sandy remnants.

He was expected. After verifying his identification, a respectful sentry accepted his uniform cap and greatcoat, and a second led him deeper into the core of the headquarters. Even this building seemed only partially occupied, with many of its offices darkened and its echoing gray corridors nearly empty.

Smyslov cleared through a second security checkpoint, and the sentry handed him off to a tense staff officer, who led him on to the innermost sanctum of the complex.

The well-appointed wood-paneled office belonged to the commanding general of all Pacific Zone Long Range Aviation Forces, but the man seated behind a massive dark mahogany desk had more authority than even that.

'Major Gregori Smyslov of the Four forty-ninth Air Force Special Security Regiment, reporting as ordered, sir.'

General Baranov returned the salute. 'Good afternoon, Major. As you have no doubt been advised, you never received those orders. You are not here. I am not here. This meeting has never taken place. Is this understood?'

'I understand, sir, fully.'

Baranov's cold gray eyes drilled into his. 'No, Major, you do not, but you will presently.' The general gestured to the chair positioned before the desk. 'Please be seated.'

As Smyslov sank into the appointed chair, the general drew an inch-thick folder onto the center of the desk's black leather blotter, flipping it open. Smyslov recognized his own *zapiska*, his service record. And he knew what its facing page would say.

Name: Smyslov, Gregori Andriovitch
Age: 31
Height: 199 centimeters
Weight: 92 kilograms
Eyes: Green
Hair: Blond
Birthplace: Berezovo, Uralsky Khrebet, Russian
    Federation

The photograph that accompanied the facing sheet would show a strong, not unpleasant mixture of blunt and angular features and narrow, rather good-humored eyes.

What else might be contained in the *zapiska*, Smyslov did not know. It might be his life, but it was the Air Force's concern.

General Baranov flipped through a few of the pages. 'Major, your regimental commander thinks highly of you. He feels you are one of the best officers under his command, if not one of the best in our service. Looking through your records, I am inclined to agree.'

The general flipped another page of the file, looking not down at it but into Smyslov's face, as if attempting to match what he had read with the man behind the words.

'Thank you, General,' Smyslov replied, carefully keeping his voice neutral. 'I have always endeavored to be a good officer.'

'You have succeeded. That is why you are here. I trust your regimental commander briefed you on the Misha 124 affair and of your duties related to it.'

'Yes, sir.'

'And what were you told?'

'That I was to be attached to a joint Russian-American investigation team being dispatched to the Misha crash site, as the Russian liaison. I will be operating with a Colonel

Smith of the United States Army, and certain other American specialists. We are to investigate the downed aircraft and ascertain if any active biological warfare agents remain aboard it. We are also to ascertain the fate of the Misha aircrew and to recover their bodies. All aspects of this mission are to be held in the highest state of security.'

Baranov nodded. 'I have recently returned from Washington, where I established those mission parameters and arranged for you to be attached to the American investigation group. What else were you told?'

'Nothing, sir. I was only ordered to proceed here' – the corner of Smyslov's mouth quirked in spite of himself – 'to this meeting that is not taking place, for a final-phase briefing on this assignment.'

'Very good. That is as it should be.' Baronov nodded with deliberation. 'Tell me this, Major. Have you ever heard of the March Fifth Event?'

March fifth? Smyslov considered, frowning. There was a girl he had known when he'd been attending the Gagarin Academy, the busty little redheaded barmaid. Her birthday had been March fifth, hadn't it? But that couldn't possibly be what the commanding general of the Thirty-seventh Strategic Air Army could be concerned with.

'No, sir. I have no idea what you mean.'

Baranov nodded again. 'That is also as it should be.'

The general levered himself up from behind the desk and crossed the office to a second door. 'Come with me, please, Major.'

The second door opened on a small, windowless briefing room, a gray steel map table centered in it. A single file folder was, in turn, centered on the table. A diagonal orange stripe ran across the file's gray cover, with a second bloodred bar down the spine.

As a security officer, Smyslov instantly recognized the document coding: Ultrasecret. Access by presidential authorization only.

Smyslov found himself wishing he still had his greatcoat.

The office and the briefing room suddenly seemed colder.

Baronov gestured toward the file. 'This is the March Fifth Event. It is possibly the single most critical state secret held by your motherland. Any unauthorized revelation of the contents of this file means an automatic death sentence. Is that understood?'

'Yes, General.'

'You are now authorized access. Read it, Major. I will return for you shortly.'

Baronov departed, locking the briefing room door behind him.

Smyslov circled the table, the room growing colder still. Sinking into a gray metal chair, he drew the file to him, his mind racing. March fifth? March fifth? There was something else about that date that he couldn't quite pull in, perhaps from a history class. Something foreboding.

He opened the untitled file.

The general gave the younger officer forty-five minutes. The file was not extensive, but Baranov recalled how, when he had been granted his authorization, he had gone through the documents twice in stunned disbelief.

In due course, Baranov rose from the desk again and unlocked the briefing room door. Major Smyslov still sat at the table, the closed file on the table before him. His face was pale under his tan, and he did not look up. His lips moved in a whisper. 'My God . . . my God.'

'It was much the same with me, Gregori Andriovitch,' Baranov said gently. 'There are perhaps thirty other men in the entirety of Russia who know of the full contents of that file. You and I are the thirty-first and the thirty-second.'

The general closed and secured the soundproof door behind him and took the chair across from Smyslov.

The younger man looked up, mastering himself. 'What are my orders, General? My true orders.'

'Firstly, Major, I can now tell you that the anthrax reservoir is still aboard the aircraft. Obviously, it was never jetti-

54

soned. However, that is far from our primary concern in this affair. The March Fifth Event is!'

Smyslov's eyebrows arched. 'I can see how that could be, sir.'

'Attached to the American investigation group, you will be our point man on Wednesday Island,' Baranov continued. 'You will be our eyes and ears. We will be relying upon you to assess the situation there. But you will not be operating alone. A Naval Spetsnaz platoon, trained and equipped for arctic warfare, is being dispatched to the island by nuclear submarine. They will land shortly before your arrival, and they will deploy and remain in concealment. You will be given means to communicate with them, and they will await word from you.'

'What . . . word am I supposed to give, General?'

'Concerning the March Fifth Event, Major. The Misha 124's political officer was under orders to destroy any and all evidence of the event at the crash site. However, he was also to destroy the aircraft and its anthrax warload as well. This plainly was not accomplished. Beyond this, all communication with Wednesday Island was lost before any confirmation of this sterilization was received.'

'So the Misha 124's crew was never rescued?' Smyslov asked, his voice quiet.

'It was not feasible,' Baronov replied with grim simplicity. 'It is our profoundest hope that they eliminated all evidence of the March Fifth Event before . . . Your mission is to verify that this was accomplished. If such is the case, or if you can successfully destroy this evidence yourself, then the joint mission with the Americans to destroy the anthrax can proceed as overtly planned.'

'But what if this evidence has not been or cannot be destroyed, sir, and what if this Colonel Smith and his people reach it first?'

'If the Americans learn of the March Fifth Event, Major, then they do not leave the island alive. You and the Spetsnaz platoon will see to this.'

Smyslov came out of his chair. 'You cannot be serious, General.'

'Word of the Event must not be allowed to reach the world at large, Major, under any circumstances.'

Smyslov groped for words, for alternatives. 'General . . . I can fully understand the critical nature of the situation, but why not have the Spetsnaz go in immediately to procure this evidence before the Americans can arrive.'

'Because we are walking on a razor's edge here! The Americans know of the Misha 124's existence. They have learned it is one of our Tupolev-4s. They know now it was a strategic biological weapons platform. If we committed our Spetsnaz team now, they could not help but disturb the crash site! The Americans will know we raced in ahead of them. They will be suspicious! They will know we were attempting to conceal something. They will begin to ask questions that must not be asked!'

Baronov lifted his hands in frustration. 'The world has changed, Major. We need the Americans as allies, not enemies. If they learn of the March Fifth Event, we shall be enemies once more.'

'Begging the general's pardon, but won't the murder of their personnel by our military accomplish the same thing?'

The flat of the general's hand slapped down on the steel tabletop. 'The elimination of the Americans is to be considered an absolute last-resort contingency, a final option to stave off total disaster! We will be relying on you, Major, to ensure that option need not be exercised!'

Baronov sighed a tired old man's sigh and leaned back in his chair. 'But if it must be done, it must be done. It is a matter of proportion and perspective, Gregori Andriovitch. If we find ourselves at odds with the United States again, the Russian Federation may yet survive. But if the world and our own people learn of the March Fifth Event, the Motherland, as a nation, is finished!'

CHAPTER EIGHT

Anacosta, Maryland

The big diesel cruiser materialized out of the Potomac mists and stood in toward the marina, ignoring the bright yellow PRIVATE NO TRESPASSING signs posted on the ends of the finger piers. A pair of marina employees, nondescript, long-haired young men in deck shoes, dungarees, and nylon windcheaters, stood by to accept the cruiser's lines as it nosed alongside.

Nothing untoward hinted that both the pier hands carried automatic pistols under their jackets or that the cruiser's helmsman had a submachine gun racked out of sight below the lip of the cockpit.

The rumble of the cruiser's engines broke into an idling whine as the propeller clutches disengaged and the bow and stern lines were deftly snubbed off. A set of boarding steps were positioned, and the yacht's lone passenger emerged from its streamlined cabin.

With a nod to the pier hands, Fred Klein disembarked and strode down the fog-dampened planks of the dock. Crossing the broad graveled expanse of the marina's dry-storage area, past the silent, tarpaulin-shrouded shapes of beached pleasure craft on their trailers and stands, Klein continued toward what appeared to be a large windowless warehouse.

The dark green metal prefab building looked new. It should. It had not been there two years before. In all probability, in another year's time, it or at least its contents would be repositioned somewhere else.

This was the headquarters and operations center of Covert One.

Concealed television cameras tracked Klein's approach, and magnetic locks clicked open as he came to stand before the heavy steel fire door.

'Good morning, sir.' The duty 'doorman' accepted Klein's hat and topcoat, neatly hanging them up beside the racked assault shotgun. 'It's a clammy kind of day out there.'

'That it is, Walt,' Klein replied amiably. 'Maggie in the shop yet?'

'About half an hour ago, sir.'

'One of these days I'll beat her in,' Klein murmured in ritual. He continued down the length of the institutional-buff central corridor. No one passed him in the hall, but an occasional murmur of voices or muffled whine of electronics leaked from behind the double row of anonymous gray doors, hinting at the quiet functionality of the headquarters.

At the far end of the passageway lay the command suite.

The outer office was Maggie Templeton's techno-lair. The entire room was a computer workstation, dominated by a large desk with no less than three twenty-one-inch flat-screen monitors positioned upon it. A second set of large-screen displays were inset on the far office wall. Her pet bonsai tree and a silver framed photograph of her late husband served as the sole reminders of Margaret Templeton's essential humanity.

The blonde looked up from her master display and smiled as Klein card-swiped his way through the security entry. 'Good morning, Mr. Klein. I hope it was a smooth voyage today.'

'It can never be smooth enough for me, Maggie,' Klein snorted. 'Someday I'm going to hunt down the sadist who came up with the brilliant notion of putting the headquarters of the world's worst sailor at a yacht club.'

She chuckled, 'You have to admit, it makes for an excellent cover.'

'Not really; my being green and nauseated all of the time could give it all away. What have we got this morning?'

Templeton instantly toggled over to her professional

mode. 'The Trent Bravo insertion appears to be going well. The team leader is reporting that his personnel and equipment are on the ground inside of Myanmar and that his point man has successfully made contact with the leadership of the Karen National Union.'

Klein nodded. Removing a handkerchief from his pocket, he polished a few fog droplets from his glasses. 'Anything new with the Wednesday Island operation?'

'Jon will be linking up with the American members of his team in Seattle tonight and with his Russian liaison in Alaska tomorrow. The equipment set has been pre-positioned, and the helicopter procured from Pole Star.'

'Any problems with Langley seconding Ms. Russell to us?'

'Only the usual moaning, whining, bitching, and complaining.' Maggie looked up from her screens. 'If I may make a point, sir. President Castilla is really going to have to make some decisions about our working relationship with our former employers in the near future.'

Klein sighed and redonned his glasses. 'Very possibly, Maggie, but in the words of the immortal Scarlett O'Hara, "I'll think about it tomorrow." Anything else for today?'

'A planning meeting with the South American Operations group at ten hundred, and you might want to have a look at your 'For your consideration' file. I've compiled a list of known illicit armament dealers believed to have both the potential interest and available resources to deal themselves into the Wednesday Island situation. It makes for interesting reading. I've also red-flagged these men and their organizations with all of our available intelligence resources. Any unusual activity on their part is to be reported.'

'Well done, Maggie, as usual.'

Every director should have an executive assistant who could both read minds and foresee the future.

His office, smaller and far less elaborately outfitted, lay beyond Maggie's. The few personalized decorations – the framed poster-sized photo of the Earth from orbit, the Elizabethan-era map prints, the large eighteenth-century globe of the world – served him as a reminder of his zone of responsibility.

There was only a single workstation monitor on his mid-grade desk, along with a tray bearing a coffee service for one, a steaming stainless steel thermos, and a single buttered English muffin on a covered dish.

Klein smiled. Removing his suit coat, he draped it neatly over the back of his chair. Settling behind his desk, he poured himself his first cup of coffee and tapped the space bar on his keyboard, calling the monitor to life.

As he sipped, a series of file headings flashed past on the screen. Maggie would have stacked the files in what she viewed as their order of priority.

**KNOWN ILLICIT ARMS DEALERS-MULTINA-TIONAL-WMD INVOLVEMENT **
KRETEK GROUP
ANTON KRETEK

A photograph followed, computer enhanced and apparently taken using a long-range telephoto camera. It showed a man, a big, ruddy-featured man, standing on the deck of what appeared to be a large private yacht, scowling in the direction of the camera.

There were many contradictions built into Anton Kretek. The thinning of his rust-colored hair contrasted with the wild profusion of his gray-tinged beard. There was obvious power in his broad shoulders and wiry, long, mus-cled arms, countered by the furry pot gut of dissipation that bulged over the waistband of his minimal swimming trunks, and while there were thick clusters of laugh wrinkles gath-ered around his eyes, those eyes were as cold and opaque as those of a hooding king cobra.

Klein decided that this man might indeed laugh a great deal, but it would be at things most normal human beings would not find amusing.

One of Maggie Templeton's deft file summaries followed, a distilled essence of the documentation on Kretek, her instincts targeting what Klein would actually want and need to know about the man and his organization:

Interpol and the other Western intelligence agencies concerned with Anton Kretek are unsure if this is the arms dealer's true name or an alias. That datum had been lost in the chaos of a disintegrating Yugoslavia. It is known that he is Croatian, from somewhere near the Italian border of that failed nation.

In the tangled eugenic lexicon of the Balkans, a 'Croat' is theoretically a Roman Catholic Southern Slav who uses the Latin alphabet, as opposed to a 'Serb,' who is a Southern Slav following the Greek Orthodox religion and who uses Cyrillic.

Kretek, to the best of anyone's knowledge, follows the tenets of no organized religion. The arms dealer is a rarity amid the deep racial, religious, political and tribal passions of Mittel Europa. He appears to be totally aracial, areligious, apolitical and atribal. As with the true criminal mentality, his own survival and well-being appear to be his sole concern. To date, in this endeavor, he has been eminently successful.

Kretek has boasted of starting his organization with a single car trunkload of rifle cartridges looted from a Yugoslavian Army depot. From this humble origin, over a period of fifteen years, he has built the Kretek Group into a multimillion-dollar criminal smuggling combine involved in the supplying and maintenance of every major and minor armed conflict in the Mideast and Mediterranean Basin.

The Kretek Group is amorphous, like an octopus that is continuously casting off and regrowing its tentacles. It is known that there is a definite head, a tight-knit trusted command cadre clustered around Kretek himself, and an ever-changing network of mercenaries, hirelings, and sub-gangs, drawn into the circle, utilized for a few operations, and then discarded.

The amorphous nature of the Kretek Group is a security measure. In addition, the liaison and contact men between these 'subcontractors' and the Kretek core cadre have a striking history of violent death and sudden disappearance, rendering a court-viable chain of evidence between Kretek and his individual operations difficult if not impossible to establish.

There is also no known fixed headquarters for the Kretek Group. Like many despots before him, he has learned the survivability of mobility. His group headquarters are continuously on the move within the more loosely regulated and unstable of the Balkan states, never providing a sitting target. While still an essential blunt-force operator, Kretek has learned to appreciate and employ modern business telecommunications to keep a grip on his far-flung enterprises.

The corpse of his native Yugoslavia provided Kretek with profitable early pickings. In the Kosovo Province, Serbian militiamen and Albaniko guerrillas slaughtered each other with ordnance provided without prejudice by the Kretek Group, and Kretek was rumored to be the primary intermediary in the covert arms dealings between the dictatorships of Slobodan Milosevic and Saddam Hussein.

With Milosevic unseated and with NATO forcing peace down the throats of the various Balkan combatants, Kretek has expanded his range of endeavor, the combatants of the Sudanese civil war and the terrorist factions of the Mideast becoming his new primary clients.

A more critical and immediate concern are the indications that Kretek is no longer content with the profit margins to be made with conventional munitions. There are now indications the Kretek Group is seeking a market entry into the ABCs: atomic, biological and chemical arms. It is feared that Anton Kretek might make as great a success of this new field of operation as he has his other criminal enterprises.

A brief segment had been highlighted at the end of the brief.

Personal Notes to the Director:

A: In the opinion of the Executive Assistant, the Kretek Group is a prime example of the kind of organization that would view the Misha 124 as a golden opportunity. They are fluid, highly adaptive, risk taking and totally ruthless.

B: Beyond the perameters of the current Wednesday Island situation, it should be pointed out that the Kretek Group is currently very much a 'one man' operation. The elimination of Anton Kretek would, in all probability, lead to the direct dissolution of the Kretek Group and an increase in stability within a number of U.S. spheres of concern. Again in the opinion of the EA, this makes Anton Kretek a valid subject for a sanctioning operation, should a lock on his position ever be established and should suitable wet assets be available.

Klein smiled grimly – the female of the species was deadlier than the male. Maggie Templeton was probably correct. This was the face of the potential enemy. Men like Anton Kretek would view two tons of loose anthrax as a glittering possibility.

And Maggie was probably correct about something else. The world would likely be a better place without its Anton Kreteks.

CHAPTER NINE

The Eastern Coast of the Adriatic

The tides were out, the seas were low, and stars glittered through a broken cloud cover above a broad strip of dark, hard-packed sand. Above the beach lay the dunes, anchored by a hog's hair–thin scattering of rank grasses and studded with a row of crudely made concrete pillboxes. Long left to the nesting seabirds, the abandoned fortifications were a physical manifestation of the paranoid delusions of the late and unlamented government of Enver Hoxha.

Beyond the dunes brooded the sullen, forested hills of Albania.

Gears ground in the night, and two vehicles, an elderly, blunt-nosed Mercedes truck and a smaller and newer Range Rover, jounced slowly down the rutted beach access road, driving by the dim glow of their parking lights.

At the mouth of the access, the little convoy paused, and two men in the baggy trousers and rough leather jackets of the Albanian working class dropped from the tailgate of the Mercedes and took up positions to cover the road. Each man carried a Croatian-made Agram submachine gun with a heavy cylindrical silencer screwed to its stubby barrel.

It was highly unlikely that anyone would venture down to this desolate stretch of seaside in the small hours of the morning. But if they did, policeman or peasant, they would die.

The trucks ran half a mile up the beach to the broadest, straightest reach of sand and halted. Half a dozen more armed men disembarked from the Range Rover and the truck cab, setting about a long-practiced drill.

As two of the men lingered beside the hood of the parked Range Rover, watching the sky, the others fanned out, creating an airfield.

Chemical glow sticks were broken and shaken into life, their butt ends inserted into short lengths of copper tubing. The men then spiked the sticks into the sand at spaced intervals in a long double row. In minutes, the flare path of an ad hoc runway glowed a dim blue-green in the night, invisible from beyond the dunes but readily apparent to anyone passing overhead.

The men fell back to the vehicles and waited, fingering their pistols and SMGs.

As watch hands crept to the appointed hour, the drone of aero engines became audible, and a winged shadow swept past, paralleling the beach, its running lights extinguished. The leader of the party, a big red-bearded man in corduroy trousers and a thick Fair Isle sweater, aimed an Aldis lamp and blazed it at the aircraft. Two short flashes, a pause, and two short again.

This was another of Anton Kretek's survival mechanisms: to stay in the field and personally supervise as many of his operations as he could. It was a good way to know whom to trust and whom to purge.

The plane, a Dornier 28D Skyservant STOL transport with twin engines and a high-set wing, ran another circuit around the beach airstrip and came in to land. With its engines throttled back to an idling mutter, it flared and settled between the rows of glow sticks, its fixed landing gear kicking up a thin, hissing spray of wet sand.

Kretek aimed and flared his Aldis lamp again, guiding the plane in to a halt beside the trucks. The Dornier's propellers continued to flicker over, but its side cargo hatch swung open, disgorging a single figure.

The man was small, dark and slender, and nervous with the world. A Palestinian Arab, his eyes moved constantly, trusting neither his environment nor his company.

'Good evening, my friend, good evening,' the larger red-haired man called over the sound of the aircraft engines. 'Welcome to beautiful Albania.'

'You are Kretek?' the Palestinian demanded.

'So I have often been accused,' Anton Kretek replied, setting the lamp on the hood of the Range Rover.

The Arab was in no mood for jocularity. 'You have the material?'

'That's why we are both here, my friend.' The arms dealer started toward the Mercedes truck. 'Come have a look for yourself.'

By the beam of a single flashlight, heavy cases of dark, waxed cardboard were being unloaded from the rear of the truck, the cases marked in the Cyrillic alphabet and bearing the international bomb-burst warning symbol for high explosives. Indicating that one case was to be set aside, Kretek flicked open a folding-bladed hunting knife and slashed through the yellow plastic strapping.

Lifting the lid revealed tightly packed brick-sized blocks wrapped in waxed paper. Opening the wrapper revealed a dense, smooth puttylike material the color of margarine.

'Military-grade Semtex plastique.' Kretek gestured at it. 'Twelve hundred kilograms' worth, all of it less than three months old and completely stable. Guaranteed to kill Jews and send your dedicated volunteers on to their seventy-two virgins with smiles on their lips.'

The Arab's head jerked up, a spark of anger in his dark, expressive eyes. The anger of the fanatic confronted with the shopkeeper. 'When you speak of the holy warriors of Muhammad and of the liberators of the Palestinian people, you will speak with respect!'

The arms runner's eyes went opaque and cold. 'Everyone is liberating something, my friend. As for me, I liberate money. You have your merchandise; now I will have my payment – and Muhammad and the Palestinian people be damned.'

The Arab started to flare but then noted the circle of grim Slavic faces drawing in around the pool of flashlight.

Sullenly he took a fat manila envelope from inside his jacket, tossing it down atop the open case of explosives.

Kretek caught up the envelope. Opening it, he counted the neat strapped bundles of euros, verifying the denominations. 'It is good,' he said finally. 'Load it.'

The ton and a half of high explosives went aboard the transport plane, the Dornier's crew balancing and tying down the lethal cargo. In a matter of minutes the last case was stowed and the Arab payoff man scrambled after it without a parting word or a look back. The fuselage doors slammed shut, and the plane's propellers revved to taxiing power, blasting the arms smugglers with its sand-loaded slipstream.

Again the Dornier raced down the faint flare path. Lifting into the black sky, it executed a climbing turn out over the Adriatic, its engines growing fainter with distance.

Kretek's men dispersed once more to collect the glow sticks. In an hour or two, all evidence of the landing would be erased by the incoming tide.

Kretek and his lieutenant trudged back to the Range Rover.

'I'm not sure if I like this, Anton,' Mikhail Vlahovitch said, slinging his Agram over his shoulder. Squatter and balder than Kretek, the pan-featured ex-Serbian Army officer was one of a very elite cadre within the Kretek Group permitted to call the arms dealer by his first name. 'You play a risky game with these people.'

Vlahovitch was also one of an even smaller cadre who had the ultimate privilege of questioning one of Anton Kretek's command decisions without being killed for it.

'What's to be concerned about, Mikhail?' Kretek chuckled fatly, slapping his second in command on his free shoulder. 'We've met their airplane. We've delivered the merchandise as we promised. We received the payment agreed upon, and they flew away. We have fulfilled our contract completely. As for what happens afterward? Who can say?'

'But this will be their second shipment lost. The Arabs are bound to be suspicious!'

'Pish, pish, pish, the Arabs are always suspicious. They are always certain everyone is out to persecute them. This can be a good thing. We can make use of this.'

Kretek paused beside the passenger door of the Range Rover. Reaching in through the lowered window, he popped open the glove compartment. 'When we negotiate our next series of arms sales to the Jihad, we will simply place the blame where it properly belongs. We will tell them that Israeli Mossad agents are operating in the Balkans and are attempting to interfere with the flow of armaments bound for the Mideast. Beyond hating everyone else, Arabs love to hate the Jews. They will be happy to blame them for the loss of their munitions.'

Kretek straightened, holding a gray metal box the size of a carton of cigarettes. He extended a telescoping aerial from the top of the box and flicked on a power switch, a green check light glowing in response.

'You will tell them about the Jews, Anton?' Vlahovitch questioned skeptically.

'Why shouldn't I? It's the truth, isn't it? The Jews are responsible. Our terrorist friends are excellent clients. They pay us good money in exchange for the weapons and explosives we sell to them. They deserve to know the truth . . .' Kretek flipped a safety guard up and off the central key on the transmitter. '. . . just not quite all of it. There's no need to mention all of the good money the Mossad is paying to see that those weapons and explosives never arrive.'

Kretek pressed with a calloused thumb. Out in the night a receiver-detonator carefully grafted inside a doctored block of Semtex reacted to the electronic impulse.

There was a flash like ruddy heat lightning over the Adriatic, and the distant thud of a massive explosion as the Dornier and its crew vaporized.

'This is the secret of doing good business, Mikhail,'

Kretek said with satisfaction. 'You must always do your best to please as many clients as possible.'

The ancient stone-walled farmhouse had been built before the birth of Napoleon and had been occupied by successive generations of the same family for almost three centuries.

In the United States this would have made it a historic landmark. In Albania this made it just another weary, over-used building in an overused land.

For the past fifty-odd years, a variety of governments had promised the occupants of the farm electricity 'soon,' but only now had it arrived, in the form of the snarling Honda generators of the Kretek Group's headquarters.

The straw pallets and crude homemade furnishings had been emptied from one of the damp sleeping rooms, replaced by the folding field desks, satellite phones, and civil sideband transceivers of the communications section. The guard force had made a billet of the barn, and their camouflaged pickets had the farm isolated from all contact with the outside world, from within or without, and the transport section had their vehicles concealed in the other outbuildings.

The members of the headquarters unit were accustomed to such temporary quarters. They never remained in the same location for more than seven days at a time. One week in a resort villa on the Rumanian coast, the next on the rented top floor of a luxury hotel in Prague, the third aboard a fishing trawler cruising the Aegean, or, as now, a dank stone farmhouse in Albania.

Never give your enemies a sitting target – that was yet another of Anton Kretek's survival precepts. The temptation to relax and wallow in the good life provided by his successes was strong, almost overwhelming at times, but the arms merchant knew that to be a road that led to disaster.

It was also beneficial for the lads to see that the Old Man still had a sharp eye and a stone fist and that he wasn't afraid to get it bloody. It was good for discipline.

'How did it go, Anton?' Kretek's chief of communications asked as the arms dealer pushed through the low doorway into the farmhouse's combined kitchen and living room.

'No difficulties, my friend,' Kretek growled amiably. 'You may contact the Palestinians and tell them their shipment is on its way. Whether it will arrive . . .' Kretek mugged a blank look and shrugged his broad shoulders.

The men seated around the rough central table knew they should laugh.

Barring the single glaring bulb of a safety light hung from an overhead beam, the room itself might have been a museum tableau from the eighteenth century with its low ceiling, its dingily whitewashed stone walls, and the broad fireplace that served for both cooking and heating, a vine-cutting fire smoldering on the blackened hearth. The puncheon plank floors were worn smooth from centuries of footsteps, and the outside entrance was a low-set, high-silled, 'skull-cracker' doorway designed to slow the initial attacking rush of bandits and family enemies.

It served as no defense to bandits invited into the house, however. The farm's owner and his fourteen-year-old daughter stood silently near the fireplace, relying on the ancient peasant's defense of unobtrusiveness.

'Ah, Gleska, my sweet, you awaited your knight's return, and with hot tea. Just the thing for a cold morning.'

Unspeaking, the girl lifted the kettle from the fireplace crane and brought it to the table, filling one of the grime-opaque glasses with powerful twice-brewed black tea. Kretek dropped into the free chair beside the glass, squeezing the girl's buttocks through her cheap cotton skirt. 'Thank you, my love. I will warm myself with your good tea, and then in a little bit, when I have finished my work, I will warm you.'

With a ferocious mock growl, he drew her in and buried his face between her almost non-existent breasts, eliciting another volley of coarse laughter from his men.

At the fireplace a flare of impotent fury flashed in her

70

father's eyes, only to be masked instantly. He had been pleased when he had rented his farm to these men for more money than he could make with five years of hard labor. He had not known then that he would also be renting his only girl child. But he was Albanian, and he understood the rule of the gun. The men with the guns make the rules, and these men had a great many guns. The girl would survive, and they would survive as Albanian peasants had always survived: by enduring.

Releasing the girl, Kretek poured sugar into his tea from the cracked bowl on the table. 'Anything new come in while I was delivering the shipment, Crencleu?'

'Only one e-mail, sir.' The communications chief passed a single sheet of hard copy across the table. 'On your personal address, in your house code.'

Kretek flipped open the sheet and studied the message. Slowly a wolflike smile broke through the brush of Kretek's beard.

'It's good news from the family, my friends,' he said finally. 'Very good news, indeed.'

The pretense of joviality passed, and he looked up, eyes distant and intent. 'Crencleu, advise our Canadian point men that the arctic operation is on and that they are to proceed with preparations with all speed. Call in the selected force team and have them rendezvous at our point of departure in Vienna. Mikhail . . .'

'Yes, sir,' his executive officer spoke crisply. It was obvious the old wolf was on the track once more, this time for the richest prize in the group's history. Vlahovich had been unsure a few days before, when he had first heard of the arctic plan. It had seemed extreme, a wild long shot. But if it could be made to work, the payoff could be astronomical. Now even the dour Serb began to catch the fever.

'Inform all headquarters sections to load and prepare to move out. I wish to be on the road in . . .' Kretek paused, and his eyes flicked toward the fireplace and the slim, silent figure standing beside it. The Albanian race had never been known for producing great beauties from among its women, and this little chit wasn't much even at that, but she was here and she was young and she was paid for. '. . . an hour and a half.'

He might as well get his money's worth out of little Gleska before she and the rest of her family perished in their tragic house fire.

CHAPTER TEN

Seattle-Tacoma International Airport

Fall meant fog in the Pacific Northwest. The landing lights of the jetliners sweeping in to the runways cut like slow comets through the sinking overcast, and the tops of the hotels along the airport strip faded out of existence in the gathering dusk, illuminated windows diffusing into a golden glow within the mist.

As the bubble elevator climbed the exterior of the Doubletree Hotel tower, Jon Smith watched the sharp edges and details fade from the night. He wore knife-creased army greens, and he was alone for the moment. That would change presently. He was en route to link up with the other members of his team, one a stranger and the other not exactly a friend.

He couldn't blame Fred Klein for his personnel selection. The director's choice had been a logical one. He'd worked with Randi Russell before. They had been thrown together on a number of missions, almost as if fate were perversely entangling their life paths. Smith recognized her as a first-class operator: experienced, dedicated, and highly intelligent, with a weirdly diverse set of talents and a useful capacity for total ruthlessness when required.

But she came with a penalty.

The elevator doors split and rumbled apart, and Smith stepped out into the dusty rose-and-bronze-themed entry of the rooftop restaurant and lounge. The hostess looked up from her podium expectantly.

'My name is Smith. I'm here to join the Russell party.'

The hostess's brows lifted, and there was a moment's

open and curious appraisal. 'Yes, sir. Right this way, please.'

She led Smith across the low-lit lounge. Silenced by the dark carpeting underfoot, their steps didn't break the murmur of subtle music and soft conversation. And then Smith understood the hostess's flash of curiosity.

Randi had selected a table in the sunken rear corner of the dining room, an isolated setting partially screened from the other patrons by a decorative planter wall. It was a table intended for privacy, suitable for the quiet planning conference to come.

But it would also serve as a very suitable lovers' rendezvous, and Smith was meeting with not just one exceptionally beautiful woman but with two.

Smith smiled wryly to himself. He hoped the hostess would enjoy her ménage à trois fantasy. She would have no idea how totally wrong she was.

'Hello, Randi,' he said. 'I never knew you could fly a helicopter.'

She looked up from the table and nodded coolly. 'There's a lot about me you don't know, Jon.'

The first few seconds were never easy. The old twist in the guts was still there. Although Dr. Sophia Russell had been the older sister, she and Randi had been like twins. With the passage of time, the resemblance had grown almost eerie.

He wondered sometimes what Randi saw when she looked at him. Likely nothing pleasant.

Randi wore black suede tonight, a jacket, skirt, and boots outfit that matched the flare of her good looks and complemented the multitinted gold of her hair. Her dark eyes held his for a fraction of an instant, then darted away. 'Lieutenant Colonel Jon Smith, this is Professor Valentina Metrace.'

These eyes were gray under a glossy fringe of midnight-colored hair, and they met his, level and interested, with a glint of humor in their depths. The professor was in black as well, black satin evening pajamas that molded to a slim yet pleasantly curved figure, hinting that there was not a great

74

deal worn underneath them. 'Checking into a motel must be hell,' she said, extending her hand to him. Her voice was low, with a hint of something like a British accent.

The hand was held palm down, not to be shaken but to have its slender fingers lightly clasped as a blood royal might accept the touch of a courtier.

It was apparent that Valentina Metrace was an attractive woman who thoroughly enjoyed being an attractive woman and who enjoyed reminding men of the fact.

The tension broke, and Smith took the offered hand for a moment. 'The spelling of the first name helps,' he deadpanned.

Smith ordered a pilsner to match Randi's white wine and Professor Metrace's Martini. 'All right,' he said, pitching his voice so it couldn't carry to the next occupied table. 'This is the word as it has been given. Tomorrow we're out of here on the eight forty-five Alaskan Airlines flight to Anchorage. Our equipment kit and our helicopter are being prepositioned there. We will also be joining up with our Russian liaison officer, a Major Gregori Smyslov of the Federation Air Force.

'From Anchorage we'll fly ourselves to Sitka. There we rendezvous with the USS *Alex Haley*, the Coast Guard ice cutter that will carry us within range of Wednesday Island.'

'Who are we?' Randi inquired – a peculiar question for anyone not in their peculiar trade.

'The cover story established for this operation will permit us to pretty much maintain our own identities,' Smith replied. 'As Lieutenant Colonel Jon Smith, MD, I'll be acting as the mission pathologist, attached to Department of Defense graves registration. My primary concern will be with the recovery and forensic identification of the bodies of the aircrew.

'Professor Metrace will also essentially be who she is, a civilian historical consultant working under contract with the DOD. Supposedly, her job will be the identification of the aircraft itself, should the wreck be of a U.S. Air Force

75

B-29. Again, supposedly, Major Smyslov is to perform much the same duty should the plane prove to be a Russian TU-4. We'll be maintaining the fiction that the bomber's origins are still unknown, at least until we reach the crash site.

'You're the tricky one, Randi. As of this moment you are a civilian charter pilot flying for the National Oceanographic and Atmospheric Administration. The Wednesday Island expedition is a multinational scientific project, and NOAA and the U.S. Coast Guard are providing the logistical support. That includes the insertion and extraction of the personnel. You and the *Alex Haley* are being sent up there to pull the expedition out before the onset of the polar winter. Your own name is probably safe, and appropriate cooked documentation will be provided with the equipment kit.'

Her gaze dropped away to the tabletop for an instant. 'Is it possible for me to know who I'm actually working for?'

Smith regretted the answer he had to give. 'You are a civilian charter pilot flying for the National Oceanographic and Atmospheric Administration.'

He could feel Randi's tension ramp up. By now, her superiors must have surmised that there was a new player in the covert operations game. A new elite outfit, working outside Langley's authority but with the pull to tap the CIA's resources at will. From past personal experience Randi must also have surmised that he, Smith, was part of that new organization. It would rankle a veteran operative to be left out of the loop in this fashion. Jon had no choice in the matter. Covert One remained 'need to know,' and to put it bluntly, Randi Russell did not need to know, just to obey.

'I see,' she continued stiffly. 'I gather I will be taking my orders from you in this operation.'

'From me or from Professor Metrace.'

Randi snapped her head around to stare at Metrace. The dark-haired mobile cipher operative merely lifted an eyebrow and her glass, taking a final sip of her martini.

This situation was simply getting better and better. Being

positioned as the junior member of the team could only further ruffle Randi's feathers. What had his mountain warfare instructor warned him of the other day, that he was forgetting how to command? Well, by God, he had better start remembering right now.

'Professor Metrace is to be considered my executive officer on this operation. Should I not be available, she has full decision-making authority on all aspects of the mission. Is that understood?'

Randi's eyes met his again, expressionless. 'Fully, Colonel.'

Their meal came and went in near silence; Smith had the salmon while Randi Russell ate lightly at a dinner salad. The only one who truly seemed to enjoy her food was Valentina Metrace, consuming her steak and baked potato with a dainty, unconcerned fierceness.

She was also the one who dove back into the mission over their after-dinner coffee.

'One of our Keyhole reconnaissance satellites got a clear-weather pass over the Misha crash site,' she said, removing a set of photo prints from her shoulder bag. 'It gives us a much better look at what we're dealing with than the ground photography from the science expedition.'

Smith frowned at his copy of the overhead imaging. It could clearly be seen that the downed bomber was indeed an exact clone of a B-29. The slender, torpedolike fuselage and the lack of a stepped cockpit were unmistakable.

'Are you sure this is one of theirs?' Randi asked, mirroring Smith's thoughts.

The historian nodded. 'Um-hum. Most of the insignia paint has been storm scoured away, but you can just make out the red star on the starboard wingtip. There's no doubt; it's a TU-4 Bull. Specifically it's the TU-4A strategic-strike variant, intended for the delivery of atomic or biochemical weapons. What's more, this one was an America bomber.'

Smith glanced up. 'An America bomber?'

'An aircraft specifically configured for attacks on targets

in the continental United States. It's been stripped and lightened to maximize its range.' Reaching across the table, Valentina traced a manicured fingernail down the spine of the aircraft. 'You can see how all of the defensive gun turrets except for the tail stingers have been removed and the mounts fared over. Most of the armor will have been removed as well and auxiliary fuel tanks installed in the wings and aft bomb bay.'

She looked up from the photo. 'Even so modified, the TU-4 had very decided limitations as an intercontinental delivery system. Striking over the pole from the nearest Soviet bases in Siberia, they could just barely reach targets in the northern-tier states. And the missions would all have been one-way. There would have been no fuel left for a return flight.'

'Missiles with men inside,' Smith mused.

'Essentially, but they were what Stalin had at the time.'

'And how did he get his hands on them in the first place?' Randi asked in puzzlement. 'I gather these were our best bombers during the Second World War. We certainly didn't just give them to the Soviets.'

'We did, but inadvertently,' the historian replied. 'Early on during the strategic bombing campaign against the Japanese home islands, three B-29s were forced to land in Vladivostok because of battle damage or engine failure. The crews and aircraft were interned by the Russians, who, at the time, were neutral in our war against Japan. Eventually, we got our aircrews back, but the bombers were never returned.

'Instead Stalin ordered Andrei Tupolev, one of Russia's greatest aircraft designers, to produce an exact copy of the B-29 for Soviet Long Range Aviation.'

She smiled ruefully. 'It was the most incredible reverse-engineering project in history. Aviation historians who've had the opportunity to closely examine examples of the Soviet Bull were always puzzled over a small round hole drilled into the leading edge of the left wing. They could never figure out what it was for. When the Russians were asked about it they stated that they didn't know what it was for, either. It had just been there on the B-29 airframe they had broken down for blueprinting.

'Come to find out, it had probably been a bullet hole made by the machine guns of a Japanese interceptor. But Stalin had specified that he wanted an *exact* copy of the Superfortress, and what Uncle Joe wanted, he got!'

Her finger continued to trace the outlines of the wrecked bomber's wings. 'She obviously hit flat and skidded across the glacier on her belly. And given the way these propellers are bent, all of her engines were still running when she went in.'

Smith scowled. 'If she still had all of her engines, what forced her down?'

Valentina shook her head. 'I, and the experts I've consulted, haven't a clue. There is no indication of a midair structural failure, battle damage, or a collision. All of the control surfaces are present and accounted for, and there's no sign of a fire before or after the crash. The best guess is that they were running out of fuel and the pilot set down on the island while he still had power for a controlled approach and landing.'

'Then wouldn't they have had plenty of time to send a distress call before going down?' Randi inquired.

Professor Metrace shrugged slim shoulders. 'You'd think so, wouldn't you? But radio conditions around the Pole can be tricky. They could have encountered a magnetic storm or a dead zone that killed their transmissions.'

Their low-keyed discussion broke as a waitress approached and refilled their coffee cups. When it was safe to resume, Randi inquired about the plane's crew.

'They lived, at least for a time.' Once more Valentina tapped the photo print. 'This was an entirely survivable landing. The crew must have gotten out. There's even evidence to that effect. The cowling of the starboard outboard engine has been removed. You can see it lying on the ice beside the wing. It was probably done to drain the oil out of the engine sump for use in a signal fire.'

'But what happened to them?' Randi insisted.

'As I said, Ms. Russell, they must have survived for a time. They would have had sleeping bags, arctic clothing, and emergency rations. But eventually . . .' Once more the professor shrugged.

The fog swirled thickly beyond the restaurant window beside them, a chill pang pulsing through the glass. It would not have been a good death, castaway in the cold and eternal polar darkness. But then, Smith knew of few good ways to die. 'How large would the crew have been?'

'For a stripped TU-4, at least eight men. In the nose you'd have the aircraft commander, the copilot, the bombardier–weapons officer, who would also have served as the plane's political officer, the navigator, the flight engineer, and the radio operator. Then, in the tail, you'd have the radar operator, possibly an observer or two, and the stinger gunner.'

A thought swirled momentarily behind Valentina's steel-colored eyes. 'I'd fancy having a look at the ammunition magazines of those tail guns,' she murmured, almost to herself.

'You'll get the chance, Professor,' Smith replied.

'Make it Val, please,' she responded with a smile. 'I only use "professor" when I'm trying to impress a grants committee.'

Smith gave an acknowledging nod. 'Okay, Val, is there any indication of the anthrax still being aboard?'

She shook her head. 'Impossible to tell. In a bioequipped TU-4A, the reservoir would have been mounted here, in the forward bomb bay. As you can see, the fuselage is intact. The containment vessel itself would have been made of stainless steel and would have been built like a bomb casing, sturdy enough to survive at least a moderate crash impact.'

'Could it have leaked?' Randi inquired. 'The reservoir, I mean. Could the crew have been exposed to the anthrax while in flight? Maybe that's what forced them down?'

Smith shook his head. 'No. That couldn't have been it. *Bacillus anthracis* is a comparatively slow-acting pathogen. Even with a high concentration of inhalational anthrax in a closed environment, the incubational period would still be at least one to six days. Anthrax also responds well to massive doses of prophylactic antibiotics. By 1953 the Russians would have had access to penicillin. A biowar crew would have been equipped to handle an accidental exposure. Anthrax only gets ugly if you aren't set up to deal with it or if you don't recognize it for what it is.'

'How ugly?'

'Very. Without immediate treatment, the mortality rate for inhalational anthrax is ninety to ninety-five percent. Once the germinated spores infest the lymph nodes and start to elaborate toxins, even with full antibiotic and supportive medical care, there's still a seventy-five percent probability of death.'

Smith sat back in his chair. 'Needless to say, I'll have enough doxycycline in my kit to treat a small army, along with a serum that can give a short-lived immunity. Working at USAMRIID I've also been inoculated with the anthrax vaccine. Have either of you?'

The two women looked at him, wide-eyed, shaking their heads.

Smith smiled grimly. 'Oh, well, if you see any fine, grayish-white powder lying around, better let me deal with it.'

Valentina Metrace lifted her elegantly sculpted eyebrows. 'I wouldn't think of denying you, Colonel.'

'My preliminary briefing indicated that there might be two metric tons of this stuff aboard that plane,' Randi said. 'That's over four thousand pounds, Jon. What would that translate to in area effectiveness?'

'Let's put it this way, Randi. You could carry enough anthrax spores in your purse to contaminate the entire city of Seattle. The Misha 124's warload would have been adequate to blanket the entire East Coast.'

'Given a perfect distribution pattern of the agent, that is,'

Professor Metrace interjected. 'That's always been the problem with any biological or chemical weapon. They tend to clump on you, and you end up wasting ninety percent of it.'

The historian's high-fashion appearance contrasted radically with her topic of discussion, but the absolute surety with which she spoke left little doubt as to her expertise. 'The Russians used a dry aerosol dispersal system with the TU-4A. Essentially the bomber was a giant crop duster. Ram airs in the engine cowlings would scoop up and compress the slipstream, channeling it through ductwork to the reservoir manifolds. There the airflow would strip the powdered spores from the containment vessel and spray them out through vents under the wings.

'A crude system with poor metering control as compared to wet dispersal, but it had the advantages of being simple and comparatively light in weight. Depending upon your drop altitude and the prevailing winds, a strip of land a dozen miles wide by several hundred long could have been rendered lethally uninhabitable for decades.'

'For decades?' Randi looked startled.

Valentina nodded. 'Anthrax spores are tough little bastards. They love organic, nitrogen-rich environments like common garden-variety dirt, and they remain virulent for a positively obscene length of time.'

She paused to take a sip of coffee. 'There was a small island off the coast of Scotland that Great Britain used for anthrax bioweapon experimentation during the Second World War. This island was only recently declared safe for human reoccupation.'

'Small areas, like individual buildings, can be decontaminated using chemical agents. Common off-the-shelf chlorine bleach works wonders against anthrax. But for large areas, like an entire city or agricultural land . . .' The historian shook her head.

'If the anthrax is still aboard the aircraft, it may have lost virulence after half a century,' Smith added. 'But it's also been sealed inside a containment vessel and exposed to the polar cold. In effect, it's been refrigerated in a dry, oxygen-free environment, as perfect for long-term preservation as you could hope for. I'm not prepared to say what state those spores may be in.'

Valentina Metrace employed her expressive eyebrows once more. 'There's one thing I am prepared to say, Colonel. I wouldn't want to be the one to have to pull the cork and look inside.'

Smith rode the exterior elevators down to the lobby level, the night and its myriad of street and building lights snapping back into clarity as the glass-bubble car dropped out of the fog layer.

He wished he could clarify his thoughts as easily. This upcoming operation looked challenging but straightforward, one that could be dealt with by simply being careful enough and deliberate enough not to make mistakes.

But there was still the sensation of being back in a fog bank. Everything in his immediate vicinity was clear and straightforward, but there was also a wall beyond which he couldn't see, and a feeling of things hidden.

What had Director Klein told him? 'Assume there are other agendas in play. Watch for them.'

He would have to stay braced for whatever might come looming out of the mist.

At least he'd have good people backing him. Valentina Metrace was . . . interesting. They certainly hadn't made professors like that back when he was going to college. There was a story to be learned about her. And as one of Klein's mobile ciphers, she had to be exceptionally good at whatever it was she did.

And he'd have Randi again. Fierce, valiant, and self-contained, there could be no doubting her. Past all personal pain or anger she would not fail him. She would do whatever she might be tasked with, or die trying.

And that was the problem within himself. Smith had seen so much of Randi Russell's life and world die, he sometimes had the feeling he was destined to oversee her death as well. Or be responsible for it. It was a personal nightmare that had grown every time they had been thrown together on an operation.

Angrily he shook his head. He must not take the counsel of that particular fear. If it was to be, then it would be. In the meantime they had a job to do.

The elevator door chimed and slid open. His rented Ford Explorer was parked out in the hotel's front lot, and as Smith passed through the lobby he diverted for a moment. Entering the glass-walled combination newsstand and gift shop, he purchased both a *USA Today* and a *Seattle Times*, as part of an agent's instinct for staying aware of his environment.

Back in the lobby he paused to study the headlines, and his operator's hackles rose.

It must have been a slow news day. On the front page of the *Times* there was a brief Department of Defense press release. It concerned the joint U.S.-Russian investigation team being sent to the crash site of the polar mystery plane, complete with its departure time from Seattle, its route, and means of travel.

The news story was entirely appropriate for the mission cover; the information given out, routine. A failure to advise the media of the operation could have aroused suspicion in its own right.

But to Smith it was a shout into the darkness, and there was no way of knowing who might overhear.

In her hotel room, Randi Russell sank down on the edge of the bed. Aimlessly running her hand over the golden-toned coverlet, her thoughts jumbled between the past and future.

Damn it, she was a good pilot, or at least a fair one, but she didn't have near the hours needed to consider herself a competent arctic bush aviator. But that was always a problem with the Agency. Admit you knew how to fix a leaky faucet, and the assumption would be that you knew how to manage a flood control project.

The compounding half of the equation was, of course, the personal pride that always choked off the words 'No, I can't do this.'

Most particularly she couldn't bring herself to say those words to Jon Smith.

What curse chained her to that man?

She would always remember the worst fight she'd ever had with her older sister, the cold fury she had felt when Sophia had appeared with Smith's engagement ring on her finger, and the searing words of betrayal she had rained upon Sophia before stalking out of her apartment.

The worst had been that Sophia had refused to fight back. 'Jon's sorry for what he's done to you, Randi,' she'd said, smiling that wise, rather sad, big sister's smile of hers, 'more sorry than you can ever know, or at least be willing to understand.'

Randi would never understand, not now.

She was starting to unzip one suede boot when a soft knock sounded at the door. Tugging the zip up again, Randi crossed to the room's entryway, carefully checking the door's security peephole.

A pair of level, narrowed gray eyes looked back.

Randi went through the motions of clearing the dead bolt and the security chain and removing the wet molded tissue wedge from the foot of the door. 'Is anything wrong, Professor?' she asked, opening it.

'I'm not sure,' Valentina Metrace replied, her voice cool. 'That's what I'm here to find out. We need to talk, Miss Russell, specifically, about you.'

A little startled, Randi stepped back, and the historian brushed past her into the room. 'Are we secure here?' she asked bruskly.

'I've scanned for bugs,' Randi replied, closing and relocking. 'We're clean.'

'Good. We can get down to it, then.' Valentina paced

85

into the middle of the room, her arms crossed. Abruptly she turned to face Randi. 'What the hell is wrong between you and Smith?'

In her casual amiability over the dinner table, Professor Metrace had not seemed quite such a formidable personality. But in attack mode now, her eyes were steel, and Randi was aware that even without heels, the brunette was an inch or two the taller.

'I have no idea what you're talking about, Professor,' Randi replied stiffly. 'There are no problems between Colonel Smith and myself.'

'Oh, please, Miss Russell. The atmosphere over that table was so charged it would have registered on a Geiger counter. I've never worked with either you or Smith before, but I gather you must have operated with the colonel in the past. I must also assume that you both must be reasonably competent members of the Club, or you wouldn't be here. But it is also obvious something has gone off between you.'

Damn it! And Randi had been priding herself on the way she'd been keeping the lid on. 'It's nothing for you to concern yourself about, Professor.'

Metrace shook her head impatiently. 'Miss Russell. I am a professional at this game. That means I don't work with people I don't trust, and right now I'm not trusting anybody. Before I take another step forward on this operation, I want to know what exactly the bloody hell is going on between my theoretical teammates – in detail!'

Randi could recognize the gambit in play: belligerence, probably feigned, and a sudden slashing assault. Metrace was not merely demanding information. She was probing, testing Randi's reaction.

The CIA operative strove to suppress her instinctive flare of anger. 'I suggest that you discuss this matter with Colonel Smith.'

'Oh, I fully intend to, darling. But he's not available at the moment, and you are. Beyond that, Smith seemed to be handling affairs better. You seem to be the one with her knickers in a knot. Illuminate me.'

This woman was infuriating, or at least that was how she desired to be at the moment. 'I can assure you that any dealings I may have had with Colonel Smith in the past will have no effect on our current assignment whatsoever.'

'I'll be the judge of that,' Metrace replied flatly.

Randi felt her control cracking. 'Then you may judge that it's none of your damn business!'

'Keeping my skin intact is my business, Miss Russell, one that I devote a great deal of loving attention to. And right now I am sensing a sour team and a mission aborted before it launches, because of personnel problems. I'm one of the mission specialists, thus, indispensable. I suspect Colonel Smith is as well. That leaves the little helicopter girl to get the black ball. I assure you that you can be replaced, darling. Now, watch me walk out of here and make it happen!'

The confrontation hovered on the verge of critical mass. But both women recognized that if a blow was thrown, it would be no scratch-and-slap cat fight; one or the other or both of them would be dead or critically maimed in seconds.

Finally, Randi took a deep, shuddering breath. Damn this woman and damn Jon Smith and damn herself. But if they were going to be operating together, Metrace had the right to ask and Randi the responsibility to answer.

'Ten years ago a young army officer that I was very much in love with was serving with a peacekeeping force in the Horn of Africa. We were going to be married when he got home. But he contracted something out of the African disease pool, something that medical science was just beginning to recognize. He was evacuated to a Navy hospital ship and placed under the care of an army doctor who was serving aboard at the time.'

Valentina relaxed minutely. 'Colonel Smith?'

'He was a captain then. He made a misdiagnosis. It wasn't really his fault, I suppose. Only a few tropical disease specialists really understood the illness at the time. But my fiancé died.'

The silence returned to the room. Randi took another deep breath and went on. 'Some time later, Major Smith met my older sister, Sophia. She was a doctor, too, a research microbiologist. They fell in love and were engaged to be married when he convinced her to come and work with him at the U.S. Army Medical Institute for Infectious Diseases. Do you remember the Hades plague?'

'Of course.'

Randi kept her eyes fixed on the blandly patterned wallpaper. 'USAMRIID was one of the first agencies called in to try and isolate the disease and find a cure. While working with the plague, my sister caught it.'

'And she died as well.' Valentina Metrace's voice softened into compassion. The test was over.

Randi could meet the other woman's gaze now. 'Since then I've found myself working with Jon on a number of different assignments. For some reason we just keep getting tangled up with each other.' She continued with a wry, self-derogatory smile. 'I've come to recognize that he's a good operative and essentially a good person. I've also come to recognize that what's happened in the past is . . . past. I promise you, Professor, that I'll have no problem working with him as my team leader. He knows his business. It's only that I have some memories to work through whenever we first come together.'

Valentina nodded. 'I see.'

She turned for the door but paused halfway through the move. 'Miss Russell, would you like to have breakfast with me tomorrow, before we get on the plane?'

She put no special emphasis on the 'we' in the sentence. It was offered as a given.

Randi's responding smile was open this time. 'I'd like that, Professor. And call me Randi.'

'And Val for me. I apologize for coming on quite so strong. I was a bit uncertain about the scenario. I wasn't sure if I might not be getting caught up in the fallout of some former romantic entanglement.'

'Between Jon and me?' Randi chuckled ruefully. 'Not likely.'

The other woman's smile deepened. 'Good.'

After Valentina Metrace had left, Randi frowned. There had been no reason for the black-haired historian to look quite so pleased with that last answer she had been given.

CHAPTER ELEVEN

Over the Straits of Juan de Fuca

The Alaska Airlines 737-400 swept over the island-studded band of water separating the Olympic Peninsula and the United States from Vancouver Island and Canada. With cloud tendrils licking at its belly, it angled away to the northwest. As the Boeing leveled off at its cruising altitude, Jon Smith loosened his seat belt. The midweek morning flight to Anchorage was half empty, and he had the dual luxuries of no seat partner and a spot in the spacious A row just behind the cockpit bulkhead.

For the first time in weeks he was in civilian clothes, his uniform exchanged for Levi's and a well-worn bush jacket. The change was a pleasant one. Glancing over the seat back, he could see Randi Russell and Professor Metrace spaced out farther back in the cabin.

Since last night Randi had apparently reestablished her equanimity with him. Looking up from the helicopter flight manual she'd been studying, she gave him a brief smile.

The professor was also reading, her nose buried in a massive bookmark-studded study of the Warsaw Pact Air Forces.

Professor. It still sounded odd.

His own briefcase rested under his seat, loaded with the latest USAMRIID downloads on the rapid diagnosis and identification of anthrax variants and their treatments. He'd get to them presently, but for the moment it felt good to sit back, stretch his legs out, and close his eyes against the warm morning sun pouring through the cabin window. Soon he'd have no time or opportunity to unload so totally.

'Mind if I sit down, Jon?'

He snapped out of the semidoze he'd drifted into. Valentina Metrace was standing in the aisle, a cup of coffee steaming in her hand and a mildly amused expression on her face.

Smith grinned back. 'Why not?'

She flowed past him to curl up in the window seat. The professor was apparently one of those women who preferred to be elegant at all times. This morning she wore a form-molding black sweater and ski pants set, and her hair was up in the sleek chignon she seemed to favor. Smith found himself wondering for a moment how far that dark, glossy cascade might flow down her back should it be set free.

Despite the pleasant distraction, he still shot a fast look around, checking the immediate environment. The seat rows across and behind them were still unoccupied, granting them a pocket of privacy.

Valentina was security wary as well, for when she spoke she kept her voice pitched below the whine of the fan jets.

'I was thinking we could use this opportunity to talk freely before our liaison joins up. Tell me, Colonel, what's your policy going to be toward our gallant Russian ally?'

It was a good question. 'Until proven otherwise, we are to assume all of the brothers are valiant and all of the sisters virtuous,' Smith replied. 'As long as the Russians appear to be playing straight with us, we'll do the same for them. But the operative word is "appear." Our instructions are to play like the deck is loaded. We're to assume the Russians have another layer on this thing.'

Metrace took a sip of her coffee. 'I think that we may call that a blinding flash of the obvious.'

They had to lean close to speak, and Smith couldn't help but note that his executive officer smelled pleasantly of Guerlain's Fleurs des Alpes. So if the Russians are trying to pull a fast one,' Smith inter-laced his fingers over his stomach, 'what is it and why? What aren't we seeing?'

'I daresay it would be better to approach this as a question of what is it they don't want us to see,' she replied. 'I've been networking with some of my fellow history buffs since catching this rocket, and I've discovered something rather interesting about the Misha 124 crash.

'Since the end of the Cold War there has been a huge . . . I suppose you could call it a glasnost under way between military historians on both sides of the conflict. Without having to worry about security restrictions, we've been asking why was this done, where, and by whom. For the most part, we've been getting answers.

'To date, our opposite numbers in the Russian Federation have been remarkably forthcoming, even about their major military bloopers like sunken atomic submarines and nerve gas spills.

'But not on this point. Prior to the discovery of the Misha crash site, in all of the ex-Soviet air force service records we've been granted access to, there has been no mention of any TU-4 squadron losing any aircraft in March of 1953, on any kind of routine exercise, anywhere.'

'And no mention of a biological broken arrow in the Arctic involving two tons of anthrax?' Smith prompted.

She shook her head, then brushed back a lock of raven hair from above her brow. 'Not a whisper, until the Russians brought the subject up with our President.

'Now, information on a bioweapons warload being carried by a specific aircraft might very well have been compartmentalized for security purposes. But this particular Bull and its entire aircrew have been completely erased from all standard Red Air Force documentation. They urgently wanted to make it go completely away. And I think the only reason the Russian Federation is admitting to its existence now is because it's sitting there in front of God and everybody.'

Smith looked past Valentina for a moment and out the glare-bright window, digesting the information. 'That is interesting,' he replied slowly. 'Here's one I've been wondering about. It seems damn peculiar to me that anyone would risk uploading a live biowar agent as part of a training exercise. Common sense would dictate you'd use some kind of harmless inert testing compound.'

Valentina shrugged. 'You'd think so, and so would I. But then, we aren't Russian. They tend to do things differently.

'Consider the Chernobyl disaster,' she went on. 'We wouldn't build a big electric power reactor with a combustible graphite core, but the Russians did. We wouldn't build a big nuclear reactor of any kind without a proper radiation containment dome, but the Russians did. And we wouldn't run a series of radical systems-failure tests on a big, unsealed graphite-core power reactor while it was up and critical, but the Russians most certainly did. I don't think we can make any assumptions on that point.'

Smith nodded. 'Then we won't. Now, let's move on to something else. I know the status of the Russian Federation's current biowar program, but you're our expert on past Soviet systems. What's the possibility that bomber might be carrying something other than plain old anthrax?'

She sighed. 'It's difficult to say. The Misha 124 was the kind of aircraft that would have been used on a one-way transpolar strike mission against strategic targets in the United States. With that as a given, and given the plane was armed, it would have been carrying some kind of ABC warload: atomic, biological, or chemical. The Soviets wouldn't expend a long-range bomber and an elite aircrew to deliver anything less potent.'

She took another sip of her coffee and squirmed around to face him directly, tucking her feet under her in the seat. 'As for the specific agent, those were the days before the exotics like Ebola and before advanced genetic engineering. You had to make do with what Mother Nature provided. The big three everyone was fooling with were anthrax, smallpox, and the bubonic plague. Anthrax was favored because it was simple and cheap to manufacture in bulk, and militarily controllable because it isn't a contagion.'

Smith frowned and considered. 'If it were the plague or

smallpox, we'd likely have nothing to worry about. The pathogens would probably be long inert by now. Besides, why lie about it? All three of the alternatives would have been equally nasty, and once we reach the crash site we'd know anyway.'

'Exactly.' Valentina gave an acknowledging tilt of her head. 'That's why it can't just be the presence of the bio-agent alone. They've already confessed to it. There must be some X factor involved that we don't understand. Beyond that, the present deponent knoweth not. But I can be reasonably certain about one other thing.'

'What would that be?'

She took another sip of her coffee. 'Something damn peculiar is going to happen when we get inside that airplane.'

CHAPTER TWELVE

Anchorage, Alaska

Three hours out of Seattle the 737 popped its flaps and air-brakes and began its descent into the Anchorage bowl. Snowcapped ridgelines and the steel blue waters of Cook's Inlet panned past the liner's windows as it spiraled down into the contradiction of a twenty-first-century American city set in the heart of an essential wilderness.

Settling on its landing gear, the little Boeing taxied to the south terminal of Ted Stevens International Airport. A uniformed Alaska State Policeman from the airport security detail stood waiting for Smith and his people at the head of the Jetway.

'Welcome to Alaska, Colonel Smith,' the state trooper said gravely. 'We've got a vehicle waiting for you out in the police lot.' He passed Smith a set of car keys. 'It's a white unmarked Crown Vic. Just leave it at Merrill Field. We'll send someone to collect it.'

It was obvious that Director Klein's invisible but potent presence had passed this way, smoothing their path. 'Thank you, Sergeant,' Smith replied, accepting the keys. 'It's appreciated.'

The trooper also handed over a small, heavy case of black pebbled plastic. 'This was also sent over for you, Colonel. Somebody seems to think you might need it.'

Smith matched the trooper's rather pointed smile. 'They could be wrong.'

They had limited themselves to carry-on luggage, so there was no need to join in the battle around the baggage carousels. Smith led his team out of the terminal building and into the crisp Alaskan noon. The oddly angled sun was warm, but the air was cool in the shadows, and the surrounding peaks of the great Chugach range were dusted with fresh snow – pointed hints that time was running out in the North.

As promised, a mud-streaked Ford with Alaskan state plates was waiting for them. After stowing their luggage in the sedan's commodious trunk, Smith tossed the keys over to Randi. She slid in behind the wheel, with Smith taking the front passenger seat and Valentina the back. Automatically they paused to arm up.

Taking the pistol case onto his lap, Smith popped the slide catches and flipped open the lid.

Since joining the profession Smith had developed a theorem about weapons preference. It was a profound personality statement about the individual and the way they related to a potentially hostile world. It was also an absolute truth because it was something one was entrusting one's life to.

He passed a black leather and nylon fanny pack across to Randi and watched as she ripped open the heavy Velcro fasteners and flipped the pouch section down and off the concealed crossdraw holster. Revealed also were the rosewood grips and stainless steel finish of a Smith and Wesson model 60, the Lady Magnum variant ergonomically optimized for a female shooter. With deft, practiced movements she dunked a speedloader of .357 hollowpoint into the revolver's chambers.

Point proven. Randi Russell was a lady, and she carried a lady's gun. But as she was a very serious lady, it was a very serious lady's gun.

For himself, there was simple mil-spec practicality, a Department of Defense alternate-issue SIG-Sauer P-226 with a stack of 9mm clips and a Bianchi shoulder holster and clip carrier. The armed forces had expended a great deal of time and effort proving up the SIG as an effective and efficient personal firearm. Smith found no reason to argue with their decision.

Finally there was a small, elongated bundle wrapped in soft black cloth. 'What's that?' Randi asked as Smith lifted it from the case.

'Those are mine,' Valentina replied, resting her chin on her crossed hands atop the seat back. 'Have a look.'

Smith opened the bundle. It contained a brace of throwing knives, but knives such as he had never seen before. Intrigued, he drew one from its nylon slip sheath.

Only eight inches long and barely the width of his ring finger, it was half haft, half blade. The blade itself was almost spikelike, with a flattened, diamond-shaped cross-section, the junctures of all four oiled facets honed to a shimmering edge. Both the doctor and the warrior within Smith were impressed. Like a rapier or one of the old triangular-bladed trench knives, it would produce a wound channel that would be a perfect horror to try and close.

There was no guard, but an indented thumb brace circled the top of the checkered hilt. And the knife hadn't been assembled; it had been carved, expertly cold-machined out of a single bar of some exceptionally heavy metal.

The knife bore a certain family resemblance to the tonki throwing darts used in Japanese martial arts, and when Smith laid it across his extended finger to test its balance he found it perfect. Except for the blade edges and a minute silver 'VM' scripted on one blade facet, it was finished in jet black.

'It's beautiful,' Randi whispered in honest appreciation. And it was. There was a sense of design and proportion to the little knife that made it a work of art beyond the weapon.

'Thank you,' Valentina Metrace replied. 'That's DY-100 steel – hellish stuff to work but incredibly strong, and if you can get an edge on it, it lasts forever.'

Smith glanced back at her. 'You made these?'

Valentina gave a modestly acknowledging tilt of her head. 'A hobby.'

Randi smiled indulgently as she buckled the belt of the fanny pack/holster around her waist. 'They're pretty,

Professor, but if a situation develops you might want something a little more substantial.'

'Never underestimate the point and the edge, darling.' Valentina accepted the knives from Smith. 'Blades have killed more people than all of the bombs and bullets ever created, and they continue to do so with undiminished efficiency.'

One of the throwing knives vanished up the historian's left sweater sleeve, the other into a boot top. 'My little pets are silent, jamproof, and far easier to conceal than a gun. You never have to worry about running out of ammunition, and they can punch through soft body armor that would stop a conventional pistol round cold.'

Randi gave her gun belt a final settling tug and cranked over the Crown Victoria's ignition. 'I'll stick with a gun, thanks.'

'Hopefully we won't need either flavor of ordnance on this job, ladies.'

'Hopefully, Jon?' Randi replied, backing the car out of its slot.

'Well, let's call it a nice thought.'

The next step was a call to a number he'd committed to memory before leaving Seattle that morning. As they worked their way out of the airport lot Smith keyed his cell phone. A deep voice speaking a mildly accented but excellent English replied, 'This is Major Smyslov.'

'Good afternoon, Major, this is Colonel Smith. We will be picking you up in front of your hotel in about fifteen minutes. A white Ford sedan, Alaska license, Sierra . . . Tango . . . Tango . . . three . . . four . . . seven, one man, two women. Civilian clothes.'

'Very good, Colonel, I will be waiting.'

Smith flipped the phone shut. This would be his next critical unknown. There had already been a couple of interesting turns in his team's makeup. What would this last member add to the already exotic brew?

*

Clad in anorak, khaki slacks, and climbing boots, Major Gregori Smyslov stood outside the lobby entrance of the Arctic Inn, his flight bag at his feet and his thoughts paralleling those of Jon Smith.

He had been briefed to expect an army doctor, a historian, and a civilian helicopter pilot. But who would they truly be? Already Smyslov had the sense they would be something more. The way Smith had set up the contact and pickup, the crisp identifiers he had given – they had the flavor of an experienced field operative.

Impatiently he lit a Camel filter with a disposable butane lighter, not of a mood to enjoy the superior American tobacco. Soon his performance would begin.

Already Smyslov didn't like the feel of this job. It had the stink of desperation about it, a stench all too common in Russian governmental circles in these days. Someone somewhere in the Moscow bureaucracy was not thinking, just reacting.

He took a hard drag on the cigarette. It wasn't his place to decide such things.

The white automobile he had been told to expect turned off the street and rolled to a halt under the hotel canopy, its license number and passengers matching the given description. Smyslov flipped the cigarette to the ground, crushing it deliberately with his boot heel. Presently he would know, or at least he would have an idea, where the Americans stood and what they suspected.

Collecting his bag, Smyslov strode out to the car.

Within five minutes Smyslov indeed knew, and any hope that the Americans might be naively accepting the Russian line on the Misha 124 crash was irrevocably gone. As he was flying a false flag, so was everyone else.

The two women might look like American fashion models, but they most certainly were something else. The taciturn, wary blonde driving the car, theoretically the 'helicopter pilot,' was maintaining a spy's situational awareness, as was the more openly relaxed and vivacious brunette 'history professor.' As she lounged in the backseat beside him, overtly chatting about the Alaskan climate, her vision scanned in a regular pattern, checking the paralleling traffic and skipping from one rearview mirror to the other, watching for potential tails.

Smyslov judged them as CIA or as members of one of the associate intelligence agencies that made up what the Americans called 'the Club.'

He wondered if the striking attractiveness of the two female agents was a mere coincidence or if one or both of them might include seductive interrogation as part of their arsenal.

That could prove disconcerting.

As for the team leader, he might be an Army surgeon but he was also American Spetsnaz, probably attached to their defense intelligence agency. The feeling of alert, focused confidence radiating from him was unmistakable, as was the bulk of the military-caliber automatic riding under his jacket. The least they could have done was to give the poor fellow a decent cover name. Jon Smith indeed!

And if he had caught their scent, they most certainly had his. When Smith had reached back over the seat to shake Smyslov's hand, there had been a glint of humor deep in his penetrating dark blue eyes, a shared, cynical joke of 'Shhh, we'll play the game for as long as you will.'

Madness!

Smyslov jerked his attention away from his thoughts. 'What did you say, Colonel?'

'I was just asking if your people had come up with anything new on the circumstances of the crash,' Smith said amiably, looking back over the seat once more. 'Do you have any better idea of what brought her down in our territory?'

Smyslov shook his head, aware of the three pairs of eyes regarding him, two sets directly and one in the rearview mirror. 'No. We have reexamined our records and we have interviewed certain personnel who were serving in Siberia at the time of the Misha 124 training flight. Communications failed sometime between two routine position reports, and no distress call was heard. There was some evidence of environmental radio interference over the Pole. We believe this is the explanation.'

'What was the last solid fix you had on her? The plane's position, that is?'

So it began. 'I don't have the exact latitude and longitude to mind, Colonel; I'll have to check my documentation, but they were somewhere north of Ostrova Anzhu.'

'We've been wondering what she was doing so far over on our side of the Pole on a training exercise.' The woman professor, (Metrace, was it?) smoothly took over the flow of the questioning. 'From what we know about the B-29-TU-4 family of aircraft, a crash on Wednesday Island would have put your bomber almost beyond her point of no return for your Siberian bases.'

Smyslov gritted his teeth for a moment and parroted the answer he had been programmed to give. 'The training flight was never intended to come close to the North American coastline at any point. We theorize that the plane's onboard gyrocompasses tumbled. Given the difficulties of aerial navigation near the Pole, the crew must have accidentally flown a reciprocal course toward Canada instead of back to Siberia.'

'That's funny,' the woman behind the wheel murmured almost to herself as she deftly maneuvered around a lumbering SUV.

'What is, Randi?' Smith said almost casually.

'It's still dark over the Pole in March, and the B-29 was a high-altitude aircraft. It should have been flying well above any cloud cover. Even if they did lose their gyros, I wonder why the navigator wasn't able to shoot a star sight and get his bearings.'

Smyslov felt the sweat start to prickle under his anorak. Now he knew what it felt like to be a mouse under the claws of a pack of exceptionally playful and sadistic cats. 'I don't know, Miss Russell. Possibly we will learn more at the crash site.'

'I'm sure we will, Major,' Smith said with a pleasant smile.

This . . . was . . . madness!

CHAPTER THIRTEEN

Merrill Field, Anchorage

Even into the twenty-first century, Alaska was essentially still a wilderness with a minimal road and rail net. Flight stitched the mammoth state together, and Merrill Field and its sister seaplane facility at Lake Hood were two of the largest civil aviation facilities in the world, central nodes in this culture of the bush pilot.

Scores of hangars lined the field taxiways, and hundreds of light planes occupied acres of parking apron. The drone of engines was a constant, and the traffic pattern was perpetually filled with incoming and departing aircraft.

As Smith and his team drew up in front of the office of Pole Star Aero-leasing, they found that a sleek Day-Glo orange helicopter had already been wheeled out of an adjacent hangar. Mounted on a set of pressed-foam arctic pontoons, it stood spotted and ready for takeoff.

'Okay, Randi,' Smith said. 'There's your piece of the action. What do you think?'

'It'll do,' she replied, openly pleased. 'It's a Bell Jet Ranger, the stretched 206L Long Ranger variant with twin turbines. It's about as stone reliable as a helicopter can get. According to the documentation, it should be fully IFR capable and weatherized for polar operations.'

'Then I may assume it's acceptable in all aspects, Ms. Russell?'

She shot a look at him along with a half-smile. 'Nominally, Colonel Smith. I'll let you know for certain when I've finished my walk-around.'

Smyslov stared out of his window at the Ranger with that

peculiar pilot's fixation, and it occurred to Smith that the Russian Air Force officer was indeed a Russian Air Force officer.

'Do you have any helicopter time, Major?' he asked.

'Some,' he replied, looking around with a grin, 'in Kamovs and Swidniks, but none in a little beauty like that one.'

'Then, Randi, you've got a copilot. Put him to work.'

Randi gave him the briefest of hesitant glances. Smith replied with a single millimeter's nod. All of the brothers were valiant, and all of the sisters virtuous . . . until proven otherwise. Beyond that, the blond-haired Russian would be riding in that helicopter along with the rest of them, and Smyslov didn't strike Smith as being overtly suicidal.

Leaving the loading and preflight to Randi, Smith touched base at the leasing office. There was little for him to do; the invisible but potent presence of Fred Klein had passed through here as well.

'The paperwork's all taken care of, Colonel,' the grizzled office manager said. 'Your bird's fully fueled and surveyed, and I took the liberty of filing a flight plan through to Kodiak for you. You've got CAVU flight conditions all the way, and the weather looks good over Cook's Inlet and the Entrances for the next twelve hours. The air boss aboard the *Haley* is expecting you, and you'll recover directly onto ship. I'll advise him when you're in the air.'

Smith knew from his briefing that Pole Star provided aircraft for a number of commercial and government research projects in the Arctic, and possibly for other purposes.

The office manager was obviously ex-army aviation. A large First Air Cavalry shield had been mounted on the flier-cluttered office wall, and the model of an AH-1 Huey Cobra sat on the desk. An ancient Vietnam-era flight jacket also lay draped over the back of the chair. Smith sensed that the older man might have been a member of the Club himself at one time or had worked on the peripheries.

'Thanks for the service,' Smith said, extending his hand

to the manager. 'We'll try to bring her back in one piece.'

'Screw it. It's insured,' the old aviator grinned back, taking Smith's hand in a strong, calloused grasp. 'I don't know what your tasking orders are, Colonel, but good luck and watch your ass. Men count. Choppers don't.'

'I'll make that my beautiful thought for the day.'

Smith stepped from the office and took a long automatic look around. The sky was blue and almost cloudless, the wind a faint cool brush against his face. In a few minutes they'd be airborne.

His team had linked up. Nothing untoward had happened on the flight to Anchorage or at the airport. No one had followed them here. No one was in sight, save for his own people and a couple of flannel-shirted locals tinkering around with a big white Cessna in a hangar across from the leasing agency.

Why was he thinking something had to be wrong?

The island and port of Kodiak lay some 270 miles west-southwest of Anchorage, down the length of Cook's Inlet and across Shelikof Strait from the Alaskan mainland, a decent haul for a small helicopter.

Randi Russell kept the Long Ranger just off the beach, steering along the densely forested shore of the Kenai Peninsula. Urban civilization fell swiftly behind them, replaced by a string of small villages spaced along the Sterling Coastal Highway like the beads on a necklace.

Randi was grateful for this opportunity to learn her aircraft. Most of her rotor hours had been in the Bell Ranger family, but few had been in the big 206 series. Now she felt her way through the Long Ranger's handling, exploring how the greater size and weight of the aircraft and the drag of the pontoons were countered by the augmented power of the twin engines. Her eyes soon found and fell into the automatic scan pattern of instrument gauges–horizon–instrument gauges–horizon of the skilled pilot.

Beyond the fishing community of Homer and the mouth

of Kachemak Bay, even the coastal villages were left behind, and the Long Ranger headed out across the broad, empty straits of the Kennedy and Stevenson Entrances to Kodiak Island. The occasional distant wake of a fishing boat cutting across the chill blue waters served as the last lingering reminder of humanity.

After the first hour airborne, the steady-state whine of the turbines and the rhythmic thudding of the rotors threatened to become soporific, and Randi found herself having to fight a backlog of transpacific jet lag. Major Smyslov's occasional interested question from the copilot's seat about the controls and handling of the Long Ranger provided a welcome stimulus.

In the amidships passenger seats Professor Metrace had succumbed. Curling up in her mink-collared leather jacket, she'd gone to sleep. Glancing up at the rearview cockpit mirror, Randi couldn't help but note the way her head had drifted companionably onto Jon's shoulder.

So it hadn't been Randi's imagination back in Seattle. Valentina Metrace obviously was not averse to combining business with pleasure, and she was also obviously interested in Smith.

Well, she was more than welcome to the man. But, damn it, did the theoretical 'historian' have to be so flagrant about it? And did she always have to go around looking like a James Bond heroine?

Randi glanced down at herself and her comfortably worn jeans and denim jacket and suppressed a soft feminine snort.

As for what Jon felt about it, Randi couldn't tell. But then, that had always been the problem with the man. Smith was one of the very few people Randi had ever met that she couldn't read. She could never be quite sure what was really going on behind those handsome, immobile features.

It had been that way even when he had been saying how sorry he was about her fiancé or telling her about Sophia.

One thing she could sense was Smith's wariness. Even with that pleasantly scented seatmate nestled against him, his head was turning with slow, repetitive deliberation, those intent blue eyes moving constantly in a fighter pilot's scan.

Did he know something he hadn't passed on, or was he sensing something? Damn it, what was going on in there?

Maybe it was just the time and environment. If someone wanted to make trouble, now, over the open sea with the Kenai Peninsula and Kodiak Island mere hazy outlines on the horizons fore and aft, would present an excellent opportunity.

Suddenly the turning of Smith's head stopped, and he fixed on something off the port side, like a gun turret locking on target.

'Randi,' he said quietly into the lip mike of his headset, 'we have traffic paralleling us. Eight o'clock high.'

Randi swore at herself for letting her own situational awareness slip. Twisted around in the pilot's seat, she looked down the bearing. There was something out there. A glint of sunlight heliographing off the windshield of another aircraft. 'I've got him.'

Everyone in the Long Ranger's cabin snapped alert, Valentina straightening up, clear-eyed and in a way that made Randi wonder if she'd been asleep at all. The team looked on as the intruder edged closer, a large, high-winged, single-engined monoplane.

'This is the direct flight path between Anchorage and Kodiak Island,' Smyslov commented, playing the devil's advocate. 'It is logical there would be other aeroplanes.'

'Maybe,' Randi replied, 'but that looks like a Cessna Turbo Centurion. He has a way higher cruising speed than we do. Why would he be station keeping on us like that?'

'Randi,' Smith said, not taking his eyes off the shadowing aircraft, 'angle us off the direct bearing to Kodiak.'

'Right. Doing it.'

She rocked the cyclic, and the Long Ranger paid off onto a slightly divergent course. Half a minute later Smyslov spoke quietly. 'He turns with us.'

The Russian tightened his seat belt, a combat aviator's instinctive ready alert gesture.

'Again, Randi,' Smith's voice sharpened. 'Turn away from him!'

She obeyed without question. She snapped the tail of the helicopter toward the Cessna. Veering away to the north-west, she tried to open the range.

The Cessna fell away astern. For over a full minute the sky around the helicopter remained clear. Then the light plane reappeared, crawling back into view half a mile to their left. Accelerating, it climbed into a dominant position off the Long Ranger's port bow, a dark silhouette against the piercing blue sky. Once more it began to sidle closer.

'He must like our company,' Valentina Metrace said, removing a small, flat pair of folding sports binoculars from her inside jacket pocket. Popping them open, she focused on their stalker. 'The starboard cargo door has been removed,' she reported. 'There's one pilot aboard and what looks like one passenger kneeling in the open doorway. The registration numbers are November . . . nine . . . five . . . three . . . seven . . . foxtrot.'

'That's it, then.' Smith's voice returned to its usual steady state. 'That's the same plane that was parked across from the leasing agency when we picked up the helicopter. Randi, put in a call to the Kodiak Coast Guard base. Tell them we may need some help out here.'

'Right.' Randi reached up to the overhead communications panel, switching her headset from intercom to radio. 'Coast Guard Kodiak, Coast Guard Kodiak, this is Nan one niner six alpha six squawking emergency, squawking emergency, over.'

She lifted her finger from the transmit key. Abruptly, electronic ice picks were driven into her ears, her headset filling with a piercing electronic warble.

'Damn! Shit! Hell!' She swatted at the selector switch.

'Randi, what is it?'

'We're being jammed! Somebody's just turned on a powerful cascade jammer out there!'

'We have descending traffic to port!' Smyslov yelled. 'He's turning in on us!'

The Centurion's wing kicked up and over. Accelerating into a shallow dive, the plane cut across the helicopter's flight path from left to right. In the dark rectangle of the plane's open cargo door, a ruddy spark danced and sputtered. Pale streaks of light blazed past the cabin.

Tracers.

'Breaking left!' Randi screamed, throwing the cyclic hard over and smashing down on her rudder bar.

The Long Ranger came up on one rotor tip and wailed into a diving turn of its own, cutting into and under the Cessna. The two aircraft flicked past one another like a pair of rapier blades.

Lift and power sagged, and Randi twisted the throttle grip to its stop, stabilizing the helicopter onto its new course. 'Where is he?' she demanded, looking around wildly for their attacker.

'Climbing out at four o'clock,' Smith replied, looking aft out the side windows. 'It looks like he's circling back, trying to get in behind us again. Can you lose him?'

She made a few rapid mental assessments and was not happy with the outcome. 'Not likely. There's no way I can extend out over open water like this. He's got a good sixty knots on us. He can also outclimb us.'

'Options?'

'Limited! With his gun firing out of his side door like that, he's got a very restricted firing arc. When he comes in on us I can evade by turning into him and diving under him, like I just did. But that'll only work for as long as we have altitude! Once he pins us down against the surface of the sea he can circle above us like the Apaches circling a wagon train. He'll cut us to pieces.'

The wave tops glittered below the Long Ranger's pontoons. They had not been flying at any great height to begin with, and their initial evasion had cost them a great deal of what they'd had. Randi had the Long Ranger shuddering at a maximum power climb, but in this game of dogfighting beggar-my-neighbor she couldn't regain what she'd expended fast enough.

'Keep on that radio,' Smith commanded. 'Try to get through to anyone.'

'It is no good,' Smyslov interjected grimly. He had been working the communications panel. 'That plane's jammer is cutting right across all of our communications bands. While it's active no one will be hearing or saying anything within twenty kilometers of us.'

'Are you sure?' Smith demanded.

Smyslov gave a bitter, ironic grimace. 'Unfortunately, yes. I recognize the interference modulation pattern of the unit. The bloody thing is one of ours! It's a Russian army tactical electronic warfare system.'

'There he is!' Valentina Metrace called from her side of the helicopter. 'He's coming around again!'

Randi felt a hand reach around the seat back, yanking her Lady Magnum out of its pack holster. She didn't have to look back to see who the hand belonged to.

'That's not going to be much, Jon,' she commented.

'I know.' There was a grim tinge of humor in his reply. 'But it's what we've got.' Randi heard the wind roar of the rear passenger window sliding open, and the chill blast of the slipstream on the back of her neck.

'Be careful you don't hit the rotors,' Randi yelled over the increased wind roar.

'I'll be lucky to hit anything!'

'Hostile at eight o'clock, high angle!' Smyslov chanted. 'Hostile is at nine o'clock, still climbing. Hostile is at ten o'clock . . . He's banking! He's turning in! He's coming in faster this time! . . .'

The tracer stream cut past the windscreen, and again Randi rolled the Long Ranger into its steep evasive break. As the helicopter rolled onto its side, there was a momentary frozen image of the attacking Cessna cutting past them, the plane's gunner half-hanging out its cargo door.

Like a Vietnam-era helicopter gunner, he was suspended from a monkey harness bolted into the door frame. Some kind of medium machine gun was strapped to his body, the belt feeding from an overhead magazine, making him a living flexible weapons mount. Looking down, he hosed death at the diving Long Ranger, the flash of an exhilarated grin glinting on his face.

Behind her, handguns crashed, both pistols firing at once, the piercing crack of Smith's automatic and the heavier slam of her revolver. Ejecting brass flickered around the cockpit, and Randi caught a whiff of gun smoke as Smith got off half a dozen rounds before the target was past.

'No chance! Missed the bastard!' It was one of the rare times she ever heard him swear.

She got the helicopter stabilized under its rotor disk and checked her gauges. 'We can do that once more,' she reported; 'then we go into the water.'

It was a simple statement of fact.

'There's a life vest under each seat, and a life raft slung under the fuselage.' Smith was equally pragmatic with his reply as he reached forward to take another speed loader from the fanny pack. 'When we go in, I'll try for the life raft. Everyone else swim as far away from the copter as fast as you can. Stay together and don't inflate your vests right off. He's going to strafe us, and you're going to have to dive to evade.'

He was only going through the drill for form's sake. Their survival time in the frigid waters of the straits could be counted in single-digit minutes.

'This would be a marvelous moment for a witty offhand comment,' Professor Metrace added dryly. 'Any volunteers?' The historian's face was pale in the cockpit mirror, but she was holding it together in her own way. Randi had to smile. Her taste in men might be questionable, but even she had to admit, Valentina Metrace had style.

Beyond the portside windows she could see the Cessna

111

climbing into attack position once again. 'Last chance,' Smith said. 'Any suggestions?'

'There may be something . . .' Smyslov's distracted murmur came over the intercom circuit.

'Major, do you have an idea?'

'Possibly, Colonel, but there is only a small chance . . .'

'A small chance is better than none, Major,' Smith snapped, 'and that's what we have now. Go!'

'As you wish, sir!' Behind his sunglasses Smyslov had his own eyes fixed on the enemy plane. 'Miss Russell, when he begins his next run, you must hold your course; your straight course; you must let him shoot at us!'

Randi spared him an instant's disbelieving glance. 'You mean we give him a clean shot?'

'Yes. Exactly! We must let him fire on us. You must hold your course to the last possible second; then you must not turn and dive; you must climb! You must cut directly across his flight path!'

That was insanity twice over. 'If he doesn't shoot us down, we'll collide with him!'

Smyslov could only nod in agreement. 'Very possibly, Miss Russell.'

The Cessna banked, lifting into its wingover and final attacking dive.

'Randi, do it!' Smith's command rang in her ears.

'Jon!'

His voice mellowed. 'I don't know what he's thinking, either, but do it anyway.'

Randi bit her lip and held her course. She felt Smyslov's hand drop onto her shoulder. 'Wait for him,' the Russian said, tracking the pursuit curve of their attacker, calculating speeds and distances. 'Wait for him!'

A tracer tentacle lashed past the Long Ranger, weaving and groping for the helicopter.

'Wait for him!' Smyslov said relentlessly, his fingers digging into her collarbone. 'Wait . . . !'

The airframe shuddered as high-velocity metal thwacked

through its structure. A side window starred and exploded inward as death screamed through the cockpit.

'Now! Pull up! Pull up!'

Wrenching her controls back to their stops, Randi lifted the Long Ranger through the flight path of the Cessna Centurion. For an instant, the whole world off the port side was filled with the nose and shimmering propeller arc of the diving plane, hanging mere feet beyond their own rotor arc. And in that frozen instant the windshield of the Cessna exploded outward.

Then it was past, and the helicopter was bucking and skidding wildly in the interlocking turbulence, on the very razor's edge of departing controlled flight. Randi fought for the recovery, a thin, angry adrenaline-spurred cry slipping from her lips as she wrestled with the pitch and collective, striving not to lethally overstress the airframe. If she could fly the Ranger out of this, by God, she could fly it anywhere.

The copter responded and steadied with a final shuddering bobble. They still had a valid aircraft. They still had life.

'Where is he?' Randi panted.

'Down there,' Smith answered.

The white Cessna was falling away beneath them in a flat spin, a thin haze of smoke streaming from its cockpit. A moment later it belly-slammed into the sea, vanishing from sight in an explosion of spray.

'Well done, Randi,' Smith continued. 'And you, Major. Exceptionally well done.'

'I'll second that,' Valentina Metrace added reverently. 'If you were a man, my dear Randi, I'd be yours for the asking.'

'Thanks, but would someone mind telling me just what it was that I did? What happened to that guy?'

'It was . . . pah, what are the words . . .' Smyslov slumped in his seat, his head tilted back and his eyes closed. '. . . target fixation. The machine gunner, he was firing his weapon from a body harness. He did not have a fixed gun mount with fire interrupters to keep him from shooting into his own airframe. Once he had you targeted, he focused on trying to hold his tracers on you for the kill. When you cut across his nose as you did, he swung with you, and turned his gun barrel right into his own cockpit.'

'And before he could get off the trigger he'd killed his own pilot and shot himself down,' Smith finished. 'Fast thinking, Major.'

Smyslov lifted his hands. 'Merest memory, Colonel. Once, over Chechnya, I had a muzhik door gunner with pig shit for brains who nearly blew the back of my head off.'

Randi sighed and glanced at the Russian. 'I'm glad he missed.'

CHAPTER FOURTEEN

Kodiak, Alaska

The spruce-shaggy slopes of Barometer Mountain mirrored themselves in the waters of St. Paul's Bay as the Long Ranger skimmed into the harbor at Kodiak. Angling past the trawlers that crowded the docks of the fishing port, the copter headed for the Coast Guard Base. The USS *Alex Haley* lay moored beside the base pier, and the big cutter was standing by to receive them. Her own helicopter had been offloaded, and her hangar bay doors gaped wide, a wandsman standing by on her afterdeck helipad to walk them aboard.

The *Haley* was a singleton, one of a kind within the Coast Guard's white-hull fleet. A staunch and stolid ex-Navy salvage ship, she did duty as both the regulation-enforcing scourge of the huge Kodiak Island fishing fleet and its rescuing angel of mercy. Sailing in the wake of legendary predecessors like the *Bear* and the *Northland*, she was the law north of the Aleutians. Also, with her powerful engines and ice-strengthened hull, she was one of only a handful of ships able to dare the Northwest Passage with winter looming.

Gingerly, Randi eased the Long Ranger aboard, compensating for the ground effect variant as she sidled over the cutter's deck. The pontoons scuffed down on the black pebbly antiskid, and she cut the throttles. For a long minute, as the turbines whined down, Smith and his people luxuriated in the sheer stability of the ship's deck. Then the cutter's aviation hands were ducking under the slowing rotor arc, and two officers in crisp khakis were approaching from the hangar bay.

'Colonel Smith, I'm Commander Will Jorganson.' As stolid and stocky as his ship, Jorganson was a fit, balding middle-aged man with intent sea-faded blue eyes and a strong, dry handshake. 'This is Lieutenant Grundig, my executive officer. We've been expecting you. Welcome aboard the *Haley*.'

'You have no idea how glad we are to be here, Commander,' Smith replied with a degree of irony. After the cramped interior of the helicopter, the open, breeze-swept freedom of the helipad felt wonderful. 'This is my assistant team leader, Professor Valentina Metrace; my pilot, Ms. Randi Russell; and my Russian liaison, Major Gregori Smyslov of the Russian Federation Air Force. Now, I have two questions I need immediate answers for, Commander. The first and most critical is, how fast can you get this ship under way and headed north?'

Jorganson frowned. 'We're scheduled to sail at 0600 tomorrow.'

'I didn't ask when we were scheduled to sail,' Smith said, meeting the Coast Guardsman's eyes. 'I asked how fast you can get under way.'

The cutter captain's scowl deepened. 'I'm afraid I don't understand, Colonel.'

'I don't either, Commander. That's why we have to get out of here right now. I trust that you have received specific orders from the commandant of the Seventeenth Coast Guard District concerning my authority on this mission under certain curcumstances?'

Jorganson stiffened. 'Yes, sir.'

'Those circumstances exist, and I am invoking that authority. Now, how fast can you get us under way?'

Jorganson had indeed received his packet of sealed orders concerning the Wednesday Island evacuation, and the two-starred signature underneath them had been exceptionally impressive. 'We are fully fueled and provisioned, Colonel. I have personnel ashore that I'll need to recall, and my engine room crew will need time to heat up the plant. One hour, sir.'

Smith nodded. 'Very good, Captain. Now, my second question leads into the reason for all of this. Is your onboard aviation detail set up to assess and repair battle damage on an aircraft?'

That finally shook Jorganson's stoicism. 'Battle damage?'

Smith nodded. 'That's correct. While we were en route to your ship, someone tried to shoot us down. We were intercepted over the Passages by a light plane equipped with a military-grade radio jammer and a machine gun. If it weren't for a bright idea by Major Smyslov and some brilliant flying by Ms. Russell, you'd be sailing to search for a downed helicopter.'

'But . . .'

'I don't know, Captain,' Smith repeated patiently. 'But someone is obviously trying to prevent my team from reaching Wednesday Island. Accordingly, I think it behooves us to get the hell up there just as fast as we can.'

'We'll take care of it, sir.' Jorganson nodded, his professional composure returning. 'The same for your helo. Whatever needs to be done will get done.'

The captain turned to his waiting first officer. 'Mr. Grundig, recall all hands and make all preparations for getting under way. Expedite! Set your sea and anchor details and advise Chief Wilkerson that he *will* be ready to turn shafts in forty-five minutes!'

'Aye, sir!' The exec disappeared through a watertight door in the white-painted deckhouse.

The Coast Guard commander looked back to Smith. 'Do you have any instructions about Dr. Trowbridge, Colonel?'

'Trowbridge?' Smith groped mentally for the name.

'Yes, sir, he's the off-site director of the university research program on Wednesday. He's up at the Kodiak Inn now. He was scheduled to ride up with us for the recovery of the expedition.'

Smith recalled the name now, and he considered his options. Dr. Rosen Trowbridge was listed as the chairman of the organizing committee for the Wednesday Island science program, a fund-raiser and an academic administrator, not an explorer. On the one hand, he would be another complication in a situation that was already growing increasingly complex.

On the other, he might prove a useful information source on the personnel, assets, and environment on Wednesday.

'If he can make it down here by the time we're ready to sail, he can come.'

CHAPTER FIFTEEN

Off the Alaskan Peninsula

With bright ice crystal stars overhead and an occasional distant shore light to starboard, the USS *Alex Haley* swept through the deepening autumn night, her engines rumbling at a steady fast cruise. The big ice cutter had a four-hundred-mile run to the southwest along the Alaskan coast before she could make her turn north at Unimak Island for the true long haul up through the Bering Sea.

Her cramped radio room smelled of ozone and cigarette smoke and was sultry with the waste heat radiating from the equipment chassis. The use-worn gray steel chair creaked with Smith's weight and the roll of the ship, and the handset of the scrambled satellite phone was slick with perspiration. Smith had the radio shack to himself, the regular radio watch having been evicted in the face of security.

'How did they spot us?' Smith demanded.

'It's not difficult to guess,' Fred Klein's distant voice replied. 'Pole Star Aero-leasing provides helicopters and light transport aircraft for a number of survey and science operations in the Canadian and Alaskan Arctic, including the Wednesday Island project. When the press release about your expedition to the Misha crash site hit the media, the hostiles must have staked out the most likely equipment sources. You were caught in an airborne version of a drive-by shooting.'

'Then somebody else must know about the anthrax aboard the Misha 124.'

'That's a distinct possibility, Jon.' Director Klein's voice remained controlled. 'We've known from the start that the

119

Misha warload would be a major prize for any terrorist group or rogue nation. That could explain the attack on your aircraft. But that's only one possible explanation. We don't know nearly enough to close out any options on this incident.'

Smith ran a hand through his sweat-dampened dark hair. 'I'll concede that point. But how did it get out? Where did it leak?'

'I don't know, but I'd suspect it's on the Russian side. We've been holding all the information on the Misha 124 tightly compartmentalized. Literally the only people state-side who know the whole story are the President, myself, Maggie, and the members of your team.'

'And as my people were the ones damn near killed in this intercept incident, I think we can safely eliminate them as a sellout source.'

Klein's voice grew emotionless. 'I said we can't close out any possibilities, Jon.'

Smith caught the caution. Smyslov . . . Professor Metrace . . . Randi. He fought back the instinctive denial. Klein was right: 'It's inconceivable!' made a wonderful set of famous last words.

The director continued. 'The other remaining option is that we had a leak on site, through one of the members of the Wednesday Island team itself. We have been assured that none of the expedition members have visited the downed bomber. Somebody may be lying. That will be something else for you to investigate, Jon.'

'Understood, sir. That brings us back to the question of who's on our ass.'

'All I can say is that we are working that problem with all available assets,' Klein replied. 'The ID numbers of the air-craft that attacked you belong to a Cessna Centurion owned by one Roger R. Wainwright, a longtime resident of Anchorage. The FBI and Homeland Security have pulled their packages on the man, and he has no criminal record and no known ties to any extremist organizations. The man's a moderately successful building contractor and pur-portedly a solid citizen. But when the Anchorage FBI office scooped him up for questioning, he confessed to occasion-ally renting his plane out under the table to other parties. After that, he stopped talking and started yelling for a lawyer. The FBI is still working on him.'

'How about the hangar across from Pole Star Aero-leasing? Who rented that?'

'The name on the documentation was Stephen Borski. The people at Merrill Field business office recall a nonde-script middle-aged man with a definite Russian accent. Possibly a Russian expat – they have a lot of them up this way. He paid in cash for a month's hangar rental. The address and phone number given on the documentation have proven to be false.'

'Was he aboard the plane that hit us?'

'Unknown, Jon. The Coast Guard has found a floating debris field where the Cessna went down, but no bodies. They must still be in the plane, and it's at the bottom of Kennedy Entrance. Given the deep waters and fast currents, it will be a while before they can locate and recover the wreck, if ever.'

Smith rapped a fingertip on the console top in frustra-tion. Even Alaska was in on the conspiracy. 'There's one other Russian connection. Major Smyslov believes that the electronic warfare system used to knock out our radio was a Russian-made military communications jammer.'

Smith tilted his chair back on its swivel, wincing a little at the piercing squeal. 'But why in the hell would the Russians be trying to stop us? They started it!'

'There are Russians and then there are Russians,' Klein replied mildly. 'We're working with the Federation govern-ment; somebody else might not be. Anchorage FBI says they get the feel of Russian Mafia or something similar, but that's just an instinct call on their part, with nothing solid to back it up. The Russian links could be purely coincidental, or they could be local hirelings fronting for someone else.

'Whoever they are, they seem to have a broad spectrum of resources available to them. That bullet recovered from the float of your helicopter was a 7.62mm NATO standard round, and the Alaskan State Police Lab identifies the lands on the slug as coming from an American Army-issue M-60 machine gun.'

God, Smith sneered at himself. And just this morning he'd been saying that this shouldn't be a shooting job? 'What are your orders, sir?'

'I've been in conference with the President, Jon. We feel that the mission and its secrecy protocols are both still necessary, more so than ever if someone else is interested in that anthrax. We also view your team as still the best asset we have in position to do the job. The question is, how do *you* feel about it?'

Smith studied the cable-bedecked overhead for a long ten seconds. If he'd forgotten how to command, he'd also forgotten about the burdens that command brought with it. He was being reminded vividly now.

'I concur, sir. The team is still good, and we still have a valid operation.'

'Very good, Jon.' A hint of warmth crept into Klein. 'I will so advise President Castilla. He's ordered you some backup as well. An Air Commando task force is being deployed to Eielson Air Force Base near Fairbanks. They'll be on call to lift in to Wednesday Island should you need them. We are also working on the identity and motives of your attackers, top priority.'

'Very good, sir. There's one other point I need to bring up: our liaison, Major Smyslov.'

'A problem with him, Jon?'

'Not with the man himself. He saved our collective asses today. Only after today's events, I'm fairly sure he realizes that we're not your average bunch of army doctors and government contract employees. And fair being fair, it's pretty obvious Major Smyslov is not your average Russian Air Force officer.'

Klein chuckled dryly. 'I think that particular fiction may be abandoned within the family, Jon. You have a fangs-out operation now and a common enemy. Putting a few more cards on the table might be in order. As team leader I'll leave that to your good judgment. You're carrying the ball.'

'Thank you, sir. Is there anything else?'

'Not at this time, Jon; we will keep you advised. Good luck.'

The sat phone link broke.

Smith dropped the phone back into its cradle and frowned. Accepted as a given, the United States and the Russian Federation did have a common enemy in this affair. But did that necessarily make them friends?

'Okay, Chief, I'm out of your hair for a while,' Smith said as he left the radio shack.

'Not a problem, sir,' the radioman of the watch replied tolerantly. The Old Man had already passed the quiet word. The Army guy and his people were to be considered VIP-plus, and don't even think about asking questions.

Smith descended one deck level into officers' country and headed aft down a gray-painted passageway. It had been a number of years since he'd last experienced the vibrant undertone of a living ship at sea, the whirr of air through ductwork, the throb of engines, and the repetitive creak of the hull working with the waves. Not since the tour he'd spent cross-attached to the Navy aboard the hospital ship *Mercy*. The cruise where Randi's fiancé . . .

He jerked his mind away from the thought. The past was dead, and there was no time for resurrections. He and his team were operating.

Smith ducked through a curtained doorway into the *Haley*'s wardroom, a small living space with scarred artificial wood paneling on the bulkheads and a collection of battered steel-tube-and-leather furnishings. Randi sat half curled on one of the settees, her feet tucked under her.

'Good evening, Colonel,' she said, glancing up from a paperback Danielle Steel, reminding him there was an individual present who wasn't supposed to know they were on a first-name basis.

The cabin's two other current occupants were seated at the big central mess table: Valentina Metrace and a middle-aged man in a wooly-pully sweater and heavy-duty cargo pants, a scattering of files open before them.

The man's rounded shoulders rendered him squat rather than stocky, and the thin frosting of graying hair over his skull was countered by a precisely trimmed salt-and-pepper beard. An expression of instinctive petulance had been ingrained on his features, and a look of automatic disapproval in his eyes, and he wore his outdoorsman's gear as though it were a poorly fitted costume.

'Colonel Smith, I don't think you've had a chance to meet my fellow academic yet, Dr. Rosen Trowbridge. Dr. Trowbridge, this is our team leader, Lieutenant Colonel Jon Smith.' A studied sweetness in Professor Metrace's voice spoke beyond her words.

Smith nodded pleasantly. He'd caught and registered the vibrations radiating from the man as well. 'Good evening, Doctor. I haven't had a chance to apologize yet for the sudden change of our sailing schedule. I hope it didn't inconvenience you too badly.'

'In fact it did, Colonel.' Trowbridge spoke Smith's rank with a hint of distaste. 'And, speaking frankly, I don't appreciate your not consulting me about it. The Wednesday Island expedition has been a meticulously planned research project, and so far it has been a success for the involved universities. We don't need any complications at this late date.'

Smith called up and applied an appropriate sympathetic smile. 'I understand fully, Professor. I've been involved in a number of research projects myself.'

Enough of them to recognize you, my friend, Smith continued silently behind his smile. *What you really mean is that your people in the field did good research while you sat in your cozy office signing off the documentation and absorbing credit by bureaucratic osmosis. Now you're probably scared to death that someone is going to upset the applecart before you can finagle your name onto the final paper.*

'You're right, Doctor.' Smith settled into a chair across from Metrace and Trowbridge. 'I should have, but it was a matter of expediency. There are certain concerns about the weather conditions we might encounter around Wednesday Island. With the winter closing in, it seemed to me the faster we get to the island the better. By gaining a little more time on station with an early sailing, I felt my team's investigation of the crash site would be less likely to interfere with the extraction of your people and their equipment.'

'Well, that does make a degree of sense, Colonel,' Trowbridge replied, not happy at being mollified. 'But still, the way this was done left a great deal to be desired. I'd like to be consulted before any further changes are made.'

Smith clasped his hands on the polished tabletop. 'I understand fully, Doctor,' he lied, 'and I promise you will be fully consulted on any further developments. It's in everybody's best interest for us to work together on this.'

'I can't disagree with that, Colonel. Just as long as it is recognized that the university expedition was there first and that we have priority.'

Smith shook his head. 'That's not exactly true, Doctor. Some other people were on Wednesday Island a long time before your expedition arrived. The job of my team is to identify them and return them to where they belong. I think they should receive a degree of concern?'

Smith found that his words were only half cover sophistry. There were men up there on the ice. Men who had been there for a long time. They had served another flag, but they had been soldiers, like Smith himself. They had also been abandoned and forgotten by the world. The fate of the Soviet aircrew might be overshadowed by political expediency, but after half a century, they still deserved to go home.

Smith kept his gaze locked on Trowbridge until the academic backed down. 'Of course, you're correct,

Colonel. I'm sure we'll be able to accommodate everyone involved.'

'I'm sure we will.'

'I've been going over the Wednesday camp setup with Dr. Trowbridge,' Valentina said, 'and the personnel roster, just to see what we might have to work with. I was thinking some of the expedition members might be able to help us with the crash site investigation.'

'If it doesn't interfere with their official duties within the university expedition,' Trowbridge interjected hastily.

'Of course.'

Smith claimed the personnel file and flipped it open. Actually Smith had no intention of letting any of these people anywhere near the Misha 124. But that didn't mean one of them might not have already paid the bomber an illicit visit. The leak about the TU-4's warload must have come from somewhere. Could it have come from the source? And had it been inadvertent or deliberate?

He'd seen these files and faces before, but now he studied them again in this new light.

Dr. Brian Creston, Great Britain, meteorologist and the expedition leader. By his picture a big, smiling bear of a man with a brown flattop and a ruddy outdoorsman's face. An accredited field researcher, he had a number of expeditions in both the Arctic and Antarctic to his credit.

Dr. Adaran Gupta, India, climatologist and assistant expedition leader. A lean, dark scholar's face peered back at Smith from the file photo. *You are a long way from New Delhi, Doctor.*

'Climatology and meteorology?' Smith commented. 'I gather global warming and the melting of the arctic ice pack were major points of concern?'

'It was *the* major point of concern, Colonel.'

Smith nodded and flipped to the next page.

Kayla Brown, U.S.A., graduate student, geophysics; pretty, delicate, almost elfin. She was hardly the classic image of the hard-bitten polar explorer. But apparently she'd had the guts and skills to claw her way onto this expedition over what must have been several hundred male applicants.

Ian Rutherford, a biology major from England, handsome in a boy-next-door kind of way, if next door happened to be the British Midlands.

Dr. Keiko Hasegawa, Japan, a second meteorology specialist. Sober, studious, a little on the plain and plump side. Possibly she'd balanced a slow social life with an exceptional dedication to her field of endeavor.

Stefan Kropodkin, Slovakia, cosmic ray astronomy; lanky, dark-haired, an amiable slaunchwise grin, and a little older than the other graduate students. *Probably you're the one giving Ms. Brown the most attention, desired or not.*

Smith flipped the folder shut. He wasn't prepared to make any assumptions on nationality, race, sex, or potential political orientation. That was a fool's game, for greed or fanaticism could wear any face. Covert One and a variety of other intelligence and law enforcement agencies would be hard at work dissecting the past lives of these six individuals. When he arrived on Wednesday Island it would be his duty to dissect their here and now.

He felt himself being regarded, and he looked up to find both Dr. Trowbridge and Professor Metrace looking at him. From Trowbridge's expression, he was puzzled. From Valentina's smile and the ironic lift of her eyebrow, she was busy reading Smith's mind.

Smith returned the file folder to the mess table. 'Professor Metrace, have you seen Major Smyslov?'

'I think he's out on deck absorbing a little nicotine,' she replied.

'Then if you will both excuse me, I need to speak with the major about a few things.'

The cutter's drive through the sea put a chill wind across her darkened decks. Gregori Smyslov flared the butane lighter within his cupped palm, touching the flame to the tip of his cigarette. He inhaled once, deeply, and let the smoke hiss slowly through his clenched teeth.

He needed to contact General Baranov. He needed to find out what in all hell was going on! He had a secure phone number that would be guarded by the Russian Federation military attaché at the embassy in Washington, but Smith's ordering of an immediate sailing this afternoon had not given him the chance to make a call.

And even if he had accessed a clear phone, would he be able to trust the person at the other end? Somebody knew! Somebody outside the *konspiratsia* knew!

But how much? About the Misha 124, obviously. They must also know the anthrax was still aboard the bomber. That would be the minimum that could conceivably justify this afternoon's airborne assassination attempt. But what other knowledge might they possess?

Smyslov took another heavy drag on his cigarette. The anthrax and the risk of it falling into the hands of a terrorist group would be bad enough. But what if there was something more? What if they knew of the March Fifth Event?

That was a nightmare worth considering. What if someone outside the circle of thirty-two knew about the Event and of the possibility that evidence of it still existed aboard the downed bomber? What if they were striving to prevent the destruction of that evidence and obtain it for themselves?

What if an organization or even a single individual gained the ability to blackmail a major nuclear power? It would dwarf the threat of even a planeload of anthrax to insignificance.

Lost in that dark thought, Smyslov started as a voice spoke nearby. 'As a physician I'm required to warn you that smoking is bad for your health.'

Jon Smith's silhouette detached itself from the shadows down deck and came to lean on the cable rail beside Smyslov. 'And now that I've performed that duty, please feel free to tell me to go to hell.'

Smyslov chuckled dryly and flipped the glowing cigarette butt over the side. 'We haven't invented lung cancer in Russia yet, Colonel.'

'I just wanted to tell you again, thanks for what you did today.'

Smyslov caught himself before he could reach for his lighter and cigarette pack again. 'We were all riding in the same helicopter.'

'So we were,' the silhouette agreed. 'So, Major, what do you think?'

'To speak the truth, Colonel, I don't know what to think.' And it was the truth.

'Do you have any idea at all who might have been behind the attack?'

Smyslov shook his head. Now he would lie again. 'None. Someone must have learned that the Misha 124 was a bioweapons platform. They must be acting on the assumption the anthrax might still be aboard the aircraft and are attempting to prevent us from reaching the crash site first. That's the only thing that would make any sense.'

'You'd think so,' Smith mused. 'But someone is certainly committing a lot of resources on a speculation.' He turned his head and looked directly at Smyslov. 'The Alaskan authorities are also speculating about the possible involvement of the Russian mafia.'

Good. Smyslov could tell the truth again. 'This is entirely possible, Colonel. It would be foolish to deny that certain criminal elements within my country have developed a great degree of power and influence within our government.'

Smyslov grimaced. 'The members of our underworld had a considerable advantage over the rest of our nation. They were the one facet of Russian society not controlled by the Communists.'

Smith chuckled in the darkness, and they looked out across the darkened wave tops for a time, listening to the hiss of the hull cutting through the water.

Finally Smyslov spoke. 'Colonel, can you tell me if my government has been notified of today's attack?'

'I really can't say for sure,' Smith replied. 'My superiors have been advised of the situation, and they've informed me that all available resources are being put to use to identify our attackers. I'd presume that includes Russian resources.'

'I see.'

Smith hesitated, then continued. 'Major, if you wish to speak directly with your superiors about this incident, I can arrange it. If you are concerned about . . . security, I can offer you my word that you will be able to speak freely. Your communications will not be monitored.'

Smyslov considered for a moment. *What can I safely say to who?* 'No, that will not be necessary.'

'As you like. The offer stands.' Smith's voice mellowed. 'So tell me, Major, hearts, bridge, or poker – which is your game?'

CHAPTER SIXTEEN

Off Reykjavik, Iceland

In another ocean, half a world away, a second ship sailed.

The captain of the deep-ocean trawler *Siffsdottar* had thought that his ship's long run of bad luck had at last come to an end. Now he wasn't so sure.

The North Atlantic fisheries had been a depressed industry for a long time, and cheeseparing and procrastination on the part of the trawler's owners had not made matters any easier. Finally, as it inevitably must, the neglected maintenance had caught up with them. *Siffsdottar* had spent most of last season held up in the yards with a protracted and expensive series of engine room casualties. The owners, as owners inevitably do, found it easier to blame the ship rather than themselves.

Siffsdottar had been facing the breakers' yard, and her captain and crew the beach when, like a miracle, a last-minute reprieve had appeared: a month-long charter by a film company for enough money to pay off the repairs and poor season both. Only they must sail immediately to meet a production deadline.

For once the owners and crew were in accord. They were happy to oblige.

But when the 'filmmakers' had come aboard they had proved to be a gang of twenty extremely tough-looking men, even by the standards of the hard-bitten trawler crew. There had also been a decided lack of camera equipment, just a good deal of electronics and radio gear.

And the guns. Those hadn't made an appearance until after they had gotten under way. Two of the 'filmmakers' lounged at the rear of the darkened wheelhouse now, each of them with an automatic pistol thrust openly in his belt.

They offered no explanation, and the trawlermen decided it prudent not to ask for one.

The leader of the filmmakers, a tall, burly red-bearded man who relayed his orders in strangely accented English, had laid in a course to the west-northwest, their destination being a set of nameless GPS coordinates deep within Hudson Bay. He had also instructed that the trawler's radio be disabled. His people would handle all communications for the voyage, 'for business reasons.'

Siffsdottar's captain now strongly suspected that his owners had made yet another bad business decision. But as the flashing point light at Iceland's westernmost land's end drifted past to starboard, he also suspected that there was little he could now do about it. Instead he would fall back on an ancient Icelandic survival mechanism: strict, stolid neutrality and a hope for the best. It had seen Iceland through a number of the world's wars essentially untouched. Perhaps it would suffice here.

Belowdecks, the Command Section had taken over the main salon as the operations center. Seated at the big mess table, Anton Kretek splashed three fingers of Aquavit into a squat glass. Taking a slurping gulp, he grimaced. This Icelandic liquor was muck, but it was the muck that was available.

'Do you have the reports from Canada Section yet?' he demanded irritably.

'Downloading now, Mr. Kretek,' the chief communications officer replied from his laptop workstation. 'It will take a moment to decrypt.'

The Internet had proven a boon to the international businessman and the international criminal alike, providing instant, secure communications from point to point anywhere on the planet. A dinner-plate-sized sat phone dish, deployed in the trawler's upper works, linked them into the global telecommunications net, and the finest in commercial encryption programs sealed their Internet messaging away from prying eyes.

A portable laser printer hissed and spat out a series of hard-copy sheets. Pushing his chair back from the communications desk, the communicator passed the hard copy over his shoulder to the waiting Kretek.

Taking a small torpedo-shaped Danish cigarillo from the ashtray, the arms merchant puffed and read, the strong tobacco smoke blending with the salon's background smell of diesel and fish oil.

Kretek frowned. There was good news and bad in the dispatches. The attempts to disrupt the joint Russian-American investigation had failed. Kretek hadn't had high hopes for the effort in the first place. The group's point man in Alaska had been forced to hire and equip whatever was available at short notice, in this case, local Russian mafia street trash.

The ad hoc interceptor dispatched to kill the investigators' helicopter had failed to return. As there had been no news reports of an attack on the government expedition, or of a plane lost, it had probably gone down at sea or in the wilderness in an accidental crash.

So be it. Let the investigation team come. If they beat him on site, he would rely on his agent on the island and on the shock effect of his main force's arrival. If a few history buffs made a nuisance of themselves at the wrong time, that would be their problem. Timing, planning, and the weather would be his allies against the outside world.

Kretek took another draw from the cigarillo, followed by a throat-clearing sip of the liquor. Unless, of course, there had been more to the investigation team than had met the eye. Was it possible that the governments involved knew of the incredible prize that was still aboard the bomber?

That seemed unlikely. If the truth was known, the Americans would be racing to secure the aircraft with all their considerable assets, and their national media would be having hysterics over the anthrax threat. The Russians must have assured them that the bomber's payload had been jettisoned, if they had mentioned it at all. The former Soviet weapons experts within the Kretek Group had assured their leader that this would be standard operating procedure.

For some reason SOP had not been followed aboard this particular aircraft, and Anton Kretek was prepared to take full advantage of the fact.

The second dispatch, from Vlahovich and the Canada group, was far more favorable. Suitable aircraft had been procured, and suitable aircrewmen had been brought in through Canadian customs. Refueling base A was being established, and sites for bases B and C were being surveyed. Very favorable. Very favorable indeed.

The final dispatch secured the arms merchant's good mood. It was from Wednesday Island, indicating that no alarm had been raised. The station staff was preparing for the arrival of the aviation historians and for their own winter extraction. No problems noted. Operations proceeding.

Now that the plan was under way, Kretek would be able to send their ETA and his final phase instructions on to Wednesday. If all continued to go as well as it had so far, it would be a most pleasant reunion.

Kretek grinned and poured another finger of liquor in his glass. It was tasting better all the time.

CHAPTER SEVENTEEN

Off the Eastern End of Wednesday Island

The stars stabbed through rents in the cloud cover, their light refracting and reflecting off the jumbled pressure ridges of the ice pack, granting hunting illumination to the great, shambling bulk that moved spectrally among them.

The polar bear was still a comparative youngster, a mere eight hundred pounds of rippling muscle and perpetual hunger thickly sheathed in glossy white fur. His instincts were driving him southward, to follow the edge of the expanding freeze up. But he had paused for a time in the vicinity of Wednesday Island. The stressed ice around the island had provided hauling-out leads and breathing holes for a lingering population of ring and hood seals, and a profitable hunting ground for a polar bear.

The bear had slain twice in the past week, crushing the skulls of his prey with swift, precise swats of his massive paws, his powerful jaws stripping the seal carcasses of the rich blubber that he needed to fuel his biological furnaces against the piercing cold of the arctic environment. But winter loomed, and the seals were fleeing ahead of it. The bear must commit to his own southward drift as well. Either that or he must explore the possibilities of his only other potential food source: the odd, decidedly unseallike animals that inhabited the island itself and that walked upright on two legs.

The polar bear was not familiar with these creatures, but the wind had carried him the scent of their sweet, hot blood, and on the ice, meat was meat.

The bear dropped down from the pressure ridge onto the

thin flat surface of a recently refrozen lead. Here, where the ice was thin and still pliant, he might find a more conventional meal: a seal gnawing its way to the surface and a breath of air. Padding silently to the center of the open lead, the polar bear paused, his head held low to the ice sheet, extending his senses, feeling and listening for the faintest hint of sound or vibration from below.

There! There was a sense of something moving below the ice.

And then came a titanic shock, and the bear was lifted off his feet and hurled through the air. Such indignities were simply not supposed to happen to the lords of the Arctic! He hit the ice sprawling. Scrambling to his feet, the bear fled in abject terror, bawling his protest to an uncaring night.

A great black axe blade pressed up from beneath the surface of the frozen lead, the shattered ice groaning and splintering as it opened, flowerlike, around it. The mammoth Oscar-class SSGN bulled its way through the pack, hatches crashing open atop its sail as it stabilized on the surface. Men poured out of those hatches, dark, weather-scarred faces contrasting against the white of their arctic camouflage clothing. Some of them swung lithely down to the ice using the ladder rungs inset in the sides of the submarine's conning tower. Dropping to the surface of the lead, they fanned out, unslinging AK-74 assault rifles as they established their security perimeter.

The others focused on hoisting their gear up and out of the red-lit belly of the undersea vessel: loaded backpacks, white equipment, and ration-stuffed duffel bags, collapsible fiberglass man-hauling sledges, and cases of ammunition and explosives. All that they would need to live, fight, and destroy in a polar environment for a protracted time.

The commanders of both the naval Spetsnaz platoon and the submarine were the last up the ladder to the submarine's bridge.

'Damnation, but this is cold,' the sub commander muttered.

Lieutenant Pavel Tomashenko of the Naval Infantry Special Forces grinned in self-superiority and repeated the old saw. 'In weather like this the flowers bloom in the streets of Pinsk.'

The submarine commander was not amused. 'I need to submerge as soon as possible. I want to give this lead a chance to refreeze before the next American satellite pass.' As was the case with all good submariners, he was a nervous and unhappy man on the surface. And he had reason to be so. He was inside Canadian territorial waters in an area forbidden to probing foreign submarines. And while the Canadian naval forces were totally incapable of enforcing this prohibition, the atomic hunter-killer boats of the United States Navy also cheerfully and routinely disregarded this restriction.

'Do not worry, Captain, we will be away in a few more minutes,' Tomashenko replied, glancing down at his men as they loaded their sleds. 'We must be under cover by the time of the next pass as well. There will be no problems.'

'So we can hope,' the submariner grunted. 'I will endeavor to keep to the communications schedule, but I must remind you, Lieutenant, I can make no promises. It will depend on my finding open-water leads for the deployment of my radio masts. I will return to these coordinates once every twenty-four hours, and I will listen for your sounding charges and your through-ice transponder. I can do no more.'

'That will be quite adequate, Captain. You run a very efficient taxi service. *Dos ve danya.*'

Tomashenko swung himself over the rim of the bridge and lowered himself toward the frozen lead.

The sub skipper only muttered his response under his breath. It galled to take such lip from a mere snot-nosed lieutenant, but these Spetsnaz types considered themselves God's anointed under the best of circumstances. Unfortunately, this particular example came with a curt set of sealed orders from the Pacific Fleet Directorate that squarely placed the sub commander and his boat at the beck and call of Tomashenko. To disregard either the word or spirit of those orders would be extremely bad joss in the shrinking Russian navy.

The sub skipper watched as Tomashenko and his platoon lined out, dark shapes against the ice, trudging toward the shadowed silhouette of Wednesday Island. He was glad to see them go. His soul and his ship were his own again for a time. He was pleased to have that particular outfit clear of his decks as well. Tomashenko's force had to be one of the most thoroughly cold-blooded – and murderous-looking crews he had ever encountered. And given his twenty years of service in the Russian military, that was saying something.

'Clear the bridge!' The submarine commander lifted his voice in a hoarse bellow. 'All lookouts below!'

As his seamen brushed past him to clatter down the ladder, he pushed the brass button beside the waterproof intercom. 'Control room, this is the bridge. Prepare to take her down!'

CHAPTER EIGHTEEN

The USS Alex Haley

Randi Russell nudged a scarlet plastic disk an inch forward with a fingernail. 'King me,' she said, staring across the game board with the focused intensity of a cougar preparing to pounce.

Muttering under his breath in Russian, Gregori Smyslov took a counter from his minimal pile of trophies and clapped it down where indicated.

'You're in trouble, Gregori,' Valentina Metrace said, munching a chip from the bowl resting beside the tabletop battlefield.

'Draughts is a child's game,' Smyslov said through gritted teeth. 'A child's game, and I am not in difficulty!'

'We call it checkers, Major.' Smith chuckled from where he sat beside Randi. 'And yes, you are in trouble.'

'Even the great Morphy would find it impossible to concentrate with certain people incessantly crunching crackers in his ear!'

'They're tortilla chips, to be precise,' Valentina said, enjoying another savory crunch. 'But your real problem is, you're trying to logic the game as you would chess. Checkers are more like fencing: a matter of finely-honed instinct.'

'Indeed.' Smyslov pounced, jumping one of Randi's red checkers with a black. 'I told you I was in no difficulty.'

The riposte was lethal, Randi's freshly minted king clearing the board of black counters in a swift, final tic-tic-tic triple assault. 'Best four out of six?' she queried with just the faintest hint of a smile.

Smyslov's palm thumped into his forehead. 'Shit, and for this I left Siberia!'

Smith grinned at the Russian. 'Don't feel too bad, Major; I've never beaten Randi at checkers, either. I don't think it can be done. Now, who's for bridge?'

Smyslov lifted his head and started to collect his dead soldiers. 'Why not? Being tortured with hot irons can't be worse than having one's fingernails torn out.'

The ice cutter was four days out of Sitka. After rounding Point Barrow she was now driving hard for the northeast and the Queen Elizabeth Archipelago. Only a certain portion of those days could be filled with briefings and brainstorming sessions about what they might find on Wednesday Island. Many hours were left to kill, and as outsiders to the tight seaborne community aboard the *Haley*, Smith and his people had been thrown together on their own resources.

Smith was pleased with this mechanism. Team building was not purely an aspect of training and discipline. It was a matter of the components learning one other. How they thought. How they acted and reacted. Minutiae down to how they liked a cup of coffee. It all accumulated into a projection of how this individual might react in a given crisis. Precious information.

Fragment by fragment, he was expanding his mental files.

Randi Russell: She was one he had known before. He had a base to build on with her. She was solid, inevitably solid. But out on the edge of perception there was always that faint, frightening whiff of don't-give-a-damn. Never about the mission, but only about herself.

Gregori Smyslov: Clearly a good soldier, but also a man thinking a great deal. And from the moods Smith caught on occasion, he wasn't happy with his thoughts. The Russian was working toward a decision. What that decision might be was something for Smith to think about.

Valentina Metrace: She was something else to think about. Specifically, just what lurked inside the history professor's vivacious, smoothly polished shell. There was some other entity in there. In his lengthening conversations with her he had caught only the slightest flavor of this alternate being. It wasn't the slipping of a mask so much as the tracing of the camouflaged gun ports of a Q-ship. 'Weapons expert' could mean any number of things.

Not that her overt personality wasn't interesting in its own right.

The cabin's overhead speaker clicked on. 'Wardroom, this is the bridge. Pick up, please.'

Smith rose and crossed to the interphone beside the hatchway. 'Wardroom here. This is Colonel Smith.'

'Colonel Smith, this is Captain Jorganson. You and your people might want to come on deck and have a look to port. We're passing what you might call a local landmark.'

'Will do.' Smith returned the interphone to its cradle. The others looked up at him from their places at the mess table. 'The captain suggests we have some sights to see, people.'

The wind on deck was piercing now, numbing exposed flesh in only a matter of seconds. Piercing also was the gunmetal blue of the sea and sky, the latter marred by only a few streaming wisps of cirrus cloud. It made a vivid contrast to the stark white castle shape drifting slowly past the cutter's quarter, the bulk of the iceberg showing as a wavering green mass below the ocean's surface. This was only the first outrider of the pack. To the north, off the bow, the horizon shimmered with a hazy metallic luster, what the arctic hands called 'ice blink.'

Smith felt someone brush lightly against his elbow. Valentina Metrace was standing close by at his side, and he could feel her shiver. Dr. Trowbridge had emerged from the deckhouse as well and stood at the rail a few feet away, not speaking or looking at Smith and his team. Other members of the cutter's crew were also coming topside, watching the passage of the pallid sea specter.

The first enemy was in sight. Soon the battle would begin.

CHAPTER NINETEEN

Wednesday Island

'Core water samples, series M?'

'Check.'

'Core water samples, series R?'

'Check.'

'Core water samples, series RA?'

Kayla Brown looked up from where she knelt beside the open plastic specimen case. 'They're all here, Doctor Creston,' she replied patiently, 'just like yesterday.'

Dr. Brian Creston chuckled and flipped his notebook shut. 'Have patience with an old man, child. I've seen Mr. Cock-up drop in on many an expedition at the last minute. There's no sense in getting sloppy in the home stretch.'

Kayla snapped the latches on the case and tightened the nylon safety strap around it. 'I hear you, Doctor. I don't want anything to come between me and that beautiful, beautiful helicopter tomorrow.'

'Really?' Creston reclaimed his pipe from the cracked chemistry retort he'd been using for an ashtray, and bent down slightly to peer through one of the laboratory hut's small, low-set windows. 'Actually, I'll rather miss the place. I've found it . . . restful.'

For the moment there was a hole in the weather over the island, and the low-riding sun struck white fire off the drifted snow outside. The Wednesday Island Science Station consisted of three small, green prefabricated buildings: the laboratory, the bunkroom, and the utility/generator shack, set side by side in a row and spaced some thirty yards apart to eliminate the risk of a spreading fire.

Established near the shore of the small frozen bay at Wednesday's western end, the station was protected from the blast of the prevailing northerlies by a shoulder of the Island's central ridge. Thus, each flat-roofed hut had been only half-buried in drift.

Kayla Brown stood up and brushed off the knees of her ski pants. 'It's been a great experience, Doctor, and I wouldn't have missed it for the world, but like we say back home, "Can we please stop having fun now?"'

Creston laughed. 'Understood, Kayla. But aren't you going up with the crash investigation team when they arrive? After all, you were the one to first spot the wreck.'

The young woman's face fell. 'No, I don't think so. I've thought about it, and it would probably be interesting, but . . . the men aboard that plane might still be up there. I'm willing to give that a pass.'

Creston nodded. Leaning back against the big worktable in the center of the laboratory, he began to lightly fill his pipe from the dwindling stock in his tobacco pouch. 'I quite understand. It might not be the most pleasant of experiences. But I must confess, I'm getting bloody curious about that old bomber, especially given how they keep ordering us to stay away from it. It makes a person suspect there might be a bit more to this story than's being let out.'

Kayla Brown braced her hands on her hips and rolled her eyes in feminine practicality. 'Oh, come on, Doctor! You know how historians and archeologists are. They hate to have amateurs fumbling around a dig, jumbling things up. You wouldn't want someone messing with your core samples or radiosonde balloons, would you?'

'Point taken.' Creston struck a wooden kitchen match. Holding it to the bowl of his pipe, he puffed experimentally. 'But trust a woman to squeeze all the mystery out of things.'

At that moment Ian Rutherford slid open the accordion door in the partition that separated the main laboratory from the little radio room that took up one end of the hut.

'Got the latest met gen, Doctor,' he said, holding up a sheet of hard copy.

'How's it look, Ian?'

The young Englishman grimaced theatrically. 'I suppose you could say mixed. We've got a mild front moving in. It might hold off through tomorrow, but for a day or so after that we're going to be spotty.'

'How big a spot, lad?'

'Variable northerly winds up to force five. Low overcast. Intermittent snow squalls.'

Kayla rolled her eyes once more. 'Oh, nice! Perfect flying weather!'

'And that's just the start,' the youthful Englishman went on. 'We've been put on a solar flare warning. Commo's going to be dicky as well.'

'Dear me.' Doctor Creston sighed a cloud of aromatic smoke. 'Someone put the kettle on. I think I hear Mr. Cock-up coming up the walk.'

'Oh, come on, Doc,' Rutherford grinned. 'It won't be that bad. Ops should only be bitched for a day or two at the most.'

'I know, Ian, but just remember who'll be waiting for us on the ship. Dear old Count-the-Pennies Trowbridge will be certain I deliberately brewed up a storm during extraction just to put him over budget.'

There was a shout from somewhere outside the lab building, muffled by the thickly insulated walls. Boots pounded in the snow lock entryway, the inner door crashed open, and Stefan Kropodkin pushed through into the laboratory, crumbs of compacted snow spraying off his Arctic gear. 'Did Doctor Hasegawa and Professor Gupta get in?' he gasped, tearing back the hood of his parka.

Creston straightened from the edge of the worktable, setting his pipe back into the retort ashtray. 'No, they haven't. What's wrong?'

The Slovakian gulped air. 'I don't know. They've disappeared.'

Creston frowned, 'What do you mean, disappeared?'

'I don't know! They're just gone! We were on the south beach, about three kilometers out. Professor Gupta wanted a last look at the ice buildup rates along the shore, and we were assisting him. The professor told me to photograph some of the formations, and he and Dr. Hasegawa went on ahead, around the point. I lost sight of them.' Kropodkin took another shuddering breath. 'When I followed after them, they were gone.'

'Damn it! If I've told Adaran once I've told him a hundred times. Keep your group together! Did they have a two-way?'

Kropodkin nodded. 'The professor had a radio.'

Creston looked to Rutherford. 'Did you hear anything on the local channel?'

The Englishman shook his head.

'Then get on the set. Call them.'

'Right-oh!' The Englishman disappeared through the door of the radio shack.

Kropodkin sank down on a stool, dragging off his heavy overmittens and gloves. Kayla Brown anxiously passed him a bottle of water. 'I went on for about another kilometer,' he continued after taking a drink. 'I called for them but there was no answer. No sign. I began to worry and I hurried back here. I thought maybe they had gotten past me somehow.'

'They must have gone inland or out onto the shore drift for some reason.' Creston scowled.

'There's no answer on the local channel, Doc!' Rutherford yelled from the radio room.

Kropodkin looked from Dr. Creston to Kayla, a mix of concern and fear crossing his features. 'There was one other thing, beyond where they disappeared. A half-eaten seal on the beach. A polar bear kill. Fresh.'

'Are you sure it was a seal?' Kayla asked, a tremor in her voice.

He nodded. 'This time.'

'Steady on, everyone. Likely we're all making a fuss over

nothing,' Creston said crisply. 'Still, it's coming on dark soon. Ian, you bring the other portable transceiver, and I'll get the medical kit. We'll take one of the hand sleds, a tent, and a survival pack with us. Kayla, I want you to stand by the radio in case we have to tell the *Haley* we have a problem.'

'But . . .' The girl caught herself. This was no time to make a fuss. 'Yes, sir.'

Kropodkin pulled his gloves on once more. 'I will get the shotgun from the bunkhouse.'

CHAPTER TWENTY

The USS Alex Haley

Jon Smith stared up drowsily at the springs of the overhead bunk, the lilting folk rock of Al Stewart's 'Sand in Your Shoes' flowing from the iPod's earphones. With tomorrow's mission launch looming, sleep had been hard to come by. Now, finally, after an hour of assiduous courting, it was almost within reach.

The urgent knock at the cabin door snapped him back to full wakefulness. He sat up, tearing off the headset. 'Yes?'

Valentina Metrace's voice issued through the glowing louvers in the door. 'We've trouble on Wednesday Island, Jon. It looks serious.'

He rolled out of the bunk and hit the light switch. 'Right. We're coming.'

Smyslov had already swung down from the upper berth and was hastily dressing. Smith pulled on a set of cold-weather BDUs and his boots, and in a few moments the two men were climbing the ladder to the radio room.

Apparently the mission launch wasn't going to wait for tomorrow.

Beyond the rumble and susurrus of the ship's routine internal white noise, an intermittent rasping and squealing reverberated through the *Haley's* frames as chunks of growler ice brushed past the hull. There was also an occasional jolting shudder beyond the beat of the propellers as the cutter's bow sheered into a thin pan of frozen seawater – sounds and sensations that had been occurring with growing frequency.

For the past three days the *Alex Haley* had been chewing

her way deeper into the thickening pack ice of the Queen Elizabeth Archipelago, keeping to the open-water leads when she could, battering through the floating drift when possible, and sidestepping the looming bergs and bleak, cliff-cragged islands when necessary.

Captain Jorganson had put all his arctic seaman's savvy into gaining ground toward their objective, but their rate of advance had slowed for every mile northward gained. The leads had been growing narrower and the berg clusters denser. Twice during the past forty-eight hours, Randi had launched in the Long Ranger, carrying one of the *Haley*'s officers on an ice survey flight, hunting for cracks in the pack for the cutter to wriggle through.

Winter was winning.

The cutter's small radio room was already crowded by the time Smith and Smyslov squeezed their way in amid the gray steel equipment chassis. The duty operator sat hunched in front of the powerful sideband transceiver, nursing the frequency and squelch dials while Captain Jorganson leaned over his shoulder. Randi Russell and Valentina Metrace were both present as well, showing signs of their own hasty awakening. Professor Metrace hadn't taken the time to pin up her hair, and a detached fragment of Smith's awareness noted that her glossy black ponytail flowed almost to the small of her back. That was one question answered.

Dr. Trowbridge had been shouldered back into an odd corner of the compartment. As did everyone else, he looked worried, but also incensed, as if this cause for concern were something that should not be happening to him.

'What do we have?' Smith demanded.

'We're not exactly sure,' Jorganson replied. 'Two members of a science party were apparently reported missing shortly before nightfall. The expedition leader advised us a search was being organized but that he was not yet declaring an emergency. Then the station was knocked completely off the air for about five hours.'

'Did something happen to their communications gear?'

'In a manner of speaking, Colonel.' Jorganson glanced toward the overhead. 'If it weren't for the cloud cover, we'd be seeing a magnificent aurora borealis tonight. A solar flare is making a hash out of everything. Even the satellite phones are going down.'

'And?'

'And when we reacquired, the science station's radio guard was calling mayday,' the Coast Guardsman continued. 'The search party has not returned, nor has she been able to contact them.'

'She?'

'It's the female grad student, Kayla Brown. Apparently she's the only one left.'

The radioman pressed his headset closer and spoke into his lip mike. 'KGWI, this is CGAH. We read you. I say again, we read you. Stand by.' The enlisted operator looked up. 'We've got another hole opening, Captain. We got her again.'

'Put it on the speaker,' Jorganson commanded.

'Aye aye.'

Interference roared and crashed from the overhead, a thin, lonely woman's voice sounding through it.

'*Haley*, *Haley*, this is Wednesday Island Station. They still haven't come back! None of them! Something's got to be wrong. When can we get help? Over.'

Captain Jorganson lifted the console hand mike from its clip. 'This is the captain of the *Haley*, Miss Brown. We understand your situation and we are coming to your assistance with all possible speed.'

Jorganson lifted his thumb from the mike trigger. 'The problem is that it might take us several days to work the ship through this last hundred miles of pack to Wednesday. We might never make it at all, given the way the freeze-up is coming on. We'll have to rely on your helicopter to render any kind of immediate assistance, Colonel.'

Smith, in turn, looked to his pilot. 'Randi, could we launch now?'

Randi Russell bit her lower lip, projecting and assessing.

'We're just barely coming into fly-and-return range of Wednesday,' she said after a few seconds. 'But we have extremely low air temperatures and potential icing conditions, and the radios are bad. I've got to say it's very marginal out there. I don't like it, but we've got to wait for daylight.'

Smith accepted her judgment without question. 'Can I have the mike, Captain?'

Jorganson handed it over.

'Ms. Brown, my name is Colonel Jon Smith. I'm the leader of the team being sent to investigate the downed bomber. We should be able to get to you shortly after first light tomorrow morning. I'm afraid you're going to have to ride it out until then. Can you give us more on your situation? Over.'

'I'm here in camp and I'm fine,' she replied. 'It's everybody else who must be in trouble – bad trouble, or Dr. Creston would have sent some kind of word back and . . . and I can't do anything! Over!'

'At the moment, you're doing everything that can be done, Ms. Brown. We'll take care of the rest when we get there. Now, I need you to answer some questions. Over.'

'Go ahead, Colonel . . . Uh, over.'

'Have you or the other members of your party seen any indication of anyone else on the island? Lights, smoke, footprints, anything like that?'

The responding voice sounded startled. 'Anyone else? No way! Other than you guys there's nobody around for a thousand miles!'

'Are you certain, Ms. Brown? There's been no sign of anybody at all?'

'What's he talking about?' Dr. Trowbridge blurted from his corner of the radio room. 'If he's trying to blame the Inuit—'

'Hush,' Valentina Metrace snapped.

'No,' the staticky voice replied. 'Nobody's mentioned anything. Over.'

'Have you seen anything else out of the ordinary?' Smith probed. 'A plane? A ship? Anything?'

'No. We see the contrail of an airliner going over the Pole now and again, but we haven't seen anything else all summer. Why? Over.'

Trowbridge tried to crowd closer to the radio. 'I'd like to know the same thing, Colonel. What is the meaning of . . .'

Damn it, he didn't have time for asides! The last rags of his mission cover were shredding away, and it was time to make the transition from totally clandestine to merely covert. Smith aimed a finger at Trowbridge, then jerked his thumb toward the radio room door. 'Captain, get him out of here.'

Stunned, Trowbridge gobbled for breath. 'What! You have no right to—'

'Yes, he does,' Captain Jorganson said quietly. 'Please leave the radio room, Doctor. I hope it won't be necessary to have you escorted out.'

Trowbridge was a man accustomed to debate. He started to formulate his first wave of verbal protest, but the cold gazes encircling him strangled his self-righteousness. Once more he sensed that he was out of his depth. Contenting himself with a muttered 'This is not acceptable,' he sidled his way to the radio shack entry.

Smith returned his attention to the radio. 'Ms. Brown, this is Colonel Smith back. I have one more question. You won't be getting anyone in trouble over the answer, but it's very important we get a straight answer. Have any of the members of your expedition visited the crash site? Anyone at all, for any reason? Over.'

'No! . . . At least not that I know of. Dr. Creston wouldn't allow it. Why? Does that old plane have something to do with my friends disappearing? Over.'

Smith hesitated over his reply. 'We're not sure, Ms. Brown. Please stand by.'

'What about it, Jon?' Randi asked, her voice soft. 'Could

the containment vessel have failed on the bomber? Could it be the anthrax?'

Smith braced a hand against the console and vehemently shook his head. 'No! It doesn't work like that! Anthrax just doesn't mow people down without an incubation period and a progressive symptomology.'

Abruptly he straightened and turned to face Smyslov. 'Gregori, for the sake of this girl and for the people on that island, now is the time to come to Jesus! Was there anything else aboard that bomber other than the anthrax?'

Smyslov felt those chill steel blue eyes drilling into him. 'Jon, I swear to you, as far as I know, the only biowar munition carried aboard the Misha 124 was the anthrax. If there was anything else, I was not briefed about it!'

Smyslov was grateful that he could fall back behind that partial shield of truth, for he suspected that he did know what was happening on Wednesday.

Those damn Spetsnaz! Could it be they had failed to stay out of sight? What if some member of the expedition had the bad luck to stumble over their encampment? If the platoon leader was some kind of bloody-minded cowboy, he might view that as justification to 'sterilize' the expedition in the name of security.

Unfortunately, a bloody-minded cowboy would be exactly the kind of commander the Federation High Command would send on a job like this!

They hadn't even set foot on the island yet, and things were already spinning out of control! If the science expedition had been wiped out, then it would follow that Smith's team would be eliminated as well. His team! People he liked and respected.

Madness!

'What's your assessment of the situation, Major?' Smith asked, his voice emotionless.

Smyslov shoved emotion aside as well. 'We must assume that some hostile force has succeeded in landing on Wednesday, presumably the same group that attempted to prevent us from reaching the island. We must also assume that they assume the anthrax store is still aboard the Misha 124 and they are intent on capturing it.'

Smith studied the Russian for a further moment before answering. 'That's likely a fair call.' He widened his attention to include the others in the radio shack. 'Now, what are we going to do about it?'

'It seems to me that the most immediate problem is, what do we do about her?' Captain Jorganson nodded toward the radio.

It was an excellent point. What do you do about one frightened young woman alone in the dark and as isolated as anyone on the planet could be?

Smith keyed the mike again. 'Ms. Brown, a twelve-gauge shotgun is listed as part of your camp equipment. What's happened to it? Over.'

'The bear gun? The search party took it with them. Why? Over.'

'Are there any other weapons in camp? Over.'

'No. Why?

'We're . . . assessing the situation, Ms. Brown. Stand by.'

Smith lifted the mike key and waited for someone, anyone, to say something.

'Get her out of there, Jon!' Randi blurted. 'Tell her to grab a sleeping bag and get out! Tell her what's going on and tell her to hide somewhere until we can get to her!'

'No,' Valentina cut in sharply. 'Tell her to stay put beside that radio.'

'Those buildings are meant to keep out weather, not people!' Randi protested. 'If we have hostiles on that island and they come for her . . .'

'If we have hostiles on that island, Miss Russell, then they've got her whenever they want her.' The historian's reply was as bleak and gray as her eyes. 'It's a safe assumption they have the science station covered by now. If they see her trying to run for it, she won't make it ten yards. But if we keep her by the radio, she might serve as an intelligence source. There's a chance she can get off a call when they come for her. She might be able to give us some idea of what we're facing.'

'So you're considering her expendable,' Randi said bitterly.

Valentina shook her head. 'No,' she replied softly. 'I consider Ms. Brown already expended.'

Randi fell silent.

Throughout this last exchange, Smith had been studying the Russian member of his team from the corner of his eye. 'How about you, Major? Anything more to add?'

Smyslov fumbled a Chesterfield from a crumpled pack and flicked fire from his butane lighter. 'No, Colonel,' he said, hissing out his first jet of smoke. 'I have no suggestions.'

'CGAH, this is KGWI,' the static-riven voice called plaintively from out in the dark. 'I am still standing by.'

Smith keyed the radio mike. 'Ms. Brown, this is Colonel Smith again. As I said, we'll be joining you shortly after first light tomorrow morning. We'd like for you to stand by the radio until we can get there. We'll be guarding this frequency continuously, and we'll be making check calls every fifteen minutes through the night. If you hear from the other members of your expedition, or if you hear or see anything unusual, you are to call us immediately. I say again, call us immediately. Do you understand? Over.'

'Yes, Colonel. I understand . . . Colonel, there's something more going on, isn't there? They aren't just lost, are they?'

What could he tell her that could provide the least little bit of help or comfort? 'We'll explain everything when we get there, Ms. Brown. We'll find your people and we'll get this sorted out. You aren't alone. We will get to you. This is CGAH, standing by.'

'Understood.' The voice at the other end of the circuit tried to sound brave. 'This is KGWI, standing by.'

Smith passed the hand mike back to the radioman. 'Sit on

that frequency, sailor. You heard me say check calls every fifteen minutes. If anyone so much as pops a mike button, I want to know about it.'

'Aye aye, sir,' the Coast Guardsman replied, resettling his headset.

'Captain Jorganson, we need every mile you can gain toward Wednesday Island before first light.'

'You'll get it, Colonel,' the *Haley*'s skipper replied. 'I'll be on the bridge if you need me.'

'I'll be in the hangar bay preflighting the helicopter,' Randi said shortly, starting for the radio room door.

'I will assist you, Randi,' Smyslov said, following her out.

Smith gave a minute, self-derisive shake of his head. To hell with it! It was inevitable that he would end up a son of a bitch in Randi Russell's eyes.

'Val, we're going to break cover, and I'm pushing the job of explaining the situation to Dr. Trowbridge onto you. I've got to get on with the director. He's going to need an update.'

'Don't worry about my fellow academic. I can take care of him.' The tall brunette regarded Smith and smiled, without humor but with empathy. 'Driving the bloody train isn't the easiest of jobs, is it, Colonel?'

Smith forced the last hint of expression from his face. 'I've been told it's good for me, Professor.'

CHAPTER TWENTY-ONE

Washington, DC

It was an ordered and lonely upper-middle-class man's bedroom in an unobtrusive town house in a quietly respectable Washington suburb. Totally unexceptional save for the bank of color-coded telephones on the Danish modern bedside table.

The piercing squall of the gray agency phone blasted Fred Klein awake, the integral lighting circuit kicking on the golden-shaded bedside lamp at the first ring. Klein had the phone in hand before he was technically awake.

'Klein here.'

The voice at the other end of the line was hollow with distance and laced with static. 'This is Jon Smith, sir, aboard the *Haley*. We have a situation.'

Sitting on the edge of the bed, Klein listened without speaking as Smith brought him up to speed in a few terse sentences.

'From what I can see, sir, somebody else has gotten there first and is moving to secure the Misha's payload.'

'If they have, they must have come in by air or by submarine, and they are very good at maintaining a low profile,' Klein replied. 'The last NSA reconsat pass over the Queen Elizabeth Archipelago indicates there are no other surface ships within five hundred miles of Wednesday and no visible activity on the island itself.'

'Understood, sir. The second possibility is that we are seeing some aspect of the Russians "alternative agenda" coming into play.'

'Do you have any idea what it could be yet?' Klein questioned. 'We're not showing anything from this end.'

'I'm not sure, sir, but I'm getting odd vibes off Major Smyslov,' Smith replied. 'I suspect he's either lying about something or he's not giving us the full story.'

'Do you consider Smyslov a mission risk, Jon?'

There was a space of dead air. 'Potentially, yes. However I'm also keeping him with the team. He seems like a good officer and decent guy, and to date he has been an asset. He also seems to be giving off mixed signals. If we do have an alternate game plan in play, I don't think he's happy about it. Properly managed, he may continue to be an asset.'

'Watch your back with him, Jon. The decent guys are the ones who can kill you the easiest.'

'Understood, sir. I am taking appropriate precautions.'

Klein rubbed the last of the sleep grit from his eyes and fumbled for his glasses on the lamp table. 'What are your intentions at this time?'

'To continue the operation as projected, sir. We will be landing on Wednesday at first light tomorrow.'

'Under the circumstances, do you consider that prudent, Jon? We've currently got that arctic ranger platoon and a RAID biowar containment team standing by at Eielson Air Force Base, along with a couple of Air Commando Ospreys and an MC-130 tanker to lift them in with. We can commit them in support.'

'No, sir, not at this time.' The reply was decisive. 'I'm not ready for them. If the intent of this mission is to prevent an international incident, we can't go completely overt yet. We don't know enough to make the call.

'Maybe the anthrax is still aboard the Misha 124 or maybe it isn't,' Smith continued. 'Maybe we have hostiles on Wednesday or maybe the search party is just stuck on a glacier with a busted radio waiting for daylight to extract themselves. We don't know. But there is one thing we can say for certain. If we go in with foot, horse, and artillery now, the operation will be blown beyond all recall. Any potential for controlling the situation will be gone. It will become almost impossible to keep this from going public.'

In spite of himself Klein chuckled dryly. 'I'm supposed to be making that speech, Jon. But what happens if you land on Wednesday and we do have hostiles present, and in force?'

'Well, sir, we'll drop off the scope and then you'll know for certain.' Klein could see the faint, wry smile that would go with the words. 'Mission accomplished.'

'Carry on, Jon, and good luck.'

'We'll keep you advised, sir.'

The link broke. Klein returned the gray phone to its cradle and picked up the yellow one next to it, the direct link to the armed men in the small security and communications center in the town house basement.

'Please have my car and the launch standing by. I will be moving to headquarters. Then give me five minutes and put me through to the National Command Authority.'

The director of Covert One rose and started to dress.

CHAPTER TWENTY-TWO

The USS Alex Haley

The hangar bay door had been retracted, and the cutter's aviation detail moved through the glare of the overhead strip lighting and the frosty mist of their own breath. The Long Ranger, with its floats cradled on a service trolley and heater cords plugged into its sleek flanks, stood ready to be rolled out onto the helipad. To the southeast, beyond the stern of the ship, the horizon lay outlined in a thin, steely streak of gray, pitching lightly with the ice-suppressed roll of the sea.

It had been a long, sleepless night, consumed in fifteen-minute bites between the radio checks with Wednesday Island, the decks shuddering and bucking underfoot as Captain Jorganson staged his last-ditch assault on the ice pack. It was good to be finally taking action.

Because of weight and space considerations, the Long Ranger's interior had been stripped of everything but the two pilots' seats. Jon Smith supervised the securing of the team's equipment to tie-downs on the cabin deck: the four backpacks and frames loaded with climbing and survival gear, the SINCGARS portable radio transceiver, and the hard-sided aluminum transport case loaded with the medical and field-testing equipment.

A pair of Coast Guard deckhands lugged the final item into the hangar bay: a dark green sausage-shaped carrier bag made out of heavy-gauge nylon.

'Here's the last of it, sir,' one of the deckhands said uneasily as they set the carrier on the deck. Possibly his unease had to do with the prominent markings on the bag:

[US ARMY GRAVES REGISTRATION BAGS-BODY-ONE DOZEN.]

'Thanks, Seaman.' The sealing tag was still in place on the carrier's zipper. The camouflage labeling had done its job well: no one had been inclined to fool with the carrier's contents.

Stepping over to the bag, Smith broke the seal and ran the zip open. As the hangar bay crew looked on soberly, Smith began to pass out the carrier's true contents, the equipment that a routine crash identification and body recovery team wouldn't have needed.

White camouflage snow smocks and overtrousers. Fanny packs containing Army MOPP III biochemical warfare suits and filter masks. And the weapons.

'I see you're an aficionado of the great spray-and-pray school,' Professor Metrace murmured as Randi checked out a Heckler and Koch MP-5 submachine gun.

'It works for me,' Randi replied briefly, clearing the breach and snapping out the stumpy little weapon's folding stock. 'Ammunition?'

'Six magazines,' Smith replied, handing her the loaded clip pouches. Lifting the next padded case out of the bag, he unzipped it and grunted in satisfaction. They'd gotten him the SR-25 tactical sniper he'd asked for. Protective lens caps were clipped over the rifle's telescopic sights, and white camo tape had been lapped around the composite stock and foregrip.

There was something oddly familiar about the feel of this particular weapon, and Smith checked its serial number. He wasn't mistaken; it was the same SR-25 he'd dialed in with and carried through his mountain warfare course. Fred Klein's meticulousness had struck again.

Valentina Metrace's brows lifted in a connoisseur's appreciation. 'Great minds work alike, Jon. I suspected it would be mountain work as well.'

The last weapon out of the carrier was a civilian sporting

rifle, and a study in contrasts. The powerful optics mounted on it were new, state-of-the-art, in fact, and the rifle itself showed meticulous care, but the scarred walnut stock also bore the patina of use and age.

'What is that?' Smith inquired as Valentina drew the weapon from its soft case.

'Something from my own collection,' she replied, flipping open the bolt in a practiced safety check. 'It's a Winchester model 70, a genuine pre-64 action mated with one of the first of the Douglas stainless steel barrels.'

Smoothly she lifted the elegant old rifle to her shoulder, test-sighting at the sunrise out of the open hangar doors. 'The scope is a Schmidt and Bender three-to-twelve-power, and the chambering is for .220 Swift. The muzzle velocity with a sixty-five-grain hollowpoint is over four thousand feet per second, the accuracy can only be described as supernatural, and bullet drop is simply something that happens to somebody else. As the saying goes, they don't make them like this anymore.'

'A varmint gun,' Randi sniffed.

'It all depends on how you define "varmint," darling,' Valentina replied darkly. 'Put a round of Swift in a man's chest and you might as well be hitting him with a lightning bolt. Put one in his shoulder and you don't get a hole; you get a sloppy amputation. I've put a full-patch slug cleanly through the brain case of a bull crocodile at three hundred yards with this old girl, and crocodiles have very thick skulls and very small brains.'

It was Smith's turn to lift an eyebrow. 'You do have some very interesting hobbies, Professor.'

Valentina smiled enigmatically as she fed sharp-tipped cartridges into the shell carrier strapped around the Winchester's stock. 'You can't even begin to guess, my dear Colonel.'

'Would you have something in there for me?' Smyslov inquired, eyeing the growing array of armament.

'We didn't pack anything, Major,' Smith said. 'But I

agree, you're likely going to need teeth.' He glanced at Valentina. 'In fact, I asked the professor to look into that.'

She nodded back and slung her rifle over her shoulder. Stepping to the open door of the helicopter, she produced a pistol belt, holster, and clip carrier from the pilot's seat. 'Nothing particularly sexy or exotic, Major, just Coast Guard standard issue, but it should do for you.'

Smyslov slid the Beretta 92F out of its holster. Balancing the big automatic in his hand he cycled the slide experimentally. 'Yes, this will do,' he replied, his voice thoughtful.

A conformal foam pharmaceuticals box was the last item in the carrier, a dozen large white-capped pill bottles fitting into its niches.

'These are our just-in-case, ladies and gentlemen,' Smith said, passing a bottle of antibiotic capsules to each of his teammates before securing the remainder in his medical kit. 'Take three now as your loading dose, then two every twelve hours, without food. They'll be good for what might ail you.'

'May I have some of those as well, Colonel?'

Parka clad, Dr. Trowbridge had been standing back with the others in the hangar bay, watching Smith's team arm up. Now he stood forward.

'I'm going . . .' he started, then caught himself. 'I would like to go with you to the island.'

'Under the circumstances I don't think that's feasible, Doctor,' Smith replied cautiously. 'We don't know what we're going to find when we get there. The situation could be hazardous.'

The academic's face tightened in resolve. 'I don't know what you're going to find, either. That's why I have to go. I don't know why this is happening or why all of this was allowed to happen, but I have responsibilities. Those are my people on that island! I helped to organize and fund this expedition. I picked the membership. Whatever has happened, I'm responsible!'

My people. Smith was coming to understand those words

quite well. He was opening his mouth to reply when a crew-man entered the hangar bay and double-timed across to the helicopter.

'Begging the colonel's pardon, sir, but Captain Jorganson wishes to advise you that Wednesday Island Station has missed its last radio check.'

Smith whipped up his wrist and shoved back his parka sleeve, checking his watch. 'How long ago?'

'Ten minutes, sir. The radio shack's been calling continuously, but there's no answer.'

Some of the arctic cold pierced into Smith's guts. Damn it! Kayla Brown had almost made it to a new day.

'Thank you. You may inform Captain Jorganson we will be launching immediately.' Smith turned back to Dr. Trowbridge. 'Three capsules now,' he said, opening his medical kit, 'then two every twelve hours, without food.'

CHAPTER TWENTY-THREE

Over the Arctic Ocean

The sky now flamed behind the Long Ranger, a gold and scarlet ribbon across the southern horizon. It served as a vivid contrast wedged between the stark black water and white ice of the fissured pack and the lowering gray of the cloud cover. The sunrise in the south was subtly perturbing, a disruption in the natural order of things that emphasized the alienness of the world they were penetrating.

'Red sky at morning . . .' Valentina Metrace murmured the first half of the old weather rhyme. With the helicopter's passenger seats pulled, she, Smith, and Trowbridge did as well as they could hunkered in among the gear lashed to the deck.

Smyslov gave up on the overhead radio panel. 'Nothing from the station. We should be within reach of their short-range sets by now.'

'What about auroral interference?' Smith inquired.

'Building again, but the ship is still receiving us. And if the ship can hear us, we should be able to hear Wednesday.'

'Why weren't we told?' Dr. Trowbridge spoke up suddenly. 'This was criminal! Leaving our expedition members exposed to biological weapons without a word of warning! This can be nothing but criminal!'

'Your people were warned,' Smith replied, 'repeatedly, as the communications logs will show, to stay well away from the crash site. And we were assured, repeatedly, by your office, that they were doing so. Besides, whatever's hit your people, it wasn't anthrax.'

'Can you be so sure of that, Colonel?' Trowbridge challenged.

'Yes, I can,' Smith replied patiently. 'Let me remind you, Doctor, that I am a physician, one with a particular expertise in this field. I've established a very close working relationship with *Bacillus anthracis* in recent years, and whatever has happened, that isn't it.'

Smith turned and stared into Trowbridge's eyes from an eighteen-inch range, going on the offensive. 'Doctor, if you and your people are concealing anything about what's happening on that island, now would be an excellent time to come clean about it.'

The academic's jaw flapped silently for a moment. 'Me? What could we possibly have to conceal?'

'I'm not sure. That's the problem. Could your expedition members have paid an under-the-table visit to that downed bomber? Could they have learned about its possible cargo of bioagent? Could they have passed that discovery on to somebody off island?'

Trowbridge gave a very good impression of a man totally stunned by a concept. 'No! Of course not! Had we had any idea that anything like that was present on the island, we would have . . . we would have . . .'

'Started looking for a buyer on eBay?' Valentina Metrace neatly double-teamed Trowbridge. As the academic twisted to face her, it was her turn to lock him up with a chill gaze. 'Doctor, I can name you half a dozen rogue states that would cheerfully empty their national treasuries to possess a bioweapons arsenal to call their very own, and it's amazing the effect a seven-figure Swiss bank account can have on ethics and morals.'

'That's why the United States and the Russian Federation didn't want word of that downed aircraft's possible payload to become public knowledge,' Smith added.

'Unfortunately, Doctor, it's apparent the word has gotten out,' Valentina slashed in once more. 'Maybe it was one of the Russians, maybe it was one of ours, or maybe it was one of yours. Be that as it may, somebody nasty knows about the filth loaded aboard that bomber, and they are out to get their hands on it. My associates and I were nearly killed because of it. Your people on Wednesday Island may have died because of it. For certain, millions of innocent lives have been placed at risk because of it!'

Valentina Metrace smiled. If the historian had possessed fangs, they would have gleamed. 'You may count on this, my dear Dr. Trowbridge. We are going to find out just who has the big mouth. And when we do, he or she is going to be very, very thoroughly chastised.'

Trowbridge had no response, but a shudder ran through the man's body.

'After Hades and Lazarus and a number of similar ugly events, the world's governments take these matters very seriously,' Smith added. 'So do I, and so do the other members of this team. And now that we've taken you into our confidence, Doctor, it is expected – no, cancel that; it is required – that you do so as well. Is this understood?'

'Yes.'

Abruptly the helicopter swayed, trying to weathervane in a gust of wind. 'It's kicking up a little,' Randi commented into the interphone. 'I think we've got a squall line out ahead of us.'

'Can we make it to the island?' Smith inquired.

'I think so. In fact . . .' She paused for a moment, peering ahead through the frost-spangled windscreen. 'We're there.'

Beyond the Long Ranger's bow, a craggy outline materialized along a sea-smoked horizon, vaster than the bergs they had been overflying, the white of its ice streaked by the gray of stone, the tips of its two distinctive peaks lost in the brooding overcast.

Wednesday Island. They had arrived.

Professor Metrace leaned forward intently. 'Can we land directly at the crash site? All it would take is five minutes on the ground to verify the presence of the warload.'

Smyslov looked back over his shoulder. 'I'm not sure about that, Colonel. That is an ugly sky north of the island. Miss Russell is correct. We have a front coming down on us.

Maybe snow. For certain, wind. Here, there will always be wind!'

'He's right, Jon,' Randi interjected. 'That saddleback would be a very poor place to park a helicopter in this kind of deteriorating weather.'

Smith could see that for himself; the darkening clouds beyond the island were drawing closer even as he watched. They were in a race to touch home before the arctic environment tagged them out.

'Okay, Randi. Advise the *Haley* that we'll be landing at the science station. We'll go up to the crash site on foot.'

Valentina moaned softly. 'And, my, isn't that going to be fun!'

Five minutes later they were orbiting the Wednesday Island expedition base. The wisdom in landing here was already becoming apparent. The Long Ranger was beginning to wallow in the turbulence boiling over the ridgeline, and the twin peaks were becoming shadows in the snow haze.

No one emerged from the buildings at the beat of the helicopter's rotors.

The camp helipad lay some eighty yards north of the huts. There the snow had been freshly compacted and marked with an 'H' of orange spray paint. A V-shaped windbreak of snow blocks had also been built to partially shelter a grounded aircraft. Aligning the Long Ranger, Randi eased into the landing site. There was a final swirling flurry of snow, and the pontoons thudded down.

Instantly Smith bailed out of the helicopter's passenger door, the SR-25 at port arms. Hunching low to stay under the blade sweep, he hastened to the end of the windbreak that overlooked the hut site. Pulling up the hood of his snow smock, he dropped to one knee and merged with the end of the snow wall, his rifle lifted and leveled.

Nothing moved, and there was no sound save for the whine of the wind and the slowing *whicka-whicka* of the rotors.

'No activity inside the hut windows,' a voice reported from a few feet away. Lithe as a snow leopard, Valentina Metrace lay in a prone firing position, her rifle muzzle swinging in delicate arcs as she scanned for targets through the Winchester's powerful optics.

'No activity anywhere,' Randi Russell commented from beside him, resting the forestock of her MP-5 on the snow wall.

'So it seems.' Smith got to his feet. Slinging his rifle, he removed his binoculars from their case and panned them slowly around the frozen cove to the west and across the ridgeline above the station. To the limit of his vision there were no other skid or float marks from a helicopter landing, no human movement. Nothing alive at all.

Around his eyes Smith felt the sting of the first hard-driven snowflakes of the oncoming squall. 'Major Smyslov,' he said recasing his field glasses, 'remain here with Doctor Trowbridge and secure the helicopter. Set your intervals, ladies. Let's see if anyone's at home.'

Their boots crunched and squeaked on the corn snow of the trail as they moved on to the station.

According to the site map they had been given, the northernmost of the three huts was the storage and utility building, shorter trails radiating out from it to the camp's flammable coal, gasoline, and kerosene dumps.

Outside the hut's door there was no need for Smith to give orders or to speak at all. He only took a covering station beside the door. Valentina twisted a knurled knob on the model 70's Pachmayr optics mounts, tipping the scope aside to clear the rifle's close-range iron sights, and Randi drew back the bolt on the MP-5. Carrying the 'short gun,' she would have the point going in. With Smith and Valentina covering from either side of the snow lock, Randi pushed through the outer and inner doors into the hut.

A moment of silence followed, then, 'Clear.'

Smith took his own fast look around inside the unheated building. There was only the camp's auxiliary gasoline generator and ranked shelves packed with equipment and stores. The reserves were somewhat depleted after a season in the field, but a sizable emergency stock remained. It was an old just-in-case for polar exploration. For a one-season stay, you supplied for two.

The central hut was the combination laboratory and radio shack. A wind turbine mounted on a short, heavily guylined mast purred nearby, pumping out electric power. A second, taller steel girder mast, carrying the communications antenna, stood atop a low ice-covered knoll some hundred yards beyond the camp area.

The last word from Kayla Brown had come from the radio shack.

Again the team repeated the entry drill.

Again, 'Clear!'

Rifles lowered, Smith and Valentina followed Randi into the hut. A smoky warmth struck Smith's face as he pushed through the inner snow lock door. This building still held life. Laboratory implements gleamed untouched on the workbenches and central table. Sample and equipment cases lay on the floor, some closed and secure, ready to load. Others were open and in the process of being filled.

The heat in the cabin issued from a small coal stove centered on the north wall. Crossing to it, Metrace lifted the stove lid, revealing glowing orange ash. 'I wonder how long one of these things can hold a fire,' she mused, adding a few chunks of glossy black anthracite from the scuttle.

'Probably for some time,' Smith commented, looking around the lab. 'There's no sign of a struggle, and there are plenty of delicate things in here to smash.'

'Um-hm,' Valentina agreed, pointing toward a row of empty hooks near the exterior doorway. 'Miss Brown must have had the chance to put on her snow gear. Apparently she left under controlled circumstances.'

Smith went on into the radio room. With her gloves off and her hood thrown back, Randi was sitting in the side-bands operator's chair, a frown on her face. The radios were still switched on. Check lights glowed green, and the thin hiss of a carrier wave issued from the speakers. As Smith looked on she pressed the transmit key at the base of the desk mike. 'CGAH *Haley* CGAH *Haley*, this is KGWI Wednesday Island. This is a check call. This is a check call. Do you copy? Over.'

The carrier hissed back emptily.

'What do you think, Randi?'

'I don't know.' She shook her head. 'We're on frequency, and the transmitter gain indicates we're putting out.' She adjusted the receiver squelch and transmitter power and repeated the test call, to no effect. 'Either they're not hearing us or we're not hearing them.'

There was a sat phone and data link at the far end of the console. Smith stepped around Randi and lifted the receiver, punching in the *Haley*'s address code. 'No joy here, either,' he reported after a moment. 'It's not accessing the satellite.'

'Could it be the antennas?'

'Possibly. That'll be something to check out later. Let's go.'

The last hut in the row was the bunk room. The leading edge of the snow squall had enveloped the station, and visibility was graying out as the team approached the building.

Once more they repeated the entry drill. Flanking the snow lock door, Smith and Metrace listened as Randi pushed her way into the bunk room. After a moment, they heard her exclaim aloud, 'Now, this is just too weird!'

Smith and the historian looked at each other and shouldered through the lock into the bunk room.

Inside, the overall layout was similar to the laboratory. There were two sets of bunk beds and a small coal heater against the north wall of the cabin. Kitchen equipment and a food preparation counter were on the south, with a communal mess table in its center. A set of women's quarters had been partitioned in the far end of the hut, an accordion-style sliding door standing half open.

The bunk room had been heavily personalized with a

variety of photographs, hard-copy downloads, and sketches, humorous and otherwise, tacked and taped to the walls.

Randi was standing beside the mess table, staring down at a plate holding a half-consumed corned beef sandwich and a half-empty glass of tea.

'I concur, Miss Russell,' Valentina Metrace said, joining in the stare at the sandwich. 'That is indeed the limit.'

Randi set her submachine gun on the table. 'I feel like I've just gone aboard the *Mary Celeste*.' She tugged off one of her leather inner gloves and touched a couple of fingers to the side of the glass. 'Still warm,' she commented.

Looking up, she tapped the rim of the glass with a finger-nail.

Jon Smith knew that he truly had a team working at that moment. None of the three in the bunk room had to say a word to understand her meaning.

The portable SINCGARS transceiver squalled and shrieked, with only the faintest fragmentary hint of human speech discernible through the clamor of the disintegrating Heaviside layer. Even with the extended-range eighteen-foot antenna strung in the rafters of the laboratory hut, it was futility.

Smith snapped off the radio. 'I think the *Haley* might be receiving us and I think they might be trying to acknowledge our call, but I wouldn't count on anything beyond that.'

'It's the same with the set in the Ranger,' Randi added. 'While we're on the ground it doesn't have enough power to punch through the solar interference. We might have more luck with the big station SSB, but I still can't figure out what's wrong with it.'

With their gear unloaded and the helicopter tarped and tied down against the weather, the landing party from the *Haley* had gathered in the laboratory hut, both to make a futile attempt to contact their mother ship and to develop a course of action.

'What do we do now, Colonel?' Smyslov inquired.

'We do what we came here to do: get a look at the crash site.' Smith glanced out of the lab window. The snow had slackened for the moment, but the wind still gusted uneasily. 'We've got enough daylight left to reach the saddleback. Major, Val, you're with me. Get your gear together and plan for a night on the ice. Doctor Trowbridge, as you've stated, this station is your responsibility. I think it's best you stay here. Randi, if you could step outside with me for a moment. I need to talk with you.'

Garbing up, they pushed out through the snow lock, making the transition from the enclosed warmth of the hut to the piercing cold of the outdoors. Smith led Randi up the packed snow trail between the cabins until there was no chance of being overheard.

'All right,' he said, turning to her. 'We have a problem.'

Randi produced a wry ChapSticked smile. 'Another one?'

'You might think so,' Smith replied, the mist of his breath swirling around his face. 'Here's the situation. I'm going to have to do something I don't want to do. I have to split my forces, such as they are, to cover both the station and the bomber. I'm going to need both Professor Metrace and Major Smyslov with me at the crash site. That means I'm going to have to leave you here on your own. I don't like it, but I'm stuck with it.'

Randi's face went dark. 'Thanks so much for the vote of confidence, Colonel.'

Annoyance cut across Smith's features. 'Don't cop an attitude with me, Randi. I don't need it. I suspect the minimum you'll be confronting down here is a mass murderer. Your only backup will be Professor Trowbridge, who, I also suspect, will be about as much use in a fight as an extra bucket of water on a sinking ship. If I didn't think you were the most survivable member of this team, I wouldn't even be considering this scenario. As it stands, I estimate you have the best chance of coming out of this job alive. Are we absolutely clear on this?'

The cold words and cold focus in those dark blue eyes jolted her back momentarily. This was a facet of Jon Smith Randi had not encountered before, either in his time with Sophia or in her chance encounters since then. This was the full-house soldier, the warrior.

'I'm sorry, Jon, I got off base. I'll cover things here for you, no problem.'

The look on his face disengaged, and Smith smiled one of his rare full smiles, resting a hand momentarily on her shoulder. 'I never doubted it, Randi. In a lot of ways this will be the tougher job. You've got to verify our suspicions about what's happened here while watching your back to make sure it doesn't happen to you. You've also got to find out how the word was passed off the island and who it was passed to. Trowbridge may be of help to you there. That's one of the reasons I brought him along. Anything you can learn about the identities, resources, and intents of the hostiles could be critical.'

She nodded. 'I have some ideas about that. I'll try and get the big radio working, too.'

'Good enough.' Smith's expression closed up again. 'But while you're about it, remember to stay alive, all right?'

'As long as it doesn't interfere with the mission,' she replied. Then she tried to lighten the Zen of her statement. 'And while you're up there on that mountain I suggest you watch your own back with that scheming brunette. I think she has designs on you.'

Smith threw his head back and laughed, and for an instant Randi could see what had enraptured her sister. 'An arctic glacier is hardly the environment for a romantic interlude, Randi.'

'Where there's a will there's a way, Jon Smith, and I have a hunch that lady has a lot of will.'

Standing outside the laboratory hut, Randi watched the three small figures trudge up the flag-marked trail, the one that led eastward along the shoreline toward the central peaks. The snow had stopped altogether, but the mist, the near-perpetual 'sea smoke' of the poles, was closing in. The arctic camouflage her teammates wore blended them into the environment until, abruptly, they were gone.

'What now?' Doctor Trowbridge stood beside her in the lee of the hut, garish in the Day-Glo orange cold-weather gear issued to the science expedition. Randi could see that the academic was beginning to regret his momentary burst of responsibility back aboard the *Haley*.

He was a man meant for the warm classrooms and comfortable offices of a university campus, not for the wild, cold, and dangerous areas of the world. She could see the fear and loneliness of this place sinking into him. It would be so even without the overlay of the Misha scenario.

He was questioning his only companion as well, this alien being with the submachine gun slung over her shoulder.

Randi felt a momentary surge of contempt for the academic. Then, angrily, she dismissed the thought. Rosen Trowbridge could no more help what he was than she could help being the bitch wolf she had become. She had no right to judge who was the superior.

'That was a computer data link attached to the satellite phone, wasn't it?'

Trowbridge blinked at her. 'Yes, that was how most of the expedition's findings were downloaded to the project universities.'

'Were the expedition members allowed access to that data link?'

'Of course. Every expedition member had a personal computer and was allotted several hours of Internet access a week for their project studies and for personal use – for e-mail and the like.'

'Right,' Randi replied. 'That would work. The first thing we do, Doctor, is to collect laptops.'

CHAPTER TWENTY-FOUR

The Southern Face of West Peak

After the first hour they had been forced to strap on crampons, and their ice axes had become something more than walking staffs. The safety line linking them together had also become a comfort rather than an encumbrance.

'This is it. Last flag. End of the trail.' Smith shot a look up the mountain slope above them, checking for unstable rock formations and snow cornices. 'Let's take a breather.'

He and his teammates shrugged out of their pack frames and sank down with their backs to the vertical wall of the broad ledge they had been following. The climb itself had not been technically challenging. There had been no piton and rope work involved, but the cold, the icy footing, and the intermittent patches of broken stone had made it physically demanding.

They'd been climbing into the overcast, and the gray haze had folded in around them, limiting their world to a fifty-yard radius. Visibility grew somewhat better-looking downward from the ledge. They could see as far as Wednesday's coastline, but the differentiation between ice-sheathed land and ice-sheathed sea was a subtle one.

'Hydrate, people.' With his snow mask tugged down and his goggles lifted, Smith opened the zip of his parka, removing a canteen from one of the large inside pockets, where the warmth of his body kept the water liquid.

With a physician's instincts he watched as his companions followed suit. 'A little more, Val,' he counseled. 'Just because you don't feel like you need water in this environment doesn't mean you don't require it.'

She made a face and took another grudging mouthful. 'It's not the input that I'm worried about; it's the inevitable outflow.' She screwed the cap back onto her canteen and turned to Smyslov. 'That's the curse of having a doctor perennially in the house, Gregori. He goes around insisting you enjoy good health.'

The Russian nodded ruefully. 'He erodes you like water dripping on a rock. The bastard has me down to ten cigarettes a day and feeling guilty about them.'

'If he starts going off on chocolate and champagne, I'm planting a cake spatula between his shoulder blades.'

'Or vodka,' Smyslov agreed. 'I will not have him attacking my national identity.'

Smith chuckled at the exchange. He didn't need to worry about team morale at any time soon. Nor about the capabilities of his companions.

Smyslov had obviously undergone the same kind of mountain warfare training and conditioning he had. He knew and could apply the simple, effective basics, with no unnecessary flash. Valentina Metrace was a tyro but with a very steep learning curve. She was quick, she kept her eyes open, and she was ready and willing to take instruction – the kind of individual who could pick up an understanding of any skill rapidly. And for all her urbane drawing room sophistication there was a startling reserve of wiry strength in that slender, long-lined body.

There were intriguing things to be learned about this woman, Smith mused. Where had she come from? Her accent was an odd combination of educated American, British, and something else. And how had she developed the odd set of talents that made her a cipher agent.

And as one of Fred Klein's ciphers, she, like Smith, must be a person without personal attachments or commitments. What disaster had made her alone?

Smith forced his mind back to immediate concerns. Unsnapping his map case, he took out a laminated sectional photo map of Wednesday Island as scanned from polar orbit. 'This is as far as the expedition's ground parties got – the official ones anyway. From here the climbing party that found the bomber started working directly upslope to the peak. We'll follow on around the mountain to a point above the glacier in the saddleback.'

'How does the route ahead look, Colonel?' Smyslov asked.

'Not bad if this map's any indication.' Smith passed the photo chart down to the Russian. 'This ledge we've been following seems to keep going for another half mile or so. At its end we can drop down into the glacier. We might need to do some rope work, but it shouldn't be too bad. The crash site's almost at the foot of the east peak, about a mile, mile and a quarter across the ice. With no hang-ups we should make it well before nightfall.'

He glanced at Metrace. She was sitting back against the rock wall, her eyes closed for the moment. 'Holding up okay, Val?'

'Marvelous,' she replied, not opening her eyes. 'Just assure me there'll be a steaming bubbly spa, a roaring fireplace, and a quart of hot buttered rum waiting for me at our destination and I'll be fine.'

'I'm afraid I can't promise anything but a sleeping bag and a solid belt of some very good medicinal whisky in your MRE coffee.'

'A distant second, but acceptable.' She opened her eyes and looked back at him, a quizzical smile brushing her face. 'I thought you medical types had decided that consuming ardent spirits in freezing weather was another biological no-no.'

'I'm not that healthy yet, Professor.'

Her smile deepened in approval. 'There is hope for you yet, Colonel.'

CHAPTER TWENTY-FIVE

Wednesday Island Station

'Shouldn't you have a warrant or something?' Doctor Trowbridge asked suddenly.

Distracted, Randi looked up from the row of six identical Dell laptops on the laboratory worktable. 'What?'

'These computers contain personal documents and information. Shouldn't you have some kind of a warrant before you go rummaging around in them?'

Randi shrugged and turned back to the computers, tapping a series of on buttons. 'Damned if I know, Doctor.'

'Well, you are a government . . . agent of some nature.'

'I don't recall saying that.'

The six screens glowed, cycling through their start-up sequences. Of the six, only two demanded access code words: those belonging to Dr. Hasegawa and Stefan Kropodkin.

'Still, before I can allow you to violate the privacy of my expedition's staff members there must be some kind of . . .'

Randi sighed, fixing a baleful gaze on Trowbridge. 'First, Doctor, I don't have anyplace to get a warrant from. Secondly, I don't have anybody to give a warrant to, and finally, I don't really give a shit! Okay?'

Trowbridge subsided in outraged bafflement for a moment, turning to stare out of the lab window.

Turning back to the computers, Randi methodically set to work, checked the four open systems first, skimming through the e-mail files and address lists. Nothing sprang out at her from the stored correspondence. Professional and personal business, letters from wives, families, and friends.

The English boy, Ian, was apparently on very good terms with at least three different girlfriends, and the American girl, Kayla, was discussing a marriage with a fiancé.

No one seemed to be openly chatting up any known terrorist groups or exchanging missives with the Syrian Ministry of Defense. Which, of course, was meaningless. There were any number of covert contact and relay nodes for such organizations infesting the Internet, just as there were any number of simple transposition codes and tear-sheet ciphers that could be used to mask a covert communication. But these days there were better ways to go about things.

Randi moved on, cross-checking the control panels and programming screens and the memory reserves of the laptops. What she was looking for could be hidden, but it would also absorb a fair-sized chunk of hard drive space.

Again nothing sprang out at her. That left the locked-out laptops.

Getting up from the stool she had been using, she stretched for a moment and crossed to her pack that she had lugged in from the helicopter. Opening it, she took out a software wallet and removed a numbered compact disk. Returning to the laboratory table, she popped open the CD drive of the first locked computer and inserted the silvery disk.

The locked laptop made the error of checking the identification of the inserted disk, and in seconds the sophisticated NSA cracking program was raping its operating system. The desktop's welcome screen came up, the system's lockout protocols erased and supplanted.

Randi began to repeat the process with the second laptop. 'Dr. Trowbridge, please don't come up behind me like that,' she murmured, not taking her eyes from the screens. 'It makes me nervous.'

'Excuse me,' he replied, his footsteps withdrawing toward the stool in the corner of the laboratory. 'I was just thinking about going over to the bunkhouse for a cup of coffee.'

'I'd rather you didn't. There's a jar of instant coffee, some mugs, and a pot for heating water in the cupboard beside the coal stove.'

The academic's voice grew heated as well. 'So I gather I'm under suspicion of something as well?'

'Of course you are.'

'I do not understand any of this!' It was a vocal explosion.

God, and she didn't have time for this! She spun around on the lab stool. 'Neither do we, Doctor! That's the problem! We don't understand how word about the anthrax got off this island. Nor do we understand who may be coming for it. Until we do we are going to be as suspicious as hell of everybody! What you apparently don't understand is that entire national populations can be at stake here!'

She turned back to the computers. There was a long silence from the far end of the lab, followed by the clatter of coffee paraphernalia.

Dr. Hasegawa used Japanese kanji script on her personal computer, and it wasn't difficult to learn the great secret she was shyly locking away from the world. The female meteorologist was also a budding novelist. Randi, who was as capable in kanji as she was in several other languages, scanned a page or two of what was obviously a sweeping and rather sultry historical romance set in the days of the shogunate. Actually she'd read worse.

As for the computer of Stefan Kropodkin, he conveniently used English, and there was nothing out of the way on his system beyond a not excessive amount of downloaded cyber porn.

But there was one blip on his scope. Almost nothing in the way of personal e-mail traffic had been saved.

'Dr. Trowbridge, what do you know about Stefan Kropodkin?'

'Kropodkin? A brilliant young man. A physics major from McGill University.'

'That was in his file, along with the fact he holds a Slovakian passport and is in Canada on a student visa. Do you know anything about his family? Was any kind of a background check done on him?'

'What kind of a background check were we supposed to do?' Trowbridge swore softly as he struggled with the lid of the jar of powdered coffee. 'This was a purely scientific research expedition. As for his family, he doesn't have one. The boy is a refugee, a war orphan from the former Yugoslavia.'

'Really?' Randi sat back on her stool. 'Then who is financing his education?'

'He's on a scholarship.'

'What kind of a scholarship?'

Trowbridge spooned coffee crystals into his mug. 'It was established by a group of concerned Middle European businessmen specifically for deserving refugee youth from the Balkan conflicts.'

'And let me guess: this scholarship was established shortly before Stefan Kropodkin applied for it, and so far, he's the only deserving refugee youth to receive it.'

Trowbridge hesitated, his spoon poised over his steaming cup. 'Well, yes. How did you know?'

'Call it a hunch.'

Randi refocused on Kropodkin's laptop. Again, that unaccounted-for block of hard drive space she was looking for wasn't present.

She bit her lip. All right, somebody was being smart again. If it wasn't locked up in one of the computers, it must be somewhere else. Where might that be?

She closed her eyes, resting her hands on her thighs. *Let's say he's being very, very smart and very careful. Where would he hide it?*

In his personal effects? No, there would be a risk in that. The same with carrying it on his person. It would be else-where.

Maybe where it would be employed.

Randi slipped off her stool. Crossing to her cold-weather gear on the wall hooks, she took her thin leather inner gloves out of her parka pocket. Donning them, she brushed past Trowbridge, recrossing the lab and entering the radio shack.

It was little more than a large closet containing only the radio console, a single swivel chair, a small filing cabinet for hard copy, and a second small cabinet containing tools and electronic spares.

It wouldn't be inside the radio chassis or in the cabinets, simply because other people might have reason to poke around in there.

The floor, ceiling, exterior walls, and interior partition were solid slabs of insulated fiber ply; the window, a sealed double thermopane. No hiding places. But where the wall and ceiling panels joined, there was a narrow ledge above man height and maybe an inch in depth. Carefully Randi started to feel her way around it.

When her fingertips finally came to rest on it, she said, 'Got you!' aloud.

'What is it?' Trowbridge had been watching her actions from a wary distance.

Randi carefully held up a chewing gum–sized stick of gray plastic. 'A remote computer hard drive. Somebody hid it in here where it would be nice and convenient.'

Randi returned to the lab table. Popping the end cap off the mini hard drive, she plugged it into the USB port of the nearest computer and called up the removable-disk access prompt.

'Got you!' she repeated with greater exaltation. Randi glanced around to find Doctor Trowbridge trying to ease a look at the screen. 'Be my guest, Doctor,' she said, stepping aside.

'What is it?' he repeated, staring at the title screen.

'It's an Internet security program,' Randi replied, 'used to encrypt e-mails and Internet files that you don't want the world at large to be able to read. This one is a very sophisticated and expensive piece of work, totally state-of-the-art. It's available on the open market, but usually you'd see something like this only in the hands of a very security-conscious business firm or government agency.'

Randi's gloved fingers danced over the keyboard for a moment. 'There's a secured document file in here as well. But even with the program, I can't open it without the personalized encryption key. That will be somebody else's job.'

For the first time she looked around at Trowbridge. 'Why would anyone at this station need something like this?'

'I don't know,' Trowbridge said, all trace of his former belligerence erased. 'There would be no reason. This was all open research. Nothing secretive was being done here.'

'That you know of.' Randi delicately removed the minidrive from the computer and dropped it into a plastic evidence envelope.

'Do you think . . .' He hesitated. 'Do you think this has something to do with the disappearance of the expedition staff?'

'I think this is the way the word about the bioweapons aboard the Misha 124 got out,' Randi replied. 'But this leaves us an even more interesting question.'

'What's that, Ms. Russell?' For the moment, in the face of this discovery, they were at a truce.

'This island has been a totally sealed environment for over six months. Somebody brought this thing here long before that bomber was ever found, for some totally different reason. Its use in this situation is a coincidence, not a cause.'

Trowbridge started to protest. 'But if it's not for the bomber, why would anyone have a reason . . .'

'As I said, Doctor, that's a very interesting question.'

Rosen Trowbridge had no answer. Instead he turned to the little coal stove with the little pot of water steaming atop it. 'Would . . . would you care for a cup of coffee, Ms. Russell?'

CHAPTER TWENTY-SIX

Saddleback Glacier

Smith studied the row of glowing green numbers in the LED strip of the handheld 'Slugger' Global Positioning unit. 'Don't quote me on it, but I think we're close,' he said, lifting his voice over the wind rumble.

Whatever weather Wednesday Island received, the glacier between the two peaks got the worst of it, the mountains channeling the polar katabatics between them. On this afternoon, the sea smoke and cloud cover had blended, streaming through the gap between the mountains in a writhing river of mist intercut with stinging bursts of airborne ice crystals too hard and piercing to be called snow.

As Smith had hoped, the rappel down the mountainside to the glacier's surface had not proved excessively difficult, but the crossing of the glacier itself had turned into a slow, painful crawl. Visibility had varied from poor to nonexistent, and the threat of crevasses had mandated a wary roped advance, probing constantly with their ice axes. Away from the shield of the mountains, the incessant winds tugged and burned, penetrating even their top-flight arctic shell clothing. Frostbite and hypothermia would soon become a factor.

They weren't in trouble yet, but Smith knew his people were tiring. He was feeling it himself. Night was coming on rapidly as well. Soon they would have to break off the hunt for the plane and start the hunt for shelter, if such existed up here.

That thought decided him. If he was thinking 'soon,' it should be 'now,' while they still had some reserves remaining. He must conserve his team's strength and endurance.

Time was critical, but squandering it by stumbling around in this freezing murk would accomplish nothing.

'That's it,' he said. 'Let's pack it in. We'll dig in for the night and hope for better visibility tomorrow.'

'But, Jon, you said we're close.' Valentina's muffled protest leaked through her snow mask. 'We must almost be on top of it!'

'It's been here for fifty years, Val. It'll be here tomorrow. We just have to make sure we're here to find it. Major, we'll try and make it across to East Peak. That'll be our best bet to find some cover out of this wind. You've got the point. Let's move.'

'Yes, Colonel.' Obediently Smyslov turned and started his hunched trudge, probing ahead with the spike end of his climbing axe and slamming his crampons into the wind-abraded ice with each step.

How's that for command, Sarge? Smith grinned to himself, telepathing the thought to his distant mountain warfare instructor.

In the saddleback, the prevailing wind was as good as any compass. They only had to keep it on their left shoulder to eventually reach the far side of the glacier. Last on the safety line, Smith's attention was centered on the other two members of his team, ready to brace and hold should either suddenly fall through into a hidden crevasse in the ice. Accordingly it took him a moment to comprehend why Gregori Smyslov came to such an abrupt halt.

'Look!' The Russian's excited yell was torn by a wind gust. 'Look there!'

Almost directly ahead of them, a towering finlike shape had materialized, ghostlike in the streaming mist: the vertical stabilizer of an aircraft, a big aircraft, the outline of a storm-scoured red star still faintly visible.

'Yes!' Valentina Metrace lifted her fists in triumph.

Wasn't that always the case? When you weren't looking for it, you found it.

CHAPTER TWENTY-SEVEN

Wednesday Island Station

Randi Russell trudged up the trail to the knoll overlooking the station. Every few feet she stopped and heaved on the heavy, weatherproof coaxial cable that led up to the radio mast, peeling a length of it up and out of the snow cover. Carefully she ran each exposed cable section through her mittened hands, looking for breaks or cuts.

It had to be the antennas. She'd checked everything else on both the sat phone and the sideband set. The little SINCGARS transceiver they'd brought with them was useless. It simply lacked the power to override the solar flare that was demolishing communications. Once they'd broken the line of sight she hadn't even been able to raise Jon and the others on the aircraft party.

She was on her own. As much as one could get. Impatiently she shook her head, displeased with the pang of loneliness that had flared within her. Giving the MP-5 a hitch onto her shoulder, she doggedly plowed another few feet up the compacted snow trail.

Reaching the base of the ice-coated radio mast, Randi knelt down and traced the last few inches of cable into the booster box at the tower base. It was intact, and all the connectors were still screwed tight. Frustrated, she rocked back on her heels. The radios should be working. Given they weren't, she was missing something. Randi suspected sabotage, but if such was the case, some very subtle methodology had been used.

Somebody was being very, very clever, and she hoped that soon she would have the opportunity to make him suffer for it.

Standing, Randi took her binoculars from her belt case. From her position on the knoll she had a fair view of the immediate cove area. Degree by degree, to the limits of the haze and the fading daylight, she made another scan of her environs, her augmented gaze lingering on the jumbled piles of pressure ice along the shoreline and on the shadows and swales of drift at the foot of the central ridge.

That clever person was out there now, somewhere nearby, possibly even watching her. He was waiting, maybe for assistance or maybe for her to make that one mistake. To defeat him she was going to have to be a little bit more clever than he was.

She had one immediate advantage. Movement in this snow-blanketed environment meant leaving obvious and unerasable tracks. The science station was centered in a straggling, lopsided web of flag-marked snow trails that interconnected the buildings, supply dumps, and more distant experiment and research sites. Randi ran her glasses down each track, seeking for fresh ground disturbances or sets of snowshoe or boot tracks angling off from the regular routes of travel.

She found one. Disconcertingly, it was almost immediately below her, branching off from the trail to the knoll she had followed just a few minutes before in her climb to the radio mast. In her intent study of the communications cable, she hadn't paid attention to the short lateral stretch of broken snow that led out to a small disturbed drift. She did so now, and a chill rippled down her spine that had nothing to do with the sinking evening temperature.

She hastened downslope to the divergent trail and followed it for a dozen yards, kicking her way along and restirring the surface. She found what she had feared: red-stained snow, covered over and hidden. Reaching the end of the trail, she dropped to her knees and dug into the drift. It didn't take long to uncover the parka-clad body.

Kayla Brown wouldn't be going home to her fiancé in Indiana. Gently Randi brushed the snow from the young woman's face. She had died from a smashing blow to the temple from some heavy, pointed object, possibly an ice axe. Traces of shock and terror, her last expression, lingered frozen on the student's face.

Kneeling beside the girl's body, Randi Russell decided that it would not be adequate for this clever person to suffer. He was going to die, and it would please her to be his executioner.

Randi reburied the body with a few sweeps of her arm. She would not tell Trowbridge about this discovery. Not immediately, at any rate. Kayla Brown would keep here for a time, at least until Randi could arrange for her avenging.

Randi continued to the hut row. The lights were already on within the bunkhouse. Doctor Trowbridge had volunteered to prepare an evening meal. Pausing on the main trail that led past the hut entrances, she judged vision angles and distances. Near the front of the bunkhouse, Randi veered off the trail, plowing out into the virgin snow for a few yards.

Then, dropping onto the snow, she burrowed and rolled, compacting a pit large and deep enough for her to lie in with her back almost flush with the surrounding surface. It brought back unbidden childhood memories of making snow angels up at Bear Lake. Her intents now, though, were quite different.

Satisfied with her efforts, she got to her feet, shook off the ice rime, and went in to dinner.

CHAPTER TWENTY-EIGHT

The Misha Crash Site

'It strikes me that a lot of people are going to feel awfully stupid if we get in there only to find that containment vessel has been lying on the bottom of the ocean for the past fifty years.' The MOPP biochemical warfare suit had been designed to fit over his cold-weather clothing, and Jon Smith suspected that he looked very much like the Michelin Tire man.

'That is a stupidity I could live with,' Smyslov replied, passing him the headset for the Leprechaun tactical radio.

'So could I.' Smith flipped back his parka hood and settled the headset in place, wincing a little as the searing chill bit at his momentarily exposed ears. 'Radio check.'

'I've got you.' Valentina Metrace hunkered down on the ice beside him, wearing a second tactical headset. 'We're all right for line-of-sight distances at least.'

The team had set up some fifty yards upwind of the crash site, behind the meager windbreak afforded by their backpacks and a low ledge of extruded ice. Evening was standing on, but there was nothing in the way of a sunset; the grayness around them simply grew darker and the wind colder. Time and environment were becoming critical.

'Okay, people, this will be a fast in-and-out to learn if the anthrax is still aboard the aircraft, and to see if anyone else has been in there.' Smith popped the plastic safety covers off the MOPP suit's filter mask. 'You two know what I should be looking for, and you'll walk me through it. There shouldn't be any problems, but I'm putting one absolute in place now. If, for any reason, something goes wrong – if I

189

don't come out, or if we lose contact – nobody goes in after me. Is that clearly understood?'

'Jon, don't be silly . . .' Valentina started to protest.

'Is that understood?' Smith barked the words.

She nodded, looking unhappy. 'Yes, I understand.'

Smith looked at Smyslov. 'Understood, Major?'

In the shadow of his parka hood, Smith could see some emotion roiling beneath the Russian's stony features, an effect Smith had noticed several times before during the past week. Again Smyslov was struggling with something down in his guts where he lived.

'Colonel, I . . . It is understood, sir.'

Smith pulled the anticontamination hood over his head, adjusting the mask straps and sealing tabs. He took his first breath of rubber-tainted filtered air and drew on the suit's overgauntlets.

'Okay.' His voice sounded muffled even in his own ears. 'Dumb question of the day: how do I get inside?'

'The fuselage appears to be essentially intact,' Valentina's voice crackled over the radio channel, 'and the only way into the forward bomb bay is through the forward crew compartment. Unfortunately the conventional access doors are located in the nose wheel well and in the forward bomb bay itself, both of which are blocked. Your alternatives are through the port and starboard cockpit windows, which would be hard to wriggle through in that outfit, or the crew's access tunnel to the aft compartment. The latter is your best bet.'

'How do I get into the aft compartment, then?'

'There is an access door in the tail just forward of the horizontal stabilizer on the starboard side. You'll have to work your way forward through the pressurized crew spaces from there.'

'Right.' Smith stood awkwardly and waddled toward the murky outline of the downed bomber.

The port-side wing of the TU-4 had been torn loose in the crash and folded back almost flush against the fuselage, but the starboard approaches to the bomber were clear. As he circled around the great aluminum slab of the horizontal stabilizers Smith found himself marveling a little. Even in an age of giant military transports and jumbo jet airliners, this thing was huge. And they were actually flying these monsters during the Second World War.

Smith approached the great cylindrical body and ran a hand over the ice-glazed metal.

'Okay, I'm here and I've found the entry door. There's a flush-mounted handle, but it looks like it's been popped out.'

'The emergency release will have been pulled from the inside,' Valentina replied. 'It should open, but you might have to pry it a bit.'

'Right.' Smith had a small tool kit slung at his belt, and he drew a heavy long-hafted screwdriver from it. Fitting the tip of the blade into the frost-clogged slit around the door, he slammed the heel of his hand against the butt of the tool. After a couple of blows there was a sharp crack as the ice seal broke. A few more moments of levering, and the door swung outward, the wind catching at it, leaving a rectangular shadowed gap in the fuselage.

'You were right, Val. It's open. Going inside now.'

Bending low, he ducked through the small door.

It was dark inside the fuselage, with only the trace of dull exterior light at his back. Smith removed a flashlight from his tool kit and snapped it on.

'Damn,' he murmured. 'I never expected this.'

'What are you seeing, Jon?' Valentina demanded.

Smith panned the flashlight beam around the fuselage interior. No appreciable amount of snow had leaked inside, but ice crystals glittered everywhere, thinly encrusting the battleship gray frames and cable and duct clusters. 'It's incredible. There's no sign of corrosion or degradation anywhere. This thing might have rolled out of the factory yesterday.'

'Natural cold storage!' the historian exclaimed over the radio. 'This is fabulous. Keep going!'

'Okay, there's a catwalk leading aft past a couple of large flat rectangular boxes to a circular dished hatch right in the tail of the airplane. The hatch is closed, and there is a round window set in its center. A couple of what look like ammunition feed tracks are set on either side of it. I guess that must be the tail gunner's station.'

'Correct. Is there anything else noteworthy back there?'

'There's some kind of a mount or pedestal with a couple of unbolted cables hanging from it. It looks like some piece of equipment has been dismantled.'

'That would be the generator set of the auxiliary power unit,' the historian mused. 'That's rather interesting. Now, just to your right there should be a bulkhead with another pressure hatch centered in it, leading forward.'

'There is. It's closed.'

'The B-29/TU-4 family was one of the first military aircraft designed specifically for high-altitude flight. A number of its compartments were pressurized to allow its crew to survive without the need for oxygen masks. You're going to have to work forward through a series of these pressure hatches.'

'Got it.' Smith shuffled over to the hatch and tried to peer through the thick glass of the port, only to find that it was frosted over. 'What should be in this next compartment?'

'It should be the crew's in-flight rest quarters.'

'Right.' Smith gripped the dogging handle of the hatch and twisted it. After a moment's resistance, the lever started to yield.

'Jon, wait!'

Smith yanked his hand away from the handle as if it had gone red hot. 'What?'

Smith heard a background muttering in his earphones. 'Oh, Gregori was just saying that it's very unlikely there would be booby traps on the hatches or anything.'

'Thank you both for sharing that with me, Val.' Smith leaned on the lever again until it gave. The hatch swung inward, and he probed with the flashlight.

'Crew's quarters, all right. There's a set of fold-out bunks on either side and there's even a john – no relation – up in one corner. The cabin appears to have been stripped. There are no mattresses or bedding in the bunks, and I can see a number of empty, open lockers.'

'That's understandable.' Valentina sounded thoughtful, obviously cogitating on something. 'The next space should be the radar-observer compartment. Let's see what you find there.'

Working his way forward, Smith ducked through a low nonpressure hatch. Here there was dim outside light. Plexiglas bubbles, sheathed in ice and hazed with decades of wind spalling, were set into the port and starboard bulkheads and into the overhead. Skeletal chairs faced the two side domes, and a third seat on an elevated pedestal was positioned under the astrodome in the top of the fuselage. In a bomber mounting its full defensive armament, Smith imagined that these would have been the gunners' targeting stations for the remotely controlled gun turrets. Valentina verified the supposition as he described the space.

'This compartment has been emptied out, too,' Smith reported. 'A lot of empty lockers, and even the padding has been stripped out of the seats.'

'All of the survival gear will have been taken, along with anything that could serve as insulation. There should also be a large electronics console against the forward bulkhead.'

'There is,' he concurred. 'The chassis has been completely gutted.'

'That's the radar operator's station. They'd have wanted the components,' Valentina finished cryptically.

'There are also two circular doors or passages in the forward bulkhead, one above the other. The larger lower passage has a pressure hatch on it. The upper one has a short aluminum stepladder leading up to it.'

'The lower hatch opens into the aft bomb bay. There won't be anything in there but fuel tanks. The upper passage is the one you want. It's the crew crawlway that runs over the bomb bays into the bow compartment.'

Smith crossed the compartment and peered down the aluminum-walled tunnel. It had been designed large enough for a man in bulky winter flight gear to negotiate, so he shouldn't have a problem with his MOPP suit.

'Going on.' He put his boot toe in a ladder step and heaved himself into the tunnel, hitching and shouldering his way awkwardly toward the circle of pale light at its far end.

The forty-foot crawl down the frost-slickened tube seemed to take forever, dislodged ice crystals raining around him with each inch gained. Smith was startled when he finally thrust his head into the comparatively open space of the forward compartment.

The last of the outside light trickled in dully through the navigator's astrodome and the hemispheric glazed nose of the old bomber, and again the state of preservation was astounding. The plane was frozen in time as well as in temperature. Ice diamonds sheathed controls that hadn't moved for five decades, and glittered over the ranked instrument gauges frozen on their last readings.

'I'm in the cockpit,' he reported into his lip mike, panting a little with the exertion.

'Very good. Is there much crash damage?'

'It's not bad, Val. Not bad at all. Some of the windows in the lower curve of the bow were caved in. Some snow and ice has packed in around the bombardier's station. A drift seems to have built up around the nose. Beyond that, everything's in pretty fair shape, although some inconvenient SOB unshipped the tunnel ladder. Just a second; let me get down from here.'

Smith rolled onto his back and used the grab rail mounted above the entry to draw himself out of the crawlway. 'Okay, on the deck.'

'Excellent, Jon. Before you examine the bomb bay could you check a couple of things for me?'

'Sure, as long as it won't take too long.'

'It shouldn't. First, I want you to examine the flight engineer's station. That will be the aft-facing seat and console behind the copilot's position.'

'Okay.' Smith snapped on his flashlight once more. 'It's a lot roomier in here than I figured.'

'In a standard TU-4 a lot of the space in the bow compartment would be taken up by the basket of the forward dorsal gun turret. That was one of the weapons mounts pulled in the America bombers.'

'Yeah.' Smith tilted his hood faceplate up. 'I can see the turret ring in the overhead. Again, I'm seeing the empty lockers, and the seat cushions and parachutes are gone. Looking toward the bow, I've got what looks like the navigator's table on my left, and another stripped electronics chassis to my right.'

'That was the radio operator's station. I suspect the plane's crew built a survival camp somewhere around here, someplace that would provide a bit more protection than the wreck's fuselage. They must have transferred all of the survival and radio gear there along with the plane's auxiliary power generator.'

'That camp will be the next thing we'll be hunting for.' Smith lumbered to the flight engineer's station and played the light across the gauge- and switch-covered panel. 'Okay, I'm at the engineer's station. What am I looking for?'

'Good, there should be three banks of four levers across the bottom of the console, a big one, a middle-sized one, and a small one – papa bear, mama bear, and baby bear. The big ones are the throttles. They should be pulled all the way back, I imagine, to the closed position. The others are the propeller and fuel mixture controls. How are they set?'

Smith scrubbed at his faceplate and swore softly as the haze turned out to be on the inside. 'They're both sort of in the middle.'

'Most interesting,' the historian mused over the radio circuit. 'There would have been no reason to fiddle with them after a crash. All right, there is one more lever I want you to check for me, Jon. It will be located on the control pedestal outboard of the pilot's seat. It will be very distinctive in appearance. The knob on the end of it will be shaped like an airfoil.'

Smith turned in the aisle between the flight control stations, peering awkwardly over the back of the pilot's chair. 'Looking for it . . . There's a hell of a lot of levers all over this thing . . . Okay, I found it. It's all the way up, forward, whatever.'

'That's the flap controller,' Valentina murmured. 'This is coming together . . . This is making sense . . .' There was a moment of silence over the channel, and then the historian continued with a rush. 'Jon, be careful! The anthrax is still aboard that aircraft!'

'How can you be sure?' Smith demanded.

'It will take too long to explain. Just take my word for it. The crew never jettisoned the bioagent reservoir. It's still in there!'

'Then I'd better have a look at it.' Smith straightened and returned to the forward bomb bay access.

In a mirror image of the rear compartment, it was a circular dished pressure hatch with a round window in its center, located directly below the crawlway tunnel. Smith knelt down.

'Okay, I'm at the bomb bay,' he reported. He paused for a moment to catch his breath and reached for the undogging lever. 'I'm opening the ha . . .' His words trailed off.

'Jon, what is it?'

'So that's why the tunnel ladder was been moved. Somebody has been here, Val, and recently. Everything in here is covered with frost. Everything but the release handle on the hatch. It's been wiped off. I can make out the finger marks.'

Smith twisted and whipped the flashlight beam around the cockpit. Now that he knew what he was looking for, he could spot the smears and scrapes in the frost cover where someone had moved around the cabin. 'He got in through the pilot's-side window.'

'Did he get inside the bomb bay?'

'We'll know in a second.' Smith got a grip on the dogging lever, twisting it. The hatch unlatched and swung open with disconcerting ease. Hunkering lower, he peered into the dark opening.

Smith's strained breath caught in his throat.

It filled the entire upper half of the bomb bay: a great lozenge shape held in place by a network of struts and braces, the iced stainless steel of the case sparkling. The latent death of entire cities whispered from within it, billions upon billons of lethal disease spores slumbering in icy suspension, waiting for revival, waiting for release.

Confronting such horrors were part of Jon Smith's profession, but he still had to suppress a shudder.

'Val, you were right. It's in here. Put Major Smyslov on. I'm going to need him.'

As he waited for the Russian to come online, he quartered the interior of the bay with his light, looking for damage to the containment vessel or for the deadly telltale gray-brown stain of spore spillage. After a few moments Smyslov's filtered voice filled his earphones.

'I gather we have a hit, Colonel.'

'We surely do, Major,' Smith replied. 'I'm looking at the reservoir now. From this end at least, it appears to have survived the crash in good shape. The bomb bay doors are partially caved in, but the casing doesn't appear to be involved. The mounts and bracings seem to be intact as well. Did Val tell you that we've had at least one snooper inside the aircraft?'

'Yes, Colonel.'

'He's been in here as well. There is an instruction plate on the front of the reservoir casing directly opposite me. The frost's been wiped from it. I can see a Soviet Air Force badge, a hammer-and-sickle insignia, and a lot of bright red writing. I'm not up on my Cyrillic, but I gather it's a bio-agent warning advisory.'

'Quite correct, Colonel. That would tell the inquisitive one everything he would need to know about the payload.'

'Then I think we've found our information leak. Now, Major, the containment vessel and the anthrax dispersal system are your babies. Walk me through what I should be looking for.'

'Very well, Colonel. If the casing is intact, you should next inspect the dispersal system manifolds to ensure that the manual containment valves on the pressurization ducts are still closed and sealed. The valves shouldn't have been opened and the system armed until the bomber was coming in on target, but . . .'

'But, indeed. From those diagrams you showed me, those containment valves should be right over my head.'

With his head and shoulders inside the bomb bay, Smith carefully rolled onto his back and found himself looking up into a tangle of large-diameter stainless steel piping.

'Okay, I'm looking up into the manifold assembly. I see two large lever valves directly above me. The valve gradations seem to just be marked with red and green zones.'

'That is correct. Those are the forward containment valves. How are they set?'

'The levers are turned all the way to the left and right, with their pointers aimed at the green zones. There appear to be intact wire seals on both valves, and the frost buildup hasn't been disturbed.'

'Very good.' Smyslov sounded relieved. 'The containment valves are still closed. The system was never armed for drop. Now, just to the right, looking aft, next to the access hatch, you should see two more levers marked and sealed as were the overhead valves. These control the valves on the dispersal vents at the rear of the reservoir.'

Smith squirmed onto his left shoulder. 'Okay, I see them. They are set vertically, in the green, and the wire seals are still in place.'

'Excellent!' Smyslov exclaimed. 'Those are all metal-to-metal knife valves with single-use lead gaskets. Nothing will get past them. We still have full containment.'

'Theoretically. I'm going into the bomb bay to do an eye-ball inspection of the whole system to make sure.'

There was some thumping and murmuring at the other end of the circuit, Valentina's voice taking over from Smyslov's. 'Jon, are you sure that's wise?'

'It's got to be done, and if I do it now, I won't have to come back later.' Smith tried to sound offhand about it. In truth he wasn't sure he could make himself come back later. Belly crawling into the freezing blackness beneath that concentration of megadeath was a singularly unappealing prospect.

In fact, he had to do it right now, immediately, or see his nerve crack. 'I'm going into the bay,' he said shortly.

Backing his shoulders out of the entry hatch, he swung his legs in and dropped to the crumpled metal floor of the compartment. Sinking to his hands and knees, he began to squirm down the length of the bomb bay, hugging the starboard bulkhead to take advantage of the space offered by the curve of the containment vessel.

Even at that, the crawl was claustrophobic in the extreme, complicated by the crash-buckled aluminum of the bay doors. Smith had to carefully plan each move, flowing himself over the torn metal, striving to protect the MOPP suit's integrity. He couldn't help but flinch each time his shoulder bumped the brooding mass of the spore-packed casing.

The hood faceplate was fogging again, hampering his vision, and he had to partially feel his way ahead. He reached forward . . . and froze. Very slowly he lifted his head, trying to peer around the edges of the visor.

'Major,' he said deliberately, 'my right arm is fouled in a wire. The wire is connected to a series of rectangular metal boxes attached by some kind of metal clip to the side of the reservoir. The boxes appear to be one foot by four inches by three, and there are half a dozen of them spaced out along the near side of the casing. I can't tell if another set is mounted symmetrically on the far side. They do not appear integral to the reservoir. The boxes and wiring are frost covered and undisturbed. They've been there for a while.'

'You are all right, Colonel,' Smyslov replied promptly. 'You are all right. Those are thermite incendiary charges. They are part of the bomber's emergency equipment. They were intended to destroy the anthrax to prevent its capture should the plane be forced down in enemy territory.'

'Fine. What do I do about them?'

'You don't have to do anything, Colonel. The charges are stable. They would have to be set off deliberately using a magneto box or a heavy battery, and if there are any batteries aboard the wreck, they would have been drained by the cold long ago.'

'Thanks for telling me.' Smith untangled his arm and paused for a moment, panting.

'This is odd,' Smyslov said. 'The bomber's crew must have deployed the incendiaries after the landing, with the intent of destroying the warload. I wonder why they didn't fire them.'

'They would have saved everybody a lot of trouble if they had.' Smith resumed his crawl to the rear of the bay. He had never considered himself a claustrophobe, but the bomb bay was getting to him, and badly. The cold metal walls kept folding around him, and it seemed increasingly difficult to breathe. He was getting a headache as well, the beating of his heart pounding at his temples. He had to force himself to focus on the job, checking the casing, inch by deliberate inch, for cracks or other damage and for spore leakage.

He made the last yard to the rear of the bay, twisting onto his back to check the rear of the reservoir and the dispenser manifolds. The fogging of his faceplate was getting worse, and the flashlight seemed to be dimming. His head suddenly seemed to be exploding, and he gulped for air, cursing weakly. This was no good! He had to get out of here!

'Jon, what's wrong?' Valentina was back on the circuit.

'Nothing. I'm fine. It's just . . . tight in here. The containment vessel is intact. I'm starting back.'

He tried to roll over and turn in the confined space. He couldn't seem to make it around. He kept hanging up on things that hadn't been there before, and his suppressed panic flared. He lost his grip on the flashlight and swore again as it rolled out of reach.

'Jon, are you all right?' Valentina's words were sharp this time, demanding.

'Yes, damn it!' He gave up on the flashlight and tried to drag himself toward the dim patch of outside illumination at the far end of the bay. Cold sweat burned in his eyes, and his arms felt as if they were encased in solidifying concrete. His breath hissing through clenched teeth, he commanded his body to move. Only his body refused to obey.

And then it reached him through his muddled mind. He wasn't all right. He was dead.

'Get away from the plane!' he shouted weakly, his lungs suddenly on fire.

'Jon, what is it? What's happening?'

'The plane's hot! I've been contaminated! There's something else in here! It's not anthrax! Abort the mission! Get away from here!'

'Jon, hold on! We're suiting up. We're coming for you!'

'No! The suits are no good! It penetrates! The antibiotics aren't stopping it, either!'

'Jon, we can't just leave you!' Beyond Val's frantic words he could hear Smyslov's demanding questions.

'Forget it!' He had to force each word with its own racking breath. 'I've had it! I'm already dying! Don't come in after me! That's an order!'

It had been bound to happen sooner or later. He'd dodged the biological bullet with Hades, with Cassandra, and with Lazarus. He had to take the fall sooner or later. That bit of his disintegrating consciousness that was still the researcher, the scientist, pushed its way forward. There was a last service he could render to those who would follow him into this black pit to learn and fight this thing.

'Val, listen . . . listen! It's respiratory. It hits through the respiratory system. My lungs and bronchial tubes are burning . . . No congestion or fluid buildup . . . no pulmonary paralysis . . . but I can't get oxygen . . . accelerated pulse . . . vision graying out . . . strength . . . losing . . . Get away . . . That's . . . order.'

There was nothing left to breathe and speak with. They were calling to him over the radio, something about the MOPP suit. He couldn't hear over the staggering hammer of his heartbeat in his ears. Was this how it had been for Sophia at the end, drowning in her own blood? No. At least Sophia hadn't been so alone. He made a final effort to drag himself toward the light, just so he wouldn't die in this hideous place. Then the light was gone, and the dark took him fully.

An eternity passed, or maybe only a second.

Smith became aware of fragments . . . Movement . . . Touch . . . Voices . . . Pressure on his chest . . . Lips, soft, warm, living, pressed against his, with urgency but without passion.

Sensation returned within himself. The lift of his chest; air, cold, pure, pouring into his lungs like water from an iced pitcher. Life stirred with its bite, radiating outward. He could breathe. He could breathe! He lay there in the suddenly pleasant cool darkness, almost orgasmically relishing each inhalation.

A small ungloved hand brushed back his hair, and those lips pressed against his again. Gently this time, pleasantly lingering.

'I think respiration has been fully restored, Professor,' an amused, accented voice commented.

'Just making sure,' a second lighter voice replied.

Smith realized that his head was pillowed on a rolled sleeping bag. Opening his eyes, he found Valentina Metrace kneeling beside him, her parka hood thrown back and ice crystals glittering like stars in her black hair. She smiled down into his face and quirked one of her expressive eyebrows at him.

Smyslov was looking over her shoulder, grinning as well. Smith realized he was lying on the deck in the forward compartment of the bomber. He was vague for a moment on just what they all were doing there; then full memory came crashing back.

'Damn it, Val! What do you think you're doing?'

Both brows lifted. 'So I'm enjoying my work?'

'That's not what I mean!' he exclaimed, struggling to sit up. 'This plane is a hot zone! There's a contaminant—'

'Easy, Jon, easy,' the historian replied, holding him down gently with her hands on his shoulders. 'There is no contaminant. You're fine, we're fine, and the plane is fine.'

'This is true, Colonel,' Smyslov interjected wryly. 'I told you before, barring two tons of weaponized anthrax, there is nothing the least bit dangerous aboard this aircraft.'

Smith sank back and found he was still in most of the MOPP suit. Beyond the glare of the electric lantern that filled the cockpit, he could see a lingering trace of daylight through the windscreen. He must have been unconscious for only a matter of a few minutes. 'Then what the hell did happen to me?'

'You almost protected yourself to death.' Smyslov held up the hood of the MOPP suit. 'It's cold in here. The moisture in your breath condensed and froze in the filters of your breathing mask. It gradually cut off your air.'

Valentina nodded. 'Something similar happened in Israel during the first Gulf War. During the SCUD bombardment, when it was feared that Saddam might be using nerve gas, a number of Israeli citizens suffocated because they forgot to remove the filter caps on their gas masks. You were rebreathing your own carbon dioxide. Only with you the effect must have come on so gradually that you didn't notice the buildup.'

Smith looked back over his clearing memories. 'Yes.

When I started to have breathing problems I first thought I was just having a bad attack of claustrophobia. Then I thought . . .'

'We know what you thought,' Valentina said softly. 'You started to report the symptomology of your own death. But when you began to give us a very good clinical description of a man dying of suffocation, we realized what was going on. We tried to tell you to take off your mask, but you were too far gone to understand.'

She nodded toward the glassed-in nose of the bomber. 'We came in through the cockpit window, and Gregori dove into the bomb bay and hauled you out. A little mouth-to-mouth resuscitation, and here you are.'

Smith grimaced. 'Pardon me while I feel incredibly stupid.'

'I shouldn't, Jon,' Valentina replied soberly. 'I can't imagine what it must have been like, climbing into that chamber of horrors. Just looking through that hatch was enough to make my skin crawl.' The historian shook her head in profound distaste. 'I love fine weapons, but that . . . thing . . . isn't a weapon; it's a nightmare.'

'I'm not going to argue the point.' Smith smiled up at her. 'I suppose I should be making a stink over you and the major for disobeying my direct orders, but I can't seem to work up much enthusiasm for it. Thank you, Val.'

He extended a hand past her to Smyslov. 'And thank you, Major.'

The Russian gripped it firmly. 'It is the duty of a good subordinate to point out factors in a situation possibly overlooked by his superior,' he quoted, still grinning.

Smith tried to sit up again, this time succeeding with only a hint of dizziness. His strength seemed to be returning rapidly. 'Well, we've got some good news and bad news. The bad news is that we still have the anthrax to deal with. The good news is that the containment vessel seems to be intact and undamaged. Just in case, we'll stay on the antibiotics, but I don't think we have any spore spillage to contend with. Val, how did—'

She stood up abruptly, giving Smith a sharp but seemingly accidental bump as she got to her feet. 'Thank God for that at least,' she chattered on. 'Do you think it's safe to fort up in the fuselage for tonight? It sounds like the weather is kicking up a bit outside.'

'Yes . . . I think that might be a good idea,' Smith replied. 'I suspect it will feel a little odd camping on top of a mound of anthrax, but I think it should be safe enough. What do you say, Major?'

Smyslov shrugged. 'I think it will still be bloody cold in here, but I think it will also be better than a tent out on that stinking glacier. I think we'd do better in the aft compartment though.'

'Marvelous!' Valentina said, offering her hand to Smith. 'Let's get our gear together and start playing house. I could use a dollop of that medicinal whisky you promised.'

Smith accepted her hand and heaved himself off the deck. 'Now that you mention it, so could I.'

Seated on the bare springs of the starboard crew bunk, Smith scowled at the walkie-talkie in his hand. 'Wednesday Island Station, Wednesday Island Station. This is crash site, crash site. Randi, can you read me? Over.'

The little SINCGARS Leprechaun tactical transceiver hissed and spat back in his face. 'Isn't that just the way of it,' Smith said in disgust. He snapped off the radio and folded the antenna back into the casing. 'You can communicate instantly with the farthest corner of the world except for when you actually need to talk with someone.'

'There is an entire mountain between us and the station.' Sitting cross-legged beside the tiny pack stove, Valentina carefully dropped a ball of hard-packed snow into the pan of water steaming atop it. Beyond melting a foot-wide circle in the frost on the overhead of the crew's quarters, the little fuel-pellet burner was incapable of measurably affecting the temperature within the compartment, but it could produce hot water for an MRE and to refill the team's canteens.

To save their batteries, the only illumination in the compartment came from a pair of chemical light sticks clipped to the bunk frames, the soft, all-encompassing green glow giving an impression of warmth.

The fuselage at least provided still air shelter from the wind whining across the glacier. The environment within the wreck would at least be tolerable for the night.

'What bunk do you want, Professor?' Smyslov asked, detaching his sleeping bag from his pack frame. 'Ladies have first choice.'

'Thank you, kind sir,' Valentina replied. 'But please indulge yourself. I'm taking the deck.'

'I'm doing the same,' Smith added, taking the last swallow of coffee from his canteen cup. 'They apparently built aviators on a small scale in those days.'

'As you wish.' Smyslov started to unroll his sleeping bag into the lower port-side bunk. 'Tell me, Colonel, now we know we do have anthrax to deal with. How do we proceed?'

'Well, I think your people had the right idea; we just take it a step farther. Since we still have full containment, I'd say we simply bring in a demolition team and pack the fuselage with a couple of tons of thermite and white phosphorous. We incinerate the whole damn thing right where it sits.'

'We most definitely do not!' Valentina exclaimed, looking up from the stove.

'Why not?' Smith asked, puzzled. 'If we can just concentrate enough heat rapidly enough around that casing, we should be able to burn every spore before there's any chance for them to spread.'

'Oh, good Lord! The blind who will not see!' She gestured expressively around the compartment. 'Given its superb condition, this plane is a historic treasure! Come spring, if we can get an ice breaker and a helicrane in here, we could lift it off the glacier essentially intact! It could be restored. In fact . . .'

The idea flared behind her eyes, 'In fact, with the components of this crash and the TU-4 that's on static display at the Gagarin Institute, I'll wager we could assemble one complete airworthy aircraft.'

She turned to face Smyslov, suddenly as excited as a schoolgirl with a new bicycle. 'You've been to the Institute! You've seen the Bull they have in the air museum there! What do you think?'

The Russian officer looked up, bemused. 'I really wouldn't know, Professor, but I'm sure it would take a great deal of money.'

'You leave the fund-raising to me, Gregori! I know of a number of wealthy war bird fanatics who would give an arm and a leg to see the *Fifi*, the Commemorative Air Force's Superfortress, doing a joint flyover with a genuine Russian B-29-ski. Champlain alone would be good for at least a quarter of a million!'

Smith couldn't help but be impressed with her vibrant enthusiasm. Valentina Metrace obviously was a cobbler who stuck to her last. He whistled softly and aimed a thumb forward toward the bomb bays. 'I'm afraid we still have certain other priorities here.'

Valentina waved a hand arily. 'Details, details! I don't care what breed of germ we might have to tidy up. No one is casually putting the torch to this aircraft if I have anything to say about it. This is history!'

'That will be for the powers that be to decide, Val,' Smith smiled. 'Not me, I'm very pleased to say.'

Smyslov looked over his shoulder at Smith, his expression intent. 'What do we do next, Colonel?'

'We know the anthrax exists and is still a factor, so reporting that is our priority.' Smith set the empty canteen cup on the deck. 'Tomorrow morning, if we have decent weather, I intend to make one fast sweep around the crash site to look for the survival camp of the Misha's crew. Then we hike for the science station. If we can't make radio contact with the outside from the station, then I'll send Randi back to the cutter in the helicopter to report.'

Smith studied Smyslov's back as the Russian unrolled his

sleeping bag in the crew bunk. 'I'm also going to commit the reinforcement group and secure the island, Major. That's going to mean bringing the Canadians on board, and a general escalation of the whole scenario. I know we promised your government that we'd try and keep this low-key, but now, with both the anthrax and the disappearance of the station staff to contend with, we may have no choice but to go overt.'

'I fully understand, Colonel. There is indeed no choice.'

Smyslov's reply was unexpressive, and Smith had to wonder if the Russian was speaking in agreement with his words or with some thought of his own.

'Ah, me! That's all for tomorrow's worry list,' Valentina said, glancing toward the hatch set in the rear bulkhead. 'In the meantime, there is something else I need to have a look at.'

'Can't it wait until morning?' Smith asked.

She looked toward Smith so the minute tilt of her head and the lift of her eyebrow would be masked from Smyslov. 'It's nothing really. Shan't take a second.'

Catching up a flashlight, she got to her feet and moved aft. Undogging the pressure door, she ducked low through it. Assorted thumps and bangs followed as she worked toward the very tail of the aircraft, followed by a few minutes of involved silence. 'Now, this is interesting,' her voice reverberated with a metallic hollowness. 'Jon, could you please give me a hand back here for a second?'

'On my way.' Smith followed Valentina into the dark of the passage. The historian was crouching on the gangway between the stinger turret's ammunition magazines. With her flashlight aimed at her face, she silently mouthed the words 'Shut the hatch.'

'Damn, Val. Were you raised in a barn! It's even colder out here.' He pulled the pressure door closed and twisted the dogging lever to the locked position. Moving back to the magazines, he sank down on one knee beside Valentina. She was turning a wicked-looking autocannon shell over and over in her gloved fingers.

'What's that?' Smith inquired over the whine of the wind playing around the tail surfaces.

'A Soviet 23mm round. From the tail gun belts,' she replied.

'All right. What's going on?'

'Something odd, Jon. Things aren't adding up, or rather, they're adding up in a very peculiar way. That's why I cut you off up in the cockpit this afternoon.'

'I thought as much,' he replied. 'What are you seeing?'

'This airplane was fully outfitted for combat. In addition to having its anthrax warload aboard, its defensive armament was also fully charged. Furthermore, this plane didn't make an emergency landing here. This was an accidental crash.'

Smith wasn't quite sure of the differentiation. 'Are you sure?'

'Quite. The bomber wasn't configured for an emergency landing when it hit the ice. Remember when I asked about the propeller and fuel mixture controls in the cockpit? They had been left at their cruise settings. Also, I asked about the flap lever. The wing flaps hadn't been lowered, as would have been done for any kind of a deliberate landing.'

Valentina rapped the top of the magazine housing with her knuckles. 'Finally they didn't eject the gun turret ammunition magazines. In a B-29 Superfortress or a TU-4 Bull, that would be a standard procedure in a ditching or emergency landing scenario.'

'Then what the hell did happen?'

'As I said, a freak crash, a total accident,' she continued. 'According to the maps of Wednesday Island, this glacier has a gradual descending gradient toward the north. The bomber must have come in from the north. They also must have been coming in at night, flying low and on instruments because they never knew the island was here. They came in between the peaks, and the terrain rose up underneath the aircraft. Before the pilots realized what was happening they struck the ground, or rather the ice. They must have been traveling at full cruising speed, way too fast for a conventional landing, but as fate would have it, the glacier's surface at that time must have been comparatively smooth, without any ledges or crevasses to trip the aircraft. So they hit flat and skidded cleanly.

'There have been similar crashes in the Arctic and Antarctic,' she continued in her whisper, 'when aircrews have lost situational awareness in whiteout conditions. To put a bottom line on this, this aircraft was not in an emergency state when it went down. They weren't lost, and they weren't landing. They were in a controlled cruise configuration, bound for somewhere else.'

'If that's the case, wouldn't they have seen the island on their charts?' Smith asked.

'You have to remember that in 1953 detailed navigational information on this part of the world was all but nonexistent. The closest thing to an accurate chart was an American military secret. Wednesday Island is also something of a freak. It's one of the highest points within the Queen Elizabeth Archipelago. At that time, whoever plotted this plane's course had no idea that a bloody great mountain would be parked out here in the middle of the Arctic Ocean.'

'It's not all that much of a mountain,' Smith mused. 'We're only about twenty-five hundred feet above sea level here. Wouldn't that be a pretty low cruising altitude for a pressurized aircraft like this one?'

'Very much so,' she agreed. 'In fact, a TU-4 or B-29 would only follow such a low flight profile for one reason: if its crew were worried about being picked up by long-range radar.'

Jon forced himself to play devil's advocate. 'Wouldn't they have seen the island on their own navigational radar?'

'Only if they were using it. What if they were maintaining full EMCON, full emission control, with all of their radio and radar transmitters deliberately shut down to avoid detection?'

If such was conceivable, it seemed to grow colder. 'So what do you think, Professor?' Smith asked.

'I don't know what to think, Colonel,' she replied. 'Or rather, I don't know what I want to think. One thing I am certain of. Tomorrow morning we have got to find the crew of this plane. It might be more important in the greater scheme of things than the anthrax.'

'Do you think this might have something to do with this Russian alternate agenda?'

He saw her nod. 'In all probability. I suspect when we find the survival camp, we'll know.'

'I suspect we'll know about Major Smyslov by then as well,' Smith replied grimly.

Out of the corner of his eye, Smyslov watched Smith disappear into the tail. All evening he had been waiting for the opportunity to act, for a moment when the others were involved or distracted. This might be the best, if not his only chance.

He headed for the crawlway tunnel leading forward, snaking down its length as rapidly and as quietly as he could. He knew exactly what he was to look for and exactly where it should be. He also had the set of fifty-year-old keys in his pocket.

Earlier in the day, when he had been in the cockpit with Smith and Metrace, he hadn't dared to search. He couldn't risk drawing possible attention to the Misha 124's official documentation until he could ascertain its status.

Bellying into the forward compartment, he removed a pocket flash from his parka. Clenching it between his teeth, he sank down on one knee beside the navigator's station and sent the narrow beam stabbing across the map safe below the table. Drawing the key ring, he fumbled with the safe's lock.

This had been a Soviet Air Force bomber, and in the old Soviet Union, maps had been state secrets, denied to all but authorized personnel.

After a moment's resistance the tumblers of the lock turned for the first time in half a century. Smyslov swung open the small, heavy door.

Nothing! The safe was empty. The navigational charts and the targeting templates that were to have been issued to the radar operator were gone.

Wasting no time, he closed and relocked the safe. The bomber's logbook and the aircraft commander's orders would be next. Moving forward to the left-hand pilot's seat, Smyslov thrust the second key into the lock of the pilot's safe located beneath it. Opening it, the Russian groped in the small, flat compartment. Again nothing!

That left the political officer's safe. The most critical of the three. He squeezed in between the pilots' stations to the bombardier's position in the very nose of the aircraft. Here the glass of the unstepped greenhouse had been caved in by the crash, and snow had drifted in and had refrozen. The bombsight itself was gone – it hadn't been needed for this mission – and the rest of the station was buried in caked semi-ice. Drawing his belt knife, Smyslov hacked his way down to the deck-mounted safe.

Damnation! The lock mechanism had been frozen solid. Swearing under his breath, the Russian tore off his gloves. Pulled his lighter from his pocket, he played the little jet of butane flame over the keyhole area. Burning his fingers, he muffled another curse and tried the key again. The stubborn lock yielded grudgingly.

Empty. The targeting photographs and maps. The tasking orders. The political officer's log and contingency instructions and the crew's postmission action plan – all were gone.

Smyslov resecured the safe door, repacking and smoothing the snow over it, trying to erase the signs of his tampering. Standing, he drew his gloves on again, his thoughts racing. It was all gone. All the mission documentation. That was how it was supposed to be. The Misha 124's political officer had been ordered to destroy every last scrap of evidence concerning the bomber's mission and the March Fifth Event.

But the political officer had also been ordered to destroy the aircraft and its payload. The thermite incendiary charges in the bomb bay were proof that he had been in the process of doing so when he had been interrupted. But what about the documents? Had he been prevented from destroying them as well?

And what of the men? Tomorrow Smith would go looking for the bomber's crew. What would be left for him to find?

Smyslov tugged down the zip of his parka and restowed the pen flash. He also removed the cigarette lighter from his shirt pocket. Not the little plastic butane he had purchased at the airport shop in Anchorage, but the other one, the stainless steel Ronson-style reservoir lighter he had brought with him from Russia. Balancing it in his palm, his mind raced through his rapidly shrinking number of options.

He could comfort himself with the thought that much of the decision making had been taken out of his hands. If the Russian Spetznaz troopers had killed the science station's personnel, fate must run its inevitable course. The coming confrontation between the United States and Russia would not be his responsibility.

He need only concern himself with betrayal on a far more personal level. Today he had saved the life of a friend in this strange cold metal room. Tomorrow he might have to kill that friend as an enemy. And the disclaimer that it wasn't his fault rang hollow.

'Hey, Major, you okay up there?' Smith's voice rang up the crawl tube from the aft compartment.

'Yes, Colonel,' Smyslov replied, his fingers tightening around the little silver box. 'I only . . . dropped my cigarette lighter.'

Several hundred feet up the face of East Peak, on a ledge that overlooked both the glacier and the Misha crash site, the wide lens of a powerful spotting scope peered out through a crevice in an artfully camouflaged stone and snow windbreak. Two men lay behind the windbreak, sheltered by an ice-encrusted white tarp spread and supported over their heads. Even with the protection it was searingly cold on the exposed mountainside. Yet the two watchers stolidly endured, the one peering through the night-vision photomultiplier attached to the spotter scope, the other listening intently to the small radio receiver he had been issued.

At regular intervals the two men conducted a survival ritual, their free hands moving between their crotches and armpits and their faces, transferring body warmth to their exposed skin, keeping at bay the vicious, scarring frostbite.

Slithering on his belly like a lizard, a third parka-clad man crawled to join the two behind the windbreak.

'Anything to report, Corporal?'

'Nothing of importance, Lieutenant,' the man at the telescope grunted. 'They have set up their camp inside the wreck. You can see lights through the windows of the rear compartment. Sometimes in the front as well.'

'Let me have a look,' Lieutenant Tomashenko said.

The Spetsnaz corporal rolled aside, making room for his platoon commander, and Tomashenko worked his way behind the night-vision scope, peering into the green and gray world it revealed. The bomber lay on the glacier below the observation post like a stranded whale. The faint wisp of illumination leaking from the downed plane's astrodomes, all but undetectable to the naked eye, was magnified to a bright kelly glow by the photomultiplier. Intermittently the glow would pulse as a figure moved past the bubble windows.

'Apparently the anthrax spores are not loose inside of the airplane,' Tomashenko muttered. 'That is something anyway.'

Tomashenko and his men had not ventured near the downed TU-4, nor had they even set foot on the glacier. The platoon's orders were specific and stringent. Keep the crash site and the investigation team under long-range observation. Conceal their presence on the island. Avoid detection at all cost. Await the issuance of the alpha command by the point agent attached to the American party. Be positioned to intervene instantly on the transmission of said command. Be prepared to withdraw to the submarine should it not be issued.

Tomashenko started to ask the radio monitor if he had heard anything, but caught himself. If the signal had been heard, he would hear. Until that moment they must wait.

CHAPTER TWENTY-NINE

Wednesday Island Station

Randi Russell lay quietly in the darkness. Beyond the partition, in the main room of the bunkhouse, she could hear the heavy slumber breathing of Doctor Trowbridge, the sound she had been waiting for.

An hour before, she and Trowbridge had banked the fire in the bunkhouse and theoretically had turned in for the night. However, in the women's quarters, Randi had only stretched out fully dressed atop Kayla Brown's bunk, refusing sleep. Now, rolling silently to her feet, she began to prepare for the out-of-doors. She squeezed three pairs of socks inside the white thermoplastic 'bunny boots.' Then came the parka and insulated overpants with the Lady Magnum and its speedloaders fitted into the holster pocket. Thin Nomex inner and leather outer gloves were pulled on, along with a white balaclava and finally the snow camouflage.

She worked in total darkness. Before shutting down for the night she had carefully positioned everything she would need and had mentally mapped out every move she would make.

Stepping to where she had left her pack, she removed a small plastic envelope from an outer compartment. Then, slinging her ammunition pouches and submachine gun, she took a folded Hudson's Bay blanket from the sleeping room's upper bunk.

Sliding open the door in the partition, she moved the length of the bunk room to the outside door, navigating unerringly by the faint rectangular lessening of black of the windows and the light brush of a fingertip on a table or countertop, easing each footstep soundlessly onto the floor. Trowbridge was still deeply asleep as she slipped through the snow lock.

Sinking onto her hands and knees, she crawled through the outer door, keeping low in the snow trench beyond the entry. Snaking down the compacted paths, she made her way to the foxhole she had molded for herself covering the bunkhouse. There she constructed her hunting hide.

The heavy Hudson's Bay blanket went beneath her, insulation between her body and the ice. The contents of the plastic envelope went over her. It was a silvered foil survival blanket, incredibly warm for its cellophane-light weight. But unlike the usual blanket of its type, the backing on this one was not high-visibility orange but arctic camo white.

Covering herself with it, Randi merged with her surroundings, making of herself nothing but an unevenness in the snow's surface.

Here, in the lee of the island, the night was almost still. Yet the wind could faintly be heard, roiling and gusting over the sheltering ridgeline. Even with her night-adapted vision, Randi could only make out the slightly variegated shades of darkness around her, the hut's solid shadow geometrics against the slightly grayish black of the snow pack. Gradually, as the minutes and eventual hours passed, she began to note a faint wavering in these shades of night. She puzzled over it for a time, then realized the northern lights must be playing somewhere overhead, a meager hint of their illumination leaking through the cloud cover above the island.

It was cold, a bitter, infiltrating cold that gradually seeped through her armor of blankets and heavy clothing. Still, as silent, patient, and invisible as an arctic fox, Randi waited, breathing as lightly as she could to minimize her breath plume.

Under the survival blanket she cuddled the MP-5 close, not to protect the rugged weapon itself – it had been lubricated with an all-environment synthetic proof against arctic temperatures – but to keep the batteries of the tactical combat light clipped under its barrel warm and energized.

Time crawled past like one of the island's glaciers. Still, she waited. If she was cold, then he was cold, and he would know there would be a warm coal fire and a cozy bed waiting for him inside, with no reason not to claim them.

Finally Randi heard the first ever-so-faint squeaking crunch of a boot step on snow. Her thumb moved half an inch, flipping the fire selector on her primary weapon from 'Safe' to 'Auto.'

An amorphous blob of total blackness moved slowly down the trail from beyond the camp. Gradually it defined itself as the upright form of a man carrying a slender, elongated shape in each hand. Moving with a stalker's care, he approached the bunkhouse entry.

The thumb that had flipped off the MP-5's safety moved to the button on the SMG's handgrip.

The figure paused for a moment outside the snow lock, taking a final protracted look around and missing the faint bumpy irregularity in the snow a few yards away. Then he leaned the elongated object in his right hand against the door frame and transferred the one in his left hand to the right. Using the freed left hand, he reached for the door handle.

Randi heaved aside the thermal blanket and came up onto her knees, the MP-5 lifting to her shoulder. Her thumb pressed the switch of the tactical light, and the narrow, dazzling blue-white beam lashed out, encompassing and paralyzing the man who stood at the bunkhouse door, his ice axe half raised.

'Hello, Mr. Kropodkin,' Randi said, her voice as cold as the barrel of the leveled submachine gun. 'Shall I cut you in two now, or should we wait until later?'

The MP-5 lay on the bunkhouse dining table, its muzzle

aimed at the dark-stubble-bearded youth seated in the wall-side bunk. Randi Russell's hand rested a short grab away from the SMG's trigger. They had both shed their heavy outdoor snow gear, and she had used a set of nylon disposa-cuffs to bind Kropodkin's hands behind his back. Now she stared at the man with ebon-eyed intensity.

'Where did you leave the bodies of the other members of the science team?'

'Bodies?' Kropodkin turned to the third party in the room. 'Dr. Trowbridge, please. I don't know what this mad-woman is talking about! I don't even know who she is!'

'I . . . don't either, really.' Trowbridge blinked uneasily in the glare of the gas lantern, smoothing back his sleep-rumpled fringe of white hair. Still clad only in thermal long johns and socks, he had been jarred awake a few minutes before when Randi had prodded Kropodkin in through the snow lock.

'Don't worry about who I am,' Randi said coldly. 'Don't even worry about standing trial for murder yet. Focus on staying alive long enough to be handed over to the authori-ties. Answering questions is your best chance. Now, who do you report to? Who's coming for the anthrax?'

'Anthrax?' The Slovakian's eyes darted once more to his only potential ally in the room. 'Dr. Trowbridge, please help me! I don't know what is happening here!'

'Please, Ms. Russell. Don't you think we might just be getting ahead of ourselves here?' The academic fumbled his glasses onto his nose.

'I don't think so,' Randi replied flatly. 'This man killed the other members of your expedition in cold blood, the teammates he'd lived and worked with for over six months. He slaughtered them all like sheep, and I'll bet for no better reason than money.'

Kropodkin's jaw dropped. 'The others . . . dead? I do not believe this! No! This is insane! I am no killer! Doctor, tell her! Tell this woman who I am!'

'Please, Ms. Russell!' Trowbridge's voice strengthened in

protest. 'You have no grounds to make such . . . drastic accusations. We have no real proof that anyone has been killed here yet.'

'Yes, we do, Doctor. Last evening I found Kayla Brown's body on the hill below the radio tower. Someone had used an ice axe on her. That one, I suspect.' Randi nodded toward the axe that lay on the table beside the submachine gun, the axe Kropodkin had been carrying. 'I have no doubt DNA testing will prove the point. They'll probably also find blood traces from Professor Gupta and Dr. Hasegawa as well. You took out Creston and Rutherford by other means, didn't you, Kropodkin?'

The graduate student half rose from the bunk, straining at the nylon bands around his wrists. 'I tell you, I have killed no one!'

Randi's hand covered the grip of the MP-5. The muzzle traversed half an inch, indexing in line with Kropodkin's chest. 'Sit down.'

He stiffened and subsided into the bunk.

Trowbridge stood watching the developing tableau, a totally blasted expression on his face. The revelation about Kayla Brown's corpse had been another of those things that shouldn't happen in his existence, another boulder in the accelerating avalanche that was sweeping his life and carefully ordered career into scandal and chaos. His only escape lay in denial. 'You have no proof that any of the expedition members are responsible for any of this,' he protested hoarsely.

'I'm afraid I do.' Leaning back in her chair, Randi caught up the model 12 Winchester Kropodkin had been carrying, the camp's polar bear deterrent. 'This shotgun has a three-round magazine capacity. It's a safe assumption that there were three shells in it when it left this camp.'

She jacked the model 12's pump action repeatedly, but only a single round of magnum-load buckshot ejected to clatter on the tabletop. 'Three shells in the gun when it left the camp, three men with this gun when it left the camp.

220

One of each came back. Do the math.'

'I fired those shells as a signal, Doctor, out on the ice pack! Will you make this woman listen?'

'The boy is right,' Trowbridge protested with growing vehemence. 'At least he has the right to be heard.'

Randi's cold stare never left Kropodkin's face. 'All right. That's fine with me. Let's hear him. Where's he been? What happened to the others?'

'Yes, Stefan,' Trowbridge interjected almost eagerly. 'Tell us what happened.'

'I have been trapped out on the damned pack ice for two nights, and I have been wondering what happened to the others!' He took a deep, shuddering breath, bringing himself under control. 'Dr. Creston, Ian, and I were looking for Professor Gupta and Dr. Hasegawa. We thought maybe they had gone out onto the pack after a specimen or to get around the ice jam along the shore. Somehow, when we went out onto the pack, I became separated from the others. The ice near the island is very broken, with many hummocks and pressure ridges.

'Then the wind shifted and a lead opened in the ice. I was cut off from the island! I couldn't get back to shore. I called for help! I fired shots. Nobody came!' Kropodkin's eyes closed, and his head sank onto his chest. 'I had no food. I have not eaten for two days. No heat. No shelter but the ice. I thought I was going to die out there.'

Randi was unimpressed. She picked the single shotgun shell up from the table. 'The standard firearm distress signal is three shots fired into the air.'

Kropodkin's head snapped up. 'We found signs of a polar bear out there! I kept the one shell for him! I didn't want to be devoured on top of dead!'

'And how did you get back?' Randi kept her words emotionless.

'Tonight the lead in the ice closed. The wind must have changed, and I managed to get back to the shore. Then I came straight back to the camp. All I wanted was to get warm again!'

'That's odd,' Randi said. 'I was out there tonight, too, and the wind seemed to be holding steady from the north, just as it's been all along.'

'Then it must have been the tide, the current, the Holy Virgin – God knows I prayed enough! I don't know! All I know is that when I finally get back to camp, someone pushes a machine gun in my face and accuses me of murdering my friends.' Awkwardly Kropodkin twisted in the bunk, looking to Trowbridge once again. 'Damn it to hell, Doctor! You know me! I have taken classes with you. You were on my selection committee. Are you a party to this insanity as well?'

'I . . .' Trowbridge stammered for an instant; then his sleep-puffy features tightened in resolve. He could not have been so totally wrong. 'No, I am not! Ms. Russell! I must protest. This man has obviously undergone a serious ordeal! Could you at least put off this inquisition until after he's had a chance to rest and have a hot meal?'

Randi's eyes still didn't shift from Kropodkin, and her slight smile held the chill of the polar katabatics. 'That's an excellent idea, Doctor. He should have something to eat.'

Standing, she removed a paratrooper's knife from the slit pocket of her ski pants and thumbed the button that snapped out the hook-shaped shroud cutter. 'Turn him loose, Doctor.' She set the open knife in the center of the table. 'He can fix himself a meal.'

Trowbridge picked up the knife. 'I'll do it for him,' he said, self-righteousness trembling in his voice.

'I said he fixes his own meal, Doctor!' Randi snapped, catching up the MP-5. 'Just cut off the cuffs and don't block my line of fire. Then go to your bunk, put on your pants, and stay out of the way.'

Wordlessly, but red-faced with anger, Trowbridge cut the disposacuffs from Kropodkin's wrists. Keeping the student covered, Randi reclaimed her knife and pulled her chair to the farthest corner of the bunk room. With her back to the wall, she settled down once more, the stock of the MP-5 tucked under her arm, and the barrel leveled.

'Okay, Mr. Kropodkin, you can stand up and fix yourself something to eat now. But don't get funny. It would be a very bad idea.'

The room went quiet beyond the wind moan and the clatter of pans and cutlery. Kropodkin heated a can of stew and a kettle of water on the bunkhouse's primus cooker. Occasionally he cast his eyes in Randi's direction, but every time he found the barrel of the submachine gun tracking him as if guided by radar fire control. Something hovered in the air of the room . . . expectancy, but her glittering jet eyes were totally unreadable and unrevealing.

'May I pick up a knife to cut myself a slice of bread?' he asked with biting politeness.

'If you make a move I don't like, you'll find out about it.'

In the far corner of the bunkroom Trowbridge finished dressing, regaining his pomposity along with his trousers. 'I think, Ms. Russell, that it is time for us to clarify a few things . . .'

'And I think, Doctor, that you had better shut up.'

The academic's voice started to lift. 'I am not accustomed to being spoken to in this manner!'

'You'll get used to it.'

Trowbridge had no choice but to subside.

Kropodkin set his dishes on the mess table and wolfed into his tea, stew, and bread, eating rapidly and glancing between Trowbridge and the woman silently covering him.

Randi let him get half the meal down before she spoke. 'Okay, let's get this finished. Your name is Stefan Kropodkin, you are a Slovakian citizen of Yugoslav descent, and you're attending McGill University on a scholarship and student visa.'

'The doctor must have told you that,' Kropodkin said around a mouthful of bread and margarine.

'He did. He also said you were a top-flight student and a very capable individual. That's how you got the posting to this expedition.' Randi leaned forward in her chair. 'Now, let's get on to what you say. You say you were on a science party with two other members of your expedition, the Professor Gupta and Doctor Hasegawa, when suddenly the two of them disappeared. You came back here and reported their disappearance. Then you went out on the search party with Dr. Creston and Ian Rutherford. You went out onto the pack ice while searching; then Creston and Rutherford vanished as well. You were trapped on the ice by an opening water lead. You just happened to be the man with the shotgun, and you just happened to fire two shots from it.

'You were stuck out there for almost two full nights; then the ice leads closed and you made it back to camp only an hour or so ago. You have no idea what happened to Gupta, Hasegawa, Creston, or Rutherford, and you have no idea who may have killed Kayla Brown here at the camp. Is this essentially your story?'

'Yes, because that is the truth,' Kropodkin replied sullenly, after taking a gulp of tea.

'No, it isn't,' Randi said matter-of-factly. 'You're a liar, and a murderer and probably a number of other unsavory things that we'll find out about.'

She rose slowly out of her chair. 'To begin with, your name isn't Stefan Kropodkin. I'm not sure what it really is, but it doesn't matter. There are other people tearing your fake past apart right now, and they'll find out. They'll also learn about the Middle European "businessmen" who are sponsoring your education. That should prove interesting as well.'

Kropodkin stared at her warily, the tip of his tongue moving along his chapped lips.

'I suspect you came to Canada, the university, and Wednesday Island for reasons other than higher learning,' Randi continued, pacing slowly between the mess table and the cooking counter. 'The collegiate ivory towers might make a convenient hideout for a man on the run. It's the kind of place the police or the security services wouldn't

224

look, granted you kept your nose out of the conventional campus radical groups. As I said, we'll learn more about that later.

'But you still wanted to have a secure mode of communications with your backers while you were laying low, just in case. That's why you brought this with you.'

Randi slipped one hand into the pocket of her ski pants and produced the transparent plastic evidence envelope that contained the mini hard drive. 'I found this where you'd hidden it in the radio shack. The correspondence files on it should be very interesting. I'll also bet you were sloppy enough to leave fingerprints.'

Randi returned the hard drive to her pocket. 'I'll also wager you were curious enough to make a private visit to the Misha 124 crash site. My friends who are up there now will find out about that. Maybe it was pure curiosity, or maybe you caught the scent of something when your expedition was warned away from the wreck. Be that as it may, you went aboard that old plane and you found out what it was carrying. You recognized that the biowarfare agent aboard the bomber would be worth several fortunes to the right parties, and somehow you knew how to contact those right parties.'

Kropodkin had forgotten about his food.

'You told them about the anthrax, and they cut you in on the deal. You were to be their point man on Wednesday. You were designated to eliminate the other members of the expedition, securing access to the anthrax before the arrival of your partners!'

'I deny this!' the Slav exploded.

Randi took a step toward the mess table. 'Deny away, but it is the truth. Your new partners weren't quite in position to make the collection yet, but the expedition's extraction ship and the crash site assessment team were on the way. You had no choice but to start the eliminations! You had to thin down the number of witnesses on Wednesday before the odds got worse!'

Her words flowed, precise, steady, and cold, accusing and then supporting each accusation, a prosecutor closing in for the kill. 'So while you were out there on the ice with Gupta and Hasegawa you murdered them and hid their bodies. Then you came back here with a story about their disappearance. And when the search party set out after them, you made sure you were carrying the only gun on the island. You led Rutherford and Creston out into the middle of nowhere and you blew them away with two of the shells that were in that gun!'

Kropodkin was crushing the chunk of bread in his hand, the crumbs and margarine squeezing out between his fingers.

'Then you came back here for Kayla Brown, and when you scoped out the camp you found her in the lab building sitting beside a live radio, talking with the *Haley*. A complication. You had to disable the radio first so she couldn't say anything she shouldn't. But you managed that and then you went in after her and you took her up on that hill and you bashed her brains out with your ice axe.'

Randi tapped the tabletop with the muzzle of the MP-5. 'Then you came back to the bunkhouse and you sat down at this table and fixed yourself a sandwich. Corned beef, plenty of mustard.

'But your snack was interrupted by the arrival of our helicopter, and you had to take off. You've been out there all afternoon, keeping an eye on us. You watched my friends leave for the crash site and you watched us turn in for the night. Then you crawled out of your hole and you came down to this hut with the intent of axing Dr. Trowbridge and me to death in our beds.'

Trowbridge stared at Kropodkin as if he had suddenly sprouted horns. 'You have no proof!' Trowbridge croaked weakly, not wanting to hear any more. He could not have been so wrong. He could not have sat across a desk from such a monster.

'Oh, I have proof, Doctor,' Randi replied so softly that

both men had to keep silent to hear her. 'For one, let's consider the state the laboratory hut and radio room were in when we found them. Totally undamaged. There was no sign of a struggle. No resistance at all. Then let's consider the state of Kayla Brown's body. She was fully dressed in all her cold weather clothing. She had been allowed to gear up and leave that hut under controlled circumstances when she started up that hill. There was no indication of haste, of flight. No indication of panic. In short, she was not frightened.'

Randi glanced at Trowbridge. 'You were in the radio shack aboard the cutter that last night, Doctor. We were talking with one very nervous and upset young woman. She knew something was very wrong on this island. I doubt she would have left the lab hut on her own, and I very much doubt she would have left so casually with a stranger. I suspect she was with someone she knew and trusted. Someone she saw as a friend. Him.'

The MP-5 barrel gestured toward Kropodkin.

'No,' the Slovakian gritted.

Randi moved to the edge of the mess table, immediately across from Kropodkin. 'Then we come to his story about being stuck out on that ice flow. It's a total fabrication. He wasn't starving for two nights running. He was forted up somewhere, chewing on the emergency rations from the survival pack the rescue party had taken with them.'

'How can you possibly know?' Dr. Trowbridge whispered, intrigued in spite of himself.

'His atrocious table manners,' Randi replied. 'Have you ever had to go hungry, Doctor? Really hungry? Several days worth of hungry in a hostile environment? I have, on several occasions. When you finally get a chance at a meal, you don't bolt your food like this gentleman did. You don't eat like you're just hungry. You eat like food is the most wonderful experience in the world. You eat slowly, getting the most out of each mouthful. Personal experience.

'And while we're on the subject of food . . .' Randi leaned

227

forward across the table. 'When we came into this hut, we found the half-eaten meal Mr. Kropodkin had left on the table. That corned beef sandwich and tea, hot tea.'

Hate glittered in the look Kropodkin aimed up at her. 'It was not mine!' he spat.

'Oh, yes, it was.' Randi's voice was almost hypnotic. 'There was something a little bit different about the way that tea had been served. You see, it was in a glass. Now, we had a group of Anglo-Saxons, a couple of Asians, and one Slav on this island. When someone of Anglo-Saxon or Asian cultural descent makes hot tea, he or she drinks it from a cup or a mug, automatically, as a cultural norm. Only an Arab or a Slav would drink hot tea from a glass . . .' The barrel of the submachine gun swung across the table and lightly tapped the rim of the steaming glass at Kropodkin's side, producing a clear ringing *ting*. 'And there aren't any Arabs on this island.'

Kropodkin grabbed for the inviting gun barrel. Randi, who had been expecting and waiting for the desperation move, yanked the submachine gun back, then smashed the muzzle full into Kropodkin's face, hurling him backward off the bench.

Screaming a curse, Kropodkin scrambled to his feet, but Randi had already rolled over the tabletop, confronting him before he could recover. To a flabbergasted Dr. Trowbridge, she moved in a golden-haired blur. Three blows were landed with the submachine gun within two seconds; a two-handed horizontal strike across the forehead with the receiver, another savage punch in the groin with the muzzle, and a final butt stroke across the back of the neck as Kropodkin folded over in agony. Randi was careful to pull the finishing blow so it would not quite fracture the spine.

Kropodkin dropped like a dynamited bridge.

Dropping to her knees beside the Slovakian, Randi first checked his breathing, then yanked his arms behind his back, applying a fresh set of disposacuffs.

'Help me get him back onto the bunk, please, Doctor.'

Trowbridge just stared down at her and at the graduate student, sprawled bloody-faced on the floor.

'I can't believe it,' he mumbled. 'I can't believe that anyone could kill so many people so casually.'

'There are more of them around than you might expect, Doctor.' Randi rubbed her eyes, suddenly very tired. 'You've been sitting in a room with two of them.'

CHAPTER THIRTY

The Misha Crash Site

Gradually Jon Smith became aware of dawn growing beyond the overhead astrodome. He also became aware of an imbalance in the warmth surrounding him, a comfortable emphasis favoring his left side. Then came a very definite snuggle.

The congealed frost of his breath rasped on the cover of his Jaeger sleeping bag as Smith lifted his head to look around the radar-observer cabin. A second occupied Jaeger bag was nestled firmly against his. Valentina Metrace, in her catlike connoisseurship of comfort, had burrowed close in the night.

Smith couldn't help but cock an eyebrow. Randi had been right. Where there was a will, there was most certainly a way.

Female companionship had not been a major factor in Smith's life for some time. At first, in the direct aftermath of Sophia's death, the concept had been too painful, too much a breaking of a faith. Then, afterward, emotional relationships had seemed an added complication in an already overly complex life. But now this particular female seemed to be making it clear in a hundred subtle and not so subtle ways that she intended to make herself a factor.

Exactly why was beyond Smith's comprehension. He had always viewed himself as a fairly prosaic individual. Any romance that might cling to him was only a reflection of his careers, and likely a misunderstood one at that. He had always felt very fortunate to have gained the love of one beautiful and intelligent woman. To have this second bold, enigmatic and decidedly attractive female move deliberately into his orbit was an unexpected phenomenon.

He felt Valentina's head lift, and she shook free of her sleeping bag's hood and face flap, peering into his face from a range of a few inches. 'I would cheerfully and without a moment's hesitation kill,' she murmured, 'for a long, hot soak in a bathtub, and a change of lingerie.'

'I could loan you a spare disinfectant towelette,' he replied.

'Your counteroffers are growing steadily more pathetic, but I suppose I'm stuck with it.'

She rested her head on his shoulder, and for a few moments they lay together in the bizarre little pocket of intimacy they had found on the ice-slickened deck of the ancient bomber. The wind outside had subsided to only the faintest intermittent whisper. In the crew's cabin aft, they could hear Gregori Smyslov snoring softly in his bunk.

The night before, Smith had been careful in the way he had arranged their gear to make sleeping room on the deck. He'd propped his loaded packframe in the hatchway between the compartments, stacking his snowshoes atop them, rendering a silent access to the radar-observer space impossible. The necessity of that action and the angular feel of his sidearm under the wadded bulk of his parka pillow pushed his momentary nonprofessional musing about Valentina Metrace into abeyance.

'What is it, Val?' he said under his breath. 'What are the Russians hiding? You have some ideas, don't you?'

She hesitated; then he felt the shake of her head, her soft hair brushing his chin. 'Not that I'm prepared to say, Jon. The historian in me is appalled by the concept of providing poor history, and the spy, of giving poor intelligence. But we've got to find the survival camp. If there are any absolute answers to be found, we'll find them there.'

'I can understand that. But that's only one set of answers. The Russians are only one factor of what I'm coming to see as a three-point equation. The other two points are who is on the island now and who may be coming for the anthrax. I left Randi hanging back there as bait for whoever may be here now.'

'Shouldn't worry, Jon. Anyone who endeavors to gulp down our Ms. Russell is going to find himself gagging on her . . . and I mean that in the best of possible connotations.'

'I know. She can take care of herself.'

'But you'll still blame yourself if anything happens to her. As you still do for the deaths of her sister and her fiancé.'

Smith scowled down at the top of her head. 'How the hell did you know about that?'

'Randi and I discussed you rather intensively one evening,' Valentina replied. 'A species of girl talk. I've also studied you for a bit, and I've come to certain conclusions of my own. You're one of those poor bastards stuck in the middle – tough enough to make the blood decisions, but with enough humanity left for it to gnaw at you. It's a difficult balance to maintain. That makes you rare and worth keeping. That's why, in due course, we're going to become lovers.'

Smith couldn't prevent the soft bark of laughter that escaped him. He had wondered, and he had been given an answer. 'I see. Don't I have any say in the matter?'

Valentina nestled contentedly again, tucking her head in under his chin. 'No, not really. Don't bother yourself about it now, Jon. I'll handle all the details.'

She had to be joking in her usual quirky manner. But there was something about the calm woman's surety in her voice that didn't seem to apply to that scenario. He couldn't help but recall the last lingering warmth of her lips on his yesterday, and he had a sudden urge to experience that warmth again.

Then the muzzy grumble and stirring of Major Smyslov in the next compartment broke the fragile bubble and returned them to the bleak reality of Wednesday Island.

It was a pale gray world atop the saddleback glacier. The

dully luminous cloud cover hid the tops of the peaks and faded the horizons to the north and south into a vague nonvisibility. The surface snow and ice had been infected by the grayness as well, losing their luster. Only the dark exposed rock of the mountain flanks stood out, extruding from the dingy-paper whiteness with an exaggerated three-dimensionality. The immediate visibility around the downed bomber and the three human flyspecks standing beside it was good, yet it was difficult to truly see. Amid the blanched contrasts it was hard to gauge sizes and distances, and something akin to vertigo intermittently tugged at the consciousness.

Jon Smith felt the effect as he panned his binoculars in their instinctive slow circle, seeing nothing either desired or unwanted.

'All right, lady and gentleman, where are they?' he asked. 'Where did they go after the crash?'

'I would say down the coast, Colonel,' Smyslov replied swiftly. 'They would need food, and there is nothing to be had here. Along the coast there would be seals and bears. There would also be better opportunities for shelter. The weather up here on the glacier would be too bad.'

Valentina shook her hooded head. 'No, I disagree, Gregori. They made their survival camp up here, probably within sight of this aircraft.'

'If they did, it's pretty well hidden.' Smith returned his binoculars to their case. 'And the major makes a pretty good case about the food. What brings you to your conclusion, Val?'

'A number of things,' she replied. 'For one, the stripped state of the aircraft. It would take a lot of work and a lot of trips to move all of that material out of the wreck. They wouldn't have carried it far. For another, they wouldn't be immediately concerned about food. They would have had emergency rations for at least a couple of weeks, and they weren't planning to stay around for that long.'

'Would they have had much choice?'

'They thought so, Jon. These people were not planning on setting up housekeeping. They intended to go home. Remember how they pulled the radio and radar systems out of the plane, as well as the auxiliary power unit? They had all of the components and expertise they needed to build one hellaciously powerful radio transmitter, one that could reach halfway around the world, and certainly back to Russia. That's another reason they'd want to stay up here. The higher elevation would increase their broadcast and reception range.'

'Then why didn't they use it?' Smith asked.

'I don't know.' Smith could feel the words the historian didn't want to speak aloud. He turned toward Smyslov. 'What do you think, Major?'

The Russian shook his head. 'I must disagree, Colonel. If they had built such a radio, they would have called for rescue. Obviously they did not.'

Whoever had chosen Gregori Smyslov had made one critical error with the man. He could lie well with his mouth, but not with his eyes or body language. The Russian's words only emphasized a subtle change that had crept into the team's dynamics overnight. Once more it had become an us-versus-them scenario, with Smyslov standing alone.

And yet, Smith pondered, if it was an us-versus-them, why hadn't Smyslov simply allowed him to suffocate in the bomb bay the previous afternoon? He'd had a blank check to kill.

'We've got to find out which one of you is right, and fast,' Smith continued. 'We know the anthrax is in the wreck. We know that someone else positively knows about it. We must assume these individuals are en route to collect it. Given that the hostiles have gone active on the island, we must also assume that we may have only hours before their main body arrives.'

Smyslov spoke up sharply. 'Colonel, given the situation, should not we immediately return to the base camp? Our priority must be to resume contact with our superiors.'

There could be no doubt about it. Smyslov wanted not to find that survival camp as urgently as Valentina wanted to locate it, and probably for the same reason.

'A valid point, Major, but we will still make a sweep up here for the aircrew's survival camp.' Smith extended his hand and swept it from north to south, covering the eastern edge of the glacier. 'Granted that Professor Metrace is correct, the crew's best bet for finding shelter should be along there, the base of East Peak.'

'The camp may have been well drifted over during the last fifty years,' Valentina added, slinging the model 70 over her shoulder. 'So I'd suggest watching for shapes, especially straight linear ones, under the surface of the snow.'

'Got it. Any other questions? Okay, let's move out.' Smith kept his own rifle cradled in his arms as they started the trudge across the ice.

Smith worked to the north, angling across the saddleback to the point where the glacier broke into a wicked blocky tumble of shattered ice, a miniature Beardmore that slumped down the front face of the island to the narrow coastal strip. From that point, according to the plan, they swept back across the gap. Advancing line abreast at twenty-yard intervals, they scouted the broken stone and ice interface along the base of the eastern peak.

Valentina kept to the inside slot, ranging along the bottom of the slope with the eager intensity of a hunting bird dog. Smith took the center point in the line while Smyslov stayed on the outer flank. In addition to watching the glacial surface, Smith found himself covering Val as she worked and eyeing the mountain slopes above for a variety of potential threats: snow cornices, avalanche chutes, and the possibility of camouflaged observers.

He also found himself intermittently watching Gregori Smyslov out of the corner of his eye. Was the Russian looking for something else beyond the remains of the lost aircrew? Who was he waiting for, and what would be the key that would trigger him into action? And what would that action be?

They passed the crash site and climbed the last hundred gently sloping yards to the central ridge of the saddleback. Smith paused for a moment in his trudging advance to survey the greater world.

The sea smoke was closing in around Wednesday once more, the mists lapping at the island's flanks, killing the horizons and enhancing the unworldly sense of isolation. For a moment the saddleback was a literal island in the sky, sandwiched in a layer of clarity between the fog and the overcast. How long it would last was questionable.

It didn't really matter. Soon they must break off the search and head back for the station. And maybe just as well. If Val was right, locating the camp of the downed aircrew might be the activation point of the Russian alternate agenda. Maybe it would be wiser to eat this apple one bite at a time, keeping Smyslov as an ally. Deal with the anthrax question first; then force the confrontation.

Smith turned and then stumbled as his right crampon snagged momentarily. Automatically he glanced down at the obstruction.

The spiked toe of his arctic boot had kicked up and exposed a short length of wire, its black insulation crumbling with age and cold.

Smith hesitated for one moment more. It would be easy enough to scrape a boot edge of snow over it and just keep going. But then, not knowing had been at the heart of this crisis from the beginning. Deliberately courting ignorance now simply didn't make sense. Smith shifted his rifle to his left hand and lifted the right over his head, the fist clinched in the rally signal.

'It's Soviet,' Smyslov confirmed, kneeling beside the exposed wire. 'A trailing antenna. The kind that could be streamed behind an aircraft for long-range communications.'

'Laying an insulated aerial across the ice has been a communications expedient used in polar environments before,' Valentina confirmed.

'But where is the radio set?' Smyslov asked, getting back to his feet. 'Where is the camp? There is nothing, only the wire.'

'The easiest way to resolve that question is to follow it.' Smith pointed toward the base of the east peak. 'Thataway.'

The antenna had melted into the frozen surface like a thread across an ice cube, but the incessant scouring of the winds had kept it buried only a few inches deep. Exposing the antenna as they went, they found that it swept in a shallow curve, having drifted with the flow of the glacier. At one point stress had snapped the thin wire, but the broken end was located only a few feet away. Surprisingly it led toward an almost sheer blank-faced wall of basalt rock, vanishing into the shoulder-high drift of hard-packed snow at its base.

'What the hell?'

Undaunted, Valentina Metrace unslung her pack and rifle and drew her belt knife. Dropping to her knees, she began to tunnel into the drift like an industrious badger. After a moment Smith and Smyslov joined her.

It swiftly became apparent that the drifted snow was packed into an overhang in the black rock, a groove rasped into the side of the mountain by the incessant sawing drag of the glacier. And then Smith noticed the texture of the snow changing. It was growing more solid, and it was as if a pattern had been worked into it.

'These are snow blocks!' Valentina exclaimed.

It was true. Someone had used building blocks of compacted snow, igloolike, to build a wall within the overhang. Over the decades, the blocks had cold-welded together into a solid glassy mass that resisted the stabbing knife blades, but their resistance couldn't prevent them from eventually yielding.

'Canvas! This is it! It's a cave!'

The snow wall and the ancient canvas windscreen behind it collapsed into darkness. And the icy dankness of long unstirred air flowed out.

Smith retrieved the big electric lantern from his pack and played the beam into the mouth of the cavern. The tunnel was perhaps six feet wide and low enough so that even Valentina would be forced to stoop to enter. Small, jagged stalactites of black rock studded the cave roof.

'A lava tube,' Smith commented.

'To be expected on a volcanic island,' Valentina agreed. 'Look, on the floor.'

The antenna wire and what looked like a hose extended from beneath the small avalanche of snow and ice they had created, to loop around a bend in the tunnel perhaps ten feet ahead.

'This must be it,' Valentina repeated. Hunching down, she started along the tunnel.

'Just a second.' Smith passed the historian her rifle, then caught up his own SR-25. 'Let's get the gear inside and out of sight, just in case.'

'I will take care of it, Colonel,' Smyslov spoke up.

'All right, we'll wait for you if we find anything interesting.' Smith removed a couple of hand flares from his pack and moved into the cave after Valentina.

Smyslov lugged the packs inside the cave, then paused for a moment outside its mouth, taking a last long look around.

The others, the members of the Spetsnaz covering force, were here. He had seen no sign of their presence, but that wasn't surprising. The men chosen for this task would be snow devils, invisible in this white world, leaving no hint of their presence or passage.

But they were present. He could feel them. They had been ordered to keep the crash site and its environs under strict observation. They would be watching him now, waiting for the one order Smyslov was authorized to give. The one command that would bring them in to kill.

If only the bloody political officer had done his bloody job!

Maybe then this all could be mended somehow. Maybe then he could regain control of the situation and stop any further escalation. But he must also be prepared to invoke the alternative. He must be ready to perform his duty.

Smyslov unzipped his parka and moved the stainless steel cigarette lighter to an outside pocket. Then he pulled the Velcro retaining tab on his belt holster and drew the model 92 Beretta he had been issued by the Americans. Ignoring the irony of readying a weapon for use against its owners, he checked the clip seating with a pop of his palm against the bottom of the handgrip. Drawing back the slide, he manually jacked a shell into the pistol's chamber.

Snapping off the safety, he returned the Beretta to its holster. Soon he would know if he would need it.

'Quite the setup,' Valentina murmured.

Around the bend in the tunnel they had found the auxiliary power unit that had been taken from the bomber. The length of hose led from the mouth of the cave to the exhaust outlet of the engine. Just beyond the generator set and connected to it via a set of batteries and power leads was a patched-together but impressive-looking radio rig.

The ever-present frost covered its exposed banks of old-fashioned vacuum tubes and control dials. Tools and unused electronics components were stacked around the set, and a transmitter key lay on a scrap-wood table positioned in front of the set, along with a set of earphones removed by an operator half a century before.

'I knew it,' she went on in a whisper. 'I knew it the minute I saw the stripped chassis in the bomber!'

The duralumin radio operator's stool had been taken from the plane, and Valentina sank onto it. Her hands lifted, but she acted as if she were afraid to touch anything. 'There's a pencil here, Jon. There's a pencil but no paper. This is a communications desk. There should be paper! A log, notes, something!'

Smith panned the wide beam of the lantern around the gut of the passage. 'Wait a minute . . .' The light fell on a blackened bucket set against the rocky wall. 'Here we go.'

He took up the bucket by its bail and set it beside the stool.

'What is it?' Valentina asked, looking down.

'It's a fire can,' Smith replied, hunkering beside the bucket. 'It's been half-filled with crushed pumice. It acts like a wick, like sand. Slosh a little gasoline in there and light it, and you'd have a steady flame for heat and cooking.'

Valentina nodded. 'And they would have a few thousand gallons of aviation fuel lying about.'

'But something else has been burned in this one.' Smith drew his knife and probed amid the charred rock. 'See that? That's paper ash, a lot of it. I'll bet that's your radio log and maybe a set of code books, too.'

'Somebody cleaned house.'

In the lantern light their eyes met, and they communicated without words for a moment. There was no reason that this radio set shouldn't have worked. There was no reason for this castaway aircrew not to have communicated with the world. There was no reason they shouldn't have summoned help.

Gregori Smyslov shuffled around the corner of the tunnel from the outside, snapping on his own flashlight. 'All is secure, Colonel.'

Smith kept his face poker-neutral. 'Okay, let's keep going.'

He turned and continued down the tunnel. A few yards farther on, the lava tube they were in broke through into a second larger, lower chamber. Slabs of basalt had been crudely aligned to create a set of uneven steps down a jagged collapsed facing. The porous black volcanic rock simply drank up the flashlight beams, and the darkness continued to predominate. It was not until Smith and his team had made the cautious descent to the floor of the chamber that they realized they were not alone.

Smith heard Valentina gasp from close by at his side, and Smyslov swore under his breath in Russian. The lantern beam panned across scattered items of survival gear, the bits of random trash produced around a lived-in camp, and finally, against the rear cavern wall, a row of huddled unmoving forms in canvas-skinned sleeping bags.

Their search for the crew of the Misha 124 was over.

Smith took one of the flares from his parka pocket and struck the igniter. Brilliant red chemical flame spewed from it, pushing back the darkness. He shoved the base of the flare into a crack in the wall.

'I wonder what got them in the end?' Valentina spoke softly, almost to herself.

'I don't think it was the cold,' Smith replied. 'They seemed pretty well set up for that.'

The sleeping bags were heavy arctic issue, and they were well insulated from the cavern floor by heavy pads of seat cushioning, life raft fabric, and parachute silk, all the materials that had been stripped from the downed aircraft. There were also several fire buckets positioned around the floor of the house-sized cavern, and a couple of gasoline jerry cans had been cached in one corner. It was obvious the bomber's crew had known their polar survival procedures.

'It wasn't starvation, either.' Valentina stepped up beside the first of the bodies and pointed to an open tin of survival ration crackers and a half bar of chocolate balanced on a small ledge in the cavern wall.

The historian glanced at the body at her feet and frowned. 'Jon, come here. Look at this.'

Smith stepped to her side and instantly spotted the point of concern.

Before going to sleep fifty-odd years before, the sleeping bag's occupant had drawn a flap of parachute silk over his face as a frost shield. A small circular hole was punched neatly in the center of that fabric.

Smith leaned his rifle against the cave wall and sank to one knee, flipping back the ice-crinkly silk. Revealed was a pleasant-featured young man's face, pale, sleep-peaceful, frozen in time. The eyes were closed, and in the center of the forehead was another small circular hole, smeared with a few drops of blood, made red once more by the flickering light of the flare.

'Well, now,' Smith murmured. 'A handgun, medium caliber, low velocity. Fired at close range, but not point-blank. No powder burns.'

'7.65mm subsonic, I'll wager,' Valentina agreed, bending down with her hands braced on her knees, 'probably fired through a silencer.'

'Probably.' Smith rose and circled to the next body. 'The same here. One shot, through the temple. Execution style.'

'Very much so,' Valentina agreed, walking slowly down the row of bedrolls. 'They were asleep, and someone just walked down the line and took the crew out, one after another . . . but not all of them.'

'Why do you say that, Val?'

'There are only six men here, Jon. The minimum complement for an America bomber would be eight.' She played the beam of her flashlight back into the shadowed corners of the cavern, beyond the pool of flare light. 'There will be at least two others . . . Ah, here we are.'

She stepped deeper into the cavern, making her way around several table-sized chunks of fallen basalt. Smith went after her. Neither of them noted Gregori Smyslov silently falling back toward the lava tube entrance.

A man clad in khaki-colored duffel pants and parka lay on the black rock floor of the lava tube. The front of his coat was black with blood and punctured by multiple bullet holes. Curled in a frozen death writhe, the dead man's lips were drawn back from his teeth in a half-century-old snarl. A few inches from his outstretched hand lay a small automatic pistol with the long cylinder of a silencer screwed to its barrel.

Smith lifted the lantern beam beyond the seventh man and found the eighth.

There was a niche in the back wall of the cave. Within it were two bedrolls, one of which was empty. An older aviation officer lay on his back, half out of the second sleeping bag, a hand-sized patch of blood frozen in place in the middle of his chest. A Soviet-issue Tokarev service pistol was still clutched in his fist.

His killer had apparently learned too late that a man with a bullet through his heart can still have fourteen seconds of life and consciousness left to him.

Valentina made her way to the seventh man. Bending down, she undid the top button of his parka and examined the insignia on the flight suit collar underneath. 'The bombardier and political officer.'

Straightening, she crossed to the eighth man and repeated her examination. 'The aircraft commander.'

'Apparently there was a falling-out among the upper echelons.'

'Apparently.' She looked back at Smith. 'It seems pretty straightforward. They'd turned in for the night, and the political officer either had the watch or he got up again after the others had fallen asleep. He walked down the line and methodically murdered his fellow crewmen. Then he came back here to kill the aircraft commander. The problem was that a silencer's effectiveness degrades with every bullet you put through it, and that last round must have made a wee bit too much noise.'

'But, damn it, Val, why?'

'Orders, Jon. It had to be under orders, given to the one member of the crew fanatically dedicated enough to the will of the Communist Party to commit both mass murder and suicide.'

Smith's brows shot up. 'Suicide?'

'Um-hum,' the historian nodded. 'I'm reasonably certain that his orders included using the last round in the clip on himself. I daresay he didn't have a great deal of choice in the matter, because it's apparent nobody was coming after them. I suspect that another aspect of his program was to torch the wreck, and probably this material along with it.'

She extended the toe of her boot and tapped a canvas-covered aircraft log and a stack of heavy buckram envelopes that lay beside the bomber commander's bedroll, some of them still bearing Soviet Air Force security seals over their flaps. 'Oh, but I wish I could read Russian.'

'Randi can,' Smith replied, shaking his head. 'But ordering one of your own aircrews slaughtered like this? That doesn't make any sense!'

'It doesn't make sense to you, Jon, and it doesn't make sense to me, but it made sense to the Stalinists. Remember the KGB barrage battalions that would follow Soviet Army units into battle. Their mission tasking wasn't to shoot at the enemy, but at any Soviet soldiers reluctant to die for the glory of the Workers' Revolution. If it was a matter of state security they wouldn't have even blinked.'

'But what the hell were they trying to hide?'

'Speaking frankly, I've been scared to think about it . . . Hello, what have we here?'

She knelt down and picked up something from beside the logbook. Smith saw that it was a man's wallet. With her flashlight tucked awkwardly between her cheek and shoulder, Valentina started to leaf through it. Suddenly she stiffened, the flashlight slipping away to bounce on the cavern floor. 'My dear God!'

Smith hastily stepped up beside her. 'Val, what is it?'

Wordlessly she thrust the wallet into his hands. Balancing the lantern on a boulder top, Smith sank down on one knee and examined its contents.

Money, American money: half a dozen twenties, two fives, and a ten. Worn, well-used bills. A driver's license, Michigan 1952, issued to an Oscar Olson. A Marquette city library card and a social security card both made out to the same name. A pair of ticket stubs to the AirView Drive-in Theater. A cash register slip for eighty-seven cents from Bromberg's corner grocery.

'Val, what does this mean? . . . Val?'

The historian was standing beside him, a blank, totally stunned expression on her face. Suddenly, without speaking, she dropped to her knees beside the body of the aircraft commander, tearing at the front of the long-dead man's flight suit. Buttons popped as she ripped it open, revealing a black and red checked lumberjack shirt. She clawed furiously at the collar, fighting the resistance of the stiffly frozen corpse. Cloth tore, and she produced the maker's tag from the back of the neck.

'Montgomery Ward!' She almost threw the tag at Smith. Then she scrambled across the cavern floor and was at the body of the Misha's political officer, forcing open his parka and flight suit, revealing a civilian suit jacket layered beneath it.

'Sears and Roebuck,' she whispered. 'Sears . . . and . . . bloody . . . Roebuck!' Her voice rose to a strangled scream. 'Smyslov, you son of a bitch! Where are you?'

'I am here, Professor.'

Smith stood up and turned at the quiet voice, and then he froze. Smyslov had come in behind them. He stood outlined in the glare of the flare Smith had left in the main part of the chamber, the ruddy light reflecting off the leveled Beretta automatic in his hand. 'Put up your hands. Both of you. Please do not attempt anything. Other Russian troops will be here shortly.'

'What the hell is this, Major?' Smith demanded, slowly lifting his hands shoulder high.

'A very regrettable situation, Colonel. If you do not resist, you will not be harmed.'

'That's a lie, Jon,' Valentina said calmly, coming to stand beside Smith, her voice and anger back under control. 'The Russians' alternate agenda is now fully in play. They can't allow us to leave this cave alive.'

The Beretta's barrel jerked in her direction. 'That's not . . . Something can be worked out . . . alternatives . . .' Smyslov gritted the words through clenched teeth.

'There are none.' Valentina's words were understanding, almost kindly. 'You know that. The Misha's political officer made a cock-up of his job. There was too much left for us to find, and you couldn't stop us from finding it. I *know*, Gregori, and, given a reference book or two, Colonel Smith could figure it out. We have to die, just like these other poor bastards in this cave had to die. There's no other way to keep the secret.'

Smyslov didn't reply.

'Since I can't figure it out, how about letting me in on it now?' Smith asked, his eyes fixed on the shadowed features of the Russian.

'Why not indeed?' Valentina replied. 'It all leads back to the attack doctrines of the Soviet Long Range Aviation Forces during the early Cold War . . .'

The gun muzzle elevated. 'Keep silent, Professor!'

'There's no sense in letting the colonel die in ignorance, Gregori.' Valentina's tone was almost bantering but with a biting edge to it. 'After all, you're going to be putting a bullet through his brain here presently.'

She glanced across at Smith. 'Remember, Jon, when I told you how all of the American bomber missions must, perforce, be one-way? The TU-4 Bull just barely had the range to reach targets in the northern states by flying over the Pole, but they didn't have the fuel to get back again. The aircrews would have to bail out over the United States after dropping their bomb loads.

'With this as a given, the Soviets decided it was a matter of waste not, want not. The America bomber crews received special training. They were taught how to speak idiomatic American English. They were cycled through the KGB's American town mock-up to adapt them to the nuances of the Western lifestyle, and they were instructed in espionage and sabotage techniques.

'It was intended that the surviving Soviet aircrewmen would merge with the masses of refugees that would be produced in the aftermath of a massive ABC attack on the

United States. Once in place, they would spy, spread defeatist propaganda, and conduct sabotage, hastening the day of the theoretical Soviet triumph. Do I have that down properly, Gregori?'

Again there was no reply.

'And the wallet, the civilian clothes?' Smith prompted.

'All part of it, Jon. The KGB were meticulous about such details. The crews would be issued American-manufactured clothing purchased in the United States, real American currency, and superbly forged identification, complete down to the inconsequential little bits and pieces a person would routinely carry in a wallet or a pocket.

'But there was one problem.' Valentina's voice flowed on, almost hypnotically. 'The raving paranoia that raged inside Stalinist Russia. The party and high presidium knew that a fair proportion of their populace, including members of their most elite military formations, desired nothing more out of life than a suit of civilian clothes, a set of documents identifying them as anything other than a Soviet citizen, and a clean run at an unguarded border.

'While the Soviets might have loaded a live bioagent aboard a long-range bomber for a simple training mission, they would never have given the flight crew their American identity kits. The potential for defection would have been viewed as too great.'

Valentina's hand stabbed at the wallet still held in Smith's hand. 'The clothing and identification would only have been issued for an actual combat operation. The real thing!'

Smith found himself staring at the wallet in his hand. 'Are you saying what I think you are, Val?'

'Oh, I am, Jon.' Her voice began to lift, growing more piercing. 'This is why the Russians were so bloody shaken over the discovery of that old bomber. That's why their official schizophrenia is over the whole subject. The damn anthrax has been a secondary concern for them all along. What they've really been worried about is our learning the truth! That the Misha 124 was a pathfinder aircraft for an all-out strategic bombing attack on the United States using nuclear, biological, and chemical weapons! The Pearl Harbor of World War Three!'

She let the words hang in the chill air of the cavern for a moment; then she tilted her head and addressed Smyslov directly. 'How about it, Gregori? I dare you to tell me I'm wrong.'

They could hear Smyslov's breath rasp, the mist it produced swirling around his head in the back glow of the flare. 'Nations make mistakes, Professor. Yours has made its mistakes. We have made ours, greater perhaps than some. Can you blame us for trying to hide the fact that we almost destroyed the world?'

'You're making another mistake now, Major,' Smith said. 'Killing us won't make things any better.'

'Please, Colonel.' There was an earnestness in Smyslov's reply. 'I give you my word! I will communicate with my superiors. I will make every effort to protect you and Professor Metrace and Miss Russell. I will get the orders changed! We will find . . . some other way!'

'You'll reopen a gulag just for us?' Smith smiled and shook his head. 'No, I don't think so.' He lowered his hands and tucked the wallet into a parka pocket. 'Put down the gun, Major. This thing is over. We've learned what we've come for.'

The barrel lifted, ominously steadying on Smith's chest. 'Don't force me to act, Colonel. I may regret the situation, but I am still a Russian officer.'

'And that's an American firearm, issued to you by us. Believe me, Major, it's not going to do you any good.'

A hint of amusement crept into Smyslov's voice. 'I trust you are not going to attempt anything as puerile as telling me you have removed the firing pin.'

'Oh, no,' Valentina said, dropping her own hands. 'You might have spotted a missing firing pin. But the Beretta 92-series automatic pistol does have an internal bar lock safety intended to prevent the accidental discharge of the weapon.

If you diddle with it a bit, it can be made to prevent deliberate discharges as well. And yes, Gregori, in addition to my myriad other gifts, talents, and charms, I am a rather capable gunsmith.'

Smyslov made the only sane and sensible reply a man in his position could make. The hammer of the leveled Beretta fell at the pull of its trigger – a flat, futile snap that echoed lightly in the cavern. 'So I see, Professor.'

'It wasn't a matter of trust, Major.' Smith took a step toward the Russian. 'It was a matter of being sensible.'

'I quite understand, Colonel.' Smyslov's hand whipped back, and he hurled the inert automatic full into Smith's face, following through with a headlong diving attack.

Smith had been fully expecting the move, and he ducked, letting the thrown pistol glance off a hunched shoulder. Still, Smyslov's grappling charge caught him low, carrying him backward to pile up with a crash on the cave floor, the Russian landing on top of him.

To further complicate matters, the flare that illuminated the central cave chamber chose that moment to burn out, plunging them into a darkness broken only by the swath of light issuing from the electric lantern.

Smith was disoriented for a moment, but he could feel the shift of Smylsov's weight and the bunching of his muscles as the Russian's arm cocked back to strike. Smith twisted his head aside, felt the brush of the blow skidding past his chin, and heard the explosive curse as Smyslov's fist slammed into the stone of the cave floor.

Smith tried to throw Smyslov off but failed, his movements hampered by his heavy swaddling of arctic clothing. Smyslov found himself hampered in the same way. He clawed for Smith's eyes but found the move rendered ineffectual by his thick-fingered gloves. He tried again, going for a grip on Smith's throat while he groped at his belt for his sheath knife.

Smith's left hand came up and closed on the collar of Smyslov's parka, giving him range and position; then he struck with the heel of his right hand, connecting under the Russian's chin, the blow snapping Smyslov's head back and raking destructively up and across his features.

The beam of the lantern swung around to cover the two struggling men, and a moment later there came the hollow clonk of a heavy blow being landed. Smyslov went abruptly limp.

'That took long enough,' Smith grunted, rolling the unconscious Russian onto the cave floor.

'I wanted to make sure who was on top, Jon,' Valentina replied, lowering the reversed model 70. 'I didn't want to do a Benny Hill and cold-knock you by mistake.'

'I can appreciate that.' Smith got to his knees and examined the prostrate Russian. Removing his glove, he checked the carotid pulse. 'He's still with us. He's out but not too deep.'

'Do you view that as a positive or a negative?' Valentina inquired.

'I'd call it a positive. He still has things he can tell us. Beyond that, the poor bastard's right – he is a Russian officer just following orders. In the meantime it sounds like he may have invited friends. Can you hold the cave mouth while I secure the major here?'

'Not a problem.' She hurried for the entrance tunnel.

By the lantern light Smith dug a Mylar survival blanket and a couple of pairs of disposacuffs out of his pockets. Binding Smyslov's wrists and ankles, he rolled the Russian onto the insulating sheet of the blanket. Glancing around, Smith noted a sizable stump of candle stuck in a wall niche by its own wax. A half century old or not, it still burned when Smith lit it, providing a scrap of long-term illumination within the cave.

Kneeling down once more, he rechecked Smyslov's vital signs. Pulse strong, breathing regular, and the slight puffiness at the back of his head indicated that the swelling from Valentina's butt stroke was developing outward. He'd live and should regain consciousness shortly. Even though

Smyslov had declared himself a member of the opposing camp and had pulled that trigger on him, Smith didn't bear a personal grudge. Smyslov was a soldier in the service of his nation, just as Smith was. It was the fortunes of war, and now, likely, it *was* war. One with no guarantees of victory for either side.

Smith caught up his own rifle and started for the cave mouth.

Valentina was lying prone behind the frozen rubble of the snow wall, using the telescopic sights of the model 70 to scan the glacier.

'Any activity?' Smith dropped beside her and drew back the bolt of the SR-25.

'I haven't seen anything yet,' she replied, lifting her face from the rifle scope. 'Of course, that may not mean all that much.'

Smith took her meaning. As both the ninja of medieval Japan and the Apache warrior of the American Southwest had proved, it was completely possible to be invisible in plain sight. It was just a matter of knowing how to go about it.

'I did find this just outside of the cave mouth, though.' Valentina held up a silver cigarette lighter.

'Smyslov's?'

'So I would suspect. Look . . .' She turned the lighter upside down and squeezed some concealed catch. There was a soft snick of a releasing spring, and a short spike antenna extended from what had looked like the filler cap. 'A radio transponder beacon operating on a preset frequency. When the penny dropped with its loud resounding clang, friend Gregori only had to push the button to call down the wolves.'

'That's a pretty small transmitter,' Smith replied, uncasing his binoculars. 'They must be close by. I wonder what's holding them back.'

'It could be they're waiting for their Judas goat to give them the final high sign.' Valentina pressed the antenna back into the lighter/transponder, then snuggled in behind her rifle sights again. 'I wonder why he tried to take us alone as he did. Grandstanding?'

'It's just barely possible he was trying to keep us from getting killed, Val,' Smith replied.

'Oh, really? You think?'

'I like to maintain a positive worldview.'

From the protection of the shadowed interior the two scanned the approaches to the cave mouth for long, silent minutes. Nothing seemed to move on the ice save for an occasional wisp of snow slithering past in the wind. Then the tracking barrel of the model 70 stopped and steadied like a pointer dog fixing on a game bird.

'Jon.' Valentina's voice was casual. 'At our two o'clock, about two hundred and fifty yards out, just beside that little uplift.'

Smith swung his binoculars onto the called target. It took him a few moments to pick up the low ridge in the glacier surface. There was nothing out there that looked like a man. But there was a small drift built up at the foot of the ridge. There was nothing exceptional about the lump of snow. Nothing outstanding. But there was something subtly wrong just the same. The drift's contours didn't quite match the fractile flow of its surroundings.

'I think there's something there,' Smith said finally, 'but I can't be sure.'

'Neither can I. So let's . . . just . . . make sure.' There was a piercing whip-crack report as the vicious little .220 round screamed on its way. The 'snowdrift' quivered under the impact of the hypervelocity hollowpoint. Then as Smith looked on, a dot of color became apparent on the whiteness. Spreading, it became a stain, the red of the spilling blood darkened by the overcast.

Valentina flipped open the Winchester's bolt, ejecting the spent brass. 'Well, now we know.'

'Indeed we do.' Smith nodded slowly. 'Probably one of their fourteen-man Spetsnaz platoons. Anything bigger would have been spotted by our satellites.'

'Um-hum.' She drew a fresh round from the shell carrier, pressing it into the Winchester's magazine. 'I'll wager they'll be out of the Vladivostok garrison, either Mongolian Siberians or Yakut tribesmen under a Russian officer. The Soviets used them to guard the gulags. They're totally adapted to an arctic environment and generally nasty to cross. Arms-wise, I think we can expect AK-74 assault rifles and at least three RPK-74 squad automatic weapons. They'll be in light marching order in this terrain, so I don't think we'll see an RPG grenade launcher.'

'But they will have rifle grenades.' Smith looked across at her. 'I figure you understand where that leaves us.'

Valentina lifted an eyebrow. 'Very much so. For the moment we've got the range on them. As long as we can keep them out there with the long guns, we're all right. But as soon as night falls or the weather closes in and they can work closer to, oh, say, about seventy-five yards, we're quite dead.'

CHAPTER THIRTY-ONE

Wednesday Island Base

'Wednesday Island Base calling *Haley*, calling *Haley*. Do you copy? Over.' Randi repeated the call for the dozenth time. Lifting her thumb from the transmit button, she tried to listen through the static that squalled from the speaker of the little transceiver.

For a moment her heart leaped. Beyond the electronic rage of the solar flare she heard a faint voice responding with what sounded like the *Haley*'s call sign. Then she caught the repetitive cadence of the transmission. It wasn't a reply. It was an interrogative.

She glanced at her wristwatch. It was on the hour, and the *Haley*'s radio operators were calling Wednesday Island, trying to establish contact from their end according to the radio schedule. And if this was the best the ice cutter's powerful transmitters could do in this anarchistic communication environment, there was no hope of the little SINCGARS set being heard.

Angrily she twisted the frequency knob to the tactical channel and lifted the mike once more. 'Wednesday Island base to aircraft party. Wednesday Island base to aircraft party. Jon, are you receiving me? Over.'

She lifted her thumb, listening impatiently, wanting to scream back at the jagged static roar issuing from the speaker.

'Jon, damn it, this is Randi! Can you hear me? Over!'

Nothing discernable.

Solar storm or not, she should be hearing from the others. They should be on their way back by now and clear of the mountain. What in the hell was going on up there? Randi had the growing sensation that things were rapidly reaching some kind of a nexus, that the situation was collapsing in on her in a way she didn't and couldn't understand.

'What will happen when they don't hear from us?' Dr. Trowbridge inquired.

Randi resumed awareness of the room around her. After a sleepless night spent keeping a vigil over Kropodkin, she had moved the station party across to the laboratory hut, where she had spent the morning fruitlessly rechecking the station's big SSB radio and satellite phone and making equally futile calls on their backup transceiver.

'Don't worry, Doctor. If we're out of communication for a certain length of time, a contingency plan goes into effect.' Randi snapped off the transceiver and replaced the microphone on its clip. 'We'll get all the help up here that we can ever use.'

'Good, perhaps we will get someone in here other than the Gestapo.'

Randi ignored Kropodkin. With his hands bound behind his back, he sat perched on a stool in the far corner of the lab. He'd spoken intermittently and ingratiatingly with Dr. Trowbridge, mostly about inconsequential matters, but he'd been sullenly silent with her, barring the occasional barbed comment.

But he was listening, his eyes intently taking in everything. Randi could almost hear him thinking. She could sense expectancy in him. Kropodkin knew that something was going to happen

Randi sank down on another of the stools and braced her elbows on the lab table. God, but she was tired. She hadn't slept or even gone off alert for two nights. She had her little packet of go-pills in her kit, but she didn't like the chemically enhanced overconfidence that came with them. She also knew that when she came down off the drug, she would crash into total worthlessness.

She rubbed her burning eyes and looked out of the frost-fogged windows of the hut. What she hoped to see was Jon coming into camp. She wanted to be able to let her guard down just for a little while. Just to close her eyes for a minute or two.

'Ms. Russell, are you all right?' Dr. Trowbridge asked warily.

Randi snapped erect. Her eyes had closed for a moment, and she had swayed on the stool.

'Yes, Doctor, I'm fine.' She got to her feet, mentally slapping herself back into wakefulness.

Over in the corner she caught Kropodkin smirking at her, sensing her growing vulnerability.

'All right,' she said, turning abruptly to face him. 'It's time somebody tells us how he sabotaged the big transceiver.'

'I did nothing to the radio! I did nothing to anything.' His words were mushy through his bruised and swollen lips. 'Or anyone.' The malevolent glitter lingered in his eyes as he met Randi's eyes, but his words were plaintive. 'Dr. Trowbridge, can't you keep this madwoman off me until I can be turned over to the proper police? I'm not eager for another beating.'

'Please, Ms. Russell,' Trowbridge began in a weary monotone, 'if the authorities are on their way, can't this be put off . . .'

Randi gave an impatient shake of her head. 'All right, Doctor, I'll drop it.'

All morning Trowbridge had been moving and speaking like a man trapped in a nightmare, with Randi as one of the premiere monsters. A modern, upscale urbanite, he lived in a world where violence and death were essentially abstracts, something to be clucked over in a television news bite or enjoyed vicariously in media entertainment. Now he was being confronted with the genuine article, up close and personal. And like the victim of a violent car crash or natural disaster, the academic was slipping steadily deeper into a state of emotional traumatic shock. Randi recognized the symptoms.

What was worse, she was the heavy in the scenario. So far, she had been the visible purveyor of the violence. In a popular culture caught up in the fad of elaborate conspiracy theories and X-File fears, she was the figurative 'woman in black.'

Stefan Kropodkin represented normality. He was the honor student, the eager face in the front row of the classroom, the recognized and comfortable name on the test paper and expedition roster. Randi was the 'agent working for the shadowy government agency,' the twenty-first-century incarnation of the boogeyman.

She could see the fear in Trowbridge's eyes every time he looked at her. She could also see Kropodkin working that fear. Any denials of the scenario she might make would be an act of futility.

Lord, what a total mess!

Catching up the MP-5, she crossed into the radio shack. Settling down before the open console, she checked the components and settings of the big sideband set for the hundredth time, making the final futile gesture of switching it on to listen to the soft hiss issuing from the set.

Randi closed her eyes and rested her face in her hands.

It had to be the antennas! The receiver circuits were working, but they weren't picking up the clamor of the solar storm. At this gain the static should be blasting the speakers off the walls.

When Kropodkin had disabled the set, it also must have been from outside. Again, the antennas. But it hadn't been anything as simple as just cutting the leads. She had been meticulous in following and checking the cable between the laboratory hut and the radio mast, checking for breaks. She had run every inch of the cable through her hands, looking for the old saboteur's trick of shorting the leads with a pin pushed through the insulation. She had made sure the all-weather connectors were screwed down tightly . . .

Randi sat up abruptly in the chair. *The connectors.*

A second later she was in the main room of the hut, hauling on her heavy outdoor shell clothing as rapidly as she could.

'What is it?' Trowbridge demanded, rising from his seat by the coal stove.

'Maybe something positive for a change, Doctor,' Randi replied, zipping her parka and hauling on her gloves. 'We'll know in a few minutes. In the meantime keep an eye on Kropodkin while I go out.'

She glanced at the suddenly alert youth in the corner. 'On second thought, just don't go near him, for any reason, until I get back. I won't be long.'

That expression of indignant truculence crossed Trowbridge's face, and his mouth opened in the beginning of a knee-jerk protest.

'I said, don't go near him!' she snapped.

Randi took a moment to make sure that the nylon disposacuffs binding Kropodkin's wrists were still tight, and then, slinging the submachine gun, she was out through the snow lock.

She hastened up the knoll behind the camp. A half foot of fresh snow had fallen and been windblown during the early morning hours, clogging the trails and making the climb to the base of the radio mast a plowing struggle. Reaching her objective, she dropped to her knees at the foot of the mast. Shoveling aside the white overburden with her mittened hands, she exposed the antenna power booster box at the mast's base. Exposed also were the weatherproof connectors that linked the cable from the radio shack to the booster box. There were two of them, the heavy main cable bifurcating into the separate leads for the satellite phone and the sideband transceiver.

Each connector was a heavy-duty screw-on piece of hardware, fully weatherproof, of a golden-tinted alloy. Randi struggled with them, and they resisted stubbornly. Swearing under her breath, she tore off her mittens and strained on the connectors with her thin undergloves. Abruptly the first connector yielded.

A shredded fragment of plastic film fluttered to the snow. Randi recognized the simple mechanism of the sabotage now. Kropodkin had unscrewed the connectors and had wrapped the thin plastic around the male end, carefully packing it in around the central prong. Screwing the female half down over the nonconductive plastic had created an insulating barrier that had broken the connection. With the excess plastic trimmed away, there was no outside hint of the tampering.

Randi swore again, both at Kropodkin and at herself. She opened the connector for the satellite phone and cleared that as well. She reassembled them both, then sat with her back against the radio mast, resting for a minute.

She'd done her job, or rather her jobs. She had learned the fate of the station crew and had secured the culprit responsible, and she had regained their contact with the outside. She could let the ship know what was going on here and expedite the arrival of their reinforcements.

Granted the weather would cooperate. Randi felt the chill grip her hands, and she drew her overmittens back on. It was growing colder, with ice crystals condensing out of the rapidly lowering overcast. Faintly, in the distance, she could hear a rising wind booming over the ridgeline.

Within a matter of minutes they were going to be socked in tight. If conditions continued to deteriorate, Jon and the others might not be able to make it down from the saddle-back tonight, much less expect help showing up from Alaska.

But every cloud, even those of a polar storm, had a silver lining. If the good guys couldn't make it in to Wednesday Island, then neither could the bad. Perhaps she could truss Kropodkin and Trowbridge up in their bunks tonight and get a little sleep.

Even the thought was soporific. The thin sift of snowflakes seemed to weigh her eyelashes down, and even here, on the ice sheathed hillside, her head began to sink down on her chest.

And then, dimly, beyond the faint rumble of the wind over the mountain, Randi became aware of something else. Her head snapped up. It wasn't truly a sound at first, more of a heavy vibration in the air. It grew in gradual intensity until it became a thudding roar that echoed between the land and the overcast.

Randi scrambled to her feet, the island seeming to shudder around her. Like a scorpion instinctively lifting its tail, she slipped the MP-5 from her shoulder and into her hands.

A huge form condensed out of the sea smoke. Two mammoth Tumanski gas turbines howled atop a great, sleek glass-nosed fuselage fully the length of an airliner. Fifty-foot rotor blades whipped the air, creating the rhythmic rib-rattling thud Randi felt in her chest.

It came in low from the south, squeezing in beneath the cloud cover; the ferocious rotor blast whipped up a tornado of displaced snow, forcing Randi to cower and shield her face as the monster passed directly over her head at a meager hundred-foot altitude.

'Oh, my God,' she whispered. 'It's a Halo!'

The Mil Mi-26, dubbed the 'Halo' by NATO, had been created during the 1980s under the Soviet military's old 'If it's bigger then it must be better' design doctrine. It was the largest and most powerful helicopter ever built and that likely ever would be built.

Following the collapse of the USSR, the aircraft had passed into commercial service and now could be found working as a heavy industrial lifter in many nations around the world. This giant wore Canadian civil registration numbers on its Day-Glo red tail boom, and the winch control cab, projecting like a growth from its port side, marked it as a sky crane derivative.

Kropodkin's sponsors had come for him and for the anthrax, and they had come in force.

As the huge flying machine began to settle into a touchdown beyond the camp, Randi broke the shock lock that had paralyzed her. She had only two options. To instantly go into escape-and-evade mode or to try for the repaired radios. She chose the radios. That was the mission. That was what she was here for, to collect intelligence and to report.

It was a nightmare's run to the laboratory hut, the fresh snow dragging at each running step like wet concrete. As she ran she mentally composed the call she would make, compressing the maximum amount of information into the absolute minimum of words. She would send until she got an acknowledgment; then, if she had time, she would try to get out, taking Trowbridge with her. She must remember to grab the lab hut's survival pack and the SINCGARS transceiver as they went out the door. She would also put a burst into Kropodkin, if for no other reason than sheer self-satisfaction.

If there wasn't time, then she would put her back to the wall and take as many of them with her as she could. Maybe it would make a difference, for Jon and Valentina if for no one else.

She fell once cutting around the hut. Scrambling to her feet, her lungs burning, she charged through the snow lock doors, the first of her intended series of commands welling up in her throat. But her instincts recognized and reacted to the threat before her conscious mind did, and she was whipping the MP-5 to her shoulder before she realized exactly what she was aiming at.

Stefan Kropodkin was cowering back in the far corner of the laboratory, holding Dr. Trowbridge in front of him, a dissection scalpel gleaming at the academic's throat. Trowbridge was tottering on his feet, barely able to stand, blood streaming down his face from a broken nose and from the cuts created by his smashed glasses.

No one spoke. No one needed to. The scene was totally self-explanatory. A pair of cut disposacuffs lay on the lab floor. Kropodkin's cunning had manipulated Trowbridge's willfulness and essential humanity.

Randi raged at herself. She never should have left the two men alone together. *Stupid! Stupid! Stupid!* But that was an irrelevancy now. She had to get to that radio. Even if she had to do it over both of their bodies.

'Don't move,' Kropodkin blurted. 'Put down the gun or I kill him!'

Outside Randi could hear voices shouting over the fading scream of the Halo's turbines. Ordering Kropodkin to put down the knife would be an act of futility. All the numbers were on his side, and he knew it!

Sorry, Doctor.

Steeling herself, she nestled the butt of the submachine gun more deeply into her shoulder, and her finger tightened on the trigger. Trowbridge could see it coming, and a faint denying moan escaped from his lips. Kropodkin could see it, too, and he cowered behind his human shield.

Then Randi's gaze slipped past the two men and through the door of the radio shack. Kropodkin hadn't been wasting any time, either. The transmitter chassis lay open and thoroughly smashed.

Slowly Randi let the muzzle of the MP-5 sink toward the floor, the bitterness of total defeat welling up in her throat. There was nothing of value that she could accomplish now. There was no reason to put Trowbridge's blood on her hands. Running figures moved beyond the hut windows. Armed men were streaming into the camp. But even before they crashed through the door behind her, she had set the MP-5 on the worktable.

With her hands raised, she laced her fingers together behind the nape of her neck as gun barrels ground into her back.

CHAPTER THIRTY-TWO

Saddleback Glacier

A ground-hugging wisp of snow flowed past the cave mouth, driven by a rising gust of wind.

'Penny for your thoughts, Jon?' Valentina said softly.

Smith shot an angled glance toward the lowering northern sky. 'We've got another front coming in.'

'It will be interesting to see which arrives first: the weather or the sunset. Granola bar?'

'No, thanks.'

The colonel and the historian lay side-by-side in the shadow and shelter of the cave mouth, watching the approaches across the glacier. Since the initial identification and elimination of the first Spetsnaz scout there had been no movement on the ice. There was only the sensation of activity, born out of the knowledge that a hostile force was upon them, an enemy that would not sit back passively and allow them to live.

Smith looked across at the odd other half of his rifle team as she munched her snack in seeming contentment. Her fine-planed, rather exotic features were relaxed within the shelter of her parka hood. 'You doing all right?' he inquired.

'Oh, yes. Quite good.' She glanced around at the black rock walls and roof of the tunnel. 'It's not exactly Cancun, but I can see marvelous development potential for winter sports.'

Smith chuckled softly and reset his attention on the cave approaches. A remarkable lady.

'Mind answering a question?' he asked.

'Why not?'

'What is that accent? It's not quite English and not quite Australian. I can't place it.'

'It's from a country that doesn't exist anymore,' she replied. 'I was born in Rhodesia – not Zimbabwe, if you please, but Rhodesia. My father was a government game control officer there before Mugabe took over.'

'And your mother?'

'An American near-zoologist. She'd been a graduate student doing research on African wildlife, but what with one thing or another, such as marrying Dad, she never went back to the States to finish her degree.'

Valentina frowned for a moment at some flash of memory. 'It did give me dual citizenship, which proved rather handy when things went to their final hell back home. I was able to refugee to America to live with my mother's family after . . . well, after.'

'I see. And how did you get here?'

She glanced at him, her lips pursed thoughtfully. 'Doesn't that question violate mobile cipher compartmentalization or something? Like the old 'one question you cannot ask' in the Foreign Legion?'

Smith shrugged. 'Damned if I know. But you're the one who said we were destined to become lovers. The question is probably going to come up again.'

'Valid point,' she agreed, looking back to the ice. 'It's a long and rather meandering story. As I said, my father was a game control officer and the commander of our local territorial commando – a hunter, a scholar, and a soldier, who probably would have been much happier living as a contemporary of Cecil Rhodes and Frederick Selous. I was born in a war zone and raised in a household where weapons were a fact and a necessity of life. My earliest memories are of the sound of gunfire beyond our compound. I was given a rifle at an age when most little girls in America were still being given Barbie dolls, and I shot my first leopard while it was trying to climb in through my bedroom window.'

She glanced wryly at Smith. 'To say the least, I grew up

with a somewhat different worldview than is the norm.'

He tilted his head in an acknowledging nod. 'I can see how that could happen.'

'My father loved history and about learning how things came to be,' she continued. 'He'd say, "To learn where you're going, you have to know where you've come from." He put that love into me, and I majored in world history at college. My doctoral paper was titled *The Cutting Edge: Armaments Technology as a Guiding Force in Sociopolitical Evolution*. Later I expanded it into my first book.'

'Sounds like an impressive topic.'

'Oh, it is, and a valid one.' Valentina's voice began to take on a lecturer's enthusiasm. 'Consider how different Europe might be today if the English longbow had not proven decisively superior to the French arbalest at the Battle of Agincourt. Or how World War Two might have played out had the Japanese not developed the shallow-water drop shroud for their aerial torpedoes, permitting the attack on Pearl Harbor. Or how the United States might never have come to exist had the British Army put Major Ferguson's breech-loading rifle into general issue during the Revolutionary War . . .'

Smith laughed softly and lifted a gloved hand. 'Points taken, but it's still *your* history I'm interested in.'

'Oops, sorry, Pavlovian reflex. At any rate, after receiving my doctorate, I found I couldn't get a decent teaching position. My views were considered somewhat un-PC in certain quarters. So, to stave off starvation, I became an authenticator, appraiser, and procurer of rare and historic weapons for museums and private collectors. It turned into a rather lucrative profession, and I found myself roving all over the world, chasing down various finds for my clients. Eventually it led to my curatorship of the Sandoval Arms Collection in California.'

'I've heard of it. But how did you get *here*?' Smith prodded gently, tapping the magazine of his leveled rifle on the cave floor.

She bit her lip lightly for a moment, the introspective look deepening in her eyes. 'That's . . . a little more esoteric. As you should have guessed by now, I am a firm member of the "If it's worth doing it's worth overdoing" school of thought.'

'I've had my suspicions.' Smith smiled.

'As my education developed I found I was not content to merely study *about* weapons. I wanted to learn how to use them and to see and feel how they were applied,' she continued. 'I studied fencing and kendo. I learned the skills of the old Western gunfighters from the champion shootists of the Single Action Shooting Society. I bribed my way into Philippine prison cells to discuss technique with butterfly-knife artists. Before his untimely death I sat at the feet of the legendary 'White Feather,' Marine master sniper Sergeant Carlos Hathcock, and learned combat marksmanship. Firearms, blades, explosives, military heavy weapons: I learned how to make them, maintain them, and employ them. Everything from the flint axe to the H-bomb.'

She lifted her hand from the action of the model 70 and flexed her black-gloved fingers, studying them. 'I found myself becoming a uniquely lethal individual, all on a purely theoretical level, of course. But then I visited Israel, following up a lead on a cache of genuine "garage factory" Sten guns from their War of Independence. And one evening I found myself having dinner with a fellow historian from Tel Aviv University.'

Valentina's voice grew softer. 'He was a totally fascinating little man who not only taught history but had lived it. He was a holocaust survivor and had seen action in the first three of Israel's wars of national survival.

'We were dining at a small outdoor restaurant near the University. I recall we were discussing the historic Mideastern Jewish communities as a possible bridge between the European Jewish and Arabic cultures. Our meals had just been brought to the table. I'd ordered steak and I'd just picked up my knife when the smartly-dressed

Arabic couple at the next table stood up and started killing people.'

Smith listened and studied the subtle emotions playing across Valentina's face. He could sense it wasn't the remembering of a fear or revulsion, but an abstract reexamination of a defining moment in a life. A time and place this woman had revisited many times before.

'I heard gunshots and I was sprayed by the blood and brains of my dinner partner as he took a bullet through the head. Then the female terrorist shoved her pistol in my face and screamed "God is great . . ."'

The historian's voice trailed off.

Gently Smith rested his hand on her back, letting the gesture grow into a few inches of caress. 'And then?'

Valentina came back into herself. 'And then I was standing over the thoroughly shredded bodies of the two Hamas terrorists. I was saturated with blood, none of it my own, and that steak knife was still in my hand, dripping. I had, in the vernacular, "flipped the switch" – spectacularly, although I have no conscious memory of doing so. My studies were no longer abstract, but very much applied.'

Smith could understand the spark that had jumped between them now; like had recognized like. He'd had his own defining moments, his own flipping of switches. 'How did you feel afterward?'

'That's the interesting point, Jon,' she mused. 'I didn't "feel" anything. They were dead and I was alive, and I was quite pleased with that outcome. I found my only regret to be that I hadn't reacted quickly enough to save my friend and the others in that restaurant. I've been told that I have the perfect sniper's mentality. I can rationally divorce myself from the emotional trauma of physical violence.'

She shrugged and made a face. 'If I work at it for a bit anyway.'

'And that incident brought you to the attention of Covert One?'

'That and a couple of under-the-table research and

267

acquisition projects I'd done for the Departments of Defense and Justice. Mr. Klein seemed to think my rather esoteric talents might prove useful to his little organization. And they have. Now I view myself as following in my father's footsteps. I'm a game control officer eliminating the rogues and man-eaters from our societal jungle. Maybe, eventually, I can make up for being slow that one night in Tel Aviv.'

'Fred Klein knows how to pick his people.' Smith smiled at her. 'I'm pleased to know you, Professor Metrace.'

'Thank you, sir.' She nodded. 'It's a pleasure to be appreciated. Some men tend to look around for the garlic and holy water after delving a little too deeply into my past.'

Smith smiled without humor and looked over the barrel of the SR-25. 'I make no claim on moral superiority.'

'That's a relief. And now, Colonel Jon Smith, what about you?'

'What about me?'

'I have a fair idea of how you ended up with Mr. Klein, but just who are you? Where do you come from?'

Smith squinted at the sky. The cloud cover was definitely edging lower again. 'My biography's not nearly as interesting as yours.'

'I'm easily amused.'

Smith was considering his answer when a small clump of dislodged snow rolled over the edge of the cave overhang, dropping in front of them with a soft *pelp*.

'Oh, dear,' Valentina murmured, her eyes going wide.

Instantly, Smith snaked his legs under himself. Then he launched out of the cave mouth in a headlong dive. Landing flat on his stomach, he rolled onto his back, sweeping the long barrel of his rifle in an arc to bear on the cliff face above the cave.

The Spetsnaz trooper in arctic camouflage was a pale wart on the frost-streaked basalt. Stealthily, he had edged out along an almost nonexistent ledge to a point some thirty feet above the cave mouth. The gloved fingers of one hand were hooked into a fissure in the rock, those of the other were closed tightly around the object he carried.

Looking down, the Russian's mouth opened in a scream as he saw Smith's explosive emergence from the cave. The sound of the cry was drowned out by the flat crash of the SR-25 as Smith squeezed off half a dozen rounds of 7.62mm as rapidly as he could pull the trigger, the copper-jacketed mil-spec slugs blasting the enemy off the cliff face.

The limp body of the Russian soldier landed almost on Smith, piling up a couple of feet to his left with a sodden, dead-meat thud. There was a second, softer thump to his right, and Smith twisted to find a hand grenade lying beside his head, a thick jacket of puttylike plastic explosive wrapped around its spherical body to enhance the demolition effect.

For an instant Smith's heart stalled in his chest; then he realized that the grenade's pin and safety lever were both still in place.

An instant more, and terror of the grenade was forgotten. Splintered ice sprayed as automatic weapons raked the glacier around him. The dead Spetsnaz trooper saved Smith's life. Convulsing grotesquely, it absorbed bullets meant for him. Valentina was screaming something, and he heard the piercing reports of the model 70 as she returned fire.

Unseen things tugged viciously at Smith as he rolled onto his stomach and scuttled backward into the cave like a frightened lobster. He made it behind the low snow wall across the cave mouth. Throwing his arm around Valentina, he hauled her down beside him, and for a long second they huddled together as a storm of vengeance-aimed gunfire sparked and shrieked off the sides of the tunnel.

Out on the glacier, clips emptied and guns fell silent. The hollow ghost-moan of the wind returned.

'Val, are you all right?'

'No hits. What about you?'

Smith noted a couple of bullet rips through the loose cloth of his snow smock. 'Close, but nobody won the cigar.'

'Cuban, no doubt.' Valentina squirmed loose and eased a look over the snow wall. 'Damn, but this lot is good! I never had a hint they were out there until they opened up and I could pick out their muzzle flashes. They have us targeted from at least half a dozen different positions.'

Smith had been given vivid proof of that. The cave mouth was covered by a complete arc of fire. Come the inevitable nightfall, that arc would begin to contract as patient, deadly men wormed closer across the ice. The climax would be a concentrated and overwhelming blast of high explosives and autofire poured down the throat of the tunnel.

He and Valentina could retreat deeper into the cave, but they would merely be rats retreating deeper into the trap, to be systematically grenaded out of existence. Nor did surrender appear to be an option.

There had to be something else. There had to be!

'Can you hold the fort here for a while, Val? I want to go check a few things out.'

'I can manage,' she replied, thumbing reloads into the magazine of her rifle. 'I don't think they'll be in a mood to play any more pranks for a time.' She nodded toward the corpse sprawled beyond the cave mouth.

'Right.' He left her the SR-25 and his cartridge belt and backed to the bend in the tunnel on his hands and knees. Beyond the bend he stood and switched on the hand lantern. For a moment he considered the generator set and the Russian transmitter, then disregarded the notion. The batteries were decades dead, and the available gasoline had been reduced to wax and varnish. Even if they could get the set operational, whom could they call who would make any difference? The only way out of this mess would be one of their own making.

Smith descended into the main cavern, working toward the small puddle of light produced by the candle he had left burning.

'Colonel?'

'It's me, Major.'

Smyslov was awake and had worked himself to a sitting position on the survival blanket. Smith knelt down and steadied the bound man with one hand. 'How are you doing? Any dizziness? Double vision?'

'Nothing bad.'

'How about the cold? Getting to you? Is your circulation being cut off anywhere?'

'No. Not bad.'

'How about some water?'

'Yes, please.'

Smith gave Smyslov a swallow from his canteen. The Russian rolled the water around in his mouth and spat a glob of congealed blood to one side. 'Thank you. A cigarette?'

'It's against my principles, but under the circumstances . . .' Smith went through Smyslov's pockets until he found the Russian's smoking materials. 'What does this one do?' he asked, holding up the butane lighter.

'It lights cigarettes,' Smyslov replied laconically.

'Good enough.' Smith slipped the filter tip between Smyslov's lips and kindled it.

'Thank you,' the Russian said around the smoke. 'What's happening? I have heard gunfire.'

'Your people made a try for us,' Smith replied, returning the canteen to its pocket.

'Is the professor all right?'

'Yeah. But your side's lost two so far.'

Smyslov closed his swollen eyes. 'Shit! This was not supposed to happen!'

'What was supposed to happen, Major?'

Smyslov hesitated.

'Damn it, this situation's already blown!' Smith said urgently. 'I'm open to the possibility that something is going on here that neither of our countries really wants to have happen. Give me something to work with and maybe we can stop this thing!'

Smyslov shook his head. 'No, Colonel, I'm sorry, but it is

already too late. The escalation has begun. It is now inescapable.'

'Then answer me one question. Why?'

Smyslov sighed heavily. 'My government has always known that the Misha 124 had gone down on Wednesday Island. They also knew that the anthrax was still aboard the aircraft and that the aircrew had survived the crash. They had succeeded in establishing radio communications with our Siberian bases. They called for rescue. But the Politburo felt that a rescue mission would present . . . difficulties. There were no atomic submarines at the time. Wednesday Island was beyond the range of the ski planes then available, and trying to reach the island by icebreaker would draw the attention of the Canadian and American militaries. It was feared that the United States might learn of our aborted attack on North America and you would retaliate with your own nuclear first strike. Accordingly the Misha's political officer was ordered to eliminate all evidence of the bomber's mission.'

'Including the crew?'

Smyslov nodded, not meeting Smith's eyes. 'Yes. The crew was considered the greatest security risk. It was feared that when they realized that no help was forthcoming from the Soviet Union, they might try to contact the Western powers for rescue. Cold and starvation are not pleasant ways to die. The Misha's political officer was instructed to . . . deal with this potential threat to the state.'

'Including himself?'

Smyslov shrugged. 'He was a political officer of the Strategic Attack Forces of the Soviet Union. Such men were fanatical party members. He would consider dying for the glory of Mother Russia and the Communist Revolution the greatest of honors, even if that death came by his own hand at the party's order.'

'But the aircraft commander apparently didn't take too well to the whole glorious-death concept.'

Smyslov half-smiled. 'Apparently. The Soviet govern-

272

ment feared that something had gone wrong when they received no final acknowledgment from the political officer verifying that he had carried out his duty, but there was nothing more they could do. They chose, as the saying goes, to 'let sleeping dogs lie.' They hoped the wreck would simply never be found.'

'But it was.'

'Quite so, and apparently intact. My government knew the wreck would be investigated. I was attached to your team to learn if the political officer had succeeded in eliminating the evidence of the Misha 124's mission. If not, I was supposed to see to its destruction myself. But the political officer and I have both failed. An alternative plan is now in effect to ensure the truth never reaches the outside world.'

Smith tightened his grip on Smyslov's shoulder. 'Can you order the troops outside to stand down? Or can you contact someone who has the authority to call this mess off before we take any more casualties out here?'

'I wish I could, Colonel. But the Spetsnaz have their orders from a higher authority, and I am outside their chain of command. Wednesday Island is now to be sterilized. All evidence of the Misha's mission is to be eliminated, including the investigation team. To my government, the threat of the anthrax is lesser than the threat represented by the truth about the Misha's mission.'

'But why?' Smith demanded. 'Why all of this for something that happened over fifty years ago?'

There was a sad irony in Smyslov's voice as he replied. 'In my culture we would say 'only fifty years ago.' You Americans are mayflies. You forgive and forget quickly. One day you make war on a nation, and the next you are giving them foreign aid and arranging for tourist groups. It is not so in Russia and in the nations surrounding Russia. Our memories are long, and we nurse the bitter ones.

'If word got out that Russia had come within a hairsbreadth of unleashing a nuclear holocaust upon the world, even after half a century, there would be a reaction: anger,

273

fear, retaliation – things my government does not want or need. Within your own country, there are political leaders who would remember the Cold War and would work to cut off the aid we are receiving from you. Even among our own people there would be outrage, enough perhaps to fuel further secessionism and a final collapse of our national authority.'

'And your government thinks there won't be repercussions for killing a team of American agents and a group of innocent civilian scientists?' Smith demanded.

Smyslov shook his head. 'I will not attempt to justify my nation's actions to you, Colonel, but our leaders are afraid, and frightened men sometimes do not react sensibly.'

'Christ!' Smith rocked back on his boot heels.

'I hope you will believe me when I say this, Colonel, but I am sorry, truly sorry, you and the others were caught up in this.'

'I'm sorry, too, Major.' Smith caught up the lantern and rose to his feet. 'But I'm like the bomber commander. I don't intend to lie down and die for the convenience of the Motherland.'

'I understand. We are soldiers, the two of us. We each do what we must.'

Smith played the lantern beam in Smyslov's face. 'Could you at least tell me why the attack was launched and then recalled at the last second?'

'I cannot do that, Colonel.' Smyslov's face was impassive as he squinted into the light. 'That is a state secret even greater than that of the Misha 124.'

Smith stepped back from his prisoner. There was nothing more to be gained here, and his time was running out.

There was one possibility he had yet to fully investigate. Smith began a slow and deliberate examination of the walls of the cavern, probing with the lantern beam into the numerous crevices and fissures in the jagged lava rock. He had almost despaired of finding anything when, high up on the tumbled rear slope of the cave, beyond the cove where they had found the bodies of the aircraft commander and political officer, he spotted something that sheened palely.

Smith scrambled up the jumbled blocks of basalt to a point near the cavern roof. The paleness was a piece of doubled parachute silk, staked out and held in place by wedged chunks of stone.

A windblock.

Smith tore out the stones and pulled the cloth aside and felt the icy, dank flow of air on his face. The lava tube continued beyond the survival camp cavern! At some time in the past there had been a rockfall that had created a natural bulkhead in the tunnel. But a gap remained, large enough for a man to crawl through to another open section that lay beyond.

Smith snaked through the gap and worked his way down the slope of the inner face. Probing ahead, the beam of the lantern faded into the darkness. The tube flared out to the size of an automobile tunnel and seemed to continue for some distance. Taking a compass from his pocket, he flipped it open and checked the glowing luminescent dial. Orienting himself and making the mental correction for the nearness of the magnetic pole, Smith judged that the tunnel roughly paralleled the outer facing of the mountain.

Maybe . . . just maybe. It depended on how far the tube ran and if there was a second way out. With deliberation he started to work his way deeper into the tunnel, trying to gauge the angle of the slope. Was he above or below the level of the glacier?

The going was slow and treacherous. Olive-tinted puddles of slick, transparent glaze ice lay congealed around furniture-sized slabs of fallen basalt. The floor of this tube section was more broken and uneven than the camp cavern, possibly an indication that it was more unstable as well. Smith had neither the time nor the inclination to be concerned about it. A hundred yards . . . two hundred . . .

There! A ribbon of white against the black rock, a spill of snow down the tunnel wall!

Smith scrambled up the glassy slope of the miniature gla-cier to where the compacting snow was being forced into the lava tube. It was at a point maybe eight feet above the cave floor and took in an area the size of a coffee table. Bracing a foot on a solid stone ledge, he snapped off the lantern and let his eyes adapt. After a couple of minutes he could make out the faintest luminescence radiating through the snow plug from the outside. Daylight!

Drawing his bayonet, Smith started to dig, tunneling his way carefully toward the outside world. The luminescence grew brighter, and Smith recognized that he was digging through another of the ice-crusted snowdrifts such as they had found caking the first lava tube entrance. This was the back door he'd been seeking.

Suddenly Smith froze. Something more was leaking in from the outer world beyond the light.

Voices – faint, muffled, and not speaking English.

Smith resumed his digging, but he moved slowly, quietly, and with infinite care not to break through the drift. He eased a last knife thrust through the ice shell, creating a sin-gle blade-wide horizontal penetration to the outside. Daylight gleamed, bright to Smith even through the heavy overcast. He squinted through the narrow observation slit he had created.

This second entrance opened into a shallow notch in the cliff face. A bare forty feet away, two armed figures in snow camouflage crouched behind the shoulder of the notch, peering around the corner toward the main cave entrance.

Like a man moving on nitroglycerin-filled eggs, Smith backed out of the snow tunnel and down to the cave floor, easing each step and testing each foot and handhold. He had found an option.

CHAPTER THIRTY-THREE

Wednesday Island Station

Randi saw it coming and was ready for it. The blows were delivered open-palm, but they were no mere slaps. She relaxed her neck and shoulder muscles and rode with the vicious left-right-left of the blows, minimizing their effect. Even so, stars flashed behind her eyes for a moment, and her skin burned.

There had been no reason for the assault. Randi had not spoken a word to her attacker, nor he to her. It was only the predictable start of the testing and breaking process, a testament on the part of her captors that they were not the least bit hesitant about inflicting pain and injury. Randi was already fully aware of that fact. She shook off the effects, straightened, and met her assailant's gaze, her features defiantly neutral.

She knew from her escape-and-evasion training that this was a bad tactic. She should be keeping her eyes lowered in submissive mode. Given the animalistic psychology of the terrorist, meeting eyes was a threat act that could trigger a violent if not lethal reaction.

But what the hell, they were going to kill her anyway.

The man who had struck her was a giant in size and in dissipation, his height and bulk enhanced by his cold-weather gear. A tangled, graying ginger beard flowed over the opened collar of his parka, and narrowed pale blue eyes peered from beneath shaggy brows of the same color, bloodshot and intent.

Those eyes studied Randi's face for a long moment; then the laughter wrinkles clenched around them and he chuckled, deep in his chest. Randi was not comforted. This man's anger would likely be more merciful than his humor.

'This is a sassy little bit,' the big man rumbled. 'What do you know about her, Stefan?'

'That she is some kind of American government agent, Uncle,' Kropodkin replied, spite heavy in his reply, 'and that the bitch owes me.'

Uncle, Randi mused grimly – so it was all a family affair. Some incredible roll of random chance's dice had placed Kropodkin's fox inside the science expedition's henhouse. The security services of the world were totally at the mercy of such flukes.

They were in the laboratory hut: Randi, Professor Trowbridge, Kropodkin, the redheaded giant, and two more of his gang – watchful, stone-featured Slavic types. Randi had been disarmed, searched, and stripped of her parka and heavy outer snow pants, and her wrists cuffed with the good old-fashioned steel variety of handcuffs.

One of the guards stood immediately behind her, and intermittently she felt the brush of a submachine gun muzzle between her shoulder blades.

'And what of him?' the giant asked, nodding toward Dr. Trowbridge.

Kropodkin's flat, dark eyes flicked briefly toward the academic, the man he had beseeched for aid and who had defended him in the face of Randi's accusations. 'A schoolteacher. He is nothing.'

Trowbridge, his hands cuffed behind him as well, was reaching the apex of his waking nightmare. He had gone so pale, his skin had a greenish tinge, and Randi feared cardiac arrest might be imminent for the man. He stayed on his feet only because of the blows and kicks that had followed when his legs buckled. The crotch of his corduroy trousers was soaked.

Randi wanted to speak to him, to say some word of encouragement or comfort, but she dared not. For Trowbridge's sake, she had to maintain a posture of complete indifference to him. If she exhibited even a hint of compassion toward the academic, their captors might view his systematic torment as a lever to get at her.

'Come, now, Stefan,' the big man said jovially. 'No one is nothing. Everyone is something.' He turned to Trowbridge. 'Come, now, my friend, you are something, aren't you?'

'Yes! Yes, I'm . . . I am Dr. Rosen Trowbridge, the administrative director of the Wednesday Island Science Program. I'm a Canadian citizen. I'm . . . a . . . a noncombatant! A civilian! I have nothing to do with . . . with these other people!'

'See, Stefan?' The big man stepped across the laboratory to where Trowbridge cowered against the wall near the stove. He gave the doctor a light slap on the shoulder. 'He is a doctor. A man of learning. An intelligent man.'

He glanced back at Randi. 'And you, my pretty pretty? Are you intelligent, too?'

Randi didn't reply. She stared past him out of the laboratory hut windows, her unfocused gaze automatically taking in the movements of the other men brought in aboard the giant helicopter, noting the supplies they were unloading, trying to spot where they might be establishing their sentry goes and guard posts around the camp perimeter.

'Hmmm, maybe the lady is not so intelligent as you are, Doctor. Who is she? What agency does she work for?'

Trowbridge's tongue dabbed at his lips as he tried not to look at Randi, as he tried to not look at anything. 'Like Stefan said, she is some kind of American government agent. I don't know any more about her than that.'

'My friend' – the redheaded giant's voice grew ominously soft – 'don't stop being an intelligent man.'

A big, hairy-backed hand shot out and engulfed the front of Trowbridge's sweater. Swinging the handcuffed man around, the terrorist leader bent him backward over the lab hut's coal stove until the bare flesh of Trowbridge's hands and wrists sizzled on the hot stovetop.

Randi's jaws clenched so tightly, her back teeth almost shattered.

After Trowbridge had stopped screaming, he started talking, the words gushing from him in a whimpering babble. There was no need for the redheaded giant to conduct an interrogation. He merely guided the flow of words with an occasional quiet, nudging question, occasionally cross-checking a given answer with Kropodkin.

Trowbridge gave it all up: Jon, Valentina, Smyslov, the *Haley*, the mission. The doctor was no trained agent. Randi could expect the hapless, terrified man to do nothing more or less.

As Trowbridge talked, Randi thought. Her mind raced, using every precious second gained to develop some kind of con or angle that might save the doctor and herself. She had been in similar situations before where she had bought herself survival time with a skillfully crafted lie or cover story. But, damn it, this scenario gave her no maneuvering room!

Between Trowbridge and Kropodkin and overt, common knowledge, these people simply knew too much. She had nothing to sell, bargain, or bluff with. In the hands and eyes of the enemy, she and Trowbridge were irrelevant and disposable.

Across the room, Trowbridge's flow of words was going dry. Randi frantically tried to telepath him a message. *Keep talking! For God's sake, make something up! Anything! Just keep talking!*

He didn't hear her unspoken entreaty. His words trailed off with a final, near-whispered, 'That's all I know . . . I'm cooperating . . . I'm a Canadian citizen.'

The big man turned toward her, those ghost-pale blue eyes speculative. 'Well, pretty-pretty? Do you have anything to add?'

Randi read those eyes and knew that he had her pegged. He understood her, and he understood that anything she might say would be merely a stratagem, offered to stave off the inevitable. She stared back as impassively as the statue of Venus, her pride and instinctive discipline blocking her despair and rage.

'You're absolutely correct, my pretty-pretty. No sense in wasting everyone's time.'

The big red-haired man turned back to Trowbridge, drawing a big Czech-made CZ-75 automatic out of the side pocket of his parka. 'Thank you, friend Doctor. You have been most helpful.' He lifted the pistol. With a flick of his head, he indicated to the guard covering Trowbridge that he should stand clear.

Trowbridge caught the meaning of the act, and a dawning, ultimate horror filled his features. 'No! Wait! I've told you everything I know! I'm cooperating! You have no reason to kill me!'

'He's right! He's not part of this!' Randi blurted. She had to speak, to protest just once, even though she knew with a sick certainty that it was useless and worse than useless. 'You have no reason to kill him.'

The aimed muzzle of the pistol wavered. 'This is very true.' The big man looked back at her and smiled. 'I have no reason to kill him . . . but then, I have no reason to keep him alive, either.'

The CZ-75 roared. The single 9mm slug embedded in the radio room partition, surrounded by a splatter pattern of blood, bone splinters, and homogenized brain tissue. Death limp, Trowbridge's body collapsed into the corner of the lab.

Randi closed her eyes, and no one heard her sob of regret and despair but herself and the universe. *Trowbridge, I'm sorry! Jon, I'm sorry! I wasn't good enough!*

She opened her eyes again to find the redheaded giant circling the worktable to confront her. So this was it. The ending place she had known she would stand in someday. It wasn't a particularly good one, but few of her kind found good endings. It was an aspect of the profession.

The CZ-75 leveled at her stomach. 'Well, pretty-pretty? Do I have a reason not to kill you?'

The man behind the gun was speaking rhetorically. Randi sensed he had already decided. He knew he needed nothing from her. Any ploy she might try now, any bargain she might offer, any attempted diversion would be recognized as sophistry. Randi reverted to silence.

'No, I suppose not.' The automatic lifted and aimed into her face.

'Wait.'

It was Kropodkin speaking. He was standing at his uncle's shoulder, and his expression was one of smug cruelty. His flat, dark eyes ran the length of her body, slipping under her clothes.

The faintest spark of hope gleamed.

'Do we have to be so fast with this one? We have a long, cold night ahead of us, Uncle. It would be a waste.'

That faint spark of hope flared as a hint of thoughtful consideration crept into the big man's eyes. The muzzle of the automatic lowered to Randi's chest, brushing lightly against the fabric of her sweater, slowly tracing the outlines.

Randi knew she was an attractive, even a beautiful, woman. Sex and seduction had been useful tools in her agent's kit, and she had no problem with employing them. But any overt coquetry on her part now would blow the fragile potential. This man was not a fool. Still, Randi inhaled slowly, a deep breath that lifted and subtly offered her full breasts.

'Yes, Stefan. This one might be worth enjoying a bit,' the red-haired man murmured.

Very carefully Randi metered a hint of fear into her expression, the promise of a chink in her iron control. Fear and vulnerability would be an aphrodisiac to men such as this. They would react to it in the way a shark would react to a drop of blood in the water. The one chance might be the briar patch tactic.

Come on, you bastards! You want it! Screw me before you kill me!

Existence balanced on a razor edge.

'Yes, a waste.' The automatic sank away from her chest and disappeared into the pocket of the parka. 'Recreational facilities are decidedly lacking on this misbegotten rock.

Remember this, Stefan. You must always look to the morale of your employees. Our men would not forgive us for denying them this charming lady's company.' The big man reached up and playfully patted Randi's bruised cheek. 'Take her back to the bunkhouse and keep her secured until this evening. Work must come before pleasure.'

Randi pretended to crack, registering an expression of sick horror. Inwardly, she exulted. They had thought with their glands instead of their brains. They were only a bunch of thugs, after all. Thugs on a world-class scale, perhaps, but thugs nonetheless. They had made a mistake a real pro outfit would never have made. They had allowed another pro to remain alive. She must now make them pay for that folly.

Wednesday Island Station had undergone a population boom. Anton Kretek had brought in a twenty-man security and technical team aboard his Halo. Now that crew was hard at work securing the mammoth helicopter against the weather and establishing a sentry perimeter.

With matters dealt with inside the laboratory hut, Anton Kretek made a tour of inspection, ensuring that his detailed ops plan was being followed to the letter. He could still make this thing work – he was certain of it, even in the face of the niggling interference of the Western security agencies – but the margin for error would be small.

His dead sister's son crunched through the layering snow at his side. Kretek was pleased with how things had worked out with him. Stefan had been a wild one a few years back. Kretek had once despaired over the boy. No discipline. No common sense, like so many of them these days.

It had been bad enough when Stefan had knifed that German student over some tourist girl in Belgrade, but he had cut the girl's throat as well. There was no putting a fix in for that. Kretek had expended a great deal of time and trouble in spiriting the boy out of Europe and getting him established under a new identity in Canada.

But the boy had made amends with this current coup. He

had acquitted himself well, and perhaps there would be a place for him in the business after all. An heir.

Stefan squinted through the growing sweep of wind-driven snow. 'We're awfully open here, Uncle. The American spy satellites could spot this activity.'

Kretek nodded to himself, pleased. The lad was thinking. Yes, he had come a long way. 'Let them look all they like. This was one of the reasons we delayed our arrival. We had to get the timing and the weather just right. We had to squeeze in just ahead of this next storm front. Now the flying conditions are impossible everywhere between us and the Canadian coast. No one can get at us.'

'But it must clear sometime.'

'Very true, Stefan. There should be a break in the weather tomorrow morning, in fact. But in this part of the world the weather breaks from the north. We will be able to take off first. I have my best explosives men with me, and they have ribbon charges already cut to fit the bulkheads of a TU-4. I have also obtained a set of schematics for the biowarfare system, and I have had a lift harness made to fit the anthrax reservoir.

'Tomorrow morning we will fly to the crash site and open up that aeroplane like an oyster. Then we will pluck out the pearl and be on our way. It should take only half an hour, maybe forty-five minutes at the most. By the time the authorities arrive, we will be gone.'

'Where do we go from here, Uncle?'

'I have three refueling sites established in isolated areas across northern Canada. We will stage through them to reach Hudson Bay, flying at treetop altitude to evade the NORAD radar. In Hudson Bay we will rendezvous with an Icelandic trawler. The helicopter will go to the bottom of the sea, and we sail for the mid-Atlantic. There, we will transfer the reservoir to one of the group ships and we will dispose of the trawler and its crew. After that, we are free and clear. We need only decide if we should sell our prize in bulk to one buyer or if there is more money to be made breaking it down into penny packets.'

Kropodkin laughed and clapped Kretek on his shoulder. 'The old wolf always has a plan.'

'Yes, but this time it was the sharp-nosed cub who sniffed out the prey.' Kretek peered intently into the eyes of the younger man. 'You are sure the investigation team didn't have the opportunity to get out a radio report on the situation here?'

'I am certain. The transmitter they brought with them did not have the power to penetrate the solar flare, and I had sabotaged the station set. It was a close thing. Very close, but they didn't radio out.'

Kretek nodded. 'This is good. As far as the outside world knows, the investigation team and the crew from the science station might still be here in the camp. The Americans won't risk cruise missiles or radar bombing through the storm if it might kill hostages. That was the last thing we had to fear.'

'I'm not quite so sure, Uncle.' Kropodkin glanced back toward the laboratory hut. One of Kretek's guards was dragging the body of Dr. Trowbridge out into the snow. Another was herding a handcuffed Randi Russell toward the bunkhouse. 'We still have the other members of the American investigation team loose on the island. If they are anything like that bitch, they could be trouble.'

Kretek shrugged. 'Pish, pish, pish! Three are only three. Worry about things worth worrying about. If they come stumbling back into camp tonight, we will kill them. If they are still up at the crash site tomorrow morning, we will kill them there. If they choose to hide from us somewhere on the island, let them hide. They are nothing as long as they do not interfere with us.'

'All but that one.' Kropodkin nodded toward Randi. 'She is something to me.' His voice was tight and as cold as the polar winds.

'I can understand that. You will be the first in her tonight. You are owed that.' Kretek gave his nephew a bearlike cuff.

285

'Just see you leave plenty for the rest of us,' he continued boisterously. 'Remember, you are a member of the firm now. Fair shares for all.'

The two men shared a warm family laugh.

CHAPTER THIRTY-FOUR

Saddleback Glacier

The black rock of East Peak loomed over the pale sheet of glacial ice, becoming one with the deepening night. At its base, the final approach began. Dark, leathery faces and dark, narrowed eyes peered from parka hoods, gauging the growing strength of the wind and the density of the snow being driven before it. As each gust blurred the line of sight between them and their objective the Spetsnaz troopers snaked forward another few meters, taking advantage of every minute concealing swale and depression in the ice, relentlessly tightening their half-circle perimeter around the cave mouth.

They were Siberian Yakut tribesmen, the ancient seed race from which the American Indian had sprung, adept at survival in this kind of savage, frigid environment. They could ignore the wind that drove through their arctic gear, turning the windward side of their bodies into a half-deadened ache. They were inured to the burning numbness of the frostbite eating into their faces. The resulting scabs and scars would be badges of honor, a testament to their ability to survive and fight in realms that would destroy lesser, softer men.

This night, if they felt anything, it was heat. The fires of revenge burned bright for the teammates who had died at the hands of those in the cave. They hoped that their enemies would not die swiftly in the initial assault. In their world-view, vengeance was something worth taking one's time over.

Lieutenant Pavel Tomashenko peered cautiously from

behind a jumble of snow-sheathed slide rock. He and his platoon sergeant had worked their way along the cliff face to within fifty yards of the objective cave. Through his night-vision monocular he could make out the body of Private Uluh sprawled on the ice outside of the cave mouth. It gave him the range he needed.

Trying to get a grenade in there that afternoon had been a mistake, but he had been angry over the loss of Scout Toyon to that sniper's shot. He had gotten impatient, and it had ended up costing him two men instead of the one.

That would make it a total of three to be avenged. The attack signal from the radio transponder carried by Major Smyslov had been their last contact with their agent within the American investigation team. The Americans must somehow have learned of Smyslov's true mission intent and killed him. It was unfortunate but also one less factor to worry about in the upcoming assault.

They were good, Tomashenko mused, the man and the woman in the cave. Probably United States Military Special Forces or Central Intelligence Agency. When he and his troopers went in after them it would be like hunting down a mated pair of Siberian tigers. They must be sure to kill them both very dead.

Full darkness settled, the beginning of a sixteen-hour arctic night. Tomashenko squinted through the monocular one last time. The photomultiplier helped against the lack of light but not the thickening snow, and now the battery was fading in the cold. His men had their orders, and the platoon would be in position. There was no sense in pro-longing this.

'Stand ready, Sergeant.'

Sergeant Vilyayskiy grunted an acknowledgment and drew the flare gun from the holster clipped to his harness.

Tomashenko slipped an RGN-86 limited-fragmentation grenade from a bandolier pouch and tugged a whistle from the neck of his parka. When he had first been assigned to the Siberian garrison he had made the mistake once of letting his whistle dangle outside on his chest on its chain. The metal of the mouthpiece had peeled the flesh right off his lips.

'Illuminate!'

The platoon sergeant fired, skidding the flare flatly across the ice so it came to rest near the cave mouth, revealing it in a blue-white glare of burning magnesium. Lifting the whistle, Tomashenko blew a prolonged, piercing blast.

Around the perimeter, the RPK-74 squad automatic weapons raved a long, focused burst, their tracer streams converging on the cave mouth. A second later half a dozen rifle grenades impacted around the cave mouth, flinging Private Uluh's body aside in a grotesque tumble. One of the grenades scored a clean hit down the throat of the tunnel, kicking a spray of snow and ice from the barricade across the mouth.

Tomashenko blew the double blast that signaled the cease-fire and the assault charge. Then he was on his feet and running for the cave mouth. For his own pride and the mastery of his platoon, he must be in the forefront of the attack.

His men were rushing the cave from all angles, pale spectral figures rising up from the ice, weapons lifted. But Tomashenko arrived first.

'Beware grenade!'

He tore the pin out of the RGN-86 and allowed the safety lever to flick away from the deadly little sphere. He counted two racing heartbeats before hurling the grenade into the tunnel mouth and pressing against the cliff face.

The heavy thud of the detonation sounded well back in the lava tube, snow and shock waves belching from it once more. Catching up his AK-74 from where it hung slung under his arm, Tomashenko pivoted in front of the cave mouth, emptying the thirty-round magazine in a single protracted burst. Sergeant Vilyayskiy was at his side, hosing out a second stream of bullets, sparks kicked up by the ricocheting slugs dancing in the cavern throat.

There was no replying fire.

As the remainder of the platoon deployed on either side of the cave entrance, Tomashenko and Vilyayskiy activated the tactical lights clipped under the barrels of their weapons.

Nothing. Beyond the swirling mist of pumice dust and picric acid fumes, this first length of tunnel was empty. The Americans must have withdrawn deeper into the cave before the attack.

Tomashenko slapped a fresh clip into his rifle. 'Corporal Vlahvitich. You and your fire team will remain here covering the cave approaches. The rest of you, follow me!'

It was not an appealing concept, but it must be done. Hunched into a single file, they plunged into the deeper darkness of the tunnel.

Beyond the first turn of the passage, they had to cautiously work their way past a jumble of old radio equipment, smashed by the grenade attack. There was no sign of life or death here, either, but ahead a gash in the tunnel floor resisted the probing beams of their tactical light – a descent into a larger, lower passage. This would be a natural choke and ambush point.

'Flare,' Tomashenko breathed.

The noncom snapped a fresh round into the projector. Together, with utmost caution, they eased up to the entrance of the lower cavern, moving as silently as well-trained warriors can move.

'Now!'

Sergeant Vilyayskiy fired the illumination round into the gut of the blackness, and Tomashenko whipped his assault rifle to his shoulder, ready to send bullets after it.

The flare hit, bounced into the rear of the lower cavern, and ignited.

Barsimoi! There were only supposed to be two of them!

Half a dozen figures stood on the cave floor, backlit by the pulsing blaze.

'Back! Get back!' Tomashenko squeezed off a wild burst and threw himself away from the cavern entry. Clawing at his bandolier, he tore out another hand grenade, Sergeant Vilyayskiy mirroring his actions.

Tomashenko hurled the grenade down into the cavern, the steel sphere ringing as it bounced off stone. It exploded with a roar and an ear-popping shock wave. The Spetsnaz troopers shrank back as shrapnel screamed and whined around the cavern interior. A second grenade followed, a third. Smoke and powdered lava saturated the air, and a fist-sized chunk of rock dislodged from the tunnel roof, glancing off Tomashenko's shoulder.

'No more!' he yelled in sudden fear. The whole damn mountain might come down. 'Cease-fire!'

The echoing reverberations and the faint, ominous grating of rock against rock faded. There was only silence from the pit of the lower cavern. Darkness as well, for the volley of hand grenades had blown out the flare.

'More illumination, Sergeant!' Tomashenko commanded.

The flare gun coughed once more, sending another scintillating ball of light bouncing around the interior of the cave.

'We got them, Lieutenant!' Vilyayskiy exclaimed. 'The bastards are down!'

They augmented the flare with their tactical lights, playing the beams across the cluster of bodies on the cavern floor.

'We only saw the two Americans. Where did these others come from?'

'I don't know, Sergeant. Be careful. There may be more.'

There was something strange about the way those bodies lay so rigidly. And then it hit Tomashenko. *There was no blood! They had killed no one! Those men down there had died fifty years before!*

Swearing, Tomashenko led his men down the lava slope to the floor of the tunnel. They had blown apart the stiff, frozen bodies of their own people! The dead crewmen of the Misha 124 had been strung up like grotesque puppets on a network of climbing rope, criss-crossed between pitons driven into the walls of the cave.

In a growing fury, Tomashenko recognized the delaying action, deftly rigged by someone who would understand the psychology and instincts of a military force in a cave-clearing operation. And he, Pavel Tomashenko, had reacted just as his enemy had hoped. Of the Americans themselves, there was no sign. Nor was there any clue to the fate of Major Smyslov.

Tomashenko became aware of an uneasy murmur passing among the enlisted men of his platoon. They were soldiers of the Russian Federation, but they were also Yakut, not far removed from the magics and superstitions of their people.

'Spread out and search!' Tomashenko roared them into action again. 'There must be another exit from this cavern! Another tunnel! Find it!'

It took several minutes of searching to find the passage into the next section of tunnel. It had been blocked with chunks of basalt stacked into it from the far side.

The Americans were buying themselves time. But to what end? They were still rats trapped in a sewer pipe. Unless . . .

'Forward! After them! Move!'

Recklessly Tomashenko dove through the gap into the next tunnel section. He must not give them the time and opportunity to set up any more of their monkey tricks. He had the numbers and the firepower. He would use them.

'Illuminate! Light this place up!'

Volleys of flares were hurled ahead, filling the tunnel with the scarlet light of hell, the chemical vapor for their combustion tainting the air and burning the lungs. This section of lava tube was as broad as a highway and as high as a two-story building. The platoon advanced fast and dirty, snaking through the jagged jumble of rock slabs on the cave floor in a leap-frogging overwatch, half the force moving while the other half covered, ready to unleash a storm of gunfire at the first sign of life or hint of resistance.

But there was none, and as the advance continued and the tunnel lengthened, Tomashenko's fears began to solidify.

And then there it was, a thick fall of pale, compacted snow drooling down the left side of the tube. The rock floor of the tunnel was slick with clear condensation ice, but this was from the outside. Damnation, there was a second exit, and the Americans had found it!

A series of steps had been axed into the face of the icefall. Sergeant Vilyayskiy scrambled up the slope for a closer look. 'There's a snow tunnel here! They must have escaped through it, then caved it in behind them.'

The Americans had logically projected that Tomashenko would tighten his security perimeter around the main cave entrance in preparation for his assault. They had simply waited for his screen to contract past their concealed escape hatch; then they had slipped away, leaving a series of delays and diversions behind to buy them running time.

'Sergeant! Get that tunnel open immediately and get after those bastards! Keep Corporal Otosek's section with you. I'll take the rest of the platoon back to the main entrance! The Americans must be heading back for the science station. You trail them while we try to cut them off. Move!'

'Yes, Lieutenant,' the Yakut noncom replied, stoically snapping open his entrenching tool. 'You, Private Amaha, get your ass up here and help me!'

In seconds, the two Spetsnaz troopers were assaulting the snow plug. Tomashenko turned and started to double-time the remainder of his force back the way they had come.

Tomashenko abruptly hesitated as the thought caught at him. The American bastards were clever. What if . . .

Private Amaha plunged his entrenching tool into the mass of loose snow blocking the route to the outside. As he scooped the burden aside, he felt a resisting tug. Glancing down in the flarelight, he saw a thin cord hooked over the blade of his shovel. He stared at it for an uncomprehending instant; then he understood and screamed.

The plastique-augmented hand grenade Private Uluh had attempted to drop into the cave entrance earlier that day fulfilled its destiny.

Concentrated by the confines of the tunnel, the concussion hurled Tomashenko face-first to the cavern floor. He tasted blood, the bitterness of high explosives, and the metallic taint of basalt. Over the howling ring in his ears he faintly heard the groans and pained swearing of the other downed members of the platoon. He levered himself to his feet and peered through the rosy haze of flare-illuminated dust that filled the cavern.

The passage to the outside had been blasted open, and the bodies of Sergeant Vilyayskiy and Private Amaha had been hurled against the far wall of the lava tube and plastered there, like bedbugs smashed under the thumb of an annoyed sleeper.

There was no curse potent enough to be worthy of the sight.

Tomashenko staggered back down the tube and clambered up to the blackened fissure in the stone revealed and emptied by the explosion.

He looked out into the storming night and couldn't believe what he found. The cave exit opened into the same cove in the mountainside he had used as his command post for all that afternoon. This man Smith must have crouched within twenty feet of him, watching and listening, and Tomashenko had never realized it! There had never been a hint!

This was a shame his career could never survive! 'Get after them!' he raged. 'They die tonight!'

CHAPTER THIRTY-FIVE

Wednesday Island Base

Randi Russell lay on her back in the lower of the two bunks in the women's quarters, her wrists over her head and cuffed around the bunk's vertical stanchion. A swath of light cut through the darkened room from the open door, issuing from the gas lantern in the main room. Intermittently the armed guard seated at the mess table glanced in her direction.

To the guard, she lay apparently unmoving, possibly even asleep. He couldn't see into the shadows at the head of the bunk, where Randi's fingers flexed and clenched slowly and continuously like a cat kneading its claws. She must not allow her hands to swell and get stiff.

Even as she had been prodded and shoved back to the bunk room that afternoon, she had been making her plans. When her captors had handcuffed her into the bunk, she had seemingly resisted for a moment, earning herself another impatient slap across the face. But in a deft bit of positional legerdemain she had also managed to ensure that when the handcuff had been resnapped around her right wrist it had closed over both the sleeve of her sweater and the heavy thermal long johns she wore underneath it.

She had worked the fabric out from under the cuff, loosening it. She had also made sure that her fists had been tightly clinched when the cuffs had been locked on, gaining herself yet another precious fraction of an inch of play.

She rolled a little on the bunk, as if hunting for a more comfortable spot. Under the cover of the movement she again found the joint in the bunk stanchion and practiced wedging the connecting links of the handcuffs into it. Then she folded her fingers in as tightly as she could and gave an experimental tug. Given enough adrenaline, it would work. It wouldn't be very pleasant, but it would work.

Her eyes scanned the semidarkness, gauging distances, plotting positions, considering the potential assets. How big was the window in the end wall of the cabin, and how thick was the thermal glass? Remember how the big boom box tape player was positioned atop the cabinet against the far wall. How deep was the snow drifted against the cabins, and how would the snow crust bear weight? Listen to the wind and gauge what the weather was like and how the visibility would be outside. What about outer shell garments? She supposed her own cold-weather gear was still over in the lab hut. She would have to improvise when the time came.

In her hours of imprisoned waiting she had made every mental and physical preparation she could. For the rest she must trust to patience, luck, and Slavic sexual propensities.

The smell of cooking rations filled the bunk room, and a growing number of shadows moved across the bar of light streaming through the door. The chief smuggler – Kretek, she had heard him called – was feeding his crew in shifts. The scent of hot food pointedly reminded Randi she hadn't eaten since a very sketchy breakfast. A meal would be a very good thing to have just now, but she didn't dare ask for anything to eat, for fear of disrupting the scenario she had built.

She recognized the voices of Kretek and Kropodkin. They were in the bunkhouse, having dinner. Russian was the lingua franca of the group, although Randi could recognize half a dozen different Balkan dialects and accents. Over their meal the shop talk was about the coming day's operation: the blowing open of the Misha's fuselage and the sling lifting of the anthrax reservoir, and the precautions that must be taken when dealing with the deadly bioagent.

They also discussed Jon, Professor Metrace, and Major Smyslov. From what Randi could gather, there had been no contact with her teammates so far. Plans were being proposed for hunting them down.

The clink and rattle of eating utensils trailed off. She smelled pipes and acrid Balkan cigarettes being lit. The conversation grew more genial, the laughter more frequent. The men were relaxing after dinner, joking, discussing women and sex.

It wouldn't be long now.

Randi heard Kretek's bull's-bellow voice say, 'Well, Stefan, you'd best get on with it. You have a lot of men standing in line for their rations here.'

So it would be Kropodkin.

She heard the ex-student laugh sheepishly, followed by a bellow of humor from around the table and a barrage of coarse suggestions and advice.

'Just don't mark up that pretty face of hers, lad.'

'Why do you worry about her face, Belinkov? What are you going to do? Draw her picture?'

'What can I say? I have a romantic soul.'

A shadow occulted the light. He was in the doorway, looking at her. She could hear his rasping breath, still hampered by the nose she had broken. She could hear the scuffle of his booted feet on the floor, smell the rancidity of his body.

Kropodkin stepped into the women's quarters . . . and drew the accordion door closed behind him, plunging the little room and the two of them into darkness.

Got you, you son of a bitch!

If Kropodkin had been a show-off or if Kretek's crew had been up for a gang bang on the mess table, Randi knew she would have been in trouble. But she had been involved in sexual relationships, both romantically and professionally, with Russians before. She knew that a strong streak of inherent prudishness still ran deeply through many of the Slavic cultures. Overt sexual exhibitionism still frequently triggered a guilt-shame response. She had been counting on this.

Kropodkin was kneeling beside the bunk now and his hands were on her breasts, squeezing and kneading them with a brutal childish eagerness. 'Things are different now, aren't they, Miss Russell?' He spat her name out like an epithet. 'You have a great deal to make up for. A very great deal. You may start begging my pardon any time you please. I might listen.'

She could make out his silhouette in the bar of light down the edge of the door and see the sparks of red light glinting in his eyes. She spoke directly to those sparks, her voice a soft whisper, audible only to him.

'Just so you'll know, I'm still going to kill you.'

Kropodkin spat out a true epithet, a counter to the chill rippling down his spine. Standing, he tore off his clothes. He would destroy the hex this deadly, beautiful witch had put on his soul with her degradation.

Then he was stripping her, dragging her ski pants, thermal underwear, and panties down to her ankles. Not bothering to force the snug garments off over her boots, he was content to hobble her with them. Then Randi's sweater and long john top were being forced up and over her head and into a wad around her wrists, leaving that firm, pale body bare save for her bra. That he tore away altogether with an angry, painful wrench, leaving her nothing.

She did not speak again or try to resist, not even in the slightest. She just looked into his face, those dark eyes glittering. It was as if what he was about to do to her simply didn't matter. As if he were irrelevant, already dead and gone.

But if it was frightening, it was also exciting. He would make this bitch notice him. He would master her and break her and make her scream and cry. He was atop her in the bunk, hunching down under the springs of the upper mattress, mounting her, feeling her back arch under the stab of his dry penetration. She would break or she would die.

*

Randi rode out the initial, tearing burst of pain. She could hear the sound of Stefan Kropodkin's breath hissing through his clenched teeth, and the laughter and shouted advice from the other arms smugglers just a few feet away beyond that paper-thin door. She felt Kropodkin's hands moving from her bruised breasts to her throat.

Above her head, the links of the handcuff chain clicked as they locked into the shallow notch in the stanchion, and the fingers of her left hand took a grip on the clothing wadded around her right wrist, so she could clear her right hand.

Kropodkin thrust savagely within her, and her pain and rage reached critical mass and exploded. Her skin tore as she ripped her right hand out of the loosened handcuff.

Lost in the sensual softness of the prostrate body beneath him and the brutality of his rape of it, Kropodkin didn't realize what Randi's convulsive movements meant. She pushed completely free of her sweater and long john top, letting them fall to the floor. Then Randi's left hand, still burdened by the handcuffs, whipped up and clenched in Kropodkin's lank hair, yanking his head back.

'Told you so.' That whisper was the last thing he heard. Then the heel of Randi Russell's right hand smashed an angled blow under Kropodkin's nose, driving his sinus cartilage into the frontal lobes of his brain, killing him instantly.

Randi felt the gush of blood over her hand, the death spasm racking Kropodkin's body. She rolled him onto the floor, clutching him in an awkward embrace to muffle the thud of his fall. Escaping from the handcuffs and killing her would-be rapist had been no major problem. Getting away afterward, with a dozen armed men a meager yard or two away beyond a flimsy unlockable door, was. It was only a matter of time, a very brief time, before they realized something was wrong in here. She faked a pained, whimpering outcry to buy a few more seconds as she wiped the blood from her hand. Hastily she redonned her clothes. She didn't have enough to wear for the outside. No doubt there was more clothing in the wall lockers, but she didn't have the time to rummage for it in the dark.

The laughing voices were trailing off out in the main bunkroom, and someone, Kretek, called out a question to Kropodkin.

She had to get out now. Kropodkin had been wearing a heavy flannel shirt with a hooded sweatshirt over it. With her night-adapted eyes she could make out where they had been discarded on the floor. They would have to do. For a fraction of a second she considered the sleeping bags in the bunks. No good. Too bulky. They would slow her down for those first few critical moments of flight.

The question from the room outside was repeated, more pointedly. Randi snatched up Kropodkin's garments, then grabbed for the carrying handle of the tape player atop the locker. Swinging it with all her strength, she smashed out the heavy thermopane of the bunkhouse window.

Mess table chairs crashed to the floor.

Randi threw the shirts over the bottom edge of the window frame as protection from the glass shards and rolled through to the outside. Behind her, the door to the women's quarters tore open.

She felt the blowing ice spicules stab at her face, and the explosion of outside cold. It all depended on that cold now. If the snow crust had frozen solidly enough in the night to support her weight, she would live. If she broke through and bogged down in a drift, she would die. Scrambling to her feet and clutching the shirts to her, she ran for the safety of the darkness.

She heard enraged shouting and started to weave and sidestep as she ran. A flashlight beam stabbed after her, and someone emptied a handgun out of the window. Bullet strikes sprayed snow around her feet. Pray that nobody in there had grabbed a submachine gun!

The toe of her boot broke through the snow crust, and for a hideous moment she stumbled; then she caught herself and ran on. Out of the light's reach, she veered sharply to her left. An Agram SMG started its angry typewriter chatter, but the gunner was firing blind, wildly spraying the night.

Randi diverted laterally again, heading away from the camp, the cabin lights fading rapidly to indistinction in the swirl of the snow. She was clear! She paused, panting, and struggled with the stolen shirts, untangling them, shaking out the glass shards and drawing them on, augmenting her ski outfit. Already she was feeling the bite of the cold. They weren't going to be enough protection out here tonight. Not nearly enough.

She ripped the tail off the flannel shirt and bound it over her face as an ad hoc snow mask and drew her already aching hands up into the overlong sleeves of the shirts. She looked around in the bleak near pitch blackness. The wind would be her compass. She would move north and try to join up with Jon and Valentina.

Randi's one course of action, her one chance, was to keep moving and somehow find the others. She would work on the premise that they had come down from the crash site to find Wednesday Island Station occupied. Given that, she would further presume that they would divert and go to cover on the island's central ridge, where they could both find shelter and keep the camp under observation. Knowing Jon, he would try to work in close during the night to try to establish the identity of the landing force and learn what had happened to her and Trowbridge.

The odds were not good. If her teammates hadn't come down from the crash site or if she couldn't find them, then she would die before morning. But the death out here looked cleaner and more defiant than the death back there. Hugging herself to conserve body warmth, Randi began her stumbling trudge through the growing blizzard.

Pouring through the broken window, the cold filled the bunkhouse like the touch of death. In the harsh white glare of the gas lantern, the naked body and bloody, ruined face of Stefan Kropodkin looked exceptionally obscene and grotesque. Kretek tore the sleeping bag from the bunk and covered his nephew.

His men stood by awkwardly, their faces impassive but with a suppressed glint of fear in their eyes. Someone had taken something from their leader. He did not react well to such acts, even in far lesser matters.

Kretek stared at the muffled mound at his feet. The one connection he'd had left to this thing called family. It was a current that ran deep through the Balkan cultures, even through a blackened soul such as his.

He had been a fool. He had made the mistake of viewing the blonde woman not as a threat but as a treat, like a bite of chocolate to be consumed casually in passing. Instead she had been a time bomb waiting for an opportune moment to explode.

He could read the signs. At her own choosing, she had torn loose, swatted Stephan like a cockroach, and made her escape. She was a professional in the deadliest possible definition of the term, and a pretty face and a nice pair of tits had blinded Kretek to this.

Stefan's hand protruded from beneath the sleeping bag, his fingers half curled in beseechment, pleading for revenge.

'Find that whore.' Kretek's words were a growling whisper. 'Get out there and find her. The only way any of you will ever leave this island is if you bring her back to me alive. Do you hear me? Alive!'

Vlahovitch, his chief of staff, hesitated only a moment before speaking. 'It will be done, Anton. Come on, the rest of you. Let's get a sweep organized. She won't get far in this weather. Move!'

Anton Kretek said nothing more as his men geared up to start the search. His thoughts were distant, planning what he would do when the golden-haired woman was brought before him.

CHAPTER THIRTY-SIX

Saddleback Glacier

Behind them, Jon Smith heard the thud of the explosion, faint in the face of the gusting wind. Straight off the Pole and unchecked by terrain, its cold was searing. Still, Smith viewed that wind and the ice particles driven before it as allies tonight. They would cut their pursuers' long-range vision and scour his party's crampon marks from the surface of the glacier.

Then there was also the subliminal human instinct to seek the easier path and turn away from a direct confrontation with that river of freezing fire, to keep your back to it. Accordingly, Smith would leave instinct to his enemies while he and his people would drive into the gale.

'Our friends reacquired their hand grenade,' Valentina commented. She was a shadow at the end of the safety line, her words muffled by her snow mask.

'Sounds like,' Smith replied. 'We'd better keep moving. They won't be too pleased with us now.'

'They weren't all that fond of us before, Jon. I see we're still angling to the northwest. Shouldn't we be turning south to pick up the flag trail back to the station?'

'We're not taking the trail back. Presumably the Russians know about it. They'll move to cut us off, or at least that's what I hope they'll do.'

'Where are we going, then?'

'To the station. But we'll be taking the scenic route. We'll drop out of the saddleback on the north side of the island and follow the shoreline around.'

'Uh, Jon, excuse me, but doesn't that mean pioneering a

303

two thousand-odd-foot descent down broken glacier fall and sheer rock cliff at night and in a bloody blizzard?'

'Essentially.'

Valentina's voice lifted. 'And you intend to do this with one total climbing tyro, i.e., me, and one trussed-up captive?'

The third member of the party had no commentary to add. Major Smyslov stood by silently, his hands bound in front of him and the safety rope knotted to his pack harness.

'Play the glad game, Val,' Smith replied. 'The Russians will never imagine us trying it.'

'With excellent reason!'

'We don't have a lot of choice in the matter. Val, you have the point and I'll take the center slot. The farther down we go on the north side of the saddleback, the more broken and treacherous the ice will become. If a crevasse should open up under you, I can go on belay and haul you out.'

'All right, but a pox upon the man who came up with "ladies first."'

Smith turned to confront his captive. 'Major, I'm counting on you not being as suicidal as the Misha's political officer. I am going to point out, however, that should you feel tempted to try any shoulder blocking from behind on any crevasses or cliff edges . . .' Smith gave the safety line a pointed tug. 'Wherever we go, you go.'

'This is understood, Colonel.' Smyslov's face couldn't be seen inside the darkness of his parka hood, and his reply was emotionless.

'Right, let's move out.'

The slow and careful advance across the glacier began. Visibility in the snow-racked night was all but nonexistent. Valentina felt her way forward, one cautious and deliberate step at a time, probing ahead continuously with the spike end of her ice axe. Smith held to his line of advance via the glowing green screen of his handheld GPS unit, carrying the precious little device next to his skin between each position fix to keep the batteries alive.

As predicted, as the descent down the glacier face steepened, the buckled, fractured ice grew increasingly unstable, the risk of crevasses escalating geometrically. Their creeping rate of advance slowed even further as they were forced to sidestep a growing number of man-devouring cracks in the glacial surface. Finally, the inevitable happened.

Valentina was edging along, forty feet ahead, a shadow silhouetted against the lesser shadow of the glacier. Then, suddenly, she simply vanished, a great puff of snow geysering around her previous position. Smith felt the heavy thud of the snow bridge giving way into the crevasse, and he was already throwing himself backward, digging in with his heel crampons. He felt the shock and snatch of the safety rope going taut as he went on belay, but he had been 'fishing' the line carefully and he hadn't given her slack enough to fall far.

It was a good belay, and Smith's brace held. With one hand twisted tightly in the line, he groped for the lantern at his belt, filling his lungs to ask if she was all right. But almost immediately he felt furious activity at the other end of the safety line.

Snapping on the lantern, he played the beam down the climbing rope to the point where it disappeared over the lip of the crevasse. He was just in time to see the head of Valentina's climbing axe whip over the edge of the ice. In seconds she had kicked herself a foothold and was scrambling out onto the surface.

'That was . . . rather interesting,' she wheezed, collapsing beside Smith.

Smith shoved his snow goggles up onto his forehead and turned his light into her face. 'Are you okay?'

'Barring a brief experiment with stark terror, I'm fine.' Valentina pushed up her own goggles and tugged aside her snow mask for a moment of serious breathing. 'What a marvelous invention adrenaline is. This damn pack weighs as much as Sinbad's Old Man of the Mountain, but when I was trying to get out of that bloody hole, it might have been a box of Kleenex!'

She took another enormous gulp of air, resuming control. 'Jon . . . Colonel . . . darling . . . I don't mean to complain, but it's getting just a tiny bit dicky out here.'

'I know.' He reached over clumsily and squeezed her shoulder. 'We have to get some rock under us. According to the photo maps there's a place a little way ahead where we can get off this glacier and traverse across to the face of West Peak. From there, a ledge stair-steps down to the beach. It shouldn't be too bad.'

Smith kept to himself the fact the photomaps were not nearly detailed enough to make a truly accurate assessment of the descent. This was yet another lesson in command presence. A good commander must always appear sure of himself and his decisions, even when he wasn't.

Switching off the lantern, Smith got himself under the load of his pack once more and stood up, offering Valentina a hand. Then he turned back to Smyslov, helping him to his feet as well. When the snow bridge had collapsed, Smith had felt the safety line behind him go taut. Smyslov had dropped into belay as well.

'Thanks, Major. I appreciated the backup.'

'As you said, Colonel . . .' The Russian's voice was still emotionless. 'Where you go, I go.'

CHAPTER THIRTY-SEVEN

Eielson Air Force Base, Fairbanks, Alaska

The two Air Commando MV-22 Ospreys had been repainted in the mottled white and gray of arctic camouflage. With their wings and propeller/rotors folded back and their long air-refueling probes thrusting forward, the VTOL assault transports lay under the glare of the hangar arc lights like a pair of beached narwhales, their Air Force ground crews swarming around them.

Down one hangar wall, Army rangers and NBC warfare specialists, likewise clad in arctic camo, sat or sprawled. Some read paperbacks; others played pocket video games or tried to doze on the cold concrete, all phlegmatically engaged in the traditional military pastime of hurry up and wait.

Outside, on the floodlit tarmac of the parking apron, an MC-130 Combat Talon brooded, an auxiliary power unit thumping steadily under its broad left wing. In the green glow of the cockpit instrumentation, a bored flight engineer held the big tanker/transport at ready-to-start-engines.

In the operations office at the rear of the hangar, the Air Commando flight crews clustered around a desk, looking on in awe as their task force commander accepted a telephone call.

Major Jason Saunders, a burly, brush-haired Special Operations veteran, barked back into the telephone handset. 'No, sir! I will not launch this mission before we have the weather for it . . . Yes, sir, I am fully cognizant of the fact that some of our people are in serious trouble up there. I want to get to them just as badly as you do, sir. But losing the rescue force because we executed prematurely is not going to do anybody any good! . . . No, sir, it is not just a matter of the weather at Wednesday Island or the weather here. It's a matter of what we'll hit in between . . . The only way we can reach that island is by using air-to-air refueling . . . Yes, sir, we are trained for it, but topping an Osprey off from a tanker aircraft is tricky under the best of conditions. Turbulence and icing are major concerns. Attempting it at night and inside an active polar storm front escalates the risks to the suicidal. If we fail to get fuel to the VTOLs, we could lose them and the landing teams over the pack. Or if we midair we could lose the whole damn force, tanker and all, and never get near that island.'

The major took a deep, controlling breath. 'In my best professional judgment, we are dealing with an impossible operational scenario at this time. I will not throw my men and aircraft away on an act of futility! Not even on your orders! . . . Yes, sir, I understand . . . I am holding the entire force at ready-to-launch, and we are receiving met updates every quarter hour. I guarantee you we will be airborne within five minutes of getting the weather . . . The meteorologists are saying sometime after first light, sir . . . Yes, sir, Mr. President. I quite understand. We will keep you advised.'

Saunders returned the phone to its cradle and collapsed face-forward onto the desktop. With his voice muffled by his crossed arms, he spoke to his squadron mates. 'Gentlemen, I am *ordering* you to never let me do anything like that again!'

308

CHAPTER THIRTY-EIGHT

Anacosta, Maryland

The windowless office offered no direct hint to the state of the world outside, and only the digital clock on his desk and his bone weariness told the director of Covert One that it was the middle of the night. Klein pushed his glasses onto his forehead and rubbed his burning eyes.

'Yes, Sam,' he said into the red telephone. 'I've been in communication with the captain of the *Haley*. He managed to close to within fifty miles of Wednesday Island before encountering solid pack ice too heavy for his ship to penetrate. He's been forced to fall back due to the gale conditions, but he intends to try again as soon as the weather improves.'

'Have they heard anything from Smith and his people?' President Castilla inquired, sounding fully as tired as Klein.

'The *Haley*'s radio watch reports they may have picked up possible trace transmissions from the island party's mobile transceiver this afternoon, but nothing decipherable. Clearly Smith has not been able to get the big station transmitter or the satellite phone back online. This could mean something or nothing. We've had one good piece of news on this point. Air Force Space Command reports solar flare activity has peaked and ionospheric conditions are improving. We should have decent communications back by tomorrow.'

'And what about strategic reconnaissance?' Castilla demanded.

'We've had one satellite over Wednesday since Smith and his team inserted, and a Navy Orion out of Dutch Harbor overflew the island this evening. Both passes were inconclusive. There's just too damn much snow in the clouds to give us a clean look at the ground, not even with infrared and thermographics. We have another sat pass scheduled for later tomorrow morning after the weather clears.'

'I keep hearing that same line from everyone,' Castilla said bitterly. 'After the weather clears.'

'We are not yet entirely masters of our own destiny, Sam. There are still forces in this world we can't even start to fight.'

'As is quite apparent.' There was a brooding pause at the White House end of the line. 'What about the FBI investigation of the Alaskan intercept incident? Is there any hint on who may have been responsible for it yet?'

'It's a literal dead end, Mr. President. We know for certain we were dealing with a Russian Mafia cell, but they were apparently acting as independent contractors. As for the identity of the true instigators, we still have no clue. The only men who could have told us died in the crash.'

The silence returned to the phone circuit.

'Fred,' Castilla said finally, 'I've decided to put the backup force on Wednesday Island. Smith and his team might just be suffering from fouled-up communications, but I'm getting a bad feeling about this situation.'

Klein suppressed his sigh of relief. 'Sam, I concur fully with that decision. In fact, I've been sitting here considering how I was going to phrase the request. I think we must have some kind of incident under way. Smith would have gotten a situation report out to us by now if he hadn't encountered trouble, bad communications or not.'

'Unfortunately, like everything else, the backup force is on hold until after the Christless weather clears!' Castilla flared into the phone. 'I just hope there's something left for them to back up.'

'Have you informed the Russians of your decision, Mr. President?'

'No, nor do I intend to, Fred. That's one of the reasons

I've elected to go overt with the operation. General Baranov, our Russian liaison, has been on call and standing by ever since we initiated the Wednesday Island operation. He's been practically hovering on the line. Now, and for about the last nine hours, he's become 'unavailable' and his aide de camp is not authorized to say anything beyond hello when he picks up the phone. I'm beginning to smell a considerable rat.'

'We've suspected the Russians have been hiding something related to the Misha incident from the beginning. Maybe Smith found it.'

'But, damn it, they came to us! They asked for our help!'

Klein sighed and flipped his glasses down onto the bridge of his nose. 'Again and again, Sam, we are dealing with the Russian government here. For a Russian political leader, *konspratsia* is like breathing; it's a survival mechanism. We are also dealing with the Russian culture. Remember what Churchill called them: 'Orientals with their shirttails tucked in.' To assume their logics and motivations will always be the same as ours is a mistake.'

'But why would they risk alienating my administration now, with so much on the table between our countries?'

'It must be something . . .' Klein paused for a moment, seeking for a word. '. . . extraordinary. I've had my people within the Russian Federation probing the Misha crash since the inception of this operation, and all they've been able to ascertain so far is that a ferocious level of security is involved. They've also encountered a term, 'the March Fifth Event.''

'The March Fifth Event? What's that?'

'As of yet we have no idea. It's a euphemism for some larger scenario within the former Soviet regime. The crash of the Misha 124 is apparently only one facet of this larger whole. The term is used almost fearfully within the current Russian government.'

'Get me more,' Castilla said flatly.

'We're already working the problem, but it may take a

while. The Russians have the lid screwed down airtight on this thing.'

'Understood.' Castilla's voice dropped an ominous octave. 'In the meantime we've stuck our necks way the hell out to accommodate President Potrenko on this. If he's backstabbing us now, whatever the reason, by God, he will rue the day . . .'

'I suggest we wait for Colonel Smith's sitrep, Mr. President,' Klein interjected quietly. 'That should give us a better idea of where we stand.'

'I only hope he'll be able to give us one, Sam. I'll be standing by at the White House.'

'I'll be remaining here at headquarters until we get a resolution, Mr. President. We will keep you advised.'

'Understood, Fred. It's going to be a long night until morning.'

CHAPTER THIRTY-NINE

The South Face, Wednesday Island

A polar environment demands that a dreadful knife-edged balance be maintained. Vigorous exercise and activity could keep the cold at bay, at least for a time. But not so much as to cause perspiration. Moisture destroys insulation. It can freeze and conduct temperature extremes. Sweat could kill you.

Randi Russell understood the mechanism and took care to stay within the boundaries of exertion as she swung wide around the Science Station and worked her way toward the ridge, moving fast but not too fast. As she semijogged through the darkness she grimly assessed her prospects.

They didn't look promising. Exercise or not, she was cold. The layers of clothing she possessed were adequate to ward off immediate hypothermic shock and to protect her from frostbite, but not over the long term. Exposure would become a critical factor within the next couple of hours. Furthermore, to keep warm she had to keep moving, and she recognized that her strength and energy reserves were already critically low.

Beyond that, twenty very nasty men on this island were out to kill her. Under other circumstances and with somewhat more lackadaisical security forces, she might hope pursuit might sensibly be put off until morning. But given she had just eliminated their employer's nephew, they'd be on her trail now and staying there.

Suddenly the sky lit up in the direction of the science station – a hazy globe of light bobbing into existence in the belly of the overcast. A parachute flare, a big one.

Randi wasn't particularly concerned. The blowing snow and sea smoke went opaque, absorbing the flare light, and the winds swept the flare to the south and away from her. It simply proved the point that they were actively in pursuit.

In a way, it was almost a favorable thing. It opened up possibilities. If there were men out here on the ice after her, there was the chance she might be able to ambush and kill one of them for his clothes and weapon.

Randi couldn't count on it, though. They would have seen Kropodkin. They would know what she was capable of. They would be afraid of her now, and their fear would make them more cautious and more dangerous.

Something else was certain. If Jon was anywhere in the vicinity, he'd know something was up. If he realized a pursuit was under way, he would know who was being pursued, and he would come for her.

Randi paused in her in-place jogging, an odd random thought darting into her tired mind.

Jon would come for her.

Always at the core of her internal bitterness toward Smith there had been the sense that he had not been there for her fiancé or her sister, that somehow he had not done enough to save them. And yet, from all she had learned and judged of the man in their random encounters over the past few years, Randi knew, without the faintest shadow of a doubt, that if Jon Smith realized she was in trouble, he would come to her aid, against all odds or orders and without regard for his own life. That was simply who he was.

Would he, could he, have done any less for Mike or Sophia?

She lacked the time to ponder the past now. She thought she could make out faint probing fingers of light in the storm. Powerful hand lanterns were panning the snow – the hunting party from the camp, tracking her. And the cold was gnawing at her, triggering an uncontrollable burst of shivering. She had to move again. Randi faced into the wind cas-

314

cading over the ridgeline and started to climb once more. Maybe she could find an avalanche she could push down on those bastards.

CHAPTER FORTY

The North Face, Wednesday Island

Smith flexed an all-environment chemical glow stick, breaking the inner capsule. Shaking its green luminescence to life, he clipped it to an outer cargo pocket of his snow smock. He could only hope that none of the Spetsnaz force had a line of sight on them. For this next evolution they had to be able to see.

A second pale green specter materialized in the swirling snow as Valentina lit off another chemical light. In the combination of the two glows they could just make out the irregular edge of a glacial precipice a few yards away.

They had reached the interface. They could descend no further on the broken, tumbled ice of the glacier. They must cross to the solid rock of West Peak, if the mountain would accept them.

Smith shrugged off his pack and drew a flare and an ice screw from its side pouches. Kneeling, he cranked the screw into the surface of the glacier, angling it away from the edge. Clipping his safety line to the anchor, he stood and edged carefully to the unstable shoulder of the ice. Striking the flare's igniter, he pitched the hissing red ball of flame into the black void below. He watched as it bounced and sputtered down the edge of the jumbled icefall to hang up on a ledge perhaps 120 feet down. In the ruddy glare he could make out the darkness of basalt, the peak facing. But beyond the ledge was the void of another, deeper drop-off.

'The photomaps were right.' Smith lifted his voice over the wind. 'There is a ledge down there.'

Valentina edged to his side, her hand on the safety line.

'It's not really all that much of a ledge, is it?'

'It widens out and descends the farther west you go, like it does on the south side. I'm just glad there's a valid traverse we can use to reach it. I wasn't sure there'd be one.'

Valentina's hood turned toward him. 'What would you have done if there hadn't been?'

'Let's just say I'm pleased the subject isn't going to come up. Once we get on that ledge it shouldn't be too much of a problem to drop down to the shoreline.'

'The operative word in that sentence, Jon, is "once."'

'We can make it.' Smith forced his confidence again, eyeing the descent. At this point, the glacier ice began its final cascade down the near vertical north wall of the central ridge, a frozen waterfall that extruded slightly from the mountain face. With luck they could work their way down to the ledge in the joining angle between rock and ice.

'I'll lower you first, Val, then the packs, then Smyslov. I'll rappel down last.'

He saw Valentina shoot a glance back toward the Russian, who stood defiantly leashed a few feet away. 'Jon, might I have a few private words with you?'

'Of course.'

They stepped away from the edge of the glacier, moving down the back trail until they were behind Smyslov. It was hard to tell with the darkness and the bulky clothing, but the Russian seemed to stiffen as they moved past him.

Valentina lifted her snow goggles and pushed down her ice-encrusted snow mask, her face underlit by her glow stick. 'We have a problem here,' she said, keeping her voice modulated to be just audible over the wind.

'Just one?' Smith replied with grim humor.

She tilted her head toward Smyslov's back, not smiling. 'I'm serious, Jon. We've got to be able to move. He's slowing us down and he's complicating a situation that's quite sticky enough as is.'

'I know it, but we don't have much of a choice in the matter.' He shifted his own mask and goggles, granting her the right of reading his own facial expressions. 'We can't just turn him loose. If he rejoined the Spetsnaz force he could be a valuable asset for them, and the deck is already stacked against us.'

'I quite agree, Jon. We can't allow him to return to his Russian friends.' Her expression was as arctic as the environment. 'But we can't very well keep him as a pet. As we lack a convenient POW camp to drop him off at, that leaves us with only one option . . .'

'Which I am not yet ready to consider.'

She frowned. 'Jon, civilization is a marvelous institution and all that, but be practical. We are up against the wall here, literally! If it's that whole Hippocratic oath thing, I can deal with it. Gregory and I can go for a little walk to admire the scenery – '

'No,' Smith replied firmly.

'Jon, we can't afford – !'

'I'm not sure if he's an enemy yet, Val.'

'Jon,' her voice lifted in protest, 'I was there this afternoon when the bolshi bastard tried to drop the hammer on you! That doesn't make him a friend!'

'I know it. Trust me on this. Something's telling me that Smyslov isn't sure just what he is yet himself. I want to give him the chance to decide. This is a command decision, Val. It's not open for discussion.'

'What if he decides he's a "them" and not an "us"?'

'Then, as the book says, we will reassess the situation and take appropriate action as the tactical conditions dictate.'

'And what if hanging onto Smyslov gets us dead, Jon?'

'Then I will have royally fucked up my job, and the failure of this mission will rest entirely with me.'

She started a heated response, hesitated, then smiled wryly. 'Well, as long as you'd be willing to admit to it,' she replied, redonning her snow mask. 'But if you get us killed before you take me to bed properly at least once, I shall throw an absolute hissy and not speak to you for an entire week.'

Smith laughed aloud in spite of himself and their situation. 'Thank you for that motivation, Val,' he replied, giving her shoulders a light squeeze. 'Now, let's get this descent out of the way.'

CHAPTER FORTY-ONE

The South Face, Wednesday Island

Randi wanted more snow and more wind, badly. As she had feared, there wasn't storm enough to completely cover her trail. Looking back, she could see the flare glows and light beams following her half-erased tracks. There must be at least half a dozen of them, and they were driving her steadily higher up the face of the ridge.

She wasn't dodging gunfire yet. That was good. It meant they didn't have a visual on her. But she couldn't see or plan for more than a yard or two ahead, and she was losing orientation in the swirling night. Randi could no longer place herself in relation to the rest of the island. She was just somewhere on the central ridge. It was only a matter of time before she found herself trapped on a dead-end ledge or in a no-exit pocket.

She must find rock, bare rock, amid a universe of ice and snow, to lose her trail on. Then she had to find some kind of shelter. She was getting tired, so incredibly tired. She stumbled over a snow-covered pile of rubble and fell, striking her shoulder against a massive boulder.

No, not a boulder. Too big. A cliff face. God, if she could only just see where she was! If she could just lie here for a second and close her eyes . . . *Jon, dammit, where are you?*

She snapped her eyes open and forced herself to her hands and knees. *Move, you stupid bitch! Don't you remember? There's no one in the world you can depend on but yourself. Everyone else dies on you. Move! You're losing time and distance! The lights are getting closer.*

Randi got to her feet and moved on, her right hand

brushing the cliff face as a guide. What the hell did the world look like around her? All she could see were differing shades and textures of darkness.

They were well above the science station now. The cliff face was on her right, so she must be going west. Off to her left would be essentially nothing, the downslope. How steep would the drop-off be along here? Somehow it 'felt' like another cliff edge. So she was on a ledge or shelf, then. What was ahead? That was impossible to say, but the ledge seemed to be tilting outward in an ominous trend.

She didn't have to look back. She knew what was behind her.

Randi could be sure of only one thing. She wasn't going to be taken. If she reached a dead end, she must find a way to make her pursuers kill her.

She heard the rattle of a machine-gun burst, and she instinctively threw herself facedown on the ledge before she realized there were no bullet strikes nearby. They weren't that close yet. Someone back there was getting trigger-happy.

Randi's relief lasted only a second. From somewhere above her she both heard and felt a deep, almost explosive *crump*. The reverberations of the gunfire had broken a snow cornice loose. Avalanche! Where? In front of her? Behind her? On top of her? It was impossible to tell beyond 'close.' She cowered and threw her arms over her face.

There was a brief whispering rumble, and the ledge trembled. Feathery plumes of sprayed snow engulfed her, but there was no crushing impact, no frozen flood sweeping her away. After a wired, panicky moment she relaxed and dropped her arms. It had been only a small one. A few tons of freed snow at most, and it had passed a few yards ahead. She shook off the thin haze of snow that had caked atop her, and got back to her feet.

The question now was, could she get over the mound of loose snow that would be heaped on the ledge without losing herself over the side? Too bad it hadn't fallen between her and the search party. It might have done her some good then.

Randi's mind locked up for a second, then raced. The slide had done her some good. Possibly it had given her a chance.

What if her pursuers found her tracks leading up to the edge of the slide and then stopping? Would they think she had been swept away? They couldn't be happy with being out here tonight, either. Maybe an excuse to quit the search would be all they'd need.

She took two or three strides forward to reach the edge of the loose slide snow. This would be it. She would have to go straight upslope from this point, and it didn't matter what the cliff face might look like even if she could see it.

And then there was the other problem: her lack of gloves. So far she'd been able to protect her hands inside the over-length sleeves of the outer shirts she wore. But she would need them to climb with. How long would she have before she started to take skin damage at this temperature? Two minutes? Three?

There was one positive. The face immediately above her couldn't be too high. The falling snow had reached the ledge in only a couple of seconds. She looked over her shoulder. The flashlights were growing brighter. She had to act, now!

Randi pulled the sleeves back from her hands and sprang upward as far as she could. Her nails scrabbled across ice-sheathed rock; one tore in a stab of pain; then she caught a handhold. Breath hissed between her clenched teeth. She hauled herself upward by arm strength alone, not letting her boots touch and mark the cliff face. Supported by her left hand for a moment, she darted her right upward, and a merciful universe let her find another grip.

Once more she hauled herself upward, shoulder muscles cracking. She was high enough to use her boots now without leaving obvious marks, and she could start hunting for and using toeholds as well. She had rock climbed before, for pleasure, but there was nothing pleasant about this. Her hands were already on fire with the cold.

Come on, Randi! You've only got your eyes closed because the Utah sun is too bright. It's ninety degrees in Zion National Park and you're wearing shorts and a halter top and you can feel the climbing harness hugging you, keeping you safe. You've got just a few yards left to go and you're at the top and you can dangle your feet over the edge and laugh and drink a cold Diet Pepsi from the cooler.

Just a few yards more.

She found a horizontal fissure she could stand in for a moment, and she beat her fists against the rock to force feeling back into them. She couldn't let them go completely numb yet. She had to be able to touch her way up!

Voices! Reflecting lights. The search party! Limpetlike, Randi plastered herself against the rock face. They had reached the slide. They were on the ledge directly below her.

This would be it. Would they buy into her accidental death, or would they suspect the trick? Would a light beam play up the cliff face, followed by a stream of bullets or just one carefully aimed shot?

Her hands! Dear God! Her hands!

They were having an argument down there! *Come on! Come on! Before I fall off and land on top of you!* Who was going to win? The tired or the dedicated? *I'm dead, damn it! Buried under an avalanche! Your red-haired bastard boss should be satisfied with that!*

They were moving. They were going back. They were leaving. After an eternity they were leaving. And no one had looked up.

Randi had to continue the climb, and she had to pray there really was only a short distance to go. She had no feeling left beyond her wrists, and she was not going to get down from here without either falling to her death or losing her hands.

Just a few yards more.

Another hunt for a foothold. She didn't care anymore if it was solid or not. A levering of her trembling body up another foot or two, again . . . again . . . Reach up once more and find something to hook those numb claws over. Something . . . soft. Fresh banked snow, the trailing edge of the broken cornice. The top! A final push and she was burrowing wormlike through the cliff-edge drift. She was out. She'd made it!

Randi came up onto her knees. Fumbling dully, she pulled her nonexistent hands back up the sleeves of the overshirts. Crossing her arms over her chest inside the shirts, she thrust her hands into her armpits. Shivering and rocking in place, she waited in dread. Slowly, slowly, she began to feel pain, the terrible fiery pain of returning circulation. It felt wonderful! And she knelt there for a long time savoring the agony, tears streaming from her eyes.

But she could feel the tears freezing. As the deadness left her hands she became aware once more of the deeper overall cold saturating her. The wind was stronger, more piercing up here, the snow being driven harder before it.

That should mean something to her, but to Randi's failing mentality it didn't. The deadly, stealthy enemy hypothermia was on her now.

Move. She had to move. Tapping the last dregs of her energy reserves, she forced herself to her feet. With her arms still crossed under her shirts, she tried to bulldoze ahead through the snowbanks. Why was the wind so much worse here? She muzzily groped at the thought. Of course, she must be right on top of the ridge. There was nothing to windward to block it anymore.

But what did that mean? Why was that important?

Randi bulled forward another yard, another step, struggling through snow and blackness; then, suddenly there wasn't anything under her left boot. She heard the crump of another collapsing cornice, and the snow around her came alive. She was falling with it, sinking into it, drowning in it.

But why was that important?

CHAPTER FORTY-TWO

The North Face, Wednesday Island

The climbing rope uncoiled as it arced outward and down to the target ledge, sinuously outlined in the light of the dropped flare.

'I'm going to double-line you down.' Jon Smith twisted a loop of the rope through a carabiner on Valentina Metrace's climbing harness. 'I'll be supporting most of your weight on the safety line.' He snapped the second rope into place. 'All you have to do is back down the bergschrund and keep the main line untangled as it feeds.'

'Fine. No problem. What's a bergschrund?'

Smith smiled patiently in the glow of their lum sticks. 'It's the interface between the mountain and the glacier.' His beard-darkened features looked tired but also confident, as if he had every certainty in the world she could pull this off. Valentina wished she could feel the same.

'I'll take your word for it. And then?'

'I'll use the main rope to lower the packs and rifles to you. Haul the gear well away from the glacier side. It looks a little unstable and we might have an icefall or two.'

She felt her eyes widen, and she glanced toward the glacial lip. 'An icefall?'

Again came that steadying smile. 'Then again, we might not. But be ready to duck, just in case.'

'You may rest assured!' Valentina knew flippancy was inappropriate at the moment, but she had used it as an effective screen for personal self-doubts and fears for so long, it was a difficult habit to break.

'I'll send Smyslov down next. Secure him well clear of the

glacier face as well. And Val, remember, he is a prisoner.'

She started to flare but caught herself. After all, she'd been the one to inject that concern into the proceedings. 'That's now a given, Jon.'

'Good enough. After that, I'll rappel down to join you on the ledge. Then we're out of here and on our way.'

Valentina suspected that for all Smith's confidence it likely wasn't going to be all that easy.

The black drop down the trough between stone and ice, with the winds clawing at her and nothing at her back but a long fall, was easily one of the most terrifying things she had ever done, and she had lived a life that held many moments of terror. Yet she could view the act almost in the abstract. Valentina Metrace had long ago learned to compartmental-ize her fears, locking them up to scream and weep in their own little mental cage while the remainder of her being dealt with the necessities of survival. She could do the same with pain, compassion, or any number of other emotions when needs required. As with her sophisticate's humor, she found it a useful mechanism.

Still, 120 feet could take a century to descend. Twice, loose ice slabs broke loose beneath her boots, crunching and clattering away to shatter on the ledge below. In each instance she paused, took a deliberate, steadying breath, and continued.

Finally, she stood on rock once more. The target ledge left a great deal to be desired. At its glacier-side end, it was barely as wide as a man was tall, and slick with glaze ice. Yet it was still an improvement over dangling at the end of a rope. Pressing back against the cliff face, she unlatched from the main line and gave it a signaling tug. It slithered back up the edge of the glacier and out of her light stick's illumination.

Valentina closed her eyes to the wind- and snow-wracked blackness of the night and took a moment to slap down that shrieking, weeping thing in the back of her mind.

A few minutes later the first of the packs skidded down to

the ledge. Signaling for more slack on the safety line, she dragged the equipment to a wider section of the ledge, beyond her judged reach of any avalanche, methodically repeating the process with the other packs and the cased rifles as they were lowered. Pausing, she studied the mound of equipment and weapons for a moment. This wasn't a particularly auspicious environment for controlling a hostile and potentially dangerous prisoner.

'Damn it, Jon,' she murmured, 'this could have been so much easier – just scrick, and over and done with.'

She took a piton and a rock hammer from the gear stack and hunted for a fissure in the cliff face at about head height. Finding one, she sank the piton into it. Taking a short hank of loose rope from one of the packs, she ran it through the fixed ring of the piton, whipping a loop and slipknot into one end.

Looking up, Valentina saw a pair of green glows at the top of the glacier. Jon's light stick and a second, starting the descent of the glacier edge, moving slowly and painfully. Smyslov was on his way down. Supporting the Russian's full weight, Smith was feeding the line through the belaying point a few jerky feet at a time.

Again Val wondered about both men, but especially about Jon Smith. Her professional survivor's instincts told her Smith was wrong about the Russian, that Smyslov was a foolish risk to be taking. And yet, maybe that was one of the things that drew her to Jon. Scruples were perforce rare within the profession. Maybe this was a man strong enough not to be totally expedient.

With a clatter of dislodged ice chips, Smyslov backed off the glacier face and onto the ledge, his bound hands gripping the main rope. Valentina flipped her safety line aside and came in behind the Russian.

She slid the M-7 utility knife/bayonet out of her harness sheath and lightly pressed the tip of its heavy blade into the small of his back. 'I'm right behind you, Gregori. I'm going to take you off the climbing rope now and I'm going to tuck you out of the way for a little bit. Colonel Smith wants to keep you alive, so let's both work toward that goal, shall we?'

'I am agreeable,' the Russian replied, his voice flat. 'What do you think about it?'

'I think I am under Colonel Smith's orders.' Cautiously she used her free hand to reach around in front of Smyslov, to unclip the climbing rope from his harness. 'But I wouldn't push the point. Now, I will step in close to the cliff face, and you will turn around slowly, facing outward, and step past me. Please recall it's still a long way down and I'm the one on the safety line. All right, let's go.'

They accomplished the maneuver like a cautious dance step, Smyslov moving past her down the ledge. Taking a grip on his climbing harness with one hand, Valentina followed, the knife poised and aimed at the base of his spine.

Valentina caught the metallic glint of the piton she had driven into the rock face. She let Smyslov move under it.

'Stop . . . Face the cliff . . . Easy, now.'

Smyslov obeyed. Valentina swiftly looped the slipknot over Smyslov's disposacuff-bound wrists. Hauling on the free end of the line, she lifted his wrists to the piton. She ran a second loop around the join of the disposacuffs and drew both tight, snubbing the rope off.

'That should keep you out of mischief,' she said, sheathing her knife.

'Why?' Smyslov asked, his voice toneless.

'Why what?'

'Why go through all this? Why not simply kill me?'

'I must confess, Gregori, the thought has occurred,' she replied, leaning against the cliff face for a moment. 'But Jon doesn't fancy the idea for some reason. When you called your Spetsnaz friends down on us last afternoon . . . Was it just last afternoon? . . . And when you tried to shoot Jon in the cave, that would have been quite good enough for me, but not for our colonel. He seems to think you are not totally beyond redemption. Or possibly he just doesn't play the game that way.'

'He is a good man,' Smyslov murmured over the rush of the wind.

'Probably better than you or I or anyone else on this island.' A wistfulness crept unbidden into her reply. 'He'll die being a good man one of these days. Well, we'll be back with you shortly. I do hope you won't mind hanging around for a bit.'

She edged back down the ledge to the glacier interface, the bergschrund, as Smith had called it. Then she remembered his final instruction. She went back to the gear cache for a second piton. Returning to the glacier face, she dropped to her knees on the ledge, searching for a belaying point. It wasn't easy; her light source was feeble, and the ledge seemed a solid slab of stone. Finally she found a narrow crack near the lip of the ledge, and she took care to drive the piton in as deeply as possible. Not wanting to unhitch herself from the safety rope, she hooked a snap carabiner through the piton ring and latched a loop of the line through that, leaving herself enough slack for free movement. Standing once more, she moved below the glacier face and gave the main rope a signal tug.

At the top of the glacier, she saw the ball of green luminance that marked Jon Smith start his bounding descent down the ice extrusion.

Not long now and he would be with her. A hundred feet to go . . . seventy . . . fifty . . .

Valentina heard a creaking groan, the yielding of inorganic matter on a massive scale, followed by a series of explosive cracks. She threw herself back against the cliff face, pressing spine to stone just as the entire vertical edge of the glacier fractured and dissolved into a thundering cascade of tumbling, grinding ice.

Val was aware of the strike and brush of ice fragments, none of them quite large enough to bludgeon her or carry her away. The big stuff, the car- and truck-sized slabs of glacier, were tipping outward, their weight and momentum carrying them beyond the shelf of rock. Then a streak of green light plummeted past en route to oblivion, and she dimly heard her own scream of denial over the grating roar of the icefall. Then something seized her with irresistible force, snatching her off her feet and hurling her to the ledge. Her head slammed into stone; white light blazed behind her eyes; then blackness took her.

Consciousness returned with the sound of an accented voice calling her name. She found herself lying facedown on the rock shelf, unnervingly near the edge, and with something stabbing uncomfortably into her stomach. Her head rang with the blow she had taken, but her thick parka hood had kept her skull from fracturing. She didn't think she'd been unconscious for long, but the cold of the stone and the wind were already creeping into her. Groggily she tried to stand but found she couldn't. It was as if she were glued down on the ledge. A moment of befuddled exploration revealed why.

It was the safety line, and the thing that was prodding her so uncomfortably was the piton and carabiner that she had looped it through. Drawn taut, the line ran from her climbing harness, through the carabiner, and over the lip of the ledge. Valentina's last few seconds of memory returned, and she recalled the avalanche and Smith's chem light falling past her.

'Jon!'

There was no answer from the black void beside her. The lifeline hung rigid, a dead weight hanging suspended from its end. She pushed and writhed, trying to draw back from the edge against the merciless drag of the rope, only to find she couldn't gain even an inch.

It was futile. Under ideal circumstances she might have been able to lift the hundred and eighty-odd pounds dangling at the end of the rope, at least for a short distance, but conditions were far from ideal. Sprawled on an ice-glassy slab of rock, there was nothing to give her leverage or purchase. She was hopelessly pinned.

Again she heard her name being called. A dozen yards

farther down the ledge she could see Smyslov leaning back against his restraints, trying to see what was happening.

'I'm here, Gregori, and from the look of things I'm not going anyplace.'

'What has happened?'

She hesitated for a moment, then realized her list of available assets and allies was ominously short. In a few terse sentences she described the situation.

'You should not have secured the lifeline like that,' he said.

'Do bloody tell,' Valentina grunted, again straining against the drag on the rope.

'Is the colonel all right?'

'I don't think so. He hasn't answered me and I don't feel any movement at the other end of the line. I'm hoping he was just knocked out by the icefall.'

'You must get him up and out of there, Professor,' Smyslov called back.

'I know it, but I can't get enough slack on the safety line to tie it off! If I cut loose, he's gone!'

'Then you must drive in a second piton and secure your climbing harness to it. You will then be able to unharness without losing the colonel.'

Valentina gave up on fighting the lifeline. 'That's an excellent idea. Only I don't have a second bloody piton!'

'Then use the spike of your rock hammer.'

She looked around within the arc of her reach and the glow of her light stick and swore again. 'I managed to lose that, too.'

'Professor, he could be injured or dying!'

'I know that, damn it!'

Smyslov said no more. Panting, Valentina rested the side of her head against the frozen stone. They would all die if she didn't do something. Trapped here, the storm and the inevitable, invasive cold would finish them all.

There was an answer, of course, obvious, simple, and easily done.

She could free herself by cutting the safety rope.

But as Jon had phrased it, that was an option she was not yet ready to consider.

She had her knives, three of them: the utility blade at her belt and her two throwing knives in the slip sheaths strapped to her forearms. Maybe she could use one of them as an ad hoc piton. But she lacked a hammer to drive the blade in solidly, and the hilts weren't meant for the task. One slip or fumble, and Jon would be dead – granted that he wasn't already.

That left Smyslov, the man she had quite been prepared to kill. But how had Jon phrased it? 'I'm not sure if he's an enemy yet, Val.'

Logic would indicate that he must be. But logic also indicated that her only alternatives were to cut Jon's safety line or allow all three of them to perish on this mountainside.

'Gregori, how good a judge of human nature do you think the colonel is?'

'A very good one, I should think,' the Russian replied, puzzled at the question.

'I hope you're right. I'm going to throw you a knife.'

It was going to be a task easier said than done. Combatant knife throwing was one of the most difficult of the martial arts to master. Were belts awarded for it, Valentina Metrace would easily be a red-belt master. Yet even the legendary William Garvin would have been challenged by this scenario: high gusting wind, miserable lighting, a bad throwing angle, and thick, hampering clothing. Most critically, there was nothing to sink the blade into.

The best bet would have been to skid the knife across the surface of the ledge to Smyslov's feet, but given the way she'd tethered him to the cliff face, he couldn't reach down to collect it.

Valentina peeled off her overmittens and gloves. Lying on her side, she pivoted around the piton to face Smyslov, the move putting her legs over the cliff edge from the knees down. She slid the utility blade out of its belt sheath, judging its throwing balance. 'Here's how it's going to work, Gregori. I'm going to try to put this knife on the cliff face just above your head. You're going to have to catch it as it slides down past you. Got it?'

'I understand, Professor. I will be ready.'

'All right, get ready. I'll throw at the count of three. One . . . two . . . three!'

She made the throw, biasing the spin of the knife so it would strike haft foremost. Over the wind she heard the *tink* of steel hitting. Then she heard his explosive curse in Russian. 'I missed it! It bounced off and over my shoulder.'

Probably that damn composite plastic grip. It wouldn't hit and lie dead.

'All right,' she replied, keeping her voice level. 'We'll try that again.'

She drew the first of her handmade throwing blades, the steel of the little weapon warmed by her own body heat.

'Ready? Again, it will be over your head. Throwing on three. One . . . two . . . three.'

Her arm whipped back and forward, easing the throw into a toss instead of a strike. Steel rang on stone again, and she saw Smyslov's silhouette lunge, trying to pin the sliding knife between his body and the cliff face. Again he cursed as the blade landed at his feet, wasted.

'I am sorry, Professor. I missed again.'

One chance left. Valentina blew into her cupped palms, flexing and wringing her aching fingers to renew warmth and sensitivity. 'Once more, Gregori, only this time we're going to work it a bit differently.'

'However you say, Professor.'

She slid the second throwing knife out of its forearm sheath. 'All right. This time, lean back.'

'Lean back?'

'That's right. Lean all the way back, with your arms extended out in front of you. Hang on to the piton.'

Smyslov obeyed, tilting his body away from the cliff face. 'Like this?' he questioned.

She studied his outline in the glow-stick light for a moment. 'Yes, just right, perfect. Now, hold still, very, very still . . . And, Gregori, one more thing.'

'What is that?'

'Sorry about this.'

She heard Smyslov's startled bellow as the steel fang spiked into his left forcarm, just above the wrist.

'I apologize again, Gregori, but that was the only place I could make the damn thing stay.'

She watched the Russian cross his bound wrists and awkwardly yank the knife out of his blood-blotched sleeve. The razor-edged blade made short work of both the tether rope and the nylon handcuffs. Now he was the one free, and she the one bound.

No matter what, at least one of them would get off this ledge alive tonight. Jon would approve. With her own knife in his hand, Smyslov loomed over her now, his face impassive. What happened next would be out of her hands. Wearily, she rested her cheek on the ledge and closed her eyes.

Smith felt himself floating, adrift, but it wasn't a pleasant, dream-state float. His body was twisted, distorted, and a broad spectrum of aches and pains stabbed at him. And there was the cold and the growing numbness. This wasn't right. He must react.

His eyes snapped open, and he saw only snow-streaked blackness. Lifting his head, he could make out a twisted tangle of rope and harness enmeshing him, greenly outlined by the chem light. There was nothing else, nothing around him. He was hanging suspended, faceup in his climbing harness, swinging slightly in the gusting wind, a single thin line extending, bar rigid, above him.

Memory reactivated. He'd been rappelling down to the ledge when the whole vertical face of the glacier had disintegrated under him. The ice, under heavy compression, had given way explosively, and simple luck must have blown him outward, so he had not been caught and carried away under the fall. Nor had he hit the ledge. He must be hanging somewhere below it.

Cautiously, he reached around himself, exploring his surrounding block of space, trying to find something solid. The fingertips of his right hand just brushed a rock wall. The mountain face under the ledge must be slightly concave. He couldn't call how far below the ledge he was suspended. Nor could he tell how much empty air was below him – possibly two feet, possibly two hundred.

He took a fast inventory of his physical condition. He was bruised and battered, but everything seemed to work. He must have ridden the outer edge of the fall, and the natural elasticity of the nylon climbing rope had absorbed some of the shock of the drop. However, both cold and weakness were settling in fast.

Unfortunately his direct-action options appeared to be limited to a hand-over-hand ascent up the safety line, and he lacked a pair of prusik rope climbers.

And what about the others? Had Val and Smyslov been caught in the avalanche? Squinting upward through the snow, he could make out a ruddy smudge of light outlining the edge of the shelf above him. The first flare they'd dropped to the ledge had gone out. Somebody must have ignited a second one up there. Somebody must have survived. Fighting the constriction of the climbing harness, he tried to inflate his lungs to yell.

Then something entered his sphere of illumination, sliding down the rigid length of his safety line. Another rope, a loop bent onto its end, had been shackled to the safety line by a carabiner. The foot loop for a Z-pulley rescue rig.

Smith caught the new rope. Unshackling it, he hooked the loop over one boot. Pulling himself upright on the safety line, he stood in the loop and gave the rescue line a haul-away tug. The rescue rig went taut, and someone on the ledge began to heave him up in incremental pulls, the slack in the safety rope being taken in as well.

As he was lifted to the ledge, Smith had plenty of time to wonder what he was going to find. One thing was certain: Valentina Metrace didn't have the mountaineering expertise to set up a Z-pulley like this one.

He reached the ledge ceiling and was distracted by having to fend himself off the cliff face. Accordingly the lip of the shelf took him by surprise. Suddenly hands were reaching down and gripping his harness, helping to heave him up and over the edge.

The feeling of rock under him was one of the grandest sensations he had felt for a long time. For a few moments he knelt on his hands and knees, luxuriating in its solidity. He allowed the trembling to take over then but fought off the recurrent surge of blackness that threatened to break over him. He shook his head like a wounded bear and looked around the ledge. By the sputtering red light of the half-consumed flare, he could make out the multiple anchors and interlacing rope loops of the Z-rig, and the sprawled bodies of Valentina and Smyslov, the two looking fully as totaled as he felt.

Smith inhaled a pull of icy air. 'Hydration and energy bars,' he said hoarsely. 'Now!'

They huddled together on the ledge, gulping down alternating mouthfuls of body-warmed water and vitamin-augmented chocolate, their metabolic furnaces catching up with the crisis load thrown on them.

Smith noted the black bloodstains on the sleeve of Smyslov's snow smock. 'How bad's the arm?'

The Russian shook his head. 'Not bad. I have a first aid pack on it.'

'Hurt in the icefall?'

Smyslov shot a wry look at Valentina. 'Not exactly. It is complicated. I'll tell you later.'

'If you say so,' Smith replied. 'Now that the rush is over, I suppose I should ask just who is whose prisoner at the moment.'

Smyslov shook his head, that self-derisive grin still on his cold-reddened face. 'It beats the shit out of me.'

'I'm a little vague on the question myself,' Val interjected, 'but may I propose that, for now, we just get down off this damn mountain. We can sort out the fiddly bits in the morning.'

'That sounds like a sensible notion to me, Major. What do you say?'

'I agree, Colonel, eminently sensible.'

'Then let's move, people. This mountain isn't getting any shorter.'

Wincing against the objections of bruised and stiffening muscles, Smith pulled himself to his feet. Val helped him up and paused for a moment, mittened hands resting on his chest. 'It appears there might be something to this scruples business after all,' she said.

'Every once in a while you can be pleasantly surprised.'

CHAPTER FORTY-THREE

The North Face, Wednesday Island

Randi Russell was on her feet and moving again before she regained true consciousness. Nor was there any clarity to that consciousness. She had no memory of how she had freed herself from the snowslide. Nor did she have any idea where she was or where she was going. It was all dying-animal reflex now.

She no longer felt particularly uncomfortable or fearful. The false warmth of hypothermia was on her, and point by point, she was detaching from the world. The imperative to keep moving was still present, but even that was fading. The next time she fell would be the last.

There were no destinations left in the cold, black emptiness surrounding her. She moved downward toward the shoreline simply because that was the easiest direction to go, the terrain working in her favor.

Randi did not realize the meaning of the jumbled piles of ice blocks she'd started to encounter. It was the broken rim of sea ice building up along the northern coast of Wednesday Island. She was only dimly aware that the searing, deadening wind was being blocked, and she turned parallel to the ghostly stacked rubble, stumbling along the snow-jacketed gravel of the beach.

The ghosts were dominating her now – sounds, voices, visions out of her past, pleasant and not, replaying in random fragments. Santa Barbara, Carmel, UCLA, Iraq, China, Russia, the lesser places in between. People known. Things experienced.

She tried to cling to the pleasant memories: playing on

the beach below her parents' home, conspiring in happy sisterhood with Sophia, Mike undressing her and lowering her to the soft grass on that first sweet, trembling time.

But the blackness and the cold kept bringing in the other occasions: standing at Sophia's side, scattering their parent's ashes. The awful pain of the open grave at Arlington, hearing taps played for the bold, smiling other half of herself. The anger and the need to strike out at something, anything, that had changed her from a CIA linguist-analyst to a wet-work field agent. The face of the first person she'd ever been forced to kill. Standing at the edge of that second grave at Ivy Hill Cemetery in Alexandria, with the last person she had to love in the world leaving her behind.

Randi's boot twisted on a frozen stone. She made no effort to catch herself as she fell. A faint voice in the back of her mind raged at her to get up, but it was too much bother to listen. She crawled a few feet into the lee of an ice mass and curled up, husbanding the last fading remnants of body warmth as the snow sifted over her.

This would be where she would die. Randi would fight it no further. There was no sense to it. She gave herself to the phantoms, reliving the dimming, fragmented kaleidoscope of memory.

The recall of Sophia became especially strong, and Randi was pleased. She was with her sister again.

But Sophia kept taking her to the wrong places. Back to Mike's death. Back to stand before that other tall, sober soldier in a black beret. Back to the one truly serious argument she'd ever had with her sister. Back to the one unforgivable thing Sophia had ever done to her.

'I'm going to marry Jon, Randi,' Sophia said again.

No!

'Jon is sorry for what he's done to you, Randi. More sorry than you will ever know or be willing to understand.'

'I don't want for him to be sorry! I want for him to have saved you!' Randi cried back, their argument flaring, as raw and as painful as ever.

'No one could have saved me, Randi. Not Jon, nor even you.'

'There must have been a way!'

Sophia's eyes filled her universe now. 'If there had been a way, Jon would have found it. Just as you would have found it.'

'No!'

'Say Jon's name for me, Randi.'

'I won't! I don't want to!'

Sophia's voice grew urgent. 'Say his name, Randi!'

Randi couldn't refuse her. 'Jon,' she sobbed.

'Louder, Randi.' Sophia's eyes were loving, frightened, demanding, 'Say it louder!'

'Jon!'

Why was her sister doing this? Randi just wanted to sleep. To go away.

Sophia wouldn't allow it. She was bending over her now, shaking her. 'Again, Randi! Call to him! Scream it! Scream Jon's name!'

'JON!'

Smith broke step and looked up, scanning the night. 'What was that?'

'What was what?' Valentina inquired, coming up behind him. Smith had taken the point, breaking trail with Valentina and Smyslov trailing on the safety line. Following the icefall, fortune had turned in their favor, and the remaining descent to the north shore had gone easily and swiftly. They had been trudging steadily along the beach, making good time in the shelter of the pressure ice, when Smith had checked at the faintest alien sounds rising above the storm.

'I don't know. It sounded like somebody calling my name.'

'Not likely.' Valentina shoved up her snow goggles. 'Who could be out here to call you?'

'Randi! Who else?' Smith unlatched from the safely line and snapped on the lantern clipped to his belt. 'Illuminate and fan out! Start looking! Move!'

They found her within five minutes.

'Jon! Over here! Hurry!'

Kneeling in a notch in the wall of pressure ice, Valentina was brushing the snow away from a huddled form. Smith was on his knees beside them in seconds, struggling out of the straps of his pack frame. Smyslov came in behind him a moment later.

'You were right!' Valentina exclaimed. 'What in all hell is she doing out here rigged like this?'

'Escape and evasion,' Smith snapped back. 'The Spetsnaz must have hit the science station.'

'That's not possible,' Smyslov protested. 'Only the one platoon was inserted on the island, the one that engaged you at the crash site.'

'Then somebody else is here.' Smith spread a survival blanket on the snow, gently lifting Randi onto it. He tore off mittens and gloves, sliding a hand under the mismatched and inadequate jumble of clothing she wore, seeking for a heartbeat.

'She's out solid,' Valentina commented, leaning over Jon's shoulder.

'She's dying,' Smith replied curtly. 'There are chemical heat pads in the packs. Two each. Get them out. All of them.'

Valentina and Smyslov obeyed with all the speed they could, flexing the heat pads to trigger the thermal reaction.

'Shove them down her sleeves and pant legs,' Smith ordered. 'When we start to move her the chilled blood in her limbs will circulate into her body core, and the shock could kill her.'

'Jon. Look at this.' Valentina had worked Randi's left arm out from under the oversized sweatshirt. A handcuff had been locked around it.

'Son of a bitch! That explains the abrasions on her other wrist. She was a prisoner.'

'But whose?'

'I don't know, Val. If it's not the Spetsnaz, then it must be the others. The ones who tried to shoot us down in Alaska.'

'How bad is she, Colonel?' Smyslov asked from behind his other shoulder.

'If we don't get her to some shelter and warmth fast, she's gone.' Smith wrapped the survival blanket tightly around Randi. They had done all they could do out here.

'I will carry her, Colonel,' Smyslov offered.

'All right. I'll take your pack. Let's go.'

The Russian lifted his new burden with care. 'It is all right, devushka,' he murmured. 'You are with friends. Don't leave us now.'

Valentina took up both the rifles. 'We've got to assume the science station's either been occupied or destroyed. Where can we go?'

'We either find another cave or build a snow shelter,' Smith replied, playing his lantern beam along the man-high stacks of pressure ice mounding along the shoreline. 'Keep your eyes open for any place that looks good.'

'Right. We might as well run ourselves out of batteries along with everything else. God, she looks like she's had a job of it.'

'I know.' His voice was as bleak as the night. 'Maybe I've finally done it.'

She puzzled over Smith's words, but she sensed this wasn't the time to ask about them.

The probing sword of Smith's lantern beam had started to cold-fade when it found the triangular gap in the ice wall. Hunkering down, he shined the light into it.

This was what he'd been seeking. A heavy slab of sea ice had been driven up onto the beach and lifted on edge by another, following shoulder of the pack, leaving a blue-white triangular cavern, twenty feet deep by six wide and high enough for a tall man to stand stooped in.

'This is it! We'll fort up here! Major, take Randi to the back of the cave; then come up here and start walling off this entrance with snow and ice blocks. Val, you're with me.'

Smith used the last of their light sticks to fill the little ice cave with a misty green chemical glow, and he took a moment to set up and light their tiny pellet stove. There wasn't much fuel left for that, either, but if it couldn't make their shelter warm, at least it could make it less freezing. As he worked with the stove he issued commands.

'Val, spread a couple of survival blankets on the cave floor; then zip your sleeping bag and mine together.'

'Right. Doing it.'

They eased the comatose Randi onto the combined sleeping bags.

'Okay Val, I'm putting you in with her. While I get Randi undressed, get out of your clothes. Everything has to come off.'

'Understood,' she replied, tugging down the zip of her parka. 'But I was hoping to hear that request under decidedly different circumstances.'

As he stripped Randi he used a flashlight to run a lightning-swift white-light examination of her body, checking for the overt ravages of frostbite. Thank God she'd at least had the arctic boots. They'd protected her feet, the point of greatest vulnerability.

Valentina squirmed out of her heavy outer shell garments. Taking a deep, deliberate breath, she whipped her sweater and thermal top off over her head. Her bra and socks followed, as did the forearm sheaths. She positioned her knives within reach near the head of the bed, then pushed ski pants, thermal bottoms, and panties off in one wadded mass. Naked, she stretched out beside Randi, her head pillowed on a pack, the cold a flame against her skin.

'Ready,' she said, clenching her teeth to keep them from chattering.

Smith supervised the nestling of the two nude ivory bodies together, Valentina shivering and Randi too deathly still. He packed the thermal pads around the women, then zipped the sleeping bags closed. He spread Smyslov's opened bag over them, along with their discarded clothing.

Valentina curled herself around the other woman's

unconscious form, cradling Randi's head against the soft pillow of her breast and shoulder. Randi stirred, whimpered faintly, and tried to nuzzle closer to the source of warmth.

'She's like ice, Jon,' Valentina murmured. 'Will this be enough?'

'I don't know. A lot depends on how much of this is simple exhaustion and how much is exposure. Hypothermia can be very mean and very tricky.' Smith rested his fingertips against Randi's throat, taking a carotid pulse. 'She's been preloaded with a massive dose of antibiotics. That'll help with any pulmonary complications. And she was keeping her hands and face covered. I don't think she's been too badly frostbitten.'

Smith shook his head, lightly stroking Randi's cheek with the backs of his fingers. 'If her core temperature hasn't fallen too far, she might be able to bounce back. She's tough, Val, as tough as they make them. If her temperature has dropped too low . . . I don't know. All we can do is keep her warm and wait.'

Valentina half-smiled. 'You care a great deal about this lady, don't you?'

Smith tucked the mouth of the sleeping bag closer around the two women. 'I'm responsible for her. Both for her being here and for her being who she is.'

'You're responsible for all of us, Jon,' Valentina replied, looking up at him. 'And may I say that's a rather comforting thought at the moment.'

Smith grinned back and lightly stroked back her dark hair. 'I hope that confidence isn't misplaced. Try and get some sleep.'

Taking the SR-25 and his medical kit with him, Smith moved up toward the mouth of the cave. En route he paused to fill an aluminum pan with ice fragments, balancing it atop the pellet stove.

Smyslov had finished walling off the entrance, leaving only an air vent at the top. Eliminating the wind chill gave their arctic clothing a chance to cope with the still air temperature, making the little cavern seem warm.

'How's the arm doing, Major?'

Smyslov shrugged. 'It isn't a problem.'

'I'll have a look at it anyway. You up on your tetanus shots?'

'I am good.'

With their backs to the opposing sides of the cave, Smith treated Smyslov's arm. Working around the Russian's blood-sodden sleeves, he removed the crudely applied field dressing. Cleaning and disinfecting the wound, he dusted it with sulfa powder and applied a fresh water-and-cold-proof bandage.

'You're lucky,' Smith commented. 'It's a nice, clean penetration.' He lifted an eyebrow at the Russian. 'In fact, it looks like it was made by one of Val's knives.'

Smyslov grimaced. 'It was, but with my approval.'

'What did happen up on that ledge while I was hanging at the other end of that safety line?'

Smyslov sketched out the chain of events from the icefall through to Smith's rescue. 'Thanks for the assist.' Smith nodded. 'It was greatly appreciated. Mind if I ask you a personal question, though?'

'Go ahead, Colonel.'

'Why didn't you just cut Val's throat and the safety rope?'

Smyslov was quiet for a moment. 'That would have been in line with the standing orders I have received from my government,' he replied finally. 'But you have a term in the American military for a situation such as I find myself in: "FUBAR." I believe it means "fucked up beyond all recall."'

Smith applied a last strip of surgical tape. 'It does.'

'Such is my current state,' the Russian continued. 'I was placed within your team to prevent an international embarrassment for Russia and a shattering of relations between our nations. The Spetsnaz were inserted onto this island for that purpose as well. But now it is all FUBAR. Even had I chosen to kill you and the professor on the mountain, there would have been no realistic way to prevent this embarrassment and alienation. Things are too out of control now. Too chaotic. Your nation would investigate, and the truth would undoubtedly come out in the end. Probably it has been so from the beginning. This I have come to recognize, and I did not wish to murder my . . . comrades in an act of futility.'

Again Smyslov gave a bitter smile. 'You see? We are not all like the Misha's political officer.'

Smith rucked Smyslov's bloodstained parka sleeve down over the fresh dressing. 'I'd already come to that conclusion, Major.'

He closed his medical kit and leaned back against the green ice wall of the cave, the SR-25 propped beside him. 'I've also come to the conclusion that you're right about the attack on the science station. The numbers don't add up for it to have been Spetsnaz. I've got to assume our third faction is now present on the island, and given the way Randi was handled, that presence is nasty and formidable.'

'I would agree, Colonel.'

'Then, given that your mission to prevent the truth being revealed about the Soviet first strike is indeed FUBAR, would you agree that we again have common cause over *our* mission, preventing the Misha's bioweapons from falling into the wrong hands?'

Smyslov smiled without humor. 'My superiors might not agree, but personally, I should like not to fuck up entirely. That anthrax could find its way into the hands of the Chechen rebels or another of our domestic terrorist groups. It could be used against Moscow or St. Petersburg as easily as against New York or Chicago. This is what matters now.'

Smith extended his hand. 'Welcome back, Major.'

The Russian accepted his handclasp. 'It's good to be back, Colonel. What are your orders?'

Smith glanced toward the rear of the cave. 'Our best intelligence source concerning this new faction is unavailable for the moment. When and if we can talk with her, then we can make some plans. For now, how about a cup of tea?'

A few minutes later the two men hunched over steaming canteen cups, letting the warmth seep in through their fingers.

'I have to admit, Major,' Smith said, 'that one question still keeps nagging at me. It's the other half of the March Fifth equation: why the Soviet attack was recalled at the last minute.'

Smyslov shook his head. 'I'm sorry, I cannot say, Colonel. I must respect the last remaining rags of my nation's security.'

'You might as well tell him, Gregori,' Valentina's voice issued from the mound of sleeping bags. 'I've figured that bit out as well.'

Smyslov's head snapped around. 'How could you?'

Valentina's sigh whispered in the ice cave. 'Because I'm a historian and because I'm very good at playing connect-the-dots. The Misha 124 crashed on Wednesday Island on March fifth, 1953, and the USSR came within a hairs-breadth of starting the Third World War on March fifth, 1953. One other major sociopolitical event involving the Soviet Union took place on that date as well. Logic indicates this one must be related to the other two.'

'What was it?' Smith demanded.

'March fifth, 1953, was the day Joseph Stalin died.' Valentina twisted around so they could make out the pale oval of her face. 'Or rather, the day he was assassinated. Your people did off the bastard, didn't they, Gregori?'

For a long moment, the only sound was the nagging whine of the wind.

'We've always suspected,' Valentina went on. 'As history currently records it, Stalin was stricken by a massive cerebral hemorrhage on the night of February the twenty-eighth, while he was in residence at the Kremlin. Supposedly he was incapacitated and rendered semicomatose by the stroke, remaining in that state until his death on March fifth. But the world has always wondered. It was held there was something "funny" about the rather sketchy account made by the

Soviet government of Stalin's death. There were also rather broad hints made by Stalin's daughter, Svetlana, that the true story of her father's demise was not being revealed.'

The historian shifted her position, trying not to disturb Randi. 'Of course, rumors and conspiracy theories cluster like flies around the death of any controversial national leader. Call it the "grassy knoll syndrome." But given Stalin's decidedly notorious nature and the nature of the Soviet regime at the time, this conspiracy theory seemed a little more solidly founded than most.

'Now, with the truth about the Misha 124 and the Soviets' aborted first strike coming out, the whole question is going to blow wide open again. I'm sorry, Gregori, but there is not going to be a plausible deniability here, and anything we guess will likely be worse than the reality.'

Disgusted, Smyslov looked up at the roof of the cave. 'Shit!' Closing his eyes, he was silent for a few moments more before replying. 'You are quite right, Professor. As you say, Stalin was stricken with a stroke, but he did not pass into a coma. He was partially paralyzed but he remained conscious, alert, and capable of giving orders. And his orders were for the immediate launching of the decisive finishing attack against the Western democracies.

'Who can say why? Possibly his mental capacities were diminished by the stroke. Possibly he foresaw his imminent death and he wanted to witness the final triumph of the People's Revolution before he died. Or possibly he just wanted the world to end with him. Be that as it may, there were other members of the Politburo who viewed such an attack as national suicide.'

'Would it have been?' Smith inquired.

'In the spring of 1953, yes,' Valentina answered. 'The West would have had a decisive edge in any nuclear exchange. By then, the United States and Great Britain possessed several hundred atomic weapons and even a couple of prototype hydrogen bombs. The Soviets had only a couple of dozen low-yield Hiroshima-grade nukes in their arsenal.

Even with the first-strike advantage and augmented by biological and chemical warfare, it wouldn't have been enough to deliver a finishing blow to NATO.

'More critically, the West had the superior delivery systems. The Soviets only had their poor old B-29skis, while the United States Air Force had the big B-36 Peacemaker, with range enough to hit any target in the USSR. The first generation of NATO jet strike aircraft like the B-47 and the Canberra were also coming into service in considerable numbers.

'Western Europe would have been made a thorough mess of,' Valentina concluded, 'and the United States would have been badly hurt. But Russia and the Warsaw Pact states would have been A-bombed into a radioactive wasteland.'

Smyslov scowled and sipped his tea. 'As I said, a clique within the Politburo fully recognized this reality. They also recognized there is only one way to impeach a dictator of Stalin's kind. I regret to tell you, Professor, that history will never know the name of the individual who held the pillow over Stalin's face until he ceased to struggle. It was most carefully not documented.'

'That's all right, Gregori. It could only have been one of three men, and I can make an educated guess.'

Smyslov shrugged. 'The clique was not able to act and secure power until after the first-strike wave was actually airborne and en route to their targets. These were the America bombers with the greatest distance to fly over the Pole. The attack was successfully recalled before it was detected by the North American air defenses, and all of the aircraft returned safely to base. All except for one biological weapons platform, the Misha 124.'

Smyslov emptied his cup. 'The great *konspiratsia* of silence concerning the March Fifth Event began then and has continued to this day.'

'Why did they have to hold it a secret?' Smith asked. 'They'd just saved the world from a nuclear holocaust, and it wasn't as if any sane individual would weep any crocodile tears over Joseph Stalin, not even in the Soviet Union.'

Smyslov shook his head. 'You do not understand the Russian mind, Colonel. Had Stalin's killers been true liberators, this might have been the case, but they were merely tyrants killing another tyrant to save their own lives and to secure their own power base. Beyond that, the Soviet state still existed, and the mythology of the state demanded that Stalin be revered as a hero of the Revolution. Even after the Soviet Union fell, its fears and paranoias lingered.'

His lips quirked ruefully, and he set his empty cup aside. 'Besides that, we Russians have something of a social inferiority complex. We pride ourselves as being profoundly civilized, and murdering one's national leader in his sickbed is simply not *kulturny*.'

Smith snapped back into wakefulness, straightening out of his dozing slouch against the ice wall. Ignoring the stabbing barrage of protests from his collection of bruises, he listened, questing with all his senses.

He wasn't sure how long he had slept; it must have at least been a couple of hours, but there was still a patch of full blackness in the entrance air vent. The sun had yet to rise, but the wind had died. The only sound from the outside was the distant creak and crack of the shifting pack ice. Inside the little cavern he could hear the deep, weary breathing of his sleeping teammates.

And a soft moan. 'Sophia?'

Smith scrambled to the rear of the cave. Snapping on the lantern, he flipped down the hood flap of the combined sleeping bags that held Randi and Valentina.

In the lantern's light Randi's face was relaxed, and the color had returned to her skin, barring a single pale patch of frostnip on one brow and the shadows under her eyes. The dreadful gray flaccidity had passed. Her breathing was easy and uncongested, and when Smith lightly touched her throat, her heartbeat was even and strong and the flesh was warm.

As he had hoped, Randi Russell was rebounding.

At his touch, she grumbled softly and her eyes snapped open, blank at first, then questioning, then aware with the wonderment of still being alive. 'Jon?'

Relief flooded through him. It wouldn't be today after all. 'You made it, Randi. You're with us and you're going to be all right.'

She looked at him almost in puzzlement, lifting her head. 'Jon . . . I called.'

'And I heard you.'

The puzzlement lingered in her dark eyes for a moment more; then she smiled. 'I guess you did.'

Valentina yawned and stretched, coming up on her elbow. 'Good morning, all. Apparently somebody's back with us.'

Startled, Randi twisted around in the sleeping bag, finding herself naked and not alone. 'What in the hell!' she yelped.

'It's perfectly all right, darling,' Valentina replied, propping her head on one slim wrist. 'Nobody waits until after they're married anymore.'

CHAPTER FORTY-FOUR

The White House, Washington, DC

President Castilla rose from the head of the long mahogany conference table. 'Gentlemen, if you will excuse me for a moment, there's a call I have to take.'

Castilla strode from the conference room, following his sober-featured Marine aide. The liaison officers from the Central Intelligence, Defense Intelligence, and National Security Agencies; the FBI; and the Office of Homeland Security exchanged silent glances, wondering what might be critical enough to preempt the morning's national intelligence briefing.

In the Oval Office, Castilla lifted the internal phone from its cradle without bothering to seat himself behind the big mesquite-wood desk. 'Castilla here.'

'Mr. President, this is the Operations Room. Please be advised, the Wednesday Island relief mission has launched and is airborne at this time.'

Castilla glanced at his desk clock. Twenty after. Major Saunders would have gotten his last weather update on the quarter hour, and true to his word, he'd been airborne within five minutes.

'Has Director Klein been notified?'

'Affirmative, Mr. President. He is monitoring the situation.'

'Do we have an ETA over the objective?'

'Roughly six hours, depending upon the weather conditions encountered en route.' The operations officer sounded faintly apologetic. 'They've got over two thousand miles to fly, sir.'

'I understand, Major. Wednesday Island is one of those places you can't get to from here. Keep me advised as things develop.'

'Will do, Mr. President. Please be advised, the Russian Special Liaison to the Wednesday Island Operation is still unavailable. Do you wish to inform the Russians of the relief operation?'

Castilla scowled at the bars of morning sunlight cutting across the rich reds and blues of the Navaho rug on the office floor. 'Negative, Major. It's apparent they have nothing more to say to us, and we have nothing more to say to them.'

CHAPTER FORTY-FIVE

The North Face, Wednesday Island

Randi Russell wasn't sure about the existence of a place called 'heaven.' But if such an environment did exist, she was now certain of two things: it would be warm, and you wouldn't be alone.

'Okay, try that,' Jon Smith said, rocking back on his heels.

Experimentally she flexed the fingers of her right hand. Jon had lightly bandaged them after applying a thin layer of antibiotic ointment. At her insistence he had done each digit separately so she could still have full use of the hand.

'It's not bad,' she replied. 'They sort of itch and tingle a little but not too bad.'

Smith nodded, looking pleased. 'That's good. I think you picked up a good touch of chilblain climbing that cliff, but I don't think you've taken any permanent damage.'

'Apparently you'll still be able count to ten without taking your shoes off.' Valentina sat up in the doubled sleeping bag, working on the handcuff around Randi's left wrist. Even clad in thermal underwear and with an unzipped parka draped over her shoulders, the professor still exuded a certain air of raffish elegance.

Randi found she couldn't be annoyed. In fact, there was almost a partylike atmosphere in the little ice cave. There was no logical reason for it. They were still on Wednesday Island, still hiding and surrounded by enemies, but the team was whole again.

Valentina gave a final delicate twist of the lock probe, and the handcuff loop snicked open. 'There you go, darling. You

'Thank you,' Randi smiled. 'It's appreciated.'

'Beyond your hands, how do you feel?' Smith went on, touching her cheek with the back of a bared hand, hunting for signs of a fever.

'I'm fine,' Randi replied in a knee-jerk response.

He continued to regard her with a disconcertingly level gaze, the very faintest of knowing smiles on his face.

Randi sighed. 'All right,' she replied. 'I feel like an old dishrag that's been wrung out too many times. It's like I'm never going to be warm inside again and I'm never going to feel not tired again and all I want to do is sleep for another thousand years. Satisfied?'

Smith's taciturn features broke into one of the rare boyish grins that involved his full face, the smile Sophia had talked about. 'That sounds about right,' he replied. 'I'm not hearing any pulmonary congestion, and your body temperature seems to be back where it's supposed to be, so I think you were knocked out more by simple exhaustion than deep-core exposure. Still, stay warm.'

'I won't argue.' Randi burrowed gratefully deeper into her sleeping bag. She was back in her own thermal long johns, and the pellet stove and their combined body heat had brought the interior of the cave up to close to freezing, but it wasn't exactly cozy. 'But still, feeling this awful now is a vast improvement over how I felt last night.'

The smile on Smith's face snapped away, replaced by a faint disapproving frown. Randi sensed it was aimed inward. 'I'm sorry about what happened at the station, Randi. I shouldn't have left you hanging like that. My fault.'

'I didn't exactly shine, either, Jon. I never should have let that little shit Kropodkin take me like he did.' She smiled wryly and then sadly. 'I'm supposed to be good. Maybe if I'd been a little better, I might have gotten Trowbridge out.'

'I'm finding you can't live on might-haves, Randi. We all have to make do on best-we-cans.'

Smyslov hunched his way back from the cave entrance

and hunkered down on his heels, joining the group at the sleeping bags. 'We have no wind outside and no snow. The sea smoke has come in heavily, but I believe it will burn off soon. It looks like it will be a lovely day, at least for the eightieth parallel.'

'As soon as he has a clear sky, Kretek will go for the anthrax,' Randi said.

Over their sketchy tea-and-energy-bar breakfast, she and the others had exchanged briefings over events at the Misha crash site and the science station. At last, they had the full picture of all they were facing. Only it wasn't an attractive one.

Valentina opened the gun cleaning kit and took the model 70 across her knees. 'What are we going to do about it, Jon?' she said, opening the bolt and dumping the shells out of the magazine trap.

'Frankly, that's an excellent question. We've got two bands of hostiles out there, both of whom outgun us and both of whom have a vested interest in killing us on sight.'

Smith closed the heavy-duty zip on his medical kit and slouched back against the ice wall. 'One valid strategy is to do nothing. We've got good concealment and shelter here, and last night's storm would have erased our trails. We've also been out of communication for too long. There was a Mike force standing by in Alaska, and it's probably inbound right now. If we sit tight and stay quiet for the next few hours, the odds are we won't be found until after the cavalry arrives.'

Randi came up on one elbow. 'But that concedes the anthrax to Kretek. He's expecting the arrival of outside forces. He's wired that into his planning. I heard his people talking about it. By timing off the weather and the flight distances, he figures he can get up to the wreck, pull the bio-agent reservoir, and get out before he can be interfered with. And given the way he's outfitted, I think he has a pretty good chance of doing it.'

Smith nodded. 'I'll agree with that assessment. If Kretek

is going to be stopped, we have to be the ones to do it.'

Smith shifted his position and idly fished something silver out of his pocket, Smyslov's cigarette lighter/radio transponder. 'Major, here's a question for you. Could you bring your Spetsnaz over to our side? In the face of the threat of the anthrax falling into terrorist hands, could you get them to help us against Kretek and his people?'

An expression akin to despair crossed the Russian's face. 'I have been thinking of this as well, Colonel. But in the eyes of my government the bioweapons aboard the Misha are entirely secondary to the security of the March Fifth Event. That was made most clear to me in my own mission briefing. The Spetsnaz platoon commander will no doubt have been given specific orders to this effect from a higher command. I have no authorization to change those orders, and he will be aware of it. He will view you and your knowledge as the primary threat, not the anthrax.'

'What about getting those orders changed?' Smith insisted.

The Russian shook his head. 'Impossible within our time frame and probably impossible altogether. I would have to contact the Spetsnaz force, then I would have to arrange a rendezvous with the submarine that transported them here to get access to long-range communications. Then I would have to convince my superiors to overturn a fifty-year-old standing security policy.' Smyslov grimaced a bitter smile and shrugged. 'Even if I somehow succeeded in this miracle, the anthrax would be gone long before I could get the orders changed. In all probability you and the ladies would be long dead as well.'

'How about working on the tactical level, leaving your government out of it? What are the odds of us convincing your platoon leader that it's in the best interest of all involved to focus on the anthrax threat?'

Again Smyslov shook his head. 'You might find that degree of flexibility among the Special Forces commanders of your army, Colonel, but not of mine. In the Russian military, good junior officers do not think, they obey, and this Spetsnaz leader will be a very good junior officer.'

'What about you, Major?' Valentina interjected, running a cleaning rod down the Winchester's barrel. 'You're thinking.'

Smyslov smiled wearily and shrugged. 'Dear lady, I'm thinking maybe I am not such a good Russian military officer. Beyond that, you shot the hell out of that Spetsnaz platoon yesterday and you humiliated its commander. He is not going to view you with favor.'

'I can empathize with his feelings.' Smith idly flipped the top of the transponder lighter open and shut with his thumb, his eyes drifting around the green-lit interior of the little cave, taking stock of his available assets.

Randi ran her own mental inventory. Two rifles, one pistol, maybe two hundred and fifty rounds of ammunition, and four combatants, one of whom was disabled by cold and exhaustion, and another crippled by conflicting interests.

It didn't make for an impressive army.

'Well, Sarge,' she heard Smith murmur under his breath. 'If I can pull this one off, I guess you'll say I've learned how to command.'

'What did you say, Jon?' Randi inquired, puzzled.

'Nothing.' The repetitive *click-ching click-ching* of the lighter top filled the interior of the cavern.

Valentina slid the bolt back into the model 70. 'Here's a lovely thought,' she said. 'Perhaps when Kretek and company arrive at the crash site they'll waltz into a Russian ambush just as we did.'

'A lovely thought indeed,' Smith replied. 'Only our friends up at the wreck are probably miles away from the crash site by now, hunting for us.'

Silence returned, except for the rhythmic *click-ching* of the lighter top. Then it stopped. Thumb still extended, Smith sat dead still for a long moment, staring intently into nowhere.

'Jon, what's wrong?'

The lighter top snapped shut decisively a final time, his features going back to their fixed focused impassiveness. 'Randi, do you think you're up to moving?'

She sat up in the sleeping bag. 'I can go wherever you need me to.'

'Right, then. Major, let's get the gear together. I want to be out of here in ten minutes. We have some positioning to do. Ladies, a favor, please. When you get dressed, exchange your outer clothes, Randi's for Val's. Got it?'

'You have a plan, my dear Colonel.' Valentina made it a statement, her eyes bright with interest.

'Just possibly, my dear professor. It says in the Bible that a man can't serve two masters at the same time. But it doesn't say a damn thing about his not being able to fight two enemies.'

CHAPTER FORTY-SIX

Over the Arctic Ocean

The patterns of pack ice below and boiling cumulus clouds above were frost white, while the sea and sky shone a steely blue. Intermittently the MV-22 Osprey VTOL bucked and shuddered like a heavily laden truck on a potholed road. The storm front had passed, but the turbulence of its passage lingered.

With the Combat Talon tanker holding its course ahead and above the Osprey, Major Saunders stalked the refueling drogue streaming from the larger aircraft's wingtip. It was an exceptionally precise piece of flying machinery. With its wingtip engine pods rotated into horizontal flight mode, the danger of putting the shuttlecock-shaped drogue through the arc of one of the Osprey's huge prop-rotors was very real. The result, to say the least, would be spectacular.

The intermittent jolts of clear-air turbulence and the fuel gauge bars dipping toward empty only compounded the challenge. Saunders had given his wingman first pass at the tanker, and it had taken the number two VTOL over twenty minutes to make the hookup, burning through most of Saunders's meager fuel reserve.

The long refueling probe extended from above the cockpit of the Osprey like the horn of a techno-unicorn. For the dozenth time, the Air Commando leader aligned it with the bobbing, weaving mouth of the drogue as a Stone Age hunter might aim a spear. With his knuckles white on the joystick and throttles, he waited for the instant his target might hold steady. It came, and he nudged the throttles forward.

This time, the probe slipped smoothly into the drogue and locked, linking the fuel-starved VTOL with its tanker. Beneath the wing of the big MC-130, command lights shifted pattern to green. 'We have locks, pressure, and transfer,' Saunders's copilot announced.

Saunders exhaled luxuriously. With the drogue secured and kerosene cascading into his fuel tanks, he could relax by a minute increment.

'Nav, how are we doing?' he called over his shoulder to the officer crouching before the GPS console.

'In the groove, sir,' the navigator replied. 'We're clearing the tail of that front now and we'll be angling east at our next waypoint.'

'ETA to objective?'

'Maybe another three hours to touchdown, sir, depending on the winds.'

'Three hours it is.'

'I touched base with the cutter a few minutes ago, Major,' Saunders's copilot commented. 'The Coasties report clear air, but they aren't hearing anything from the island yet. I wonder what we're gonna find.'

'Maybe not a damn thing, Bart. That's what's worrying me.'

CHAPTER FORTY-SEVEN

Saddleback Glacier

Crouching inside the cave mouth, the Russian demolitions man studied the lava ceiling and the explosive charges he'd planted, double-checking his placements. His orders had been explicit. He must collapse the entrance in a way that would present the appearance of a natural rockfall. It was an interesting technical challenge, especially in the roiling of the fall so that explosives-uncontaminated rock would face outward. It wouldn't do to leave detectable chemical traces. Lieutenant Tomashenko had been very insistent about this, and today would not be a good day to fail his platoon leader.

Satisfied, the demolitions man knelt and crimped an electric detonator cap to the end of the spliced bundle of primer cords. Some of the cord lengths led to the overhead charges; others ran deeper into the cavern within the mountain.

Pavel Tomashenko felt the cold sweat gathering down the center of his spine beneath his parka. He knew it was only partially due to the golden ball of the sun bobbing above the southern horizon. He was on the verge of losing this mission. Like a hockey goalie seeing the puck skimming past beyond his block, all he could do was try to stretch for that last critical millimeter.

He, his radioman, and the second member of his demolitions team stood out on the glacier some fifty meters from the mouth of the cave the Misha crew had used as a survival shelter and the Americans had used for a fortress.

Even standing out on the glacier face in the open daylight was an admission of crisis. Like any other commando unit, the Spetsnaz were normally creatures of secrecy and concealment. But Tomashenko had lost both the cover of night and weather to the more critical factor of time. He must act decisively now, utilizing the scraps remaining to him. With the clearing skies, the outside world would be reaching in to Wednesday Island.

'Have you been able to contact the submarine?' Tomashenko snapped, then silently berated himself for the display of nerves. If his radioman had been able to establish communications, he would have reported it at once.

'No, Lieutenant,' the stolid Yakut replied, crouching beside his tactical transceiver. 'There is no longer any interference, but there is no reply. They must not have found a lead in the ice for their antenna.'

'So be it.' Tomashenko forced his voice into normality. 'We will try again at the noon schedule.' It was just as well. It would give him a couple of additional hours to salvage this mess and conceal his failure. 'Get me through to White Bird team.'

'At once, Lieutenant.'

Using the radio so promiscuously was another symbol of disaster, as was the splitting of his meager command. But again Tomashenko had no choice. He must clean up things here at the crash site, and at the same time he must find and eliminate those damn American intelligence operatives!

At the base of East Peak the senior demolitions man emerged from the cave mouth. Trailing the detonator wire behind him, he backed across the sun-brightened surface of the glacier toward Tomashenko's temporary command post. The number two demo man took the detonator box from the explosives sled and began setting it up.

'Lieutenant, I have White Bird leader.'

Tomashenko tore back his parka hood. Hunkering down beside the radioman, he accepted the headset and microphone.

'White Bird, this is Red Bird. Report!'

'Red Bird,' the radio-filtered voice whispered in the

earphones. 'We have no contact. We have swept the south descents and the main trail approaches for a second time. We have found no trace of them. They are not on the glacier and they have not climbed down on this side of the ridge. They must have descended the north face, Lieutenant.'

The descent Tomashenko had said was impossible the night before.

'Very well, White Bird,' he spoke curtly into the handset. 'Commence a sweep toward the west end of the island and the science station. Engage on contact. We will be joining you shortly. Red Bird out.'

'Understood. Executing. White Bird out.' Tomashenko passed back the headset and mike. The Americans must have headed for the station. There was nowhere else to go. If so, there was still a chance they could be taken and eliminated. Even if it cost him another third of his command, the secret of the March Fifth Event would be kept.

The demolitions team had the charge leads wired into the detonator box now, and the lead man was cranking up the key. 'Ready to fire, Lieutenant.'

'Carry on. Blow it.'

The demo man rested his gloved thumb on the detonator button and hesitated, looking over his shoulder at his platoon leader. 'Lieutenant, those men in the cave . . . Sergeant Vilyayskiy and our people. Shouldn't something be said . . . some words?'

'The dead are deaf, Corporal. Fire it!'

The detonator box magneto zipped, and thunder rumbled deep within the belly of the mountain. Ten thousand tons of basalt fractured, shifted, and resettled, sealing the crew of the Misha 124 and the four lost members of the Spetsnaz platoon in a black rock eternity. A brief burst of lava dust jetted from the cave mouth, only to be overwhelmed by the cascade of disturbed ice and snow flowing down the flank of East Peak, erasing the last trace. Even those who had been inside the lava tube would have a hard time finding it again.

As the misting avalanche cloud dissipated, the demolitions leader spoke, his words flat. 'Your orders, Lieutenant?'

'Retrieve the detonator leads and let's move out. I want to join up with the search party as soon as possible.'

The demo man gestured toward the wreck of the Misha 124 a half-mile distant across the saddleback. 'What about the plane?'

'We leave it as it sits. The Americans know of it, and to burn it now would only make for more questions. Let's move!'

At that moment, the radio operator stiffened. Tilting his head he pressed his earphones tighter to his head. 'Lieutenant, I hear a signal on the transponder circuit! It is the radio tracer beacon Major Smyslov was carrying!'

Tomashenko bent over the radioman's shoulder. 'Are you certain?'

'It is the proper frequency and code pattern. It must be the same tracer.'

'Get a bearing!' Smyslov must still be alive and possibly pointing the way to his captors. As the radioman plugged the RDF loop into his set, Tomashenko squatted on the ice. Spreading out an island map, he readied a compass and a straightedge from his chart case.

'Signal bearing approximately two six six degrees! Signal strength five!'

Tomashenko's all-weather pencil slashed across the map. A little south of west. That bearing would put Smyslov either on top of East Peak or on the south coast between this position and the science station. It must be the science station! At signal strength five it might be three or four miles out. Maybe his luck was turning.

'Radioman! Contact White Bird leader! Tell him the enemy is on the southern coast and they are heading for the station! Tell him to pursue with all speed! Corporal! Cache and conceal the radio and the other heavy gear, on the double! Light marching order! Weapons and ammunition only! We'll have these bastards yet!'

CHAPTER FORTY-EIGHT

Wednesday Island Station

'We destroy the station when we leave,' Kretek ordered. 'We burn it all.'

'Is that necessary?' Mikhail Vlahovitch looked up from the data file he had been glancing through. He was no man of science, and he did not understand the columns of carefully noted meteorological readings. But neither was he, by instinct, a wolverine.

'It will muddy the waters and destroy evidence, Mikhail. Besides, the people who scribbled all of that down are dead. What will it matter to them?'

'No doubt you are right.' Vlahovitch tossed the folder on the laboratory worktable. It was a wise time to be agreeable with his employer.

Through the lab hut's windows, men could be seen at work, gray shades moving through the rapidly thinning fog. Preparations for departure and the final big job were under way. Down at the helipad, heater tents had been erected around the Halo's engine pods, prewarming the heavy-lift copter's turbines for flight. The riggers were connecting the heavy nylon strap sling to the belly hard point, and the members of the demolitions team were laying out their ribbon charges on the snow, checking the connectors and fusing.

'How do you think we are coming on time, Anton?' Vlahovitch had to ask again.

'I've told you, we have enough,' Kretek replied irritably. 'They are coming, but if we make no more mistakes we will be well away before they arrive.'

'We should be ready to start engines within the next fifteen minutes.' Vlahovitch hesitated. 'Anton, what do you wish to do about the boy's body?'

'Leave it in the bunkhouse. It would be excess weight, and when it is found it will confuse matters even further.'

Kretek's explosion of familial anger had passed, and his professional objectivity was returning. He would gladly kill his nephew's killer, but he couldn't be bothered with his corpse.

'No one will know exactly what happened here,' the arms dealer continued. He peered into his second in command's face; his ice-colored eyes narrowed. 'At least, no one will know as long as that girl is indeed dead.'

Vlahovitch ran his tongue across cracked lips, not liking the feel of that intent, cold stare. 'I told you, Anton, she was swept away in an avalanche.'

'You are sure?'

'That was how it looked.'

'That might be how it looked, Mikhail, but is that what actually happened? You saw no body!'

'How could we?' Vlahovich lifted his voice. 'It was at the bottom of a two-hundred-foot cliff, in the dark, in the middle of a blizzard! Besides, if she didn't die then, she died later. She couldn't have survived last night dressed as she was.'

Kretek maintained his glacial gaze for a moment longer, and then he smiled and gave Vlahovitch a bearlike slap on the shoulder. 'Pish, pish, pish, no doubt you are right, my friend. What does it matter when she died, as long as the bitch is dead? Come, let's be about the day's work.'

The two men geared up for the cold, zipping parkas, donning gloves and taking up arms. Kretek had claimed the MP-5 the blonde girl had carried. Waste not, want not. The Heckler and Koch was a fine weapon, decidedly superior to the Croation-made Agrams he had issued to his men. Still, as he slung the SMG's carrying strap over his shoulder, a muscle in his bearded jaw jumped. He did not like having things – people, money, or opportunities – taken from him.

Kretek swept a shelf full of hard-copy files onto the lab hut's floor. Bracing a booted foot against the heater, he rocked it off its mounts. With a smoky clatter of falling stovepipe, it tipped onto its side, spraying burning coals. A score of flame tongues sprang up amid the scattered papers. The two men filed out through the snow lock, leaving the legacy of Wednesday Island Station to burn.

Outside, the quiet air seemed mild in comparison to the cold-fanged wind of yesterday. Directly overhead, the blue of a clear sky filtered down through the mist and the terrain around the station was swiftly regaining definition and color. As was frequently the case, the morning's sea smoke was dissipating as rapidly as it had come on. The men's voices lifted in exuberance, and their movements quickened in automatic response to the coming sun.

Kretek and Vlahovitch were just starting their trudge out to the landing ground when one of the perimeter sentries yelled an alarm.

A figure stood atop the antenna knoll – a small, slender figure clad in red ski pants and a floppy, oversized green sweatshirt, its hood drawn over her head. She looked down at the station and its startled inhabitants for a moment more; then she turned and was gone, dropping out of sight down the far side of the hill, a hasty burst of gunfire futilely chasing after her.

Kretek turned on Vlahovitch, massive fists engulfing the front of his lieutenant's parka. For a moment Vlahovitch thought he was a dead man.

'So if she didn't die then, she had to die later!' Kretek's glare burned red-eyed with the focused rage of a charging boar. 'I want her dead this time, Mikhail! For certain! Now!' He converted his grip into a shove. 'Get after her!'

'At once, sir! Lazlo! Prishkin!' Vlahovitch lifted his voice in a half-strangled shout. 'You and your fire teams, follow me! Move, you bastards! Move!'

Unslinging his submachine gun, Vlahovitch fled as much as he started to chase, laboring up the hill toward the place where the figure had disappeared. You simply did not fail Anton Kretek in this kind of catastrophic fashion and survive. Even if he succeeded in catching and killing the girl now, the odds of his getting off Wednesday Island alive were not good. But if he failed to bring her head back, they were nonexistent.

Valentina Metrace kept to the hard-packed and flagged station trails. Wallowing in the soft unbroken drifts would be slow death. There were several inches of fresh snow in the bottoms of the trail troughs, but she had the legs and lungs to cope with it. She kept in trim by running two or more miles daily, and not mere roadwork, but steeplechase orienteering over broken ground. In the field, she could match the old ivory hunter's standard of twenty miles from dawn to dusk, walking and trotting, while carrying a light rucksack and a heavy-caliber rifle.

For this run though she was traveling light: clothes, knives, a single white camo survival blanket, and a steel signaling mirror. It enhanced her mobility edge over her more heavily laden pursuers.

After allowing herself to be seen, Valentina had angled down to the main trail along the island's southern shoreline. Heading eastward, she alternated between an easy jog and a fast walk, carefully managing her breathing, ground coverage, and energy reserves. She had the edge here as well. She knew how far she had to go, how rapidly she needed to get there, and what was going to happen once she arrived.

She stayed focused on the trail ahead, taking care with each step and keeping to the easiest, safest, and most efficient path. For the moment a fall and a twisted ankle was all she needed to fear.

Looking back over her shoulder would be a waste of energy and distance. She'd had a good hundred yards' lead at the start, and by the time her surprised pursuers could have reached the hilltop to acquire her trail, she would have lengthened that out.

The men coming after her would also be 'blown' by their climb and would need to get their breath back. More time and space in her favor. As long as she kept moving, there was little chance they could get within pistol-caliber range before she'd drawn them into the target zone. All she had to do was to stay in their sight and keep them chasing and not thinking.

Of course, all this was predicated on Jon's plan working and on Randi's observation that the arms smugglers hadn't brought a sniper with them. If either of them were wrong . . . There was no sense in worrying about it. If they were, she'd find out presently. As she ran along the landward edge of the piled shore ice she tossed a three-fingered Girl Guide's salute to the rocky point of land a mile ahead.

CHAPTER FORTY-NINE

South Coast, Wednesday Island

'How are you doing?' Smith glanced across the compacted snow foxhole.

'I say again, I'm just fine!' Randi snapped back. 'God, Jon, don't hover!'

'You're getting cranky,' Smith approved. 'That's a good sign.'

'I'm not . . .' She caught herself, then grinned sheepishly. 'Really, I'm okay. You're a good doctor.'

They were forted up atop a point of land that buckled outward from the southern flank of the island, a position that gave them both concealment and an overwatch of the shoreline to the east and west. Over the past few days the grip of the pack had solidified, the only differentiation now between the sea and shore being that the sea ice was the more broken and irregular.

He lifted an eyebrow. 'Thanks. I've been out of general practice for a while and I was afraid my technique was a little rusty.'

Randi lifted a hand off the stock of Valentina's model 70 and wriggled her gloved fingers. 'None of them have fallen off yet.'

'Still, I want you to see a good dermatologist when we get out of here. You might sluff some skin, and your hands are going to have to be watched for infection.'

Randi sighed in a swirl of vapor. 'Jon, trust me, your technique isn't rusty in the least. You can fuss as well as any doctor I have ever known! Sophia would be proud of you.'

There was a silent pause; then Randi took the awkwardness

out of the moment with another smile. 'She really would be, you know.'

The moment was broken by the scrabble of boots and gloves on ice. Staying low in a fast hands-and-knees crawl, Gregori Smyslov snaked into the foxhole beside them. The Russian had established a second observation post deeper along the point that provided a better view eastward.

'It has worked,' he said, panting a little. 'Spetsnaz. Coming toward us along the coast trail.'

'Where are they?

'About a kilometer out, at the foot of the trail down from West Peak.'

Smith glanced first at his watch and then toward a mound of snow at the edge of the foxhole. The cigarette lighter/transponder sat atop it, its antenna extended. 'It's working. We're tolling them in. And the timing should be pretty good. How many?'

'Six. They must have split their force again.'

'Damn! I was hoping for the whole platoon.' Smith reached across and collected the transponder. Collapsing its antenna, he pocketed it. It had served its purpose.

'The others are probably following,' Smyslov added.

'Maybe, but they might not get here in time to do us or themselves any good. Let me have the glasses.'

Smyslov unslung the binocular case and passed it to Smith. Coming up on his knees, Smith aimed the field glasses westward toward the science station, tracking along the flag-marked coastal trail.

'Can you see her yet, Jon?' Randi inquired.

'Not yet . . . Wait a minute. Yeah! There she is. She's running.'

In his magnified field of view he could make out Valentina trotting along, seemingly at ease, the red and green of her clothing, or rather Randi's clothing, making her stand out against the sun-washed white of the terrain. Again the timing was about what he had hoped for. Elevating the glasses farther, he could make out the knoll with its radio

372

mast that overlooked the science station. Smoke seemed to be rising from behind the hill, and on the side facing them flyspeck figures moved. A line of men hastened down toward the shoreline, pursuing that other small, colorful dot that moved toward Smith's position.

'Val's pulling in her share! Five . . . six . . . eight – damn, not as many as I'd like there, either.'

Smith swiveled around 180 degrees and ran a scan down the east shore. There was the other half of the equation, the Spetsnaz force. Only one man followed the compacted pathway; the other five had fanned out on either side, scuffling along on snowshoes. The Russians were closer than the force advancing from the science station, but they were also moving slower. And so far, with the point blocking their line of sight, neither converging force had become aware of the other. Smith mentally computed times and distances. Yeah. It was going to be just about as good as they had any right to expect.

'Ladies and gentleman,' he said, lowering the binoculars, 'it's coming together. Randi, give Val the word.'

Randi gave the stainless steel signaling mirror a final quick buff on her sleeve. Squinting through the tiny sighting hole in its center, she acquired the dot on the snow that was Valentina Metrace. Angling the mirror, she produced a single flash that might be mistaken for a sun strike off the snow were you not looking for it.

After a few moments the pursued dot glinted back.

'She's acknowledged,' Randi reported.

'Right. That's all we can do here. Let's move out.'

'I don't like this, Jon,' Randi spoke vehemently under her breath. 'I don't like this part at all!'

'I'm not crazy about it myself.' Through the glasses he could make out Val as a human figure moving effortlessly as if she were out for a morning's jog. *Leading your troops into battle is easy, Sarge. Having to leave them there, on their own, that's the real bear.*

'She doesn't even have a gun, damn it!'

'She didn't seem to think she'd need one.' Smith slammed the binoculars back into their case.

'I do hope you realize that woman is just a hopeless showoff,' Randi said, binding on her bear-paw snowshoes.

'Oh, yes, most definitely. And speaking about guns . . .' Smith drew his sidearm from the holster pocket of his parka, passing the automatic to Smyslov, butt first. 'You might find use for this today, Major. This one works, guaranteed.'

Smyslov grinned and accepted the P-226, stowing it in his pocket. 'That is good to hear. I had a most disappointing experience with an American firearm not long ago.'

Valentina Metrace was a predator and huntress by both instinctive nature and personal preference. But as a successful predator, she also understood what was required of a successful, i.e., survivable, prey animal.

Staying alive as prey mandated you not only knew when to run but when, where, and how to hide, and the moment to break trail and disappear was almost upon her.

The single mirror flash from the top of the point had told her Jon Smith's plan was on track. The Spetsnaz were moving into the killing zone from the other side of the point. Two flashes would have meant a scrub and for her to keep going, pulling her pursuers under the fire of the long guns atop the point.

As it was, their unknowing allies, the Spetsnaz, would hopefully do the job for them.

Smith had orchestrated his engagement well. On the landward side a thirty-foot cliff rose above a narrowed boulder-strewn beach, while to seaward the point acted like the prow of a ship, building up an exceptionally jagged and tumbled pile of pressure ice. It was a natural choke point and a superb killing ground, leaving neither force room to maneuver or successfully disengage.

All she had to do now was to squirm out from between their two fires, and the pressure ice jumble provided a magnificent maze to disappear into.

Now Valentina started looking back. The men chasing her were perhaps a quarter mile behind and slowly closing. She'd been deliberately sandbagging her pace, allowing them to overtake her, dangling the prospect of bringing her within gun range as a lure.

It was working.

She had no clear idea of how close the Spetsnaz were, so she dare not waste any time. The instant she rounded the tip of the point, breaking the line of sight with her pursuers, she broke laterally into the sea ice, scrambling over the man-high pressure ridge at the beach edge.

Crossing from the trail, Valentina carefully plotted each step and handgrip, hopping from one slab of snow-bared ice to the next like a person crossing a stream on stepping-stones, striving to minimize the trail she left. It would be impossible to leave no trace at all. Her pursuers would see where her boot tracks stopped on the main trail, but she was striving for confusion, to hold this one facet of the enemy in the killing zone for the arrival of the second.

Working her way roughly twenty yards offshore, she swung westward again, like a canny white-tail buck circling behind its stalking hunter. Out here, the sea ice was a living thing – softer, green-tinged, buckling and breaking with the rise and sink of the tides and the drag of the currents. Whipping out the survival blanket she carried, Valentina donned it as a camouflage cloak, wearing the white side out. Sinking down, she wormed along on hands and knees, staying below the outer edge of the pressure ridge.

She moved silently, but once she was almost startled into a yelp when a mushy emerald puddle of ice crystals erupted in front of her and she found herself literally nose to nose with an equally unnerved ring seal. Snorting in her face, the seal plunged back through his breathing hole, leaving her to reestablish her own breathing.

Then she heard the voices to shoreward. Her hunters had come to the break in her trail. That was it. The time for running was over. Drawing the white protective sheeting closer, she merged into a notch in the pressure ridge. Drawing her legs up tightly against her chest and wrapping her arms around her knees, she assumed the *pu ning mu* position, the 'hiding like a stone' of ninjutsu. She also drew the neck of the sweatshirt up and over her mouth and nose, breathing down into the garment to kill her breath plume. Valentina Metrace became just another block of ice.

The pack beneath her creaked and sighed. The voices faded to an occasional fragmented mutter. By now the arms smugglers must have figured out what she had done and where she had gone. By now someone would be standing atop the pressure ridge, scanning with binoculars.

He'd be looking for color and movement. If she denied her hunters both, she'd be immune, at least for a time. Unfortunately Randi Russell had given these men the slip in much this same way before. It was questionable that they'd just give up twice. They'd look. They'd think. They'd talk it over for a minute. Then they'd start probing into the sea ice after her.

At least until the Russians walked in on them.

Valentina focused on breathing without chest movement. This was no worse than sitting it out in a leopard blind, only she couldn't see, and she was the one being set for. She pushed her other senses out beyond the second skin of the survival blanket, listening for the rasp of exertion breathing or the vibration of a footfall on ice. Her fingers eased into the sleeve of her sweater, their tips touching the hilt of the knife strapped to her forearm.

Jon and the others should be well on their way by now. They'd be moving toward the station along the base of the ridge. With this batch of guns drawn off and theoretically engaged by the Spetsnaz, they'd have a better chance when they put the station and landing ground under sniper fire. Divide and conquer. Good strategy, Jon.

She gulped and wished she could sneak a mouthful of snow. Let's see, what to do should the Spetsnaz not show? Don't wait to be fallen over. Jump and knife the nearest man. Drop the second closest with a throw. Commandeer a submachine gun and ammunition. Keep to the cover of the pressure ridge, maximize casualties, and buy Jon and Randi their time yourself.

There, that was something of a plan anyway.

Where in the hell were those bloody Russians? Wasn't that just the way of the world? There was never a Bolshevik around when you needed one.

Someone nearby gave a startled yell and an SMG chattered. Valentina went stark stiff for an instant, then realized there had been no shock of a bullet impact. Another automatic weapon replied – the sharper, more piercing crackle of a small-caliber assault rifle. Valentina recognized an AK-74. The Spetsnaz had just put their foot in it!

More shouts followed. A scream trailed off. The exchange of gunfire built explosively.

Valentina allowed herself a full, deep breath. Blinking for a moment in the snow-refracted sunlight, she slipped out from under the camo blanket. Drawing one of her knives, she began to slither on her belly through the buckled ice, moving toward the heart of the burgeoning firefight.

Jon's orders had been specific. When their enemies engaged each other she was to fall back and disengage immediately. But Valentina had decided upon a loose definition of 'immediate.' She intended to linger a bit, extending military assistance to both sides of the conflict.

At the first crash of automatic weapons fire, Jon Smith had drawn up sharply and looked back. Then, when it was returned and built in volume, he managed a grin. That was a battle, not an execution.

They'd been double-timing along the base of the central ridge, keeping out of sight of the shoreline trail. It had been snowshoe work and hard going, but they'd already covered a fair portion of the distance back to the science station. Now if they could only make the high ground overlooking the helipad and Kretek's helicopter without being seen, they'd stand a chance of bitching somebody's works.

The question marks were Val and Randi. Would Val be able to get clear and rejoin, and could Randi keep it together? Randi was slumped against Smyslov with her eyes closed and with the concerned Russian half-supporting her as she gasped for breath. She was carrying neither pack nor weapon, and he couldn't doubt her will. But running in snowshoes was murderous even for someone who hadn't already been half-killed by hypothermia.

'Randi?'

She looked up, her shadow-rimmed eyes fierce. 'Go!' she whispered. 'Just go!'

Three plumes of smoke rose over Wednesday Island Station. All three huts had now been torched. The remaining security teams had been pulled in tight around the Halo, the flight and demolition men were on board, and the heating tents around the engines had been stricken. Kretek paced warily beside the big aircraft, his sense of unease growing.

He glanced down at the submachine gun he carried. The MP-5 was a professional's weapon, and the woman who had carried it had been a consummate professional. What of the others he had been told of? This history professor, the Russian and American military officers. Had they been of the same breed as the lethal little blonde? What of the team leader, this Jon Smith? Obviously it was the crudest of cover names. Who was he really?

For the thousandth time Kretek's eyes swept the high ground above the station, tasting the blood from his cold-cracked lips. He could smell more than the smoke of the burning huts. He could smell the stink of an operation going rotten.

This was wrong. He'd acted without thinking when he'd sent Mikhail after the girl. Appearing above the camp at that moment had been too convenient, and he had snapped at the dangled bait too rapidly. Somebody was setting something up.

On an ordinary job, any other job, he would abort and run. But this was the job. The one that would never come again.

Abruptly he stopped his pacing and yelled up through the Halo's open fuselage door, 'Prepare to start the engines.'

One of the demolitions men leaned out of the hatch. 'I haven't rigged the time fuse on the other helicopter yet, sir.'

Because of its proximity to the parked Halo, the smaller Jet Ranger couldn't be blown until after they were in the air.

'Then get on with it!' Kretek snapped back impatiently. 'We're taking off.'

'What about Vlahovitch and the others?'

At that instant the faint ripple of distant gunshots reverberated over the knoll – automatic weapons exchanging fire, many of them.

Everyone froze in place, listening. Then Kretek broke the lock with his bellow. 'Everyone aboard! Everyone aboard now! Get those goddamned engines started! We're getting out of here!'

The gas turbines began to crank with their hollow baritone moan, the huge rotor blades sweeping past overhead. The security perimeter collapsed in on the helicopter, men hurling their weapons through the open side hatch and scrambling in after them. Kretek was last aboard as displaced snow started to swirl, tornadolike, around the mammoth heavy lifter.

Kretek raced forward to the cockpit. 'Get us in the air!' he yelled, leaning in between the pilots' seats. 'Take us to the crash site!'

The pilot twisted in his seat, looking back at his employer. 'Aren't we going after the others?' He was a former Canadian naval aviator who had been cashiered for wife beating. He had fallen a great distance, but he still remembered how things had once been done.

'The sea is frozen,' Kretek said, glaring out of the windscreen. 'They can walk home.'

*

They were half a mile short of the station when they saw the gleaming red bulk of the Halo lifting from behind the antenna knoll. The big machine swung parallel to the ridge, climbing under full power. Instinctively, Smith and the others went facedown flat on the snow, camo-merging into their background. The aircraft thundered almost directly overhead, heading for the central peaks and the saddleback between.

'Damn it!' Smith raged, scrambling to his feet and staring after the departing helicopter. 'I'd hoped splitting them up would keep them pinned! They're bailing out on their own men!'

Randi shook her head, coming up onto her knees. 'They don't give a damn, Jon. They're criminals, not soldiers. They well and truly don't give a damn.'

'What do we do now, Colonel?' Smyslov asked.

'We fall back to Plan B.'

'What is Plan B?'

'That depends on what's left at the station. Let's go!'

Mikhail Vlahovitch fumbled the little Belgian-made pocket grenade out of his parka, feeling the bullets hitting on the far side of the ice slab he crouched behind. Pulling the pin, he let the safety lever flick free, counted two, and pitched overhand. He waited for the flat crack of the grenade detonation, then lunged out from behind the slab, rolling across the frozen beach to get the angle on the men who had been firing on him.

Vlahovitch came up onto his knees, saw a wounded Spetsnaz trooper kneeling beside a second downed man, and leveled the Agram, emptying the submachine gun in a single prolonged figure-eight burst that engulfed both the wounded and the dying.

As the bolt clicked open on an empty chamber, Vlahovitch was caught by the silence. His had been the last gun firing. The only sounds remaining were the creak and whine of the pack ice and the hiss of his own breath.

Staggering, he got to his feet, drawing a fresh clip out of his belt pouches.

The Russians had come out of nowhere while Vlahovitch and his men had been distracted by their search for the woman. The Spetsnaz had apparently been taken as much by surprise by the presence of the arms smugglers as the reverse. It had been an unexpected-meeting engagement, inevitably the most chaotic and savage of battles.

'Lazlo,' he yelled, ejecting the empty and forcing the reload into the Agram's magazine well. 'Lazlo! . . . Vrasek! . . . Prishkin! To me!'

No one answered. Blood streaked the ice. The scattering of bodies lay unmoving. Their men and his.

'Lazlo! . . . Prishkin!'

He turned in place slowly, looking around. It was a wipe-out. A mutual massacre. He was the only one left of either side.

'Lazlo?'

Then he heard the distant, rhythmic thudding of rotors. It was the Halo. He couldn't see it from the base of the point, but he could follow the sound of its flight. It was heading up to the glacier. Kretek was going after the anthrax, and Vlahovitch knew without the faintest shadow of a doubt that he wouldn't be coming back.

And Vlahovitch finally acknowledged something else that he had known down deep in his belly for a long time: that Anton Kretek would eventually betray and abandon him like this.

'Kretek, you bastard!' He almost burst his throat with the scream.

'He's not a very nice man really.' The voice was conversational, feminine, and coming from directly behind him.

Vlahovitch spun to find the woman standing some twenty feet away. She hadn't been there a few moments before, but she was there now, her materialization as silent as the arrival of a stalking cat. She wore the red ski pants worn by the blonde they had captured the day before, and the green sweatshirt she had stolen from the body of Kretek's nephew, the overlong sleeves rolled up. But this wasn't the brown-eyed American blonde. The thrown-back hood of the shirt revealed high-pinned raven black hair and chill gray eyes, and the accent to her words was vaguely British. She stood relaxed with her arms held loosely crossed over her stomach.

'But then, *you* really aren't a very nice man, either,' she went on. And then she smiled.

A strange, uncontrollable horror welled up within Vlahovitch. There was no justification for it. He was a man cradling a loaded machine gun, and she an unarmed woman. Yet he was stricken with the fear a condemned prisoner feels when he hears the approaching footfalls of his hangman. He brought up the Agram, trying to draw back the SMG's bolt, his terror making him fumble.

The first thrown knife sank into his right shoulder, paralyzing his arm. The second struck in the center of his chest, driving through his breastbone and into his heart.

Valentina Metrace allowed herself that single, deep, deliberate breath. An enemy was dead and she and her friends were alive, and that was how it should be. She knelt down beside Vlahovitch's body, reclaiming her knives. She cleaned each blade with a handful of snow, drying them on the clothing of the arms smuggler before resheathing them.

She'd started to salvage the man's weapon and remaining ammunition when a new factor intruded. From this position, she had a fair view down the eastern side of the point. Standing, she shielded her eyes against the growing sun glare and peered down the revealed reach of the shoreline trail. 'Oh, dear,' she murmured under her breath.

CHAPTER FIFTY

Wednesday Island Station

'Jon, look!' Randi exclaimed, pointing. 'They didn't torch the copter!'

From their position atop the antenna knoll they could look down on the ruins of the science station. All three of the prefab huts were in flames, but beyond the camp, at the helipad site, the Long Ranger sat apparently intact under its protective shroud of snow-covered tarpaulins.

Smith kicked free of his snowshoes and unslung the SR-25. 'If they didn't wreck it some other way we may still be in business. Let's go, but keep your eyes open for any stay-behinds.'

Weapons readied, they dropped down off the hill to the station area. The low-lying smoke stank of burning plastic and hot metal, and there was a faint tinge of roasting pork to it that all three recognized but none commented on.

It took only a few moments of wary inspection to prove that the station's ruins were deserted. 'They've pulled out,' Randi commented, lowering Valentina's rifle, 'bag and baggage.'

'They must have bolted when they heard the firefight. They realized more was going down around here than they'd figured.' Smith looked across at her. 'How about it, Randi? What are the chances they're aborting?'

She shook her head. 'I think the guy running this show, Kretek, would be willing to risk everything at this point but the anthrax. I think he's operating in bull-in-the-china-shop mode now. He's going for it.'

'Then so do we. Let's look at the copter.'

They had to circle wide around the blazing lab hut. As they did so Smith almost tripped over a form half-buried in the snow.

'Ah, hell!'

It was the body of Professor Trowbridge, casually kicked aside out of the camp walkways and frozen solid in an undignified sprawl. Smith was glad the previous night's snowfall had encrusted the dead man's face so that he didn't have to look down into Trowbridge's accusing eyes.

'I'm sorry, Jon,' Randi spoke quietly, coming to stand beside him. 'I kind of made a hash of things here.'

'It's not your fault. I set up the situation. I let him come with us.'

The final lesson, Sarge. When you command, you don't just live with your decisions for today, but forever.

'He asked to come, Jon,' she said, looking at the still form, 'and it was his call to make. None of us knew what was waiting for us here.'

'I guess that's true enough.' He glanced at her, a grim half-smile crossing his face. 'Does it make you feel any better?'

She shook her head. 'Not really.'

They moved on.

When they reached the helipad, they found only a single set of tracks leading up to the Long Ranger through the fresh snow. They also found an ugly brick-sized package strapped around one landing gear strut with electrician's tape. Smith and Smyslov froze when they saw it, but Randi dropped to her knees beside the float, intently examining the charge. 'It's plastique,' she reported after a moment, 'and it hasn't been fused. Let me have a knife, please.'

Smith passed her his bayonet. 'They were probably interrupted by the firefight.'

She carefully cut through the tape binding the charge to the helicopter. Standing, she pitched the explosives as far beyond the wind berm as she could. 'It stands to reason that if they were going to blow up the Ranger they wouldn't bother with sabotaging it as well.'

'That'll be for you and the major to check out.' Smith looked back toward the burning camp. Where in the hell was Val? After she finished her decoy run she was supposed to rejoin. 'How long will it take for you to get this ship airworthy?'

Randi frowned and brushed back her parka hood. 'It's been sitting out here cold-soaking for two days. The book says at least two hours for warm-up, prep, and preflight in this kind of environment.'

'The book doesn't exist on this island.'

'Right. I'll see what I can do. Major, help me get the tarps and engine covers off.'

Smith twisted the handle on the Long Ranger's side hatch. Sliding it open, he peered inside the cabin. Everything looked intact and as they had left it, including the big aluminum case of lab equipment they had left strapped to the deck. A fat lot of good that had done them.

He unslung his pack and swung it into the cabin, laying Valentina's model 70 beside it. The sight of the rifle reminded him again of the weapon's owner.

She'd been so sure she could pull off an escape and evasion on her own. What if she'd been wrong? Smith felt his guts knot. He didn't want her to become another of those failed things he'd have to live with.

'Colonel, look!' Smyslov threw aside one of the engine covers and pointed. A small figure had appeared beyond the burning huts, coming around the knoll and running – no, staggering – along the shoreline trail. Smith caught up his own rifle and ran to meet her, Smyslov following a few steps behind.

They intercepted her just short of the huts. 'Are you all right?' Smith demanded as Valentina half-collapsed in the curve of his arm.

'Fine,' she gulped and wheezed, bracing her hands against her knees. 'Just winded . . . but we have . . . complications, Jon . . . Complications.'

'What's happening?'

She forced herself erect, still panting from her sprint. 'Our arranged mutual ambush worked magnificently . . . almost a draw. I hung back to tidy up and maybe acquire a spare weapon or two . . . but I was . . . interrupted . . . and had to take off.'

'By?'

'The other section of the Spetsnaz force. There were only six taken out in the firefight with the smugglers. Four more are coming in behind me, and I strongly suspect they are not pleased with current events.'

'Did they spot you?' Smith demanded.

'Not sure. Maybe.'

'How long do we have?'

'They stopped to check their dead. I think we've got about ten minutes.'

'Christ! Now they show up!' Smith paused to rub his aching eyes, wondering if he'd ever not be tired again. 'All right. Major, you and Randi have got to get that helicopter ready to fly. Val, your rifle's back at the Ranger. I want you to cover the helipad approaches from there. I'll stay here and put the trail under fire.'

Valentina swiped a sweat-damp lock of hair back from her brow. 'Jon, these fellows likely know the old German infantry trick of maintaining the unit firebase. The survivors will swap out their assault rifles for the squad automatic weapons taken from their dead. They may have lost seventy percent of their platoon manpower, but they'll still possess eighty percent of their firepower.'

'That's why I'd like that helicopter ready before they get here.'

'Jon, we are talking about three bloody machine guns!'

'That's a given, Val. Get going!'

'Colonel,' Smyslov said slowly. 'May I suggest an alternative?'

'I'll be happy to consider one, Major.'

'Let me go out to meet them. Let me order them to stand down.'

Smith's eyes narrowed. 'I thought you said you didn't have the authority for that.'

'I don't, but I can try. Maybe I can reason with them' – Smyslov shrugged and gave his wry grin – 'or maybe just bullshit them. Even if I fail, maybe I can buy you and the ladies enough time to get out of here.'

'Those Spetsnaz might not be too pleased with you at the moment, either, Major.'

The Russian's face went sober again. 'I suspect my entire government is not too pleased with me at the moment, Colonel, but we must stop Kretek from getting that anthrax. And maybe, this way, no more Russian soldiers will have to die.'

Smith hesitated. Now was no time to stop trusting. 'Val, you help Randi with the helicopter. I'll fall back and join you when you start engines. If I do not rejoin by the time you're ready to take off, take off anyway. That's an order! Your absolute priority will be to report the situation here on Wednesday Island. After that, act as you see fit. Go!'

She gave him a beseeching look but strangled down her protest. Obediently she dashed off toward the helipad.

Smith turned back to Smyslov. 'Good luck, Major. I hope you're a silver-tongued devil today.'

'I shall try to be, sir.' He drew Smith's sidearm from his pocket and handed it back. 'If I am not, you may have more use for this than I.'

Smyslov took a step back and came to attention, his European-style heel click muffled by the snow as his hand whipped up in a precise salute. 'Colonel Smith, may I say it has been a privilege serving under your command.'

Smith's rigid fingertips touched his brow in the response. 'Anytime, anywhere, Major. The privilege has been mine.'

Randi fought back a momentary surge of dizziness as she leaned into the engine compartment. The mental haze of the previous night threatened a return, and she fought to stay focused on tightening the knobs of the battery reconnects.

On the voyage north she had come to know this Long Ranger intimately, and she knew that it had been 'polarized' by its leasing company to the best extent possible. All the gaskets and seals were cold-resistant plastics and composites. The lubricants were arctic environment multiviscosity synthetics. The fuel had been heavily laced with an anti-jelling agent, and the batteries were all ultraheavy-duty, deep-charge gel packs, the best on the market.

But it wasn't enough.

The little aircraft's power train and controls should be warmed inside a heating tent for several hours to bring them back up to a decent operating temperature, and the batteries freshened by a quick charger.

But the tent, heaters, and charger were burning in the supply hut, and there would have been no time for them anyway.

She took a final checking look around the interior of the battery compartment, then slammed the outside door, forcing herself to take deliberate care with each of the Dzus fasteners.

Light running footsteps came around from the far side of the helicopter, and Valentina Metrace appeared.

'What's happening?' Randi demanded.

'The last batch of Spetsnaz are coming in. Maybe five minutes. Gregori's gone out to chat them up, but I don't think it's going to work. Jon's gone all self-sacrificial on us and is preparing to do his Horatio-at-the-bridge number. We are under orders to get this ridiculous contrivance running now!'

The sickness welling up within Randi didn't all have to do with her recent bout of exposure. She swallowed the mouthful of chill saliva and forced her mind back to clarity. 'Okay, do a walk-around. Drag those tarps farther away and make sure there are no foreign objects near us that could get sucked into the intakes.'

'Right.' There was no time for either of them to be fearful or concerned, or at least to admit to it.

Randi ran around to the pilot's door and hauled herself up into the cockpit, the frozen leather of the seat biting into her thighs. She propped the preflight checklist against the windscreen; she didn't dare to trust her memory. Then she hit the main switches. Behind the frost-hazed glass lenses, instrument needles stirred and lifted sluggishly.

There would be three crises to surmount. First, there must be enough power left in the batteries to force the cold engines to crank up and start. The second would come at the moment of ignition, when the frozen, brittle components of the propulsion train would either spin up to speed or fracture and explode.

The third and final crisis would occur after liftoff, when the helicopter's flight controls would either work or fail, throwing them out of the sky.

And they would have only one chance at each.

Lieutenant Pavel Tomashenko moved with the steady, ground-devouring trot of the Zulu warrior or Special Forces soldier, his AK-74 cradled across his chest. His eyes scanned ahead, like an automated radar tracking system seeking for the next ambush. The rest of his mentality was lost in rage.

Even he was willing to admit to his failure as an officer and soldier. Again he had allowed his men to walk into a trap. The bulk of his command had been wiped out, and he had not even been near the fight. He was finished. He could expect nothing but disgrace and a court-martial. Better by far at least to die with his jaws locked in the throat of the enemies who had shamed him.

Burdened by the heavy RPK squad automatic weapons and their loads of ammunition, the two men of the demolitions team and the platoon radioman trotted behind him, stolidly unquestioning. They were Spetsnaz.

Ahead, Tomashenko saw the smoke of burning buildings rising from the area of the science station. He did not know what might be happening there. Nor did he know the identities of the strange body of armed men who had wiped out and been almost wiped out by his own advance scouting force. Nor did he know where they had come from. But through his binoculars Tomashenko had seen the last enemy survivor fleeing in this direction.

As they rounded the hill with the radio mast at its top, Tomashenko slowed their advance to a stalking walk, dispersing his remaining men with silent curt gestures. The science station's huts were blazing, thick streamers of dark smoke smearing into the chill blue of the sky.

And from the base of the smoke plumes a man walked in their direction, his hands lifted shoulder high.

Tomashenko lifted his own hand, halting the advance. Shifting the strap of his assault rifle so it rode leveled at his waist, the Spetsnaz commander waited, his hand curled around the AK's trigger group. To the right and left, his troopers went prone, hunching into the snow, their bipodded weapons aimed.

The man with the lifted hands met them about a hundred yards out from the burning station. The hood of his parka was thrown back, and blond hair could be seen. Tomashenko recognized him from the photographs he had been shown. It was Smyslov, the Air Force officer who supposedly was subverting the operations of the American intelligence group from within. The man who should have been dead by now. Tomashenko's eyes glittered as they narrowed.

Smyslov came within ten feet and dropped his hands. 'I am Major Gregori Smyslov of the Russian Federation Air Force,' he stated crisply. 'You will have been briefed about my presence. And you are?'

'Lieutenant Pavel Tomashenko of the Naval Infantry Special Forces. I was briefed about you, Major. I am pleased you have escaped.'

'It is not a matter of escape, Lieutenant,' the Air Force officer replied. 'The parameters of this mission have changed, and your original orders concerning the American intelligence party are no longer relevant.'

'I have received no instructions from my superiors concerning this.'

'Our superiors are not aware of the true situation here. As the senior officer present I am changing your orders on my own authority, Lieutenant. You will break off this operation immediately. I will accompany you back to your submarine, where I will make my report and see that your orders are updated.'

'Major, my orders concerning the American intelligence team came from the highest possible national authority. As you should be aware, they have placed critical state secrets at risk. They are to be stopped at all costs.'

'And I said, those orders are no longer relevant, Lieutenant!' Smyslov took another step forward. 'You will not, I repeat, not interfere further with the Americans. You and your men will return to the submarine.'

Tomashenko's voice cracked. 'They've killed my men!'

'The incident at the crash site was ... regrettable,' Smyslov replied, continuing his advance. 'As for the fight that has just occurred, you may rest assured that your men fell honorably in battle with the enemies, the true enemies, of Russia.'

'I have some questions as to just who our true enemies are, Major.' Tomashenko spat out Smyslov's rank.

'As you should, Lieutenant.' Smyslov's green eyes bored into his. 'Now, stand down your men and I will tell you.'

'No, Major. I will obey my standing orders and deal with the Americans! Then I will communicate with my superiors about a number of things, including treason!'

'I'm sure it will be a very interesting discussion, Lieutenant. But for now you will obey my orders and stand down!' Smyslov extended his hand to straight-arm the Spetsnaz trooper. Tomashenko's finger, already curled around the trigger of his slung assault rifle, tightened. The AK-74 crashed out a single shot.

Major Gregori Smyslov buckled and fell unmoving to the snow of Wednesday Island.

The Spetsnaz officer had no more than a second or two to look down in triumph at the body of the fallen man. Then the numbing shock arrived a moment before the sound of the second, distant gunshot. Tomashenko looked down to find a palm-sized spray of scarlet in the center of his chest. Oddly enough, his last sensation before the blackness took him was one of great relief. He would never have to answer for failing the Motherland.

A hundred yards away, kneeling in the trail rut beside the bunkhouse, Jon Smith lowered the smoking SR-25 and swore in bitter futility at governments, secrets, and lies. Then he threw himself flat as a bullet stream kicked up a line of snow jets beside the trail.

More slugs snapped low over his head as a second squad automatic opened up, raking his position. Dragging his rifle behind him, he hunched backward down the trail a few yards, pressing low in the meager shelter of the compacted snow. Coming up onto his knees again, he spotted the movement of a Spetsnaz trooper crawling toward the station. Smith squeezed off two hasty shots before the covering gunners shifted fire to his new position.

Smith recognized a losing scenario when he saw one. The battery of light machine guns he faced could simply throw too much lead too fast. By using alternating over-watch fire, the Russians could keep him pinned while they worked around to a kill position on his flanks. It was only a matter of time.

Gregori Smyslov had traded his life for a few precious minutes of that commodity. Now it was his turn. He had to keep fire off the helicopter. He had to protract his death long enough to give Val and Randi their chance.

The two women heard the sudden hammer crash of gunfire beyond the station.

'Randi?'

'Get in!'

As Valentina threw herself on the deck behind the pilots' seats, Randi ran a final eye over the cockpit instrumentation. She didn't like what she saw, especially the battery rates. But nothing was going to get any better. She set her throttle position and energized the starter.

Overhead, in the power pack, the turbines sluggishly started their spin-up against the drag and inertia of cold metal. Slowly a rotor blade swung past, too slowly. Randi willed the tachometer needles upward into the green ignition zone. The battery amperage flickered ominously as the drain grew.

'Shit! Shit! Shit!' She got off the starter before the final dregs of battery power bled away.

Valentina thrust her head and shoulders over the pilot's seat. 'Miss Russell, as the saying goes, failure is not an option here!'

'I know, damn it! Let me think!'

There had to be something! But it wouldn't be anything in the book. The book said it was impossible to get airborne under these circumstances. The book said they were all going to die on the ground. It would have to be something else. An anecdote read once about a peculiarity of the Bell Ranger family of helicopters. What had it been? What had it been?

'Spin the tail rotor!' Randi screeched.

'What?'

'Spin the tail rotor by hand while I crank it! It's connected through a direct driveshaft to the transmission. It'll take some of the load off the starter motor!'

'What the bloody ever!' Valentina called back, scrambling out of the open side hatch.

In the cockpit sideview mirror Randi watched as Valentina positioned herself at the end of the fuselage boom, hands braced on the small, vertically mounted blade of the tail rotor.

'Ready!' the historian called.

'Right! Cranking now!'

Once more the starter whined. As the tail rotor began to spin, Valentina shoved down on it with all her weight, kicking it around. Shifting her grip, she repeated the move again and again. As the RPMs climbed she began to ride the blades single-handed, adding her strength to the electric starter.

In the cockpit Randi watched the tachometers as Valentina's efforts were magnified by the transmission gearing. The needle edged upward, not quite to ignition range. Not quite. Not quite. The ammeter needles began to quiver.

'Get clear!' she screamed. 'Get clear!' That was as good as it was going to get.

Randi saw Valentina throw herself backward and out of the way, and she shoved the starter switch into the ignition detente. Flame flickered in the engine throats. A soft, rising vacuum cleaner moan supplanted the starter whine, and the engine temperature gauges snapped to attention.

'Yes!' Randi twisted the throttle grip on the collective, and the turbines screamed in response, the main rotor blurring into its thudding beat, the Long Ranger coming to life.

Laughing, Valentina scrambled back into the cabin. Throwing her arms around the pilot's seat, she administered a gleeful hug.

'What were Jon's orders?' Randi yelled over her shoulder.

'Oh, he said a lot of things! Let's go fetch him!'

Smith felt the contrast of the heat beating on his back, and the cold beneath his belly. He'd gone prone beside the flaming frame of the bunk hut, using the swirling smoke for cover. Two of the surviving Spetsnaz were still out ahead of him somewhere, firing short, economical bursts. The third was off to his right at about two o'clock and still working steadily around to an enfilade position. Soon the third man would be in position to lay down suppressive fire, and the first two men could start working in.

Rolling onto his side, Smith squeezed off half a dozen rounds offhand toward the third man, emptying the magazine and driving the Russian to ground momentarily. Snaking back a couple of yards, he found another shallow depression in the snow and reloaded.

This was getting nasty. In another minute he was going to have to fall back to the lab hut, and the smoke cover would start working in favor of the Spetsnaz.

In an action movie this would be an excellent time for the relief force to come thundering over the horizon. But Smith didn't believe in Hollywood anymore. Incrementally he lifted his head and peered around, judging his terrain. No, on second thought, he wouldn't fall back any farther. If the Russians reached the first hut, they'd have a line of sight and fire on the helipad. He'd make his stand here.

It was interesting, he noted, how abstractly a person could decide on his dying ground. The scientist and diagnostician within him said it was due merely to the numbing effect of shock and emotional overload. Psychologically, he was not actually comprehending the concept of his own death.

The romantic and the soldier counterpointed that one man's life really wasn't that important in the greater scheme of the world, and if it could be expended in the saving of things and people one cared about, the spending was not so bitter.

Behind him he heard the rising metallic whistle of a helicopter's engines. *Good girl, Randi, you always manage.* That bastard out at two o'clock would have the best angle of fire on a departing copter, so Smith nestled his cheek against the chill stock of the SR-25. Laying the sighting crosshairs on the knob of snow the Russian was crouching behind, he started knocking chunks off it.

The whine of the turbines intermixed with the drone of lifting rotors. That was it. His people were out of it and clear.

And then Smith realized the drone wasn't drawing away; it was coming closer. He twisted around and bellowed an incoherent curse.

Hovering in ground effect at a mere ten feet altitude, the Long Ranger was sidling in over the station, snow and smoke swirling in the lift wash. A slender gun barrel protruded from the open side hatch, the venomous crack of Valentina's Winchester echoing as she put fire in on the Spetsnaz positions.

To rage, hesitate, or even think would see them all dead. One end of the laboratory building was not yet fully involved; its roof not yet burning. Scrambling to his feet, Smith backed toward the lab hut, emptying the SR-25's magazine, not hoping to hit, but just to keep hostile heads down for a few critical seconds.

The bolt slammed on an empty chamber, and he turned and sprinted the last few yards. He threw his rifle at the rooftop, swearing again as it rebounded and skidded off. There was no time to fool with it. He vaulted for the roof edge, straight-arming himself onto the unburned section. It proved to be not nearly as stable as it had looked, and flame licked at him.

Randi had him spotted, and the Long Ranger moved in, easing past the wind turbine tower, the starboard pontoon pushing closer through the smoke.

Wind-whipped embers seared Smith's face and charred his clothing. He sprang again, throwing his arms over the top of the float, the helicopter bobbling wildly as his weight came aboard. Squad automatic fire tore into the compressed foam beside him. 'Go! Go! G—' His yell strangled off as Valentina grabbed the hood of his parka, heaving furiously to drag him in through the hatch.

Centrifugal force swung his legs out as Randi pivoted the Long Ranger around its rotor mast, putting its tail to the enemy. The nose dipped as she firewalled the throttles, powering away from the firefight.

Smith got a leg up on the float and lunged into the helicopter's cabin, collapsing on the deck. Valentina collapsed next to him, glaring.

'Don't start about us coming back for you, Jon!' she yelled

over the growing wind roar. 'Just don't even bloody start!'

The last two members of the Spetsnaz platoon, the radio operator and the junior demolitions man, watched the small orange helicopter buzz away over the central ridge. The senior demo man had died spectacularly in the last moments of the fight. Standing to fire at the aircraft, his head had exploded like a bursting balloon, struck by a bullet traveling at some ungodly velocity.

There was nothing to be done for him, and the pair of survivors were unsure of what they could do for themselves. At the moment they were among the most helpless of men: Russian soldiers without an officer to give them orders. They exchanged a few quiet words in their native Yakut tongue; then they started to trudge back toward the dead body of Lieutenant Tomashenko and the stranger he had shot down.

The stone- and snow-streaked flanks of the central ridge wheeled past below the Long Ranger. Randi's hands hurt, but she could cope with it. Far more importantly, in the face of the cold start and the gunfire, all the instrument gauges were where they were supposed to be.

'How does it look?' Smith said, pulling himself up between the pilot seats.

'It looks like Bell builds a pretty good helicopter. Where do you want me to head, Jon?'

'The Misha crash site, as fast as you can get us there.'

'We're on the way. What are we going to do when we get there?'

There was no sense in not telling her the truth. 'I have no idea, Randi. We're going to have to see what we've got and how it plays.'

Valentina pulled herself up beside him. 'What happened to Gregori?'

Smith hated the sound of his own voice, cold and flat. 'His own people shot him.'

'God, and I wanted to kill him myself once.' Valentina rested her forehead on the back of the pilot's seat. When she straightened her voice had gone cold as well. 'Once we've sorted out that lot at the crash site, I'd like to go back there and tidy up a few things.'

'You don't have to. The issue has been dealt with.'

The Long Ranger swept around West Peak, and the jagged slopes fell away to the dirty gray white of the glacier.

'Stay high, Randi. We may have guns down there.'

'Understood. It should be right over on the far side of the saddleback, shouldn't it?'

'Yeah, we should be over it in another second.'

And then they were.

'You bastards!' Valentina screamed in helpless rage, smashing her fists down on the cabin deck. 'You filthy, stinking bastards!'

The scattered ruins of the Misha 124 lay on the ice below. The entire forward fuselage of the ancient bomber had been ripped open, first by shaped explosive charges and then by the enormous lift and leverage of Kretek's flying crane. Chunks of aircraft skin and bulkheading lay scattered like discarded Christmas wrappings, and they could look down into the TU-4's forward bomb bay.

The bioagent reservoir was gone, lifted out of the wreck like an egg out of a crumpled aluminum nest.

Randi let the Long Ranger slip into a hover over the crash site. 'Oh, God, he's got it!' she exclaimed, her voice despairing.

Two metric tons of weaponized anthrax. Half a continent's worth of death in the hands of a man who cared less than nothing for human life.

Smith looked away from the crash site and toward the south, toward the threatened world, and in the distance he caught the faint repetitive flicker of rotors in the sunlight.

CHAPTER FIFTY-ONE

Over the Arctic Ocean

'This is Black Horse Lead calling any Wednesday Island station. Black Horse Lead calling any Wednesday Island station. Do you copy?'

Major Saunders had repeated the call so often it had started to lose meaning for him. They had completed their final top-off from the tanker, and in the Osprey's cargo bay the ranger strikers and the ABC men were tightening harness and running their final equipment checks. Soon they'd be coming in on their objective. For the first time in days the radio bands were clear of solar interference. But Saunders was beginning to suspect there was no one out there to answer.

'This is Black Horse Lead . . .'

'Black Horse Lead, this is Wednesday Island Point,' a crisp, businesslike voice crackled clearly into Saunders's earphones. 'This is Lieutenant Colonel Jon Smith. I am coded Cipher Venger Five. Do you read me, Black Horse?'

Saunders's thumb crushed the transmit button on his joystick. 'We read you, Colonel, four by four. We are your Mike force. What is your situation?'

'We are off Wednesday and airborne at this time. Situation on the island is critical and unstable. What is your ETA, Black Horse, and do you have fighter assets attached?'

'We are approximately twenty-five minutes out from Wednesday. Negative on fighter assets; we are lift and tanker only.'

'That's not going to do us any good then,' the voice replied. 'Be advised Wednesday Island should be considered a potentially hot LZ. Hostiles may include Russian Spetsnaz elements. Also be advised the Primary Package is verified. I say again, the Primary Package is verified. Primary Package is also off the island and is being sling carried by a Mil 26, that is Mary . . . India . . . Lima . . . two . . . six, Halo heavy-lift helicopter, Canadian civil registry, Golf . . . Kilo . . . Tango . . . Alpha. Halo is now heading south-southeast from Wednesday Island at approximately ninety knots. We are in pursuit at this time. Require immediate interceptor launch. Engage and destroy Halo at all costs. I say again, engage and destroy at all costs!'

'Understood, Wednesday Point. We will relay intercept request, but it's going to take a while. Even the jets will need a couple of hours to get out this far.'

'Roger that, Black Horse, understood.' There was a fatalism in the reply. 'We'll do what we can until they get here.'

Anton Kretek peered down from the crane operator's cab on the port side of the Halo. Seventy feet below the huge helicopter, the lozenge-shaped containment vessel twisted slowly at the end of its heavy Kevlar cable. Torn wiring and ductwork trailed raggedly from either end of the silvery reservoir, and the lifting harness wasn't as secure as it might have been, but the pearl had been stolen from the oyster.

It had been a tough, sloppy job, but what did it matter? It was the last. It had cost him a number of his best men, including his chief of staff, but that might have worked out for the best. Mikhail would have had to have been liquidated in due course anyway. The man simply knew too much. Now was as good a time as any to have done with it.

There was, of course, the chance he might be captured back on the island, along with his knowledge about the remainder of the anthrax retrieval operation, but Kretek had prepared for even that eventuality.

Then there was also the unavenged death of his sister's son, but pish, be damned to the woman. The boy was dead. What profit was there in fussing about it now?

Kretek groped in the pocket of his parka for his Balkan-blend cigarettes and lighter, then recalled the big half-empty blivett of jet fuel filling the helicopter's central cargo bay. Telling his nicotine-starved nerves to be patient for a few hours more, he went forward from the crane cab to the cockpit.

The demolitions men and the surviving members of the security force slouched on the cargo bay deck, their heads resting on their knees, or sprawled on the fuel blivet, using it as a waterbed. In the cockpit the Canadian pilot was on the controls while his Byelorussian copilot intermittently stuck his head into the observation bubble set in the cockpit side window, checking on the status of the sling load.

'There is a change in plans.' Kretek lifted his voice over the thrum of the rotors. 'We won't be returning to the trawler. We will turn directly south at the second refueling depot.'

'Whatever you say.' The pilot's reply was laconic. 'Where are we heading?'

'I will give you the GPS coordinates later.'

'However you want it.'

Kretek approved of the man. A true professional, he asked no questions. Were Kretek staying in the trade, he would have considered keeping the fellow around. Such men were useful. As it was, he, his crew, and his aircraft would end up at the bottom of an isolated Canadian lake instead of Hudson Bay.

As for the anthrax, it would be left well camouflaged near a logging road in the Canadian Northwest Territories. In a few months, after the heat was off and after he had negotiated a sale of the merchandise, it could be extracted by truck. This was the secondary plan that not even Mikhail Vlahovitch had known about. It meant sacrificing the men he'd left on the trawler as well, but so it went. He no longer needed them, either. A momentary smile tugged at Kretek's mouth. What did they call it, 'corporate downsizing'?

The arms merchant leaned against the side of the

cockpit, bracing himself against the intermittent low-altitude turbulence, and again fought down the urge for a cigarette. He would rather miss the trade, but with the sale of the anthrax it would not be wise to continue. He would be too rich, too complacent. The wise man knew when to call enough.

The Halo's copilot suddenly gave an explosive curse, staring out of the portside cockpit window. They were no longer alone in the sky. Another aircraft was paralleling their course, half a kilometer off. The small Day-Glo orange helicopter, the one they had left back on the island. The one he had been in too much of a rush to destroy.

Kretek echoed the copilot's curse. Complacency was already biting him in the ass.

The arms merchant dove back into the cargo hold. Twisting the quick release handle on the escape hatch, port side, just aft of the cockpit, he took a grip on a grab bar and kicked the hatch out of its frame.

'Get two men with machine guns here!' he bellowed over the roar of the slipstream. 'Then two others at each of the other hatches. Move, you bastards! Move!'

The Long Ranger held warily on the hip of the heavy lifter. Slowed by the ominous cylindrical shape dangling beneath its belly, the Halo hadn't been difficult to overtake.

'It's rather like a dog chasing an automobile,' Valentina mused as they studied the giant Russian-built helicopter. 'Once you catch the damn thing what do you do with it?'

The larger aircraft stolidly continued its lumbering retreat away from Wednesday Island. To the southeast, the cloud-capped outlines of the next rank of arctic islands thrust above the horizon.

'This is not good, Jon,' she continued, kneeling on the deck beside the open side hatch. 'If he drops down to fly nap-of-the-Earth inside of the archipelago, the DEW Line will never be able to pick him up amid that tangle of islands and channels. It'll be blind luck if the interceptors can find him.'

'I know it. That's why we've got to stay on him.'

Randi looked back over the pilot's seat. 'Just letting you know, Jon, we don't have all that much of a fuel reserve.'

'I know that, too.' Again they were running out of assets, and every minute and mile was taking them deeper into the frozen wastes of the Queen Elizabeth Archipelago and farther from allies and aid.

'Watch it!' Valentina exclaimed. A black rectangle had suddenly appeared in the Halo's fuselage, the jettisoned door fluttering away toward the pack ice below. 'He's opening his gun ports!'

Sparks of muzzle flame danced inside the open doorway, and gun smoke streaked down the flank of the heavy lifter. Randi countered, flaring the Long Ranger back. Climbing and sideslipping, she put her smaller, nimbler machine above and behind the shield of the larger helicopter's blade arc, positioning so that Kretek's gunners could not fire on them without damaging their own rotors.

Below them, the Halo weaved sluggishly, like an elephant waving its tusks at a prowling lion, the containment vessel swinging, pendulumlike, at the end of its tether.

'Wouldn't it be lovely if they developed a bad case of butterfingers and just dropped the damn thing?' Valentina commented.

'A nice thought, but it's something we can't count on,' Smith replied. 'Randi, what are the odds of our shooting out one of their engines?'

The blonde shook her head. 'Not good at all! The Halo is built to Russian mil spec. It's a flying tank, designed to absorb a lot of battle damage.'

'There's got to be some point of vulnerability!' Smith insisted.

Randi frowned in thought. 'Maybe the Jesus nut, the main rotor hub. If you can cut a push-pull rod or fracture a blade hinge, that might do it.'

'Val, it's your rifle. What do you think?'

The historian looked dubiously at her old Winchester. 'I

don't know. The .220 Swift is an excellent man killer but a stinkin' antimateriel round. There's too much velocity and not enough penetration.'

'Can you do it?' Smith insisted.

'I can but try. No promises, though. Randi, bring us in, close as you can and as steady as you can.'

She lay down on the deck in the prone firing position. Twisting the sling of the model 70 around her forearm, she aimed out of the side hatch, nestling in behind the sights.

Stacked almost on top of each other, the Long Ranger and the Halo thundered through the arctic sky, a crow mercilessly harrying a vulture. In the Halo's cockpit, the deck below Kretek's feet swayed ominously, the arcing swings of the containment vessel at the end of the cable wrenching at the heavy lifter.

'They're firing at us!' the arms dealer bellowed into the ear of the Halo's pilot. 'Do something!' With the escape hatches kicked open, the interior of the big helicopter was a welter of wind roar and engine shriek.

'I can't maneuver with a sling load!' the pilot yelled back. 'The only way we can evade is by cutting loose!'

An automatic pistol appeared in Kretek's hand. 'Try it and I'll kill you.'

It was no idle threat, as the Halo's pilot was well aware. But the threat presented by that other rotor-winged gadfly was not idle, either. There was the tap and screech of a bullet strike on the upper fuselage.

'Climb, you bastard!' Kretek snapped. 'Climb above them so we can shoot back!'

Gritting his teeth, the pilot twisted his throttle grip to maximum war power, pushing the Tumanski gas turbines to their limits and sending the tachometers and temperature gauges swinging up and into their red zones.

Randi Russell made the Long Ranger dance, maintaining her position and distance from the lumbering Halo as if connected to it by an invisible boom, keeping behind the invisible shield of the larger helicopter's rotor plain, denying the hostile gunners a target.

Valentina Metrace worked her own skills to their limit as well. Lips curled into a snarl of concentration, she worked the model 70 like an automaton, tracking on target, jacking the bolt to eject the empties, and firing on the split-seconds the sight picture became right. Three times she paused to feed fresh shells into the rifle, but as the third magazine emptied, she lowered the weapon, shaking her head.

'It's no good, Jon,' she yelled. 'I'm connecting, but the damn bullets just explode when they hit. Too much vel. It's not going to work.'

'What else can we try?'

She looked up at him from the deck. 'We try for the pilots. There's the same velocity-and-penetration problem, though. I'll have to first blow out the windscreen and then fire through the hole to get at the men.'

'If that's what we've got, we go with it.'

'One additional problem.' She shoved her hand into her sweatshirt pocket. When she removed and opened it, three slender, sharp-nosed cartridges gleamed in the palm of her glove. 'That's the lot. Then the cow's dry.'

'Like I said, if that's what we've got. Randi, set us up.'

She had been listening to the exchange. 'I'll have to drop below the rotor arc to give you a line of fire into the cockpit. They'll get to shoot back.'

'I'll say yet again, if that's what we've got.'

'Where are they?' the Halo's pilot demanded, eyeing his sideview mirrors. 'Where'd the cocksuckers go?'

'I do not know.' His copilot twisted in his seat and peered out the side bubble. 'They dropped behind us.'

'What is it?' Kretek demanded from over the pilot's shoulder.

'I don't know,' the pilot replied shortly. 'They're back on our six. They're trying something.'

Then he felt the vibration through his controls as a second blast of rotor wash interfered with his own. A shadow tore over the cockpit as the floats of the Long Ranger flashed past, mere feet overhead, in a shallow accelerating dive. Pulling a couple of hundred feet ahead, the smaller helicopter skidded in midair, presenting its open side hatch to the Halo.

'What the f—'

The left side of the cockpit windscreen exploded in a hailstorm of pebbled glass. The copilot screamed incoherently, clawing at his shredded face. Then his scream was abruptly cut off as the second murderously precise rifle slug caught the Byelorussian in the throat, almost decapitating him.

A combat flier's instincts took over, and the pilot locked his controls over. The nose of the Halo came around, sluggishly but quick enough to put the third bullet past his shoulder instead of into his head.

The Halo continued its wild turnaway, shuddering on the verge of a rotor stall. The pilot could hear the door gunner blazing wildly back at their attacker as he fought with the cyclic and collective, trying not to further stress the Halo's critically overloaded airframe. His hand went to the T-grip handle of the emergency sling release.

'No!' The muzzle of Kretek's automatic jammed into the pilot's throat. Glaring like a wild boar at bay, the arms merchant wedged himself between the cockpit seats, his left arm a bloody ruin from the hypervelocity bullet that had missed the pilot. 'No!'

Grimly Randi held her course until she heard Val's rifle crack out its last shot. The Halo was turning on them like a ship of the line presenting its broadside, automatic weapons fire lashing from its side hatches. Submachine gun slugs dotted the flank of the Long Ranger. With her windscreen starring with bullet hits, Randi kicked up onto a rotor tip and dove under the firestreams.

In the cargo bay, Smith locked one arm around a seat brace and the other around Valentina as the radical evasion threatened to hurl them both out of the plunging aircraft. For a fragment of a second they could see the anthrax reservoir lashing wildly at the end of its sling cable, threatening to sweep down on them like Thor's hammer. Then they were past and diving clear, beneath and behind the Halo.

Smith stuck his head out into the slipstream, looking after the fate of the stricken heavy lifter, hoping, praying to see the sling cable breaking or the big helicopter spinning down out of the sky. For a few heartening moments the Halo did seem to stagger on the verge of departing control. Then it stabilized and resumed its remorseless drone to the southeast.

The outer islands of the archipelago lay very close now.

Randi swung in behind the larger helicopter once more, climbing for position. When she called back, her voice was light. 'I don't know about you guys, but I've had it with this. I'm just going to go up there and stick a pontoon in his rotors. We'll land a little lopsided, but that's okay.'

It was the casual declaration of a kamikaze run. Tapping the Halo's rotor with one of the Ranger's floats would indeed finish the job. But the odds of the Long Ranger surviving the resulting kinetic explosion and spray of disintegrating blade fragments were almost nonexistent.

Randi knew this full well. So did Smith and so did Valentina. The black-haired historian gave him an ironic smile and a faint throwaway shrug of her shoulders. It was the way of the trade. It must always be the job and getting the job done. Survival was not mandatory, especially with the lives of thousands in the balance.

There was no sense in prolonging matters. Randi had them positioned above and behind the lumbering Halo once more, poised to strike. Before giving the word, Smith took a final look around the Long Ranger's interior, seeking for some asset, some option, that he might have overlooked.

There was simply nothing left. Only the big aluminum

carryall of lab gear and his half-emptied backpack, a few loops of well-used climbing rope drooling out of it.

And then Jon Smith grinned, a tight, humorless, feral grin.

'What are they doing now?' It was growing harder to yell over the engines. Kretek could feel the weakness creeping upon him. The crude tourniquet on his shattered arm was only slowing the growth of the blood pool at his feet.

'How the fuck should I know?' the pilot raged back, casting a longing look at the release lever. 'They're hanging behind us again.'

'Hold your course.' Kretek stumbled back toward the crane cab amidships. From where they huddled near the open doorways he could feel his men's eyes upon him. They were starting to fail; they were beginning to fear death more than they feared Anton Kretek. And Kretek felt the first shadow of that fear himself.

How could he be beaten by someone called Jon Smith?

Somehow the arms merchant knew it was the American team leader from Wednesday Island back there. The man the college professor had spoken of but whom he, Kretek, had never met face to face. Who was he? Who was this anonymous man with the bland name to end so many dreams and plans?

Painfully Kretek hauled himself into the glass-walled crane cab, looking astern.

There it was! The Long Ranger was almost on top of them again, diving in like a striking hawk. And this time there was something suspended beneath the smaller helicopter.

As if it were aping the Halo and its sling load of anthrax, a silver metal case dangled below one of the Long Ranger's pontoons on a rope. And a man was braced in the side hatch of the Ranger, feeding the rope over the side. Kretek had an impression of dark hair flattened in the rotor wash, and hard, fine-planed features and narrowed, intent eyes that cut across the distance between them like a cold blue death ray. This, then, was Smith. This was his executioner. Kretek bellowed a wordless cry of denial and rage and horror.

The heavy equipment case dipped into the Halo's rotor sweep. Smith felt the end of climbing rope smoke out from between his gloved hands as the case was smashed and hurled away by a blade tip.

Smith rolled back into the Long Ranger's cargo compartment, Valentina helping to drag him through the side hatch. 'Randi,' he yelled, 'get us out of here!'

A savage, racketing vibration jackhammered through the Halo's frame as Kretek staggered back toward the cockpit. The pilot was fighting with the blood-smeared controls, his dead copilot looking on, his near-severed head shaking sardonically.

'That's it!' the pilot screamed. 'We've got to jettison and land!'

'No,' Kretek fell back on the threat of his leveled automatic. 'Keep going.'

'You stupid son of a bitch! We've taken a major blade strike! The fucking rotor assembly's coming apart! If we don't land now we are going to fucking die!'

The pilot grabbed for the sling release, and Kretek used the last of his strength to smash his gun butt down on the groping hand.

'No!'

Then all time for debate was past. The Halo's tortured transmission exploded like a howitzer shell. Centrifugal force hurled fifty-foot rotors away like thrown sword blades, and the Halo pitched over into its death dive, the white ice and black water of the pack below filling the shattered windscreen as it rushed toward them.

Anton Kretek screamed like the trapped animal he was. Emptying his pistol into the pilot, he denied the Canadian an extra second or two of life.

They watched as smoke and sparks streamed back from the Halo's engine bays; then the rotor assembly came apart and tore away, and the massive helicopter assumed the flight dynamics of a filing cabinet.

Pitching over onto its nose, it plummeted toward the sea ice. With gravity's tension off the sling tether, the bioagent reservoir seemed to float beside the falling hulk of the heavy lifter, the maimed aircraft and its canister of death tangled in an entwining, dream-slow dance.

Then they hit, and a mushroom of black and scarlet flame sprouted and grew over the huge hole blasted through the ice.

'What about the anthrax, Jon?' Valentina inquired, watching the fireball.

'Flame and seawater,' Smith replied. 'You couldn't ask for two better spore destroyers.'

'That's it, then?'

'That's it.' Smith looked forward into the cockpit. His throat was raw from yelling and his lungs burned from the cold. As his adrenaline load burned out he was suddenly aware of the aching bruises from the previous night's icefall. It was becoming harder to force the words out. 'Randi, do you think you can find the *Haley* from here?'

'With the radios working, it shouldn't be too much of a problem.'

'Then take us back to the ship. Somebody else can pick up the pieces back on Wednesday.'

'I hear that!'

Smith slammed the side hatches shut and collapsed with his back to the pilot seats. Unbidden, his eyes closed, and he was only dimly aware of a warmth beside him: Valentina's head resting lightly on his shoulder.

CHAPTER FIFTY-TWO

Ascension Island

It was early spring in the South Atlantic, but a storm had rolled in with the sunset. The ghost blue runway lights of Wideawake Field glowed through a watery mist, and rain dripped from the wings of the two huge jet transports sitting side by side on the most isolated parking apron of the joint UK/US air facility. One, a Boeing 747 wearing the blue and white livery of the Presidential Squadron; the other, an Ilyushin 96, it's opposite number from the Russian Federation.

The world at large did not know of the presence of the two aircraft here, nor of the meeting between the two national leaders they carried. As armed sentries circled the sodden parking apron, a confrontation without records or witnesses took place in a soundproof, electronically screened briefing room aboard Air Force One.

'I recognize it's sometimes necessary for a President to lie to his constituency,' Samuel Castilla said coldly to the lean, aristocratic figure seated across the conference table from him, 'but I damn well don't like having to abuse the privilege. I especially don't like having to lie to those people about how their family members died. It leaves a sick taste in my mouth.'

'What other choice do we have, Samuel?' President Potrenko replied patiently. 'To rip open the healing wounds of the Cold War? To set the rapprochement between our nations back by decades? To play into the hands of the hard-liners on both sides who say the United States and Russia are meant to be hereditary enemies?'

'You spin that line very smoothly, Yuri, and so do my advisors and the State Department, but even if I accept it, I still don't have to like it.'

'This I can understand, Samuel. I know you to be a man of conscience and honor' – the corner of the Russian's mouth quirked – 'possibly too much so for the realities of our profession. But we need more time. We have to let more of the old Cold Warriors die, and we have to move the fear further into the past. But at least you will have the consolation of knowing the truth will come out in the end.'

'Oh, it will, Yuri. You can bank on it. We're in agreement that in twenty years' time all documentation on the Wednesday Island incident and the March Fifth Event will be unsealed and there will be a full joint disclosure by both governments.'

'It is agreed.'

Castilla pressed the point home. 'Said pact to be made over our signatures and with the two of us accepting the full responsibility for the secrecy lockdown and the whitewash.'

Potrenko's eyes flickered toward the tabletop; then he nodded. 'It is agreed. Until that day, the members of the Wednesday Island science expedition perished in the tragic fuel dump fire that swept through the station. The members of our Spetsnaz platoon were lost in a training accident. The crew of the Misha 124 will simply not be found, their disappearance becoming one more mystery of the Arctic. And the aircraft itself was destroyed when an old onboard demolition charge was accidentally triggered. All eventualities are covered.'

'I doubt it will be quite that easy,' Castilla replied dryly. 'Lies seldom are. No doubt Wednesday Island will become yet another conspiracy theory haunting the Internet. Maybe we can take a page from John Campbell and Howard Hawks and blame it on a flying saucer.'

Castilla took a sip from the glass of branch water sitting beside his place and wished the shot of bourbon were sitting beside it. 'Why couldn't you have told me the truth in the beginning, Yuri? We could have rigged this somehow. Nobody had to die. We didn't have to come within a hairs-breadth of loosing that anthrax on the world.'

Potrenko continued his silent study of the maroon leather tabletop. 'No doubt things could have been man-aged . . . more effectively. But I cannot apologize for being part of the Russian bureaucracy or for the protocols set by my predecessors. We are all still very much "slaves of the state," and we are likely to remain so for some time to come. I can only apologize for allowing this situation to slip so far out of control. Certain . . . individuals within governmental and military chains of command exercised poor judgment. They are being dealt with.'

'I daresay they are,' Castilla replied, his voice arch. 'Now, there's one last point for us to cover. When our relief force occupied Wednesday Island, the body of one man was not accounted for, that of Major Gregori Smyslov, the Russian Air Force liaison officer assigned to our inspection team. Do you have any information on him?'

Potrenko frowned. 'That need not be a point of concern, Mr. President.'

'Colonel Smith, our team leader on Wednesday, seems to think differently. When I spoke with him, he asked specifi-cally that I inquire about the fate of Major Smyslov. I am inclined to favor his request. What happened to him, Yuri?'

'The major was . . . injured during events on the island, but he survived. He was evacuated to our submarine. He is now being held for trial on a variety of charges.'

'Stemming from the fact he sided with Colonel Smith and against your government?' Castilla's voice softened in an ominous manner. 'That is not acceptable, Mr. President. You will see that all charges against Major Smyslov are dropped immediately and that all ranks and privileges are restored to him without prejudice. If you feel that to be impossible, you will turn the major over to our ambassador in Moscow for repatriation to the United States. If you don't want him, we'll be glad to have him.'

'That is impossible!' Potrenko snapped. 'Major Smyslov has been charged with mutiny and a massive breach of state security. These are very serious matters! I am warning you, Mr. President, these are strictly the internal affairs of the Russian Federation!'

Castilla smiled back without humor but with some pleasure. 'And I just hate having to violate the internal affairs of the Russian Federation, Yuri, but then, I'm having to do a lot of things today that I'm not pleased about. What's one more?'

'This man is a Russian citizen and military officer of the Federation!'

'Colonel Smith seems to feel the major is also still a member of his team, and as I said, I am inclined in the colonel's favor at the moment!'

'This matter is not open for discussion!'

'Then forget it!' Castilla half rose from his chair. 'The whole deal is off! Upon returning to Washington, I'm calling a press conference and I'm blowing the whole thing: the aborted nuclear war, Stalin's assassination, the anthrax, the attack on our investigations team, the cover-up – the whole nine yards goes public!'

Potrenko's face went bloodless. 'You're mad! You would not do this thing! You would not trigger this catastrophe between our governments over the fate of one man!'

Castilla sank back into his chair. 'Yuri,' he said, peering coldly at Potrenko over the frames of his glasses, 'I'm not a happy camper. Humor me.'

CHAPTER FIFTY-THREE

Seattle-Tacoma International Airport

The cabdriver glanced in his rearview mirror at the tall, quiet man in the Army greens and black beret. Since 9/11 he'd carried a lot of soldiers to the airport, some of them heading home, others heading out to somewhere. From the multiple rows of ribbons on this man's uniform coat, there had been a lot of somewheres, and from the weariness etched in his face, he'd been to one not long ago. But like most of the best, he wasn't saying much about it.

The cabbie smiled to himself, looking back on his own somewheres, among them the rice paddy south of Bear Cat where he'd exchanged his right hand for a steel hook.

The Yellow Crown Victoria swept around the great curving reception bay of the terminal building, finding an unloading slot amid the milling streams of traffic. The soldier dismounted, drawing his barracks bag and briefcase out of the backseat. Stepping up to the front window, he reached for his wallet.

The cabdriver reached over with his prosthesis and zeroed the meter. 'Forget it, Colonel. This one's on the house.'

The tall soldier hesitated and then smiled. 'If you insist.'

'Damn straight I do,' the cabby called back, pulling into traffic with a blare of his horn. 'Eleventh Cav, 'sixty-seven. Good luck, sir.'

The shift manager wouldn't mind. He was an ex-Marine, and he'd been some places, too.

Jon Smith pushed through the glass doors of the terminal to

the ticketing counters, the luggage check-in, and the sluggish shuffle of the security inspection lines. The wait didn't bother him particularly. At the moment he was in no rush.

He recognized the phenomenon, a combination of the biological backlash of the past week's extreme exertions and the usual postmission psychological letdown. It would pass. At his last long-distance debriefing with Fred Klein, the director had told him to stand down and take some of his backlog of leave. The director had even waved his magic wand and arranged for it to happen.

The problem was, Smith didn't feel like going anywhere or doing anything particularly. And back in Bethesda there was only the house that had never had the chance to become a home.

Snap out of it, Smith. You don't need a leave. You need to get back to work.

But that brought up another point for consideration. Just exactly what was his work now? When he had accepted his position with Covert One, he had viewed himself as a research microbiologist performing an occasional specialist's assignment for Fred Klein. Now, though, it was feeling more and more as if he was the dedicated operator and his position as USAMRIID was the filler.

And hadn't he taken that research slot to begin with specifically so he could work with Sophia? So they could be together? Since the Hades plague that wasn't going to happen. That idealization was gone forever. Why the hell was he still going through those motions?

The X-ray machine and the security shakedown was a welcome distraction, his uniform and his government ID rating him the most cursory of inspections. He strode on down the concourse toward the United boarding gates. He was early for his flight to Dulles. Maybe he had enough time to get himself a cup of coffee before boarding. Not a drink in the mood he was in, but a cup of coffee.

'Jon, hey, Jon! Hold up!'

Randi Russell was trotting toward him, towing a squeaking piece of wheeled luggage. The white ladies' gloves she wore contrasted with her comfort-faded denims. Coming to a halt, she smiled up at him, an open, happy, pleased smile, very different from when they'd met across the street at the Doubletree.

'I saw that dermatologist you wanted,' she said, holding up her gloved hands. 'He said they might be a little sensitive to cold from now on, but he doesn't think there will even be any scarring.'

Smith found himself smiling back. 'I'm glad to hear it, Randi. Where are you off for?'

She made a face. 'I can't really say. You know the drill.'

He nodded. 'I do. I'm glad we at least have the chance to say good-bye. It was good working with you again and just good seeing you again.'

'The same for me.' She hesitated for a moment, glancing around at the other hurrying occupants of the concourse, and then seemed to make a final call on some debated question.

'Could you come with me for a second?'

'Sure. Why not?'

She led him over into a small pocket of privacy behind an advertising kiosk. 'I was hoping for the chance to tell you about something, Jon,' she said, 'something that happened on the island. I feel kind of strange talking about it. But after thinking about it for a while, I guess it's something you should know.'

'What is it?'

She hesitated a moment more, then looked into his face, her dark eyes sober. 'Remember that night on the north beach when I just about froze to death? You know, when you found me after I'd called out to you?'

'Of course,'

'This is the strange thing. I wasn't . . . alone out there, Jon. Sophia was with me. I know it sounds crazy, and maybe I was or am crazy, but for a minute Sophia . . . came back.

She told me to call out for you. She made me call out. If she hadn't, you'd never have found me.'

She dropped her eyes. 'There, now go ahead and call me a nutcase.'

Smith frowned. 'Why should I do that? Sophia loved you very much.' He lightly rested his hands on her shoulders. 'If you were in trouble and if there were any way in this universe for her to help you, she would. I don't think it's crazy, Randi. I'm not even particularly surprised.'

Randi looked up and gave a sheepish grin. 'Well, she loved you a whole lot, too, Jon Smith. So don't be surprised if she shows up for you sometime, too.'

He nodded thoughtfully. It wasn't a displeasing notion. 'Maybe that explains why we keep bumping into each other. We're bonded through her.'

'It must count for something.' She came up on her toes and lightly brushed her lips against his cheek. 'I have to run. They're calling my flight. You take care, Jon, till next time.'

'Till next time.' And he knew there would be a next time.

Smith found his shoulders squaring and his mood lightening as he finished the walk to the boarding gate. It improved further when he found someone else waiting for him at the United jetway.

Valentina Metrace wore heels and a pleasantly snug gray knit dress that matched her eyes, and a number of other male travelers shot disgruntled looks at Smith as she smiled and stood to greet him.

'Hello, Colonel.'

'Hello yourself, Professor.' He set his briefcase down beside her small pile of carry-ons. 'Are you bound for Washington?'

'No, I'm pleased to say.' She nodded up the concourse. 'I'm on Southwestern a couple of slots farther on. I'm off to Palm Springs for a few days. I find I need to melt a bit of residual ice off my soul.'

'Palm Springs.' Smith nodded thoughtfully. 'It would be nice down there this time of year.'

'Oh, it is, I assure you. There's a swimming pool I know of, shaded by real palm trees and fed by one of the real palm springs. During the day I intend to lie beside it, wearing a swimsuit or less, and at night I will drink champagne and sleep between satin sheets. It will be a life of great beauty.'

She held out her hand to him. 'I've been thinking . . . it would be nice to share it with someone.'

There was no coquetry in the invitation, no challenge, no dare to her offer, only a hint of wistfulness, an echo from the lonely operator's existence that Jon knew and understood.

He hesitated for a last moment. Val would be different, so very different from anyone he had ever known before, and so would any roads they might walk down together. But different wasn't necessarily a bad thing.

'I'll need to look into something first,' he replied.

'What's that?'

He drew Valentina in to him. Putting a hand into her thick, rich hair, he kissed her, letting it linger, learning the softness of her lips, the delicate touch contours of her face.

Val's eyes closed into the kiss and when they opened again he could see that she had been pleased with the result as well. It had been different from one of Sophia's kisses, but that too was as it should be.

It was time. It was time and past time for a great many new things.

Smith went to change his ticket.

EPILOGUE

Anacosta, Maryland

The Wednesday Island operation wound down in the screen-lit dimness of Margaret Templeton's office, coming to its conclusion against the soft purring backdrop of computer cooling fans.

'We've done the partial-truth feed to both the Canadian authorities and Interpol,' Templeton said from her desk workstation. 'To wit, Anton Kretek and his people were involved in some armaments smuggling venture, the exact nature of which remains unknown, when their chartered helicopter went down in Hudson Bay. There were no survivors, but the appropriate wreckage has been recovered.'

'Is it selling?' Fred Klein inquired, testing the soil of Maggie's bonsai tree with a probing finger.

'So far. The general consensus seems to be, the man is no great loss to anyone. We've also located and cleaned up Kretek's refueling depots.'

Klein nodded absently, adding a jet of water to the little planter from the squeeze bottle beside it. He was seated beside Maggie's desk, watching the bank of flat-screen displays on the far office wall. His features were softened by a faint haze of gray beard, and his tie had been loosened a couple of casual inches. It was the end of another average twelve-hour day. 'What about the getaway trawler?'

'Successfully dealt with, sir. The USS *MacIntyre* placed a SEAL team on board the vessel. The Icelandic crew were essentially hired help. Likely they were viewed by Kretek as a disposable asset. They knew nothing about the true nature of the Wednesday Island operation. Accordingly they have been released to the Icelandic authorities.'

'And Kretek's men?'

Maggie's even-featured face was worthy of a championship poker table. 'An operational accident. While they were being taken across to the destroyer, the whaleboat carrying the arms smugglers capsized in a rogue wave. The guards and the coxswain were wearing antiexposure suits and lifejackets and were rescued; Kretek's men weren't. Hudson Bay is a very dangerous body of water, sir.'

'Very much so, Maggie. Here's hoping we won't have to work up that way again for a while.' Klein snugged his tie tight once more. He and Maggie would finish this up and then, for certain, call it quits for the night. 'How are our people doing?'

Maggie's hands danced across her keyboard, the file photos of Jon Smith and Valentina Metrace windowing up on the wall screens. 'Physically, they are recovering from exhaustion, exposure, and a variety of minor injuries. Psychologically, they appear to be stable and still comfortable with operating. Given a reasonable period of rest and recuperation, I feel they will be deployable again. In my opinion both Jon and Professor Metrace continue to be valid mobile ciphers.'

Klein nodded. 'I concur. I'm pleased with the way they seem to work in harness together. I've always been a bit concerned about Metrace, she tends toward being a bit of a cowboy at times. I think Jon's a steadying influence on her. The chemistry's good.'

In the screen glow, Maggie's lips quirked into a slight smile. 'In a number of ways. They've spent the last week together in Palm Springs.'

'Indeed.' Klein frowned, not in disapproval, but in consideration. 'Normally, I don't like to see off-mission fraternization between our prime ciphers, but in this instance I think we'll make an exception. If Jon's good for Metrace, I think Metrace may be good for Jon.'

'I agree, sir. Now, there's one other personnel point I'd like to bring up.'

'What's that, Maggie?'

His executive officer's fingers clattered across her keyboard again, and a third wall screen lit, filling with the image of Randi Russell. 'I think we had best declare this young lady radioactive. I don't think we should ever tap her as an outside asset again.'

'Why so, Maggie? According to Jon's report, Ms. Russell's actions have been exemplary. She has a history of successful operations with him.'

'Yes, sir, but she's CIA, and the Agency knows Covert One is out here now. They don't know exactly who or what we are yet, but they don't like our authority and the way we keep tapping their assets. They're starting to sniff around, hunting for a line on us. Ms. Russell can bore-sight two of our prime ciphers, and we could get some comeback through her. I think we need to keep her distanced in the future.'

Klein shook his head. 'I disagree. I believe we have another option.'

'What's that, sir?'

'We don't distance her. We absorb her. We bring her all the way in.'

Maggie lifted an eyebrow. 'We recruit her as a mobile cipher?'

'Why not? Ms. Russell has the package. She has an excellent set of skills. She has the experience, and she doesn't have any connections or attachments.'

'Except to the Agency.'

'We can work around that.' Klein smiled to himself, like a fencer flexing a new foil. 'In fact, we may be able to make use of it.'

'As you wish, sir.' Maggie sounded dubious. 'Do you want me to set up a recruitment approach?'

'No . . . not quite yet. But let's keep an eye on her. Silver-flag her file and redesignate her as a special asset; then have her placed under a loose assessment surveillance. We'll wait for another opportunity to team her with Smith and Metrace, and then . . . we shall see what we shall see.'

'Very good, sir.'

A silver border blipped into existence around Randi Russell's photo. Fred Klein leaned forward in his chair, his hands clasped, his expression intent. 'Welcome to the firm, Ms. Russell,' he murmured to the blonde woman's image.

Have you read them all?

The **Covert-One** *thrillers listed in the order in which they first appeared:*

The Hades Factor

Introducing Lt. Col. Jon Smith, a research scientist with the US army. An unknown virus takes the life of his fiancée. But this was no accident. Millions of lives are threatened. Smith must find the virus' evil-genius creator.

The Cassandra Compact

Lt. Col. Jon Smith is now an agent with the highly secretive Covert-One agency. His colleague is gunned down in Venice. Smith's investigations lead to a deadly bacteria. And a terrifying global conspiracy.

The Paris Option

A science lab in Paris is destroyed. A 'super computer' is assumed lost. But then US fighter jets disappear from radar screens. Utilities cease functioning. Lt. Col. Jon Smith must uncover the evil plot.

The Altman Code

The docks of Shanghai: a photographer records cargo being secretly loaded. He is killed. Lt. Col. Jon Smith races against time to uncover the truth about the ship and its deadly cargo.

The Lazarus Vendetta

Anti-technology protestors turn violent at a research institute in Santa Fe. Their leader is Lazarus. Lt. Col. Jon Smith must uncover his identity. And prevent him from making his most deadly move yet.

The Moscow Vector

One of the world's wealthiest men has created an incurable bioweapon. Lt. Col. Jon Smith must stop the murderous conspiracy. And thwart the Kremlin's bid to restore Russia to her former power.

The Arctic Event

The wreckage of an old Soviet bomber lies on a mountain glacier. Its cargo is weaponised anthrax. Lt. Col. Jon Smith discovers that it also contains a devastating secret that could trigger a Third World War.